VENGEANCE

A DARKHURST NOVEL

GAIL Z. MARTIN

CONTENTS

VENGEANCE

A DARKHURST NOVEL

By Gail Z. Martin

eBook ISBN: 978-1-939704-74-0
Print ISBN: 978-1-939704-75-7
Vengeance: Copyright © 2018 by Gail Z. Martin.

Cover art by Sam Gretton.
Additional cover work by Melissa Gilbert.
SOL Publishing is an imprint of DreamSpinner Communications, LLC

To my agent, Ethan Ellenberg, who has believed in me from the beginning.

CHAPTER ONE

"Duck!"

A chair sailed through the air, thrown by unseen hands. Rigan Valmonde shouted the warning to his brother Corran and dropped to the floor seconds before the chair slammed into the wall behind him hard enough to splinter into pieces.

Setting a child's vengeful ghost to rest hadn't sounded like a difficult job when Corran and Rigan took on the task from the village elders. The reality turned out to be far different from what they had been led to expect.

"Finish the banishing circle before she kills us!" Corran climbed to his feet after the angry ghost had thrown him across the room. His iron knife might be able to disrupt the ghost if he could see the spirit to know where to strike.

"Great idea——why didn't I think of that?" Rigan replied, sarcasm thick in his voice. "Trying not to die right now." He reached toward the container of salt, aconite, and amanita powder to lay down a protective circle for the banishment, but the spirit materialized just long enough to hurl the container to the far side of the small cabin before he could grab it.

"At least we know for sure that she's got enough strength to be behind the murders." Corran dove for the salt mixture, only to see it skid along the wall as if the vengeful spirit were baiting him.

"Yeah, but why?" Rigan got to his knees and brushed the splinters out of his dark hair. Getting thrown around by a wrathful ghost had been an occasional danger when he and Corran were undertakers in Ravenwood City. Now that they were outlaw monster hunters, bodily injury had become an everyday occurrence.

Before Corran had a chance to answer, a force slammed him against the wall and pinned him, immobilizing his arms and legs. "Ask her," he croaked, as the pressure tightened against his chest. "You're the one who can confess the dead."

The force pressing against his chest grew stronger, and Corran gasped for breath. Rigan scrambled to his feet. Corran's eyes widened with fear, and his whole body trembled, then his head fell forward, and the spirit let him collapse against the wall, but not before carving four deep gashes across his chest.

"Corran!"

Usually they contained a restless spirit before Rigan attempted to contact the ghost, either trapping the revenant inside a salt circle, or drawing signals and the circle to protect them from its anger. This time, the ghostly child attacked as soon as they crossed the old cabin's threshold with a fury they had seldom seen even from much older spirits. They had seriously underestimated the danger, and that mistake might cost them their lives.

Rigan reached into his pocket for a handful of loose salt mixture. He did not have enough to draw a circle, but what he threw into the air where the child's ghost last materialized was enough to break her grip on Corran, who freed himself from the wall. The ghost struggled to show herself, momentarily weakened by the protective mix of materials.

"Corran!" Rigan shouted again, terrified when his brother did not respond. Then he heard a groan and felt dizzy with relief as Corran pushed himself up on his hands and knees, scowling in anger. Blood stained his shirt from the cuts, and the skin around his throat had already begun to bruise.

"Cover me," Rigan said, closing his eyes and gathering his grave magic. Though he and Corran were brothers, and both had grave magic that let them see and hear spirits, only Rigan could take their final confessions and send them into the After.

Corran gripped his iron blade and moved closer to watch Rigan's back. He circled warily, unsure where the ghost would show herself.

"Are you crazy? You'll get yourself killed—"

A window shattered, sending a hail of glass shards flying. Corran dipped his head, turning so that the worst of the pieces hit his back and shoulders, sliding off the leather coat. He swore under his breath as he tried to get close enough to protect his younger brother from the vengeful spirit.

Rigan ignored Corran's protests and reached out with his power to the spirit. "How did you die?"

Everything stilled. For a heartbeat, Rigan wondered whether she heard him.

I couldn't breathe. The thin, reedy voice came from behind him, and he wheeled to face the ghost. Rigan motioned for Corran to remain where he was.

"What happened?" Rigan asked. "Were you alone?"

The ghost flickered several times before a hazy shape materialized and held its form long enough for Rigan to take in the details. The girl looked to be about ten years old, wearing a torn and dirty dress. Livid bruises around her neck could only have been caused by a man's tight grip.

It brought me here. She did not move, regarding him with a wary, baleful gaze. *It killed me like it killed the others, and it chewed on my bones.*

Rigan repressed a shiver. "It? Not 'him'?"

The ghost girl nodded solemnly. She fit the description the village elders had given Corran and Rigan, of both a missing child and the angry apparition. Rigan had thought at first that the spirit might be vengeful because she did not know how to move on to the After, or because she was afraid, not knowing she was dead. No one had even hinted at the possibility that she might have been murdered. Now,

Rigan wondered whether the elders did not know, or merely wished to be rid of the evidence.

He looked like a man, but he changed.

Rigan took a deep breath, trying to quiet his impatience. Spirits spoke haltingly when they could process words. Long, detailed descriptions would be difficult even for the ghost of an older person or a spirit that had been dead for many years. He would have to adapt to what this revenant could give him.

"Changed how?"

Like a dog, but he had four eyes.

Rigan had heard tales of shape-shifters and werewolves, though he and his hunter friends had yet to encounter such a creature. But none of those were said to have four eyes. "You said there were others?"

She nodded solemnly. *I can show you.*

Her image flickered out, only to reappear on the other side of the cabin, near the back door. Rigan gave a nod to Corran, and followed, careful to keep his distance so that he did not alarm the spirit. After her attack on Corran, he had no intention of trusting the ghost.

"Not sure this is a good idea," Corran grumbled, his voice raspier than usual as if it hurt to talk.

"I think there's more to this than we were told," Rigan murmured, keeping his eyes on the girl's ghost. "And if she has unfinished business, I can't confess her."

The spirit vanished, and Rigan thought she meant to trick them, but then he made out her form several yards behind the shack. He grabbed the container of salt mixture from where it had landed and drew his knife with the other hand, in case whatever had killed the girl awaited them outside.

The ghost led them down a slope through tall grasses that bent and swayed with the breeze. Rigan caught a glint of something in the afternoon sun, down at the bottom of the hill. Sure enough, the ghost materialized again by the edge of a stagnant pond filled with algae-green water. She pointed, meeting his gaze somberly.

"Is that where it put your body?" Rigan asked.

She nodded, and held up a hand, splaying all five fingers wide.

"Five bodies?" Rigan did not try to keep the shock from his tone. The ghost nodded.

Rigan exchanged a look with Corran. "They hired us to get rid of a ghost. How did they not notice five missing children?" He had a suspicion that the elders might get more than they wanted out of banishing the restless spirit.

"The people you hurt—why them?" It worked best to keep his questions short and direct. Spirits—especially the newly dead—seemed to get confused easily.

They knew.

Rigan felt a flare of anger, certain now that the elders had not been honest with them. "You hurt them because they knew about... it?"

The ghost girl nodded. *Knew. Didn't stop.*

"We have to fix this," Corran growled.

A glance at his brother told him Corran was attempting to rein in his fury. "The other children, were they before you?" Rigan asked. Again, she nodded confirming his guess. "But they can't come back as easily as you can?"

She shook her head. *Too little.*

The thought that a ten-year-old girl would be the avenger for murdered children younger than herself made Rigan grit his teeth. "Tell me who did this," he said, trying to keep his voice level.

Elkin, the wheelwright, the ghost replied.

"We'll find him and stop him," Rigan promised. "And then I'll help you pass over to the After. The others, too, if they haven't already." The girl nodded, then raised her arm to point at the algae-covered pond and vanished.

"You think the elders knew when they hired us?" Rigan asked.

Corran cursed under his breath. "They had to suspect something. The village is small enough that everyone would know about missing children." He rubbed a hand over his bruised throat. Even at a volume barely above a whisper, his voice sounded rough.

"That's what I figure, unless whatever did this covered its tracks, made it look like a wild animal snatched them, or that they wandered off," Rigan said. He ran a hand through his hair, trying to come up with a plan.

"Wouldn't they have noticed if the wheelwright had four eyes and looked like a dog?"

"Maybe the creature only takes its true form when it kills," Rigan replied. "We've found references in the lore books to monsters like that." He, Corran, and their friends had been hunting monsters for less than a year, though it felt like an eternity. They still had a lot to learn.

Now that the ghost no longer posed an immediate threat, Rigan grabbed Corran's arm. "Let me see the damage."

"We don't have time."

"You're still bleeding." Rigan pushed Corran's jacket open and hissed through his teeth at the sight of the gashes. "Damn. Those are deep."

"Aiden can fix me up when we get back."

"You're losing too much blood. Give me your shirt."

Corran scowled but complied, watching impatiently as Rigan tore the ruined garment into strips and then bound up the gashes.

"Can't do anything about the pain, but at least you'll have some blood left when we're done," Rigan said. He purposefully kept his gaze away from the bruises on Corran's neck that looked like the fatal markings on the ghost child's throat.

That was too close, he thought. *If I had been any slower, it might have been Corran's ghost I'd have to banish.* He turned away, clenching his jaw.

Corran headed back up the trail. "Come on. I thought I saw some hay rakes in the shed. If the pond is shallow enough, we might snag the skeletons of the others. Then we can salt and burn them after we show the elders."

"No wonder she attacked the people she did," Rigan replied. "If they knew and did nothing—"

"So why did she attack us? She'd never seen us before," Corran asked as he trampled the high grass on his way up the hill.

"She's a little girl, she's alone and frightened, and something awful happened to her," Rigan said, understanding despite his anger over

Corran's injuries. "Can't blame her for fighting first and asking questions later."

They found the wooden hay rakes leaning against the wall in the shed, and went back down the slope, intent on finding evidence in the slime-coated water. Neither spoke, though Rigan felt certain their thoughts followed the same path. Only once before had they been called in to banish the spirit of a small child, and then it had been a wailing toddler who had perished in a fire and did not realize that he and his whole family were dead. No confessions to hear, no awful secret to reveal, just a simple ritual to send the wayward ghost into the After to find peace. Rigan much preferred that closure to what lay ahead of them today.

"Got something," Corran said after he dragged the rake through the shallow edge of the pond. He grimaced as the muck-covered tines pulled up a water-stained, pitifully small skull.

"Sweet Oj and Ren," Rigan murmured, doing his best not to be sick. A few minutes later, his rake caught on something, and he pulled gently, retrieving a child's rib cage.

Corran's mouth set in a hard line, and his gaze went cold. "Bastard just threw them in, knew no one could see down to the bottom and no one would have reason to wade out."

"We don't know where the creature killed them," Rigan pointed out, anything to take his mind off his awful task. Again and again, he reached beneath the surface of the water, making his way slowly around the edge. Dry weather had evaporated the shallows so that Corran and Rigan were standing on ground that would have been submerged in the wettest months. Rigan's boot caught on something in the dust and revealed a fragile femur. "Damn," he muttered, rucking up the dirt with his rake to reveal more bones.

A candlemark's work yielded a grisly harvest. Five small skulls stared out from the heap of discolored bones. The ghost had told the truth; the other four victims had been much younger.

"I think it's time to go see the wheelwright," Corran said, setting the rake aside. "Take care of whatever he is, and then come back here and handle the bones."

"Sounds good. I'm in the mood for a fight," Rigan agreed. Dangerous as it was to go up against a monster, after their gruesome discovery he needed to burn off the rage that filled him.

They headed back to the village and agreed to say nothing about their discoveries thus far until the matter had been settled. Corran waited with a stash of their most obvious weapons while Rigan ambled a few blocks to the village green. If the villagers wondered why their pants were wet to the knee, no one cared enough to ask. Getting directions to the wheelwright's workshop required only a question to a passerby.

"Edge of town, set back a bit. I'm guessing he has plenty of room with no one around to see, and not close enough for neighbors to pay much attention to noise," Rigan said as he reported his conversation to Corran. "Let's go."

By the time they reached the outskirts of the village, the late afternoon sun cast long shadows. Rigan chewed his lip in thought when the found the turn to the dirt lane leading back to a wooden barn. The location was even more remote than he had imagined, offering a perfect place for murder.

"What do you think he is?" Corran asked as they walked.

"Not sure. I know we came out here to deal with a ghost, but Aiden and I have looked through the lore on monsters many times," Rigan replied, mentioning the healer-witch who traveled with their group. "Doesn't sound right for a werewolf or shapeshifter, although I guess one might have specific tastes." He curled his lip in disgust. "Same with a vampire or strix—too difficult to hide, and much more likely to take adults. It might be a *capcaun*—that would fit what the ghost said about the creature having four eyes."

"Never heard of that one."

Rigan shrugged. "It's not real common, but there was a sketch in one of the old books. It's about the size of a man—and can disguise itself as a person if it wants to—but in its true form, it's got a dog's head and four red eyes."

"How do we kill it?" Corran asked.

Rigan rubbed the back of his neck. "The old books didn't say. But it's a good bet that iron, steel, and salt won't make it happy."

Between them, they carried an impressive array of knives, swords, and stakes, as well as the salt mixture, a bag of iron filings, pouches of herbs for spells, and some vials of green vitriol that burned flesh on contact. Few creatures natural or unnatural could stand against their weapons or Rigan's magic, but the randomness of luck and fate could change the outcome of a hunt in a heartbeat.

Corran and Rigan glanced at each other and walked forward. They moved as silently as possible up the dirt lane, and as they closed on the barn, a familiar, sickly-sweet smell hung in the air.

More bodies, Rigan thought. *Not fresh ones, either.*

Corran wrinkled his nose, showing that he caught the scent, and came to the same conclusion. He gripped a steel sword in one hand and an iron knife in the other. Rigan had his sword ready as well, and the knife he held had runes carved in the handle and the blade that might offset any magic the creature possessed.

Rigan and Corran threw open the main doors and heard an echoing bellow from inside. Enough light came through the cracks between boards and an opening to the loft above to reveal the majority of the large open first floor. A heap in one corner covered with flies suggested what had become of the real wheelwright. His tools lay scattered across the floor, and the worktable had been overturned.

A powerfully built creature crouched in the middle of the workshop, muscles tensed to fight. The monster stood, revealing itself to be the height of a tall man, but more powerfully built. Leathery gray skin with patches of sparse brown hair covered its naked body. Its arms were muscled like a dockhand, with equally massive thighs. The feet looked like the paws of a big dog, while the hands had thick fingers that ended in claws. The wolf-like face and head and the four red eyes confirmed Rigan's guess. *Capcaun.*

Training and practice had Rigan moving left while Corran went right. The *capcaun* tracked them both, showing no sign of fear. Rigan grounded his magic, calmed his thoughts, and raised one hand, focusing all his will on his intention.

A stream of fire lanced from his hand, striking the *capcaun* in the chest. Rigan set his jaw and narrowed his gaze, widening the flame jet, forcing it to burn hotter. The smell of burning hair filled the workshop, and the *capcaun* roared in anger, but though its skin blistered and charred, the fire did not destroy him.

Rigan's heart pounded in his chest. They had agreed to lead with their strongest defense, seeing no reason to get hurt working up to a magical assault. He knew with certainty that the fire would have immolated a normal man, and more than one type of monster would have fallen to the flames as well. Yet the *capcaun* stood before them, damaged but undeterred.

Corran and Rigan charged, swords leveled. The *capcaun* swung a massive arm sending Rigan flying backward. Corran struck from behind, bringing his blade down with enough force to sever a man's arm, but the creature's thick skin turned what should have been a maiming blow into a deep gash.

Rigan rose to a crouch, then ran at the monster at full speed. The *capcaun* blocked the sword with its forearm, nearly tearing the weapon from Rigan's grip. His spelled knife sank into the creature's belly, and Rigan spoke the words of power to activate the runes even as the beast's arm sent him sprawling.

Corran came at the creature again as Rigan continued to chant, and he tackled the *capcaun* from the rear, striking for the neck with his iron blade. Corran cut deep, and the iron burned the creature's flesh, sending up tendrils of foul-smelling smoke. The *capcaun* roared again, and Rigan saw that the glowing runes of the spelled knife had grown brighter, while around the blade, sunk hilt-deep into the monster's body, the flesh changed color from a corpse-gray to a livid purplish-red.

Corran grappled to stay on the *capcaun's* back, sawing at its thick neck with his iron knife. The creature tried to buck him off, but Corran hung on, wild-eyed and resolute.

"Get free!" Rigan yelled, and Corran gave one more jab with his knife and spike before he leaped clear, scrambling to get beyond striking distance of the monster's powerful arms.

Rigan mustered his magic once more, and this time, he sent it toward the spelled blade sunk deep into the monster's innards. He concentrated on force, not fire, sending a narrow stream of cold white power to meld with the glowing runes, stretching along the blade and then into the *capcaun's* body, where he released some of the pressure that concentrated the power and allowed it to expand.

The *capcaun* shrieked as its abdomen distended, and its whole form shook. In the next instant, bloody gobbets and a spray of gore rained down, propelled by the force that had torn the monster apart from the inside. The explosion slung bits of flesh and bone at them hard enough to bruise, and the backlash sent Rigan staggering.

When Rigan's head cleared, he realized that blood soaked him from head to toe, dripping from his hair and plastering his clothing to his body. Corran, too, looked like he had escaped a charnel house.

"Damn, what did you do?" Corran shook off the pieces of monster that clung to his face and arms.

"I might need to rein it in a little, next time," Rigan admitted. He withdrew the vials of green vitriol from his belt as Corran took out the salt from his pack. Together they used some of the wheelwright's ruined tools to scrape together as much of the monster's body as they could. Just in case the *capcaun* could magically reform from its scattered bits,

"Did you know *capcaun* could take someone else's form?" Corran asked, reaching up to pick a piece of bone from his hair.

"The stories weren't very clear on that point," Rigan replied, trying to scrape the worst off of his ruined shirt with the back of his blade, screwing up his face in distaste as he swallowed back bile.

Corran laid down a circle of the salt mixture around the bloodied chunks, then poured a liberal amount over the savaged flesh. Rigan retrieved his knife, and sloshed green vitriol onto the pile, watching in satisfaction as it began to burn through the corpse. The head of the creature they stuffed into a burlap sack as proof, figuring they could burn it once they reached the village.

Corran glanced over at the decomposing heap that had been the real wheelwright. "Poor bastard," he muttered. "Probably never saw it coming. Looks like he's been dead quite a while."

"So why did the girl say that some of the villagers helped the monster?" Rigan asked, watching the *capcaun's* remains smoke and sizzle until he was satisfied that the creature would not revive.

"If they saw it, maybe they agreed to provide victims to save themselves," Corran replied, wiping down with a rag he found on the workbench. "Or maybe it controlled them. We probably won't know unless we run into another of these things—which I'm hoping won't be for a long, long time."

They walked back in silence to salt and burn the bones of the victims. Corran bent down to mark sigils on the bones with the ochre, black, blue, and white pigment from pouches on his belt. Before they were outlaws and monster hunters, they had been undertakers, as had their ancestors. While Rigan's abilities to do magic and confess the dead were inherited from their mother's side, both brothers shared the grave magic essential to their trade.

Rigan sprinkled the salt, aconite, and amanita mixture over the skeletons which would set their spirits free. Corran gathered enough wood for a small pyre. As Corran struck flint to steel to put spark to kindling, the image of the young girl they had seen in the shed flickered beside the pile. With her were four boys and girls, who stared at the brothers with dark, solemn gazes.

"It's over," Rigan told her. "The creature is dead. He can't hurt anyone else. You can go now. All of you—you can rest."

The girl nodded, her gaze sad.

"Tell us your names," Rigan said. "That way, we can let your families know that you've gone on."

"Annie."

"Benny."

"Cora."

"Thom."

"Betta."

Rigan nodded, committing the names to memory. "Go now," he said, and then as Corran set the pyre ablaze, they joined their voices in the chant they had said so often over the bodies of the dead before they left their profession behind. The fire rose higher as the song continued, but as the sparks climbed into the sky, the ghostly images thinned and faded, then vanished altogether.

"Let's collect our money and get out of here." Corran twitched his shoulders uncomfortably beneath his shirt that was stiff with blood. "I imagine they'll be happy to be rid of us. We smell like a slaughter-house and look like something out of a nightmare."

"I'll make a note of what worked, in case we run into one of those things again," Rigan replied as they walked back the dirt lane. Getting thrown by the *capcaun* had twisted his back, and he could tell that Corran noted his limp with a worried glance.

"That's nice. Right now, I want a hot bath and a warm dinner, then a clean bed," Corran said. "And the next time you decide to blow a monster up with your magic, give me time to get well away from the blast."

"We'll need to get more salt soon," Rigan remarked. "Probably good to get Aiden and Elinor to be on the lookout for more aconite and amanita as well since we can't count on finding a patch of those when-ever we need them."

The walk back to the village to collect their fee gave Rigan time to think. From the set of Corran's jaw, he guessed his brother turned the matter over in his mind as well. They found the mayor who hired them in the pub, surrounded by the village elders. The mayor looked up as the brothers entered, and he smiled in a way that did not reach his eyes.

"Did you find the ghost? Could you get rid of it?"

Rigan caught a warning glance from Corran, but his temper burned too hot for him to care. "We found the ghosts—all five of them. And the monster who killed them. Did you know the wheelwright was the creature? Did you give him the children to save your own skins?"

For an instant, shock and fear glinted in the mayor's eyes before cold calculation took over. "I don't know what you're talking about."

Rigan's slammed the burlap sack down on the table, and the men jumped, sliding back in their chairs. The rest of the crowd in the common room fell silent.

"I think you knew," Rigan said, looming over the mayor until the man had to crane his neck and his multiple chins to see. "The ghosts said people in the village helped the monster. Supplied the children for it to eat. Who else could go unnoticed for so long?"

"You're crazy. That's... insane," the mayor sputtered.

"You found them? The missing ones?" A man stood near the back of the pub. From his clothing and the dirt streaks on his pants, he looked like a farmer, probably stopping for a meal after bringing goods to market. His broad shoulders and muscular arms spoke of hard work, and while sun and hardship had weathered his features, Rigan guessed the man might only be a few years older than Corran.

"We found the skeletons of five children, dumped in the pond near where the ghosts appeared," Corran replied, anger clear in his voice.

"One of those that went missing was my Annie," the man said. "Is it true, Mayor? You knew?"

The mayor's pale, fleshy face flushed and sweat beaded on his forehead. "No, of course not. They're lying—"

"We killed the creature," Rigan continued. "A *capcaun*. It can take the appearance of someone else, like the wheelwright. But it couldn't have snatched that many children without help. So I'm guessing that someone made a deal—sacrifice a few children, keep the monster away from everyone else."

The townspeople looked on in horror, and while Rigan's magic did not let him read minds, their reactions came too naturally to be false. The mayor, on the other hand, sat tensely in his chair, gripping the armrests.

"Is it true?" one of the mayor's companions asked, a tall man with gray hair and prominent cheekbones who from his clothing might have been a shopkeeper. "You told us the guards searched for them. You blamed it on wolves or Wanderers."

"What about my sister's boy, Benny?" a man asked from near the bar. "He went to fetch water and never came back. Did the monster get him, too?"

"Annie. Benny. Cora. Thom. Betta," Rigan repeated and saw the faces of the customers go pale. "You never told us any of their names. They did, when their ghosts confessed to me."

By now, most of the men at the other tables were on their feet. The mayor's companions pushed their chairs back even farther, leaving him alone at the table.

"You could have found that out from anyone," the mayor said. "It's a trick. We hired you to get rid of a ghost, and you want more money."

"We didn't make this up." Rigan reached into the bag and pulled out the head of the *capcaun*. The mayor's associates scrambled away at the smell, as if only now realizing why both Rigan and Corran were drenched with dark, dried blood.

"What deal did you offer it?" Corran asked, placing a hand on the mayor's shoulder to push him back down in his chair when it looked like he might bolt. "A child every so often, if it would ignore your cows and sheep?"

"You don't understand." Fear shifted to anger and the mayor's round face reddened. "It might have murdered us all. I'd never seen anything like it; no one had. How was I to know it could be killed? It wasn't greedy. Just a brat now and again, nothing anyone would miss."

"Nothing we'd miss?" Annie's father took a step toward them, fists clenched at his side. "I miss my Annie. My wife almost went mad with grief."

"You tell my sister she don't miss Benny," the man at the bar said, slipping down from his stool to close in on the mayor.

"I'm the mayor. It was my decision. I had to do what was best for everyone—"

"Lettin' a monster live among us and kill our children was 'best' for us?" A large man with arms and shoulders like a blacksmith came to stand next to Annie's father. "I was one of the people who searched all night for those kids, and here you knew where they were, knew what happened to them all along? Served them up like a sacrifice?"

"You'd have done the same thing in my position," the mayor argued.

"No, I don't think we would have," the blacksmith said.

"What about the ghosts?" Annie's father asked. "Where are they?"

"We're undertakers," Corran replied, still keeping a firm hand on the mayor's shoulder. "Once they saw the monster die and told their story, we helped them pass over to the After."

The grieving man swallowed hard and nodded. "So they're at rest now?"

"Yes," Corran said. "And we burned their bones as well as the monster's body, to make sure they won't come back." He nodded toward the severed head in the middle of the table. "Should burn that too."

"Not yet," the blacksmith said. He seemed to be a man others followed because five or six of the pub's patrons had come to stand shoulder to shoulder with him. "Not until everyone's seen it and knows what he did."

The mayor's gaze flickered from one man to another, and he licked his lips. "We can work this out—"

Annie's father kicked a chair halfway across the room, and the noise made everyone jump. "All right then," he said. "Give me my Annie back, and we'll call it square."

"I can't—"

"Of course you can't!" the grieving father roared. "You can't because you paid a monster with her, and then thought you'd get rid of her ghost by having these two send her on. But you didn't figure ghosts could talk, did you?"

By now, a dozen angry men circled the mayor, whose former companions had abandoned him and now looked on in shock and horror. Corran and Rigan stepped back.

The pub owner came out of the kitchen, and his gaze went immediately to the brothers. "I need a word," he said, with a twitch of his head toward the room behind him. Corran and Rigan exchanged a dubious look but followed him.

Whatever Rigan had expected, having a fistful of coins shoved at them wasn't part of it. "Here," the pub owner said. "Since you won't be getting' your pay from the mayor, and you more than earned it. Some of us thought there was something wrong about those children going missing, but there was nothin' to prove it. It's a harsh truth, but it had to be told. Now people can move on."

"Thank you," Rigan said, pocketing the coins. A glance told him they totaled twice what the mayor had promised.

"Best you leave by a different route," the pub owner said, with a wary glance toward the other room where voices rose. "I saw the mayor talkin' with two rough fellows who got here not long after you went off to do what you did. Didn't like the look of the men, or the look on the mayor's face."

The pub owner swept his gaze over them, taking in their dirty, worn clothing, their weapons and their bag of gear. "I imagine the guards think ill of what you do," he said. "It looked to me like the mayor struck a deal with those strangers, and since you two are the only other folks not from around here—"

Shit, Rigan thought. *Bounty hunters.*

"We appreciate the warning," Corran replied.

The pub owner smiled. "I never did trust the mayor. Can't say I dislike seeing him get what's comin'. As for your horses," he went on, "I had my stable boy lead them out the other way, to the back road. Don't know where you're going, and you might have to wind around a little, but didn't think with what you'd done you wanted more trouble."

Rigan opened his mouth to thank the man, but the pub owner shook his head. "We owe you for settling this. Now git, before those ruffians come back looking for you."

CHAPTER TWO

"It's them!"

Rigan guessed the bounty hunters knew about the back road because two men on horseback came galloping from beneath the shadow of a stand of trees outside the village. Both wore swords, and one sent a crossbow quarrel flying far too close for comfort as Rigan and Corran pushed their horses as fast as they could run.

Corran cursed. "You think the pub owner set us up?"

"Nah. I think they were smart enough to know there'd be more than one road."

They had a lead on the bounty hunters, enough for now to stay beyond the range of their quarrels.

"Can you blast them?" Corran asked, as he crouched low over his mount's neck and urged the gelding faster.

"Not while I'm riding and trying to aim at the same time. I'm pretty spent, after what we did back there," Rigan admitted. He knew he didn't have the magic right now to do anything powerful enough to stop their pursuers, and neither of them was in much shape for an all-out fight after the battle with the *capcaun*. Worse, they had no way of knowing whether the two ruffians behind them had allies and whether more attackers might be waiting up ahead.

"We can't outrun them forever."

This road wasn't as wide or as well kept as the main road leading into the village. Rigan guessed few aside from local farmers and peddlers came this way. Old trees with thick, tangled branches overhung the roadway, casting the length in shadows. The sun had almost set, and twilight made it difficult to see.

"I've got an idea," Rigan said. He eyed a large tree with heavy, twisting limbs that sprawled almost from one side of the road to the other.

The bounty hunters' faster horses let them gain on Corran and Rigan. The one with the bow nocked another arrow. He would be in range in seconds, and at this distance, he couldn't miss.

Rigan sank his power into the land around them and fixed his attention on the huge old tree. He *pulled* with all the magic he had remaining and felt the trunk move. The ground at its base gave way, ripping up the roots, and the whole thing came crashing down, so close on their heels that the smallest branches whipped Rigan's back like a flail. The crack and thud of the falling tree mingled with the cries of the bounty hunters and the screams of their terrified horses.

"Ride!" Rigan gasped, falling forward and clinging to the reins and his horse's mane to steady himself.

Rigan's head spun, and it took full concentration not to fall from his horse. It wasn't just dispelling the ghosts of Annie and her fellow victims and dispatching the *capcaun* that drained him. They had hunted too often without enough rest, and Rigan was finally feeling the aftermath. Corran had nagged at him to take more time to recover, but the situations always seemed urgent and they needed the money to get by, so Rigan kept on pushing until he had finally pushed too hard.

"Godsdamn it!" Corran growled. "There are more men ahead."

"I'm done in," Rigan panted. "Go cross country. I'll distract them."

"To the gods with that," Corran muttered, grabbing the reins of Rigan's horse. "We go, we go together. Hold on."

A wagon turned sideways blocked the road ahead, and four heavily armed men waited for their quarry to ride into the ambush. Corran dug his heels into his mount's sides and snapped the reins, leaping a ditch and taking off across a meadow.

Rigan held on with his hands and knees, feeling every jolt as they covered the ground at a pace that could only end with a lame horse and a thrown rider. It took their pursuers a few minutes to mount up and come after them, but Rigan knew their horses, sweat-soaked and foam-flecked, could not go much longer.

Corran changed course abruptly, and Rigan wondered what had caught his eye. Then he spied a tall oak standing alone in the middle of a clearing surrounded by crude markers, and understood.

He felt Corran's grave magic rise around them, as his brother began to chant. Rigan sent what little power he could muster, as Corran slowed their horses to a stop on the far side of the small graveyard.

Rigan was the one to confess ghosts and summon unwilling spirits; Corran usually only helped to banish them. Together, they could offer the dead something rare and precious out here, far from the city and the Guilds. Undertakers in the farm country were few and expensive, so many bodies went without the proper rites that sped their souls to the After. Most would eventually find their way, while others became lost and eventually, vengeful. Now, Corran called to those restless spirits, offering them proper passage, if only they would send the bad men away.

The ghosts came, old and young, more than Rigan guessed the burying yard held. Soldiers from a long-forgotten battle stood next to farmers and elderly women. The temperature fell, and the wind picked up, sending leaves and dust flying. Without Corran and Rigan's magic, the ghosts might not have been able to manifest so clearly, but now they stood as a gray, shimmering line between the bounty hunters and their prey.

Then, without warning, the ghosts swept down the meadow toward the ruffians, and the wind howled along with them, strong enough to send a man reeling. The bounty hunters shouted curses as rocks and sticks pelted them, then turned and fled as the angry spirits pursued them nearly to the edge of the road. The ghosts did not vanish until the brigands had turned their wagon and ridden off, then they winked out from their spot near the highway and reappeared once more beneath the oak.

"Thank you," Corran said. He dismounted and laid a hand on Rigan's shoulder to indicate he should stay where he was. Corran looked drawn and tired, his face streaked with sweat, dirt, and the *capcaun's* blood. He walked out into the midst of the ghosts and raised his hands in benediction.

One of the ghosts pointed toward the far side of the clearing, where Rigan could barely make out a break in the trees that might have been a farm road. Corran nodded, and Rigan realized the spirit had provided them with an escape route that led away from the bounty hunters.

They had none of the usual materials a proper burial required, but these were not bodies to be prepared, just ghosts long overdue for their rest. Corran withdrew four wooden stakes from his saddlebags, each marked in woad, ochre, chalk, or soot with one of the sigils they used to send the dead on to the After.

Corran pushed the stakes into the ground in a straight line, leading toward the horizon where the last glow of the setting sun lingered. He raised his voice once more in the passing over ritual, joined by Rigan's ragged whisper. The sigils glowed, and the ghosts moved like marchers at the end of a long trek, walking shoulder to shoulder toward the place where the shadows deepened, and the brothers' grave magic opened a portal to the After. Singly or in pairs, the ghosts passed beyond, until the wind stilled, the shadows lightened, and Corran and Rigan were alone once more in the quiet of the night.

"When we get home, you're going to heal and rest if I have to lock you in your room or have Aiden knock you out and keep you unconscious," Corran grumbled, checking on Rigan to assure he hadn't gotten worse.

"There's been too much going on—" Rigan protested, though his voice barely rose above a whisper.

Corran helped Rigan on to his horse, and then swung up to his saddle and took both their reins once more. "Forget that. Let Ross or Trent or Calfon take the next job and the job after that. And once you're better, we're going to talk about this 'drain myself dry for a good cause' approach to magic," Corran growled. "We didn't come through everything just to bury you because you don't know your limits."

"I know them," Rigan said.

"Yeah, and you go right past them until you fall down," Corran snapped. "No more. You can protect people without making yourself a godsdamn sacrifice."

Too tired to argue, Rigan let Corran vent. Corran had a point, and Rigan felt a twinge of guilt as he looked at the situation from his brother's perspective. Rigan's magic, still not fully trained, remained both a weapon and a danger to himself. And while Corran rarely hesitated to throw himself in harm's way in a physical fight, he disliked Rigan doing the same where it involved magic.

Later he would argue again with Corran and try to bring him around. Tomorrow, or maybe the next day, depending on when the pounding in his head finally stopped.

———

BY THE TIME they returned to the abandoned monastery, Rigan had recovered enough to take back his reins and sit up, though more out of stubbornness than from a second wind. Both Rigan and Corran felt the day's injuries and the hard ride. They stabled their horses and limped up the broken stone steps, winding through the ruined entranceway and front rooms, a familiar path that seemed longer than usual today.

Rigan felt for the clasp that unlocked the hidden door to the monastery's lower levels. He leaned heavily on the railing as he staggered down the stairway. Corran's uneven gait told him without looking that his brother was feeling every impact from the attack. Rigan would not be surprised if they were both bruised all over. His aching body felt like it.

"Did you get her?" Calfon, one of their fellow hunter-exiles, looked up as they entered the large open room at the bottom of the steps.

Rigan nodded wearily. "Turns out there was a lot more to the story than anyone knew." He sagged into a chair, and Corran found a seat next to him.

"You look like you got your asses handed to you." Mir, another of their hunter friends, glanced at them from where he sat sharpening a collection of knives and swords that covered an entire table. Back in Ravenwood City, Mir had been a blacksmith, and it showed in every line of his body. Even now, he took care of shoeing their horses and mending tools, and the times when he fired up a forge and worked hot iron were when Rigan thought he seemed free of the loss that seemed to shadow him.

"Feels like it, too," Corran agreed ruefully, running his hand back through his blond hair. Since they fled the city, he had grown his hair long enough for curls to brush his collar. Rigan pushed a strand of his dark hair from his eyes. Rigan and Corran bore a family resemblance most strongly in the shade and shape of their blue eyes. Rigan took after their mother, tall, thin, and angular with chestnut brown hair, while Corran favored their father with ash blond hair and a stockier build. Corran stood half a head taller, too.

"All right, let's see how bad the damage was this time." Aiden bustled out from one of the back rooms with Elinor close on his heels. He stopped in front of the brothers, giving them an appraising look.

"Fix Corran first," Rigan said, unable to hide the weariness in his voice. "He's hurt worse than I am."

"You hit the wall awfully hard," Corran protested.

"You're bleeding," Rigan countered.

Aiden glared at them. "If you're well enough to fight, I'm not worried either of you is close to death," he observed drily. Elinor chuckled in agreement.

"How about I start with the bloody one and Rigan can tell us about the adventure," Aiden said, opening the bag he carried with him. By the time Aiden and Elinor finished cleaning and treating Corran's wounds, Rigan had filled the others in on the hunt.

"Your turn," Aiden said to Corran as Rigan fell silent. Elinor gave Rigan's hand an affectionate squeeze, then watched everything Aiden did, taking her apprenticeship to the healer seriously. Rigan felt their magic as they worked on him, sensing it in their touch as the cleaned gashes and smoothed liniment over aching muscles. Aiden's magic was as strong in its own way as Rigan's, and Elinor's subtle abilities had grown more powerful now that exile meant their lives depended almost daily on their wits and skills.

"So you went for a ghost and ended up with a completely different sort of monster," Mir observed, never breaking the rhythm of steel against whetstone.

"Do you think it was natural or summoned?" Calfon asked. He still had the look of a stonemason, with muscular arms and a back broadened by heavy loads. The sun had bleached his short sandy hair and tanned his skin from days spent outdoors.

"Natural," Rigan replied as Aiden passed cups of whiskey to both him and Corran. He took a sip, and let it burn down his throat. "The *capcaun* is smarter than the ghouls and beasts the blood witches controlled. Creatures like it have probably been around forever, long before the mages started tampering with nature."

Calfon's expression darkened. "We need to have more of a plan," he said. "It's too damn close too many times. We didn't even know you were heading out until—"

"I'm not going to ask permission." Corran's flat tone made it clear he wasn't up to rehashing the old argument.

"It's not permission, it's… organization," Calfon snapped. "Not having you two go one way and Ross go haring off on one of his damn jaunts—"

"We coordinate when we need to work together," Corran argued. "This was supposed to be a simple haunting. Something Rigan and I did before we ever started hunting monsters. When have we ever taken more than two of us after a ghost?"

"You're missing the point," Calfon said, pushing away from the table in anger and turning his back.

"It's not like it was back in Ravenwood City," Corran said quietly. "Everything had to be tightly structured to keep from getting caught because we were trying to hide in plain sight, in a crowded city, with guards everywhere. And you led us well. You're still a good leader," he coaxed with more patience than Rigan could tell he felt. "But things are different out here. *We're* different. It's not going to work the old way."

"And look how well it works doing it the new way," Calfon said before he strode from the kitchen and slammed the door behind him.

"That went smoothly," Mir muttered, rolling his eyes.

"He'll cool down," Rigan said, too tired for the same old pissing match. Calfon had led the hunters before Corran joined, but the dynamics shifted when they fled Below for their lives and both brothers—and magic—came into the fight. Corran had no desire to be in charge of anything, but he had a level head and kept his temper better than Calfon. Rigan's powers, and their shared grave magic, often put the two of them at the forefront when a fight needed both a witch and a warrior. Maybe Calfon liked giving orders, or maybe he felt at a loss out here beyond the city walls, without a trade. Rigan did not doubt Calfon's friendship, but the ongoing friction got old, especially when they shared tight quarters and had little time away from one another.

"Did they pay you?" Polly broke the mood with her question. She stepped out of a doorway on the other side of the room; her red hair tucked up under a cap. From the sheen of sweat on her face and the traces of flour on her apron, Rigan guessed she had been cooking over the hearth in a back room.

"Better than they originally intended," Rigan replied with a tired laugh. "After we found the five victims and a monster the mayor didn't want to admit knowing about. Although there were a few complications."

"Have you heard from Trent and Ross? Shouldn't they be back by now?" Corran asked with a glance toward Mir, worry clear in his tone. "That son of a bitch mayor sold us out to bounty hunters. Probably figured that if we did find anything out about the *capcaun* and the real reason the children went missing, we wouldn't be able to tell anyone about it, and he wouldn't have to pay us."

Mir shrugged. "You know what a hunt is like. They all look simple until you're in the thick of it." Worry haunted his dark eyes. "Did you kill the bounty hunters?"

Corran shook his head. "We were both hurt, and there ended up being at least six of them. Rigan knocked over a tree, and we ran."

"I hate knowing they're circling out there, like buzzards," Mir replied.

Whatever Corran might have said in response went unspoken as Polly came to the doorway once again. "Dinner's ready. Get your ungrateful asses in here before the food goes cold," she added with a grin. "I'll make a plate for Calfon. I'm not going to chase him down when he's in a snit."

Lanterns lit the underground rooms of the secret basement. Soot streaked the whitewashed plaster and blackened the ceilings. The old monks and their builders had been clever, bringing in fresh air with ducts that led to hidden vents outside, providing fresh water with cisterns, and taking pains to build chimneys that hid the smoke from the fireplaces.

Despite the warmth of the cook fire and the close space of the kitchen, Rigan shivered. He caught Corran's worried glance and shook his head tiredly.

"Nothing's wrong. It just reminds me of Below down here."

"Yeah, except Below was a lot bigger," Aiden replied, overhearing his comment. "More like a city where it was always night. This basement feels like... a basement."

Rigan and the others had taken refuge Below before the final battle against the Lord Mayor. Below was a warren of paved-over and forgotten streets beneath Ravenwood City. People went there to lose themselves and to stay lost. The hunters and rogue mages had fit right in.

Polly tapped her wooden spoon against the table, hurrying them to their places. She was nearly fifteen, a spitfire of a girl, and her time as a tavern server gave her a tart tongue and a well-honed survival instinct. "Come on, come on. Slaved over a fire down here in the dark, the least you could do is eat while it's hot," she teased.

"It really does smell good," Elinor said, taking the seat next to

Rigan. "I'm amazed at what you can do with the provisions we've been able to gather." Underneath the table, Rigan reached over and took her hand, giving it a squeeze.

"Onions, salt, cabbage, and butter go a long way," Polly replied, sitting down only after the others were settled. "Those chickens you brought in cooked up real nice."

Rigan watched Polly and had to look away as a lump formed in his throat. Corran and Rigan's younger brother, Kell, had been sweet on Polly, and Rigan did not doubt they would have made a remarkable pair. That dream ended the night the Lord Mayor's guards and monsters killed Kell—when he had the bad luck to be in the wrong place at the wrong time.

Corran bumped his elbow as if guessing his thoughts. Rigan managed a wan smile and went back to his food. "You going to save any for Trent and Ross?" Corran asked.

Polly gave him a withering glance. "Yes, but only because I'm generous that way," she replied, playfully stern. "It would serve them right to go hungry, coming late to supper."

"Not that late," a voice said from the doorway, as Trent and Ross crowded into the room.

"Sorry," Ross added. "Had a bit more excitement than we counted on."

Now that Rigan got a good view as they came into the lantern light, both men were streaked with dirt and blood, appearing about as worn as he and Corran had been when they had returned from their battle. Calfon trailed in behind them and sat, having gotten his temper under control.

"Do I need to tend to you now?" Aiden asked, putting down his fork and appraising them with a worried expression.

Ross shook his head. "Looks worse than it is. Most of the blood isn't ours. Thought we had a Black Dog, and it turned out to be a small nest of ghouls."

"Did you ask the grateful villagers for coins or provisions?" Polly asked, raising an eyebrow. She, Elinor, and Aiden saw to most of the provisioning, since the three of them supported the others with magic and research, but did not go on as many hunts. Elinor had discovered the remnants of an old herb garden behind the monastery, as well as some berry bushes and fruit trees. Aiden had a gift for setting snares, which put meat on the table, and he occasionally ventured to a nearby lake to fish. "Or goats," she added. "I wouldn't mind having a couple of goats. Good for milk, and easy to take with us when we need to move again."

"I'll remember to ask for our pay in goats next time," Ross replied, barely hiding his amusement. "The villagers were happy enough about us stopping the attacks on their cows that they paid me in silver, if that's all right with you."

Polly gave a theatrically imperious sniff, raising her chin. "I guess. It'll do," she said, then broke into a broad grin. "Silver is fine. I'll come up with a list of what we need the next time one of you is some-place near a market."

Three months ago, all of them except Aiden and Polly had been tradespeople, Guild members in the walled city of Ravenwood, respectable citizens and business owners. Ross had been a farrier, Trent a butcher. Calfon's family made lamps, and Mir was the son of the blacksmith. Elinor was an apprentice dyer, and Polly a kitchen girl at one of the local inns. Aiden's healer magic had forced him into hiding, but he carried on his practice in secret, taking care of the sick in the forgotten subterranean warren of Below. Never had any of them expected to find themselves squatting in the ruins of an old monastery, roaming the countryside battling monsters.

"Anyone hear news about the city?" Elinor asked between bites. "Surely the peddlers and tinkers have gossip."

"Last I heard from anyone, things were still a mess," Trent said. "Rebuilding what burned, chasing down the monsters that didn't die the night of the battle, and trying to calm down the Guilds."

"In some ways, I think we've got it a bit better out here than inside the wall," Mir added. "Something's gone wrong, and I heard a peddler say the ships from Garenoth aren't coming into the harbor like they used to. I bet the Guilds are mad as wet hens over that."

"Has a new Lord Mayor been chosen?" Corran asked.

"From what people say, Crown Prince Aliyev himself has stepped in to straighten things out," Calfon said. "At least, that was the word down at the pub we stopped at on our way back from the last hunt. Maybe that's a good thing. He might be more honorable than Machison."

"He couldn't be much less honorable," Trent replied.

A moment of painful silence followed, with knowing glances. They'd all lost people they loved to the monsters and had been forced to take matters into their own hands when the guards did nothing. It wasn't until much later they learned that the unnatural predators weren't the true enemy—it was Lord Mayor Machison and his blood witch Thron Blackholt.

Machison sent guards and assassins after the hunters and burned out their homes and shops. Four of Corran and Rigan's friends died in the battle to destroy the Lord Mayor and Blackholt and free Raven-wood of the tyranny of their summoned monsters. It had been a night filled with blood, fire, and death. When dawn came, the Lord Mayor and Blackholt were dead, riots had broken out over the mayor's heavy-handed crackdown, and much of the city went up in flames. Dispossessed and sought by the remaining guards, Rigan, Corran, and their friends fled.

Now they were outlaws, with a reward set for their capture, disavowed by their Guilds, hunting monsters in the forests and farm-lands outside the city wall for whatever pay they could muster.

"We got some leads on a few more hunts," Ross volunteered as he scraped the last of the food from his plate. He gave a hopeful glance at Polly, but she shook her head, tipping the empty serving bowl to let him know everything had been eaten. He relented with a sigh. "The men at the pub were talking about a string of deaths by one of the lakes nearby. Seemed to think there might be a monster of some sort involved."

"If you know which lake, we can check it out," Corran said.

"And then the tinker I asked for directions got chatty and wondered if I'd heard about how the young women over in Eiler-town seem to be going missing," Mir added. "Too many to chalk up to eloping. Thought it sounded like something we ought to look into."

"Did you say Eilertown?" Elinor looked up at Mir startled.

Mir nodded. "Yes. Why?"

Elinor stole a glance at Rigan and Aiden before replying, swallowing nervously when Aiden gave her a slight nod. "It's just, Rigan and Aiden and I have been working on something. We thought maybe if monsters have some magical abilities, maybe they affect the magic around them, like ripples on a pond."

She looked nervous, now that the others were all paying attention. "It's something we've been toying with, nothing definite, but Eilertown was one of the places where we picked up 'ripples' in the magic."

Corran raised an eyebrow. "Interesting. That could be a big help if it works. Sounds better than having to spend the night in the pub listening to tall tales."

"Speak for yourself," Rigan said with a chuckle. "I for one don't mind gathering information at pubs. Be willing to sacrifice a whole evening, for the good of the hunt," he added, grinning. He slipped an arm around Elinor. "Been a while since we've been out on the town."

She gently elbowed him. "We've never been out on the town. You didn't get serious about wooing me until we'd both become fugitives."

"I'm serious now," he added with a grin, ducking in and pressing a kiss to her temple that had her smiling, blushing, and pretending to slap him away.

"If you're done?" Corran said, clearing his throat with mock sternness, his amusement clear in his eyes. "We have monsters to fight." Rigan and Elinor settled into their seats.

"We've barely started looking for those 'ripples,'" Aiden said, moving past the distraction with a roll of his eyes. "Right now, it's probably only as reliable as those men at the pub—maybe not as much. But Elinor's right—I think it's got potential, not just to find us monsters to hunt, but to give us warning about where the monsters are so we can avoid them when we aren't hunting."

Rigan and Corran exchanged a glance. Not coming upon monsters by accident would make traveling much safer. They were all new to this life of monster hunting, but since they could hardly ply their old trades in exile and on the run, it seemed like a way to do some good and earn enough coin to survive. Every time they went out on a hunt, they learned by trial and error, and in their new line of work, mistakes could easily be fatal. Any edge magic could give them would be welcome.

"Give us a day to rest, and then we'll move. Sounds like we've got ourselves another couple of hunts," Corran said.

CHAPTER THREE

"WE DON'T KNOW what sort of evil this is, but it can't go on." The older man had a careworn expression, and his shoulders slumped as if he carried a great burden.

"Tell us what's been happening. If there's a monster behind it, we'll take care of it," Corran said.

Mahon, the leader of the village council, gestured for Rigan, Aiden, Calfon, and Corran to sit. They took their places and waited for him to continue.

"Every year, people die up at the Bourn Lake," Mahon said. "How many die varies by the year. Sometimes one or two, sometimes more."

"All people from your village?" Corran asked, leaning forward to listen closely.

Mahon shook his head. "No. Some travelers from the road nearby, and some from other towns. But they all drown—and none of them had reason to be near the water."

Calfon frowned. "Why do they go to the lake? To fish?"

"No. There hasn't been good fishing in Bourn Lake in a long time. Most people know to stay clear of the lake. They know it's dangerous up there."

"So what draws them?" Rigan asked.

"Suicide," Mahon replied. "All of them."

"That makes no sense," Aiden countered. "Why would so many people have cause to want to kill themselves?"

Mahon's eyes flashed. "That's the thing. They didn't. Something about the lake lures people close, and then it either kills them or makes them kill themselves."

Rigan chewed his lip for a moment as he thought. "Have you tried putting up a fence?"

Mahon snorted. "Of course we did. Something always tears it down."

"How long has this been happening?" Calfon asked.

"At least twenty years," Mahon replied. "Maybe longer. If it went back more than twenty years, it wasn't a regular thing, not every year. Didn't happen to as many people, either. Seems to have gotten worse as time went on."

Corran watched the older man carefully. Nothing about his manner or voice made Corran doubt his story. Bourn Lake had shown up as a ripple in the magic when Rigan and the others looked closely. That had been enough for Corran to pull a team together to have a closer look. It had only taken asking a few questions when they first got to the village to have Mahon bustling out to see what was going on. Corran had expected Mahon to be suspicious, but to his surprise, the councilman almost seemed relieved to have the hunters show up.

"Was there something that happened around the time the suicides began that might have changed things?" Aiden asked. "Anything out of the ordinary?"

Mahon leaned back and crossed his arms. "Not much out of the ordinary happens around here, ever. We're a quiet little farming community. We're not on a main road, so people who come through this area usually have business with someone who lives here."

"Could someone from the village have done something to cause this? Maybe worked a curse or some dark magic?" Corran pressed.

Mahon looked at Corran as if he had lost his mind. "Curses? What do you think we are, son? Farmers don't need to curse nobody—the damn weather and blight do a good enough job on their own."

"There are always rivalries," Rigan ventured. "Or jealousy. Petty arguments that escalate. People have affairs and want to punish the unfaithful."

For a moment, Mahon went red in the face as if he intended to defend his village's honor. Then he deflated and shook his head. "Those things happen, sure, like they do everywhere. But even so, Bourn is pretty tame. Folks here have too much hard work to do for them to have time to be causing a lot of trouble for each other. Fist fights, sometimes, if a man looks at another man's wife the wrong way. There's been a time or two when a cow or a few goats turn up dead or missing after there's been a big argument. Had a shed burn down once. But the only magic around here is what the healers and the midwives do, and what the farmers learn to keep their animals healthy. Nothing like what you're talking about."

Corran believed him, or at least believed that Mahon told the truth as he knew it. "So nothing unusual happened twenty years ago? Nothing at all?"

Mahon looked off into the distance, thinking. "We had a bad winter that year. More snow than usual, especially in the high country. That spring, when it melted, everything flooded. The streams and the lake damn near swallowed up everything around them. Lost some livestock with the flooding, and some damn fools who wouldn't leave the low places. Then everything dried up and went back to how it was before."

"What about the lake?" Rigan asked, seizing on the information. "Did it change after the flooding?"

"Not after the flooding, no," Mahon replied. "For a while there, it practically doubled in size, what with the overflow from the streams gushing in. Quite a sight to see."

"If there's nothing else you can tell us, I think we'd like to have a look at the lake for ourselves," Corran said.

"Of course," Mahon said, standing. "We've heard of you hunters, what you've done for some of the other towns. If you can help us with this, we'd be much obliged."

"It's too late in the day for us to do more now than get our bearings," Calfon said as they rose from their seats. "We'll need lodging and food tonight, and then there's the matter of our fee."

Mahon shifted uncomfortably. "We're farmers," he repeated. "We don't have a lot of coin. But if you're willing to take payment in trade, we can do that. Fix you up real good with fresh vegetables, eggs, cheese."

"Perhaps a goat or two, maybe some chickens?" Rigan asked.

Mahon nodded. "Yes. Easily. If you can stop what's killing our people, we'll be in your debt."

Mahon walked them to the edge of the village and gave them directions to Bourn Lake. The group said little until they were some distance from town.

"Do you think he's telling the truth?" Rigan asked.

"I don't think he's lying," Calfon replied.

"Which isn't the same as saying that he's got his facts right," Aiden added. "I agree that I think he believes what he said. But there may be more to it than he knows, and we're likely to find that out the hard way."

Corran led the way. Rigan and Aiden followed, and Calfon brought up the rear. Bourn was a day's ride from the monastery, so they had brought their weapons with them, unsure of what to expect. Rigan and Aiden packed in as many magical supplies as they could carry, along with a few lore books and plenty of the salt mixture.

As they walked, Rigan and Aiden debated what sort of creature they might find waiting for them. "I think the flood had something to do with it," Rigan said. "Maybe it washed something in from another location."

"Or woke something up that hadn't been disturbed in a long time," Aiden replied. "Might explain why there aren't any fish in the lake."

"You mean whatever is living there likes a snack in between suicides?"

"Sounds likely to me."

Corran moved carefully along the overgrown trail. From the look of it, the path had very little traffic. Not surprising, considering the lake's reputation. He strained to listen for any sounds out of the ordinary. All around them, birds chirped and underbrush rustled as small animals scurried out of their way. That boded well; dead silence meant the wildlife had fled to give a top predator space.

Under other circumstances, Corran might have enjoyed the walk. The forest's lush green, the scent of the trees, and the clear blue sky above made for a beautiful day. Although the sun hung low in the sky, the temperature remained mild, and a slight breeze ruffled Corran's hair. Still, he could not shake the restless feeling that had grown stronger since they left the village.

It could be nerves, he told himself. *After all, we don't know what kind of monster we're facing.* He was glad Rigan and Aiden remained deep in conversation, knowing his brother would sense the shift in his mood with a glance.

The idea of being monster hunters instead of undertakers still made Corran uncomfortable. He knew they could never return to Ravenwood City, not after killing the Lord Mayor and his witch. Exile was the price they paid for freeing the city of the conjured monsters Blackholt and Machison called down on their friends and neighbors.

But undertaking was the Valmonde family business, passed down to them by their father and grandfather, back many generations. Until the aftermath of Kell's murder forced them into hiding Below, Corran had assumed that he and Rigan would carry on the profession all their lives, passing it on to their heirs. Kell died, the guards came for them, and Rigan and Corran had barely escaped with their lives as their home and workshop burned behind them.

After three months, the loss still felt like a fresh wound. Corran tried to focus on the good he and the others were doing, how putting their hard-won abilities as monster hunters to use here in the rural areas saved lives. He took cold comfort from the thought. Hunting gave their little band of exiles a purpose, something to hang on to, and for now, that was enough.

The trees thinned, revealing Bourn Lake. The water shimmered in the afternoon sun. The lake stretched into the distance, much longer than it was wide. Mahon steered them here because it was the closest access point and the place where most of the bodies had washed up on shore.

"Doesn't look evil," Aiden observed as he and Rigan came to stand on either side of Corran, looking out over the water.

"I don't imagine it's the lake that's evil," Calfon replied, standing with his back to them, watching the treeline. "It's whatever's in the lake."

Corran looked to Rigan and Aiden. "Picking up anything with your magic?"

Both men closed their eyes, concentrating enhanced senses on the lake. Aiden opened his eyes first. "I can sense something, but it's either shielding itself, or it's far away. Mahon said the lake is a couple of miles long."

"But I was right—it's not the water itself?" Calfon asked, still not taking his eyes off the forest.

Aiden nodded. "As far as I can tell, yes. Mahon didn't say anything about people being harmed by drinking the water or touching it. Just drowning—on purpose."

"I'm still not sure about that part," Corran said, running a hand through his hair. "I mean some of them, yes. There were witnesses, according to Mahon. But the ones who came out here alone—how do we know they didn't fall in by accident? Or decide to cool off with a swim and go down with a cramp?"

The longer they stood by the lake, the more uncomfortable Corran became. Kell's absence loomed large in his thoughts, the grief strong and tangible. Many nights he had lain awake, his own voice a tireless accuser, faulting him for having let Kell down, having paid too little attention to their younger brother, not protecting him enough. All of his reasons and protestations died in the face of those accusations, and he knew them to be the awful truth. He'd let Kell down the same way he had failed to protect Jora, the way his mistakes had cost the lives of the friends and hunters who died in the city.

Corran stared at the glitter of the sun on the water and thought about the blessed silence he might find if he let himself sink beneath that rippling surface. He couldn't change the past, couldn't be absolved of his mistakes, but he could make a sacrifice—

"Corran!" Aiden's voice sounded distant, but something in the tone made Corran hesitate. A sharp pain in his upper arm brought him out of the daze.

"What in the name of the Gods did you do that for?" he snapped, seeing a bloodied knife in Aiden's hand and realizing the blood came from his bicep where Aiden had cut him.

"Look where you're standing," Aiden said, and Corran glanced down to see that he had moved almost to the edge of the lake from where he had been several feet away.

"It had you," Aiden answered his silent question. "Whatever was going on in your mind, it had you, and it would have pulled you in. I had barely stopped Calfon from doing the same, and turned around to find you ready to take a dive."

Calfon had retreated from the water's edge, but he eyed the lake like a viper, and his face looked pale and drawn.

"Guilt," Corran said thickly. "Mistakes. Things I didn't do, could have done better—"

"Lies," Aiden countered. "Blown out of proportion, calculated to do damage."

"Why aren't you affected?"

Aiden reached beneath his shirt and lifted a variety of bone, silver, and iron charms. "I wear them all the time. Looks like I should make more."

"They came because they thought they had to." Rigan's voice sounded strained and oddly distant. Corran glanced at him sharply. Rigan's eyes were open but staring glassily at the lake, as if he were locked inside his head instead of seeing what lay before him. He held one arm out in front of him, focusing his magic.

A chill went down Corran's spine, remembering the last time he had seen Rigan like this, just before they both almost died in the battle against Blackholt.

"Rigan?" Corran called in a quiet voice, afraid to startle his brother.

"It called to them, and they came."

Aiden gasped, and Corran shifted his focus from Rigan to the lake shore. At least a dozen ghosts stood at the edge of the water. Adults, children, young and old, all of them perhaps claimed by the lake's curse. The apparitions looked like their corpses must have appeared to those who dragged them from the water, bedraggled and bloated, garments plastered to their skin, lank hair in their eyes. The ghosts stared at the hunters, and Corran felt his heartbeat speed up at their accusing gaze. The air around them had been pleasantly warm, but now the temperature plummeted until they could see their breath.

"Why can't I hear them?" Corran asked.

"It's taking all my magic to help them manifest, and they're only strong enough to speak in my mind," Rigan replied.

"Let me help," Corran started, but Rigan cut him off.

"No. I've got this. Save your magic. We might need it."

"Ask them," Corran managed to croak the words through his dry mouth. He knew Rigan could not maintain his link to the dead for long. "Ask them what killed them."

"Cold and strong," Rigan relayed, his voice taking on a dreamlike sing-song. "Dark. Fast. Too big to see, or... too much churned up from the bottom."

"Did they mean to kill themselves?" The urgency was clear in Aiden's voice. He looked at Rigan worriedly, watching for signs that the magic that enabled Rigan to hear the confessions of the dead might be taking a toll on him.

"Yes," Rigan said, his eyes narrowed with concentration as if he were straining to hear the responses. "It called to them. They had their reasons. All of them had... reasons."

"Why? What reasons?" Aiden pressed. "Why did they think they needed to kill themselves?"

Rigan's face tightened, lips thinning as if concentration had turned to pain. Rigan flinched, and his whole body tensed, snapping his head to one side as if slapped. His outstretched hand clenched, curling the fingers in until they became a fist.

"Lies... failures... mistakes... disappointment... different for all of them—"

"That's enough!" Corran grabbed Rigan's outstretched arm and felt how tense his muscles were. "Let it go, Rigan. We've heard enough. Let go before you hurt yourself."

"So much pain," Rigan murmured as if he had not heard Corran. "They were all in so much pain—"

"Rigan!" Corran moved to stand in front of his brother and grabbed him by the shoulders, giving him a shake. "Let them go."

"I'm not sure he can, Corran," Aiden said quietly. "Has he ever tried to confess a crowd of spirits all at once?"

Corran shook his head, staring at Rigan and feeling fear rise in his throat. "No. Not to my knowledge. Just calling one at a time usually knocks the wind out of him."

"I don't know much about grave magic," Aiden said. "But it has to be draining his energy quickly, dealing with so many spirits at once."

Confessing the dead wasn't regular grave magic. Their mother had Wanderer blood, and this was part of Rigan's legacy from her, something he and his brother did not share.

"There are at least a dozen ghosts on the shore," Aiden replied. "And if they all want to unburden themselves to him, it's going to drain him dry." He licked his lips nervously. "I think he's created a bond with them somehow. They're holding on to him, even if he's trying to let them go."

"Do something!"

"I don't know what it will do to Rigan if I break the connection," Aiden snapped.

"We're pretty sure it's going to kill him if you don't."

"It's getting dark," Calfon said from behind them. "And I don't want to have to get through the woods when we can't see what's out there—in case the monster in the lake doesn't have to stay in the water. So make up your mind, but do it soon."

"I think—" Aiden said before he got a far-away look in his eyes that spoke of anchoring and concentration, and he reached out and clasped his hand around Rigan's outstretched fist. Then he pulled out an iron knife from his belt and sliced it across Rigan's forearm in a shallow, bloody cut.

Immediately, the ghosts on the shore vanished. Rigan gave a muffled cry and collapsed.

Aiden staggered and came back to himself. "I think... I think we should get out of here," he said, planting his feet wide to keep himself upright.

"Rigan?" Corran bent over his brother and felt for a pulse, relieved when he felt the beat beneath his fingers. Rigan did not stir.

"We're losing the light," Calfon cautioned.

"Calfon's right," Aiden said. "We need to get out of here. We still don't know enough about what the monster can do, but I think I've got some new leads. I think I saw something in the lore books that might help. Right now, we have to get Rigan back to town. We'll sort the rest of this out later."

Corran got Rigan up over his shoulder, grunting with the effort. Rigan might be slender, but he was all muscle, and heavy. "Got him," Corran managed. "Let's go."

The trek back through the woods seemed to take forever, and Corran swore Rigan grew heavier with every step. Together, he and Aiden could handle Rigan's weight easily, but the thick underbrush would make carrying him between them impossible. Corran took comfort in the steady in and out of Rigan's breathing, assuring himself that the drain from the magic had not been too much.

"Almost there," Aiden said, leading the way. Calfon trailed behind, weapons ready as if he expected the ghosts to follow.

The walk back to the village seemed much longer than it had on the way out. After the second time Corran stumbled and nearly fell, Calfon wordlessly stopped in front of him and transferred Rigan to his shoulder for the remainder of the trek.

Mahon had arranged for them to have a room to themselves upstairs at the local pub. When Corran opened the door, he found a lantern already lit. A single bed sat up against one wall, but Mahon had seen to it that the innkeeper dragged enough straw-stuffed mattresses in so that each of them had a place to sleep with pillows and rough woolen blankets.

Without a word, Calfon crossed to the bed. Corran helped steady Rigan as Calfon gently eased out from beneath his weight. "Did he come around at all?" Corran asked, feeling for a pulse again.

"Not that I could tell," Calfon said.

"Let him sleep it off," Aiden advised. "We'll make sure he eats and drinks before we try to do anything else."

"Is he hurt?"

Aiden stretched out his hand, fingers splayed, palm down, and let it hover over Rigan's chest. After a moment, the healer shook his head. "No. Just exhausted. Although I don't want to think about what might have happened if I hadn't been able to break the bond." He looked ruefully at Rigan's injured arm and pulled some linen bandages from his bag, wrapping the cut after he had cleaned and treated it.

Corran stared at Rigan lying motionless on the bed, and the sight brought back too many memories of other fights, other injuries, times when Rigan nearly did not make it back.

"Don't," Aiden said as if he could read Corran's mind. "That was then; this is now. He's tired. There's no internal bleeding; no significant drain on his life force—"

"No *significant* drain?"

Aiden gave him a patient look. "When you wear yourself out until you can barely stand up, what do you think you're draining? The energy to move and think and breathe is part of your life force. He's pushed himself as if he ran ten miles. He needs to sleep it off and eat. That's all."

Even after nearly a year of knowing about Rigan's extra abilities, Corran still had difficulty wrapping his mind around the magic. What they did as undertakers, the chants and songs to help souls pass to the After, even Rigan's ability to hear the confessions of the dead, those he understood. But the other uses, like summoning fire or force, seemed foreign. That alienness did not make him afraid of Rigan; he knew and trusted his brother. It made him afraid *for* Rigan, that one day he would push too far and not recover.

Kell and their parents were dead. He could not lose Rigan, too.

"How do we fight that thing?" Corran asked.

After depositing Rigan, Calfon had gone to fetch food and drink, leaving them alone to get him settled. Corran could tell that Calfon still chafed about not being the one in charge, and that accounted for his surly mood. But right now, hurt feelings seemed the least of their concerns. Or perhaps Calfon's sour mood stemmed from whatever visions the monster in the lake had drawn out of his head, the fears and insecurities that made sliding beneath that dark water seem like a good idea.

The dinner hour was long past, and if not for his worry about Rigan, Corran guessed he might be hungry. Now, all he could think about was the battle that still loomed, and how they might be able to win without destroying themselves.

"There are some references in the books Rigan and I brought with us," Aiden said, moving away from the bed. "They're old histories and some bestiaries. Pretty sure some of the stuff is pure legend, but then again, most stories have a kernel of truth in them."

Corran saw weariness in Aiden's face and realized they were all tired, frightened, and worried. "You think there's a way to kill that thing, without burning yourselves up?"

Aiden ran a hand back through his hair. "Yeah. Rigan and I both did, or we wouldn't have agreed to take the job. But we know a little more about the creature now, how it works, and that might narrow down what's in the lore, help us get it right the first time."

"I'll sit with Rigan," Corran said. "Go do what you need to do. Let's hope Calfon brings back something good to eat and some ale to wash it down with." *And fixes his attitude. We've got bigger things to worry about.*

A few candlemarks later, they sat around a small table covered with old manuscripts. "I think it's a *nokk*," Aiden said and glanced at Rigan for confirmation. Rigan nodded. "Odds are good it came from one of the larger lakes upstream, and got carried down here by the big flood Mahon mentioned."

"The *nokk* feed on emotion," Rigan continued. He looked drawn and tired, but after sleeping for most of the evening and eating his dinner, Rigan refused to stay in bed. His eyes were haunted and held a pained look that worried Corran, making him wonder what dark lies the creature in the lake had whispered to his brother, what reasons it might have supplied to draw him below the water. "That can be something as simple as the fear of an animal being hunted by predators. Up in the high country, these things probably don't have much contact with humans, so terrified deer will do. This one—"

"Got swept downstream into a damn banquet," Calfon finished for him. "But how does it target its victims? Do that many villagers want to kill themselves?"

Aiden leaned back. "No, at least, I don't think so. I don't know how it picks its prey, but I doubt all those people intended to commit suicide when they got lured to the lake. For all we know, it fed just fine on their fear when it drowned them."

"It likes guilt." They turned to look at Rigan. Calfon paled, and his jaw set, but Corran saw fear glint in the man's eyes. Corran forced his mind away from the poison that had slithered through his mind and guessed from Rigan's shadowed gaze that he had experienced the creature's lure himself. "Guilt, uncertainty, insecurity—the dark emotions feed it." Rigan shivered and rubbed his hands on his forearms to get warm. "It's good at finding weaknesses."

"So how do we kill it?" Corran asked. He felt too edgy to sit still, and his left leg bounced up and down hard enough that he realized he was shaking the table.

"Anointed steel," Aiden said, pointing to a paragraph in one of the yellowed manuscripts. "It kills the prey before eating it. Blood from a living person on spelled steel weakens it enough that we can take it down the regular way—chop it to pieces."

Aiden reached into his pocket and pulled out a handful of amulets on leather straps. Some were crystals, while others were bits of wire and bone or sigils made from bent iron nails. "Elinor and Mir made these," he said. "There's enough for each of you to wear several like I do. I figured we'd need them before we go back. I'll be damned if I'll let that thing get into your heads again. I should have thought of this beforehand."

Corran reached out to clap Aiden on the shoulder. "I think we've had enough of guilt. Not your fault that you can't foresee everything." Aiden managed a self-deprecating smile.

"You know how it is with healers," he said. "We don't take the advice we give to everyone else."

"The sooner we get rid of this creature, the better," Calfon said, and Corran guessed he was channeling his fear into defiance.

"Sounds good to me." Corran reached for his tankard of ale and took a long draught. "Any particular time of day that's especially good for *nokk* hunting?"

Aiden managed a tired smile. "All the books say is 'after the sun has hit its zenith,' so not in the morning."

"What sort of 'blessing' do the blades require?" Calfon asked.

"Everything we found suggests a prayer to the Elder Gods and a request for their favor in the hunt," Rigan replied. His gaze slid to Corran. The night Kell died, they had called on Eshtamon, one of the Elder Gods, for vengeance and sworn their souls and service to him. Their battle against Machison and Blackholt had been successful. Corran strongly doubted they had discharged their oath so easily. A god's favor was rarely so cheaply bought.

"Can't say I'm a praying man myself," Calfon admitted, "but this sounds worth the effort. Any suggestion on which of the Elder Gods might be inclined to care?"

"I doubt it would be Colduraan," Aiden replied. "He's partial to chaos, and the monsters are definitely chaotic. Ardevan and Balledec haven't been prominent in a long while. That leaves Doharmu—god of death, Oj and Ren—the Eternal Mother and Forever Father, and Eshtamon—bringer of vengeance. Take your pick."

"As an undertaker, I can tell you that it's never wise to approach

Doharmu outside his temple," Corran cautioned. "He can be... unpredictable."

Calfon rubbed the back of his neck uncomfortably. "All right. And I'm not keen on bothering the two most powerful Elder Gods. But Eshtamon sounds like a possibility. What do I have to do?"

"Spill three drops of blood on the blade you plan to fight the *nokk* with, and ask Eshtamon's favor in the hunt," Aiden replied. "And hope for the best."

Later, after they had asked the ancient gods to bless their weapons and shuttered the lanterns, Corran lay awake on his pallet, listening to the sounds of the night. Calfon snored and rolled over. Aiden lay still as a dead man on his belly. In the cot next to him, Rigan moved restlessly before settling into a new position and quieting.

He had wondered when he and Rigan asked Eshtamon to bless their swords and knives, whether the god would speak to them again or show himself as he did that night they swore their oath in the graveyard. But when they worked the ritual tonight, Eshtamon did not appear to them. Nothing happened.

Except, that's not completely true, Corran thought.

Because he had felt something, when he did the working. He felt a shiver and remembered the sense of awe and power that had come over him, that awful night at the cemetery when Kell lay newly dead and buried, and their world was about to go up in flames. He had felt a presence, and in his mind heard that same resonant voice he'd remembered from before.

The task is not yet done.

Corran had glanced at Rigan then and saw the same fearful, wide-eyed look on his brother's face that he imagined was on his own. That was when he knew he had not imagined the voice; he felt certain Rigan had heard it too. He wanted to ask, but the words caught in his throat. *Later. After the hunt. We'll figure out what Eshtamon meant, how in the name of the gods we aren't done when we killed the bastards that ordered Kell's death.*

He lay awake a while longer, trying to figure out the meaning until the stress of the day finally caught up to him and he fell into a restless sleep.

Dark dreams found him. *The creature barreled into Corran, knocking him to the floor before he could get in a good swing with his rake. The thing that attacked him looked like a withered corpse, but moved swiftly and fought savagely. Sharp teeth snapped inches from his throat; a bony hand pinned his left arm, digging its nails through his shirt and deep into his flesh.*

"Get out of here, Jora!" Corran yelled, twisting to evade the creature's snapping teeth. He thumped the ghoul hard on the head with the handle of his rake and brought his knees up into its belly.

Jora swung the shovel with all her might. The iron blade came down hard on the ghoul's back, with enough force to break bone. The creature shrieked, but it did not release its hold on Corran.

"Go get help!" he shouted.

"I'm not leaving you." With that, Jora swung, and the blade of the shovel clanged against the creature's skull.

Corran gritted his teeth as he ripped his arm free and rolled out from beneath the ghoul. He swung his rake, sinking the sharp metal tines into the creature's side.

The ghoul grabbed Jora's arm and threw her aside with inhuman force, before backhanding Corran hard enough to blur his vision and set his ears ringing. Jora scrambled to her feet, coming back at full speed, swinging her shovel for a killing blow. The ghoul wrenched the shovel from her hands, grabbed her by the throat, and twisted. Her neck snapped with a sickening crunch, and her body fell to the ground.

In the next instant, the scene changed. Corran was back in the workshop of their undertaking business in Ravenwood City. A chill went down his back, and he knew with certainty what he would see when he turned to the tables where they prepared corpses for burial.

Rigan marked a sigil in ochre on Kell's abdomen, a dark orange gash against his pale skin, the mark of "life." He drew another compli-cated marking with white chalk on the chest, above the linen strips that bound Kell's ribs, this time for "breath." Blue woad sealed Kell's lips with another sigil, the sign for "spirit." The final rune was drawn in soot on Kell's forehead, for "soul."

"It's done," Corran said, his voice tight. "I just wish we could say goodbye."

A strange look crossed Rigan's face. "Maybe we can."

"What are you talking about?" Corran asked, uneasy at the new determination in Rigan's eyes.

Rigan stretched out his hand, palm down, over the first sigil. His eyes closed, his tear-streaked face tight with concentration. After a few seconds, the ochre sigil began to glow.

"What are you doing?" Corran stared at the glowing rune.

Rigan's hand hovered above the second marking, and the white sigil glowed almost too bright for Corran to look at. Next, the blue mark that sealed Kell's lips burned like the summer sky. Finally, Rigan held his hand steady above the soot mark on Kell's forehead, and pinpricks of light shone from the darkness like stars.

"I'm sorry."

The voice startled both of them. Kell's apparition stood at the head of the table that bore his body. Corran stepped back, heart thudding. Rigan opened his eyes, his expression a mixture of amazement and satisfaction.

"Is it really you?" Corran managed to ask, though his mouth was dry.

Kell's ghost nodded. "I can't stay. But I wanted to say goodbye. And I'm sorry that I got caught. Thanks for—" he gestured toward the preparations they had made for his corpse.

Corran's knees felt weak, and his chest ached. "It's too soon. This wasn't supposed to happen."

Kell's expression was somber. "I don't want to leave. The guards loosed the monster to cover up the killings. They're using the creatures. Stop them."

Kell looked as if he were about to answer, but the image began to waver, fading. The image winked out, as quickly as it had appeared.

Rigan slumped to the floor.

"Oh, gods! What did you do?" Corran dropped to his knees beside

49

his brother, realizing that throughout the exchange with Kell's ghost, Rigan had said nothing. "Come on!" Corran urged with a note of desperation in his voice. Rigan lay still, deathly pale and unresponsive, breath slow and shallow.

"Dammit! I'm not losing both of you! Come on, Rigan! Stay with me." He felt for a pulse, and found one, though Rigan's erratic heartbeat and clammy skin fueled his panic.

Corran grabbed a bucket of cold water and a bottle of whiskey. He doused Rigan with the frigid water. To his relief, his brother sputtered and roused, blinking through the icy rivulets that ran down his face. Corran knelt and forced Rigan's mouth open, trickling the strong whiskey between his lips. Rigan gasped, turning his head, and motioned for Corran to stop.

"What did you do?" Corran demanded.

"I learned how to summon spirits as well as banish them," Rigan replied in a harsh whisper. "It's like confessing the dead, only a bit different. I've been using it to find out more about how magic is being used to summon the monsters. The spell works, but there's a cost."

"What kind of cost?"

"A thread of my soul."

Corran stared at Rigan, speechless and stunned. Finally, he found his voice. "Why didn't you tell me? Why did you risk yourself?" How many threads are in a soul?

Corran woke with a start, sitting bolt upright and catching his breath sharply in the darkened room. The others slept on, undisturbed. Corran passed a hand over his face, trying to calm himself, feeling his heart pound. *Jora. Kell. I let them down. I failed them. I was supposed to keep them safe, and I failed. And look what's become of us. Tonight, I almost lost Rigan, too. I failed. Jora and Kell are dead, and Rigan nearly died, and it's all my fault.* He did not need the *nokk* to drown in his failures and mistakes. He'd been doing that on his own for months.

Corran glanced around, fearful he had woken the others, then sagged back onto his pallet when he realized they slept on, undisturbed. Nightmares about Jora's death and the night they lost Kell were not uncommon. Frequently, a hunt pushed memories to the surface, and while Corran could push those thoughts away while awake, he had no recourse against them while he slept.

Gradually, his heartbeat calmed, and his breathing slowed. The sheen of sweat on his forehead grew clammy. Corran lay still, afraid to shut his eyes, fearful of the torments to which sleep would deliver him. He had learned the hard way that nightmares came in clusters.

Rigan murmured something in his sleep and turned over. Calfon's snore reached a window-rattling crescendo and broke off abruptly. Aiden slept on, unaffected. Corran knew he needed to rest, knew that he could pose a danger to the others in the fight if he were groggy, but his whole body thrummed with energy as if he had drunk too much coffee.

Maybe the guards will lose interest eventually. After all, Machison is dead. Sooner or later, they'll have something more important to do. We just have to stay out of reach until then. When that happens, we won't have to always keep moving. We can find a village, settle down, and go back to our trades if we want. The Guilds have little actual power out here; most of the towns would be glad to have our skills. We have to survive long enough to get to that point.

Corran had been certain that he would remain awake, but sometime in the darkness, sleep claimed him.

"Time to go." Calfon nudged his leg with the toe of a boot. "It's daylight. We've got enough time to eat and then go back and finish the job."

Corran hauled himself to his feet, groaning as his back protested. Despite the pallet, a night on the floor made him stiff. He remembered the nightmares, and despite his best efforts, knew they would cast a pall over his mood. A glance at Rigan's empty cot told him that his brother had already risen, and he tried to focus on that as being a good sign.

"Rigan's fine," Calfon said, guessing Corran's thought. "He and Aiden went down and rustled up coffee and breakfast and brought it back. You're the last one up."

"Never could sleep well on the floor," Corran said, unwilling to admit the real reason for his grogginess, and embarrassed that he lagged behind.

Calfon shrugged. "I'm not up long myself. Aiden got me a few minutes ago." He paused. "Hope I didn't snore." Calfon had the good grace to look embarrassed.

"Not that I noticed," Corran lied. "Come on; we've got a lake monster to hunt."

———

IT ALL WENT wrong so fast.

They stood on the lakeshore, waiting as Rigan and Aiden reached out with their magic, troubling the water with their power, nudging the creature that lay beneath the surface. Poking the beast.

When the *nokk* rose from the lake's depths, they fell back, discovering that the authors of the ancient manuscripts lacked firsthand knowledge of their subject. The monster loomed larger than they expected, and it bore scant resemblance to the woodcut image in the lore book.

The *nokk* looked like a man astride a horse, if both had been flayed to raw, bleeding muscle and conjoined. White, pupilless eyes fixed on them as the creature emerged from the water, bearing down on them as if it knew they had come looking for a fight. Chillingly, Corran could make out no features on the faces of either the rider or the steed. No nose, no mouth. Then he remembered; the thing did not need to bite or rend to feed.

They had wondered whether the *nokk* could navigate on dry land; now they had their answer. It left the safety of the depths, trailing water and slime behind it. The legs ended in paws rather than hooves, and the beast had a powerful tail that lashed from side to side behind it. To Corran's relief, the charms Aiden made for them kept the creature's dark seduction at bay, though he could feel a storm looming at the edges of his consciousness.

"Careful," Calfon cautioned as the hunters moved to surround the creature. Corran stood closest to the water, with Rigan to his left and

Calfon to his right and Aiden directly opposite. The monster regarded them in silence, giving no suggestion that it considered them to be a threat. Calfon gave the signal, and the hunters attacked in unison.

Damn, that thing is fast! Corran dove forward with his blessed blade and spelled knife, only to discover that the *nokk's* hide proved tougher than expected. The creature snapped its powerful tail one way and another, sending Calfon flying several feet to land hard on the ground. Corran threw himself to one side, barely missing the muscular appendage that swung past him with sufficient force to break bones.

The *nokk* charged forward, nearly trampling Rigan as he and Aiden lunged at it with their blades. Corran scrambled to his feet, and from this angle, he could not see if their blows landed. This time, the four men staggered their attack, trying to keep the monster off balance, dodging in and out only long enough to score a gash on a shoulder or flank, to thrust a blade deep and pull free.

"It's working—keep it up!" Calfon shouted, grinning triumphantly as his knife tore a long, ragged line down the *nokk's* side. The creature bled dark ichor from wounds all over its body, but nothing so far had crippled it.

"Do we strike the man or the horse?" Corran yelled. "What kills it?"

"The lore said to hit the heart," Aiden called back. "It didn't say where that was." Aiden fell back a few steps and used his shorter blade as an athame, closing his eyes and concentrating his magic. Corran knew what they had discussed, that Aiden would attempt to disrupt the creature's functioning, to slow the heart or cut off the breathing. After a few moments, Aiden lowered his hands and shook his head.

"There's nothing for me to lock onto," he said. "Or whatever is there is too far from human to recognize. My magic just slips away."

"What about the spells and the blessings and the blood?" Calfon danced backward as the creature turned its attention toward him. "Why isn't it doing anything?"

"Maybe it is," Rigan countered. "Maybe we haven't hurt it enough."

Corran threw himself forward, aiming his sword to slip between the ribs of the lower body, to hit where the heart would be on an actual horse. His blade sank hilt deep, spraying Corran with cold ichor, and the whole beast trembled, then wrenched free and shifted its hindquarters, swinging its muscular tail as Corran stumbled backward.

The tail caught him in the stomach, lifting him off his feet, driving the breath from his lungs and tossing him into the air toward the lake. Corran thought he heard Rigan scream his name, but the impact when he hit the water drove everything from his mind.

He sank. Fully clothed and heavily armed, Corran felt the water drag him under. His woolen jacket soaked up the water and sturdy boots made his legs leaden. Stunned by the force of his landing, Corran gasped for air and choked as water filled his lungs.

The memories from the night before enveloped him as he fought to breathe. Jora, dying in the barn, staring lifelessly at him as if to accuse him for failing her. Kell's savaged corpse, bloodied and bound, slashed by the guards' swords and ripped open by one of the Lord Mayor's monsters. Another memory took hold of him, of Rigan beaten nearly to death by the guards, spent from using too much magic, dying. And then another image, of Rigan collapsing after the fight against Blackholt, pale and bleeding, barely breathing, so close to death—

I'm so sorry. I failed. All my fault. I've lost them— Grief, guilt, and sorrow clinched in his chest as he sank through the cold, dark water, and Corran did not fight the reprieve offered as everything began to turn gray. *They're dead because of me. I deserve to pay...*

A strong hand locked around his upper arm, hard enough to bruise, and then Corran felt himself begin to rise. He had no strength left to fight or assist, and overcome with the memories and loss; he did not care what happened. He hung limp in the grasp of whatever gripped him, and he wondered if the *nokk* had returned to the water to claim its victim.

He barely registered the fact that he broke the surface of the water. Cold air stung his face, and the bruising grip on his arm wrenched his shoulder as it dragged his sodden body toward shore.

"Corran! Don't you die. Don't you dare die!"

Corran knew he should be able to recognize the voice, but his ears were full of water, muffling sound, and his head felt stuffed with cotton. Seizures wracked his body as he strained for air, trying to purge the water from his lungs and managing only a gurgle.

He hit the ground hard, on his side, and water gushed from his mouth. Blows struck his back, forcing more of the water out of him. Corran could make out more voices shouting, and then he rolled onto his back, heaving for breath.

Once again someone grabbed him and hauled him away from the water, leaving him sprawled on the sparse, dry grass. "Drive it back toward the lake!" He heard Rigan shout, and a moment later, a fiery blast lit up the air.

Corran managed to turn onto his side, enough to see Rigan standing between him and the monster. Fire lanced from Rigan's outstretched hand, engulfing the *nokk* in flames. The beast flailed, its limbs stomping in the shallow water, flesh charring and peeling. Yet it did not fall. The tail thrashed from side to side, skimming across the water and sending up a blinding spray that did not quench the fire.

"Rigan, be careful!" A voice shouted.

"This is for trying to kill my brother," Rigan growled. Bright blue-white light arced from Rigan's palm, forking to strike the *nokk* in both of its chests.

Lightning. Corran's head had not completely cleared from his near-drowning, but he recognized the blinding energy that enveloped the monster. Violent shaking wracked the *nokk*, and even through Corran's fuzzy thoughts, he realized that the creature stood knee-deep in water.

Corran felt the same shiver as a cold tendril of thought formed in his mind—*guilt, bad, failed, lost, all my fault, betrayed them*—but this time, the touch felt muted.

"It's too close, and throwing everything it's got at us," Aiden warned, an edge of strain in his voice. "The amulets aren't strong enough. You've got to fight it."

Corran gasped at the violation, gripping his temples with his hands. He still struggled to breathe, coughing up water, but instinct took over, and he fought the alien thoughts. The air smelled like burned flesh and the tang after a storm. He heard shouting in the distance, and the persistent sizzle of the lightning Rigan sent against the *nokk*.

In a heartbeat, the assault ended. The cold tendrils vanished from Corran's mind, the hiss of the lightning fell silent, a heavy object hit the water with a great splash, and Rigan collapsed in a heap next to him.

Corran clung to consciousness, and dug his fingers into the damp ground, trying to drag himself to Rigan's side. Footsteps pounded nearby. Aiden fell to his knees next to Rigan.

"You stubborn son of a bitch," Aiden muttered as he rolled Rigan onto his back and began to examine him.

In the next instant, Calfon knelt next to Corran, pushing him onto his chest. Corran resisted, not wanting to lose sight of Rigan, but Calfon easily overpowered him and began slapping his back with hard, open-palm strikes.

"Same goes for you," Calfon grumbled. "Thought we were going to lose both of you, and Aiden and I weren't doing too well against that thing."

"Is it dead?" The water and choking made Corran's voice rough and strangled. "Did we get it?"

"Yeah," Calfon said, glancing over his shoulder and shuddering. "Since when can Rigan hurl lightning?"

"Since that damn thing tried to kill my brother," came the answer. Rigan sounded tired and weakened, but there was a note of triumph in his voice that made Corran smile.

"Once we're safe back home, we'll discuss the wisdom of throwing lightning when you're soaking wet," Aiden snapped. "You could have fried yourself as much as you cooked that thing."

"But I didn't." Rigan's hazy tone suggested he had a slim hold on consciousness.

"Let's get both of you home, and as soon as you're healed, I've got a mind to kick your asses," Calfon said, bending down and helping Corran to his feet as Aiden did the same for Rigan. Neither of the injured men was steady, so the walk back took longer than the trip in.

Corran stole a look at Rigan. His brother was pale and shaking, hair and clothing plastered to his body. Corran doubted he looked any better since his lungs burned and his shoulder throbbed from bearing his whole weight when Rigan pulled him clear. He could not resist shooting a grin at Rigan for defying the odds, and Rigan managed a tired nod in acknowledgment.

"You know, I don't have to thrash you," Calfon said as they neared the end of the forest road. "I think we could just take you back to the monastery and let Polly and Elinor do it for us."

"Please, no," Rigan groaned.

"I think it's only fair," Aiden teased.

Corran had no doubt that Elinor would give Rigan some stern words for taking crazy chances. As for Polly, Corran knew she would take after him with her dreaded wooden spoon on general principles.

"Did the impact knock you out when you hit the water?" Calfon asked. "Because it didn't look like you were trying to get out."

Suicides, Corran thought. *Maybe the other victims didn't go to the lake intending to die, either. Maybe it made them believe they deserved to, like it did with me.*

"No idea," he lied, and with the *nokk* dead, the truth might not really matter.

Rigan turned to him and met his gaze with a stare that told Corran his brother saw right through his deception. "Maybe we can save the talking for later," Rigan croaked. But the look he gave Corran suggested that his brother intended to pursue the topic in private until he discovered what had happened. Corran resolved to put off that conversation as long as possible.

To their surprise, Mahon was waiting for them at the edge of the forest. Their horses stood behind him, loaded with their gear.

"You can't go back to the village," Mahon said. "They're looking for you."

"Who?" Calfon asked. "The families of the victims? We killed the monster."

Mahon shook his head. "No. I mean, thank you. Very good that you killed the monster. I've brought your pay," he said, handing off a thin pouch of coins, as well as a bag filled with vegetables, cheese, and eggs, a wooden cage with two chickens and a young goat with a rope for a leash. "But it's not the families. Guards came, asking about strangers. I hid your things from them, but they searched the room and kept asking questions."

"What did you tell them?" Aiden asked.

Corran felt a chill of an entirely different sort run down his back, at the thought that the soldiers might drag them back to the city, where they would face certain execution.

"I didn't say anything," Mahon snapped. "Told them all kinds of people come through and I don't remember any of them, which is mostly true. I warned everyone not to mention you and to slow the guards any way they could. But someone is likely to have seen something, and you'd best be gone by the time that happens."

"Damn," Calfon muttered. "We've got two injured men—"

"I can ride." Corran managed to get the words out between gritted teeth. "It's not like we have a choice."

"I can, too." Rigan lifted his head, jaw set. "Don't waste time arguing. Let's go."

Corran felt his face blaze with embarrassment as he resigned himself to accepting help from Calfon to get up to his saddle. Rigan barely dragged himself into position on his own, with Aiden standing nearby, just in case.

"I'll stall the guards as long as I can," Mahon said. "I'll send them down the valley road. The bridge is out, but they won't discover that until they've already traveled a candlemark and have to turn around."

"Thank you," Calfon said before swinging up to his mount.

"You've rid us of a monster. We're in your debt," Mahon replied. "Now ride quickly, and may the gods go with you."

———

MAHON'S SUBTERFUGE SUCCEEDED in getting Corran and the others past the guards, but the tense ride back to the monastery left them all out of sorts. They took a roundabout way home, in case the guards paid spies to keep a lookout, and the extra apprehension made Corran feel as if his guts were knotted by the time they arrived safely.

When they finished telling their story to those waiting in the monastery's makeshift kitchen, Corran longed for food and sleep. Polly put out bread, fruit, honey, and cheese, while Trent poured them all whiskey and raised a toast to their success. The memory of what the *nokk* had brought to the surface of his thoughts left Corran hollow and spent, but he forced a smile and seconded the toast for good measure.

"Where're Ross and Mir?" Corran asked, realizing that they had not been present for the retelling of the day's hunt.

"Mir's on guard duty, and Ross... well, that's a good question," Trent replied dourly. "Slipped out again, and his weapons are gone, so he's probably gone on some damn fool solo hunt. I figured I'd wait up for him, and slap some sense into him."

"Good luck with that," Calfon muttered. "Boy's got a death wish. One of these days, he's not going to come back, and we won't know what happened."

Corran remembered the dark thoughts that the *nokk* had nearly used to lure him to his death, and how easily Calfon and Rigan had also been snared. They were all still reeling from their losses and mistakes, and the new reality of being hunted outlaws. Calfon fretted over pointless slights to his authority. Polly hid her fear behind relentless wit and sarcasm. Elinor barely left their small library, while Aiden and Rigan pushed themselves to the breaking point to harness more magic. Ross proved himself with hunts, and Mir drank.

I hope no one's counting on us to save the world, because if they are, the world is screwed, Corran thought.

"Keep an ear out for Ross," Corran said with a tired sigh. "I'm going to go talk to Mir and make sure no one followed us."

Corran felt far older than his twenty-one years as he climbed the steep stone steps that led out of the monastery's hidden basement. He pushed open the trap door and carefully shut it behind him, then tromped up the steps to the damaged tower where someone always kept watch.

Mir appeared to relax when he recognized him and then frowned. "Problems?"

Corran shrugged. "Rough day. Thought I'd come up and see how you were doing."

Mir turned away and looked out over the countryside. The tower gave a clear view of the surrounding area while sheltering the watcher from notice from the ground. The remnants of lunch and a jug of water attested to how long Mir had been on duty.

"It hasn't been exciting," he answered. "I'm nearly at the end of my shift." He did not turn to look at Corran as he spoke. "I kind of like it up here. Quiet. Gets me away from the tempers and hurt feelings."

Corran chuckled. "It's not that bad," he replied. "Considering what we've been through, and how we've been living in each other's pockets, we should be stark raving mad by now."

"Aren't we?" His voice sounded more lost than joking, and Corran regarded him, taking in the hunch of his shoulders, the stubble of beard and the unkempt hair.

"Could be worse," Corran said. "None of us ever bargained for this."

Mir sighed but did not turn around. "I miss my family," he said, keeping his back to Corran like a shield. "I miss the forge, and the way the coals in the furnace smelled, the heft of the iron in my hands, the sound of the hammer on the anvil. I liked being a blacksmith." He shook his head. "Didn't ever want to be a soldier."

"We didn't think that's what we were going to become when we started hunting monsters," Corran said, remembering the night Kell died when Mir came to warn them, and they had all barely escaped with their lives. "And now... I hope that when things settle down, we can go back to our trades if we want. Hard to do on the run."

"You think it ever will—settle down, I mean? Everything we find out about the monsters makes this mess bigger. Shit, Corran, we're tradesmen. What if this blood magic business goes up to the crown princes? The nobles? The king himself?"

Corran leaned against the rough stone tower wall. "I ask myself the same thing, and I don't have a good answer. But we can't quit right now even if we turned our backs on the monsters, because we're outlaws. We can't stop running until they stop chasing us."

Mir dropped his head, and Corran saw defeat in his shoulders. He knew his friend remained sober for his watch duty, but afterward, Corran had seen Mir drown his memories in rough whiskey even more than the rest of them.

"I wish there was some way to know that they're all right—the ones we left behind," Mir continued in a voice barely above a whisper. "You and Rigan and Aiden and Polly, everyone you've got is right here. But Elinor had Parah, and Calfon and Trent and I still had family back there. I wish I could send them a message, let them know I'm alive, even if I can't ever go home again. And I wish something fierce they could just let me know that the guards didn't burn them out or string them up. That's what I can't get out of my head, what I dream about. That what we've done brought destruction down on them."

"I don't have an answer for that," Corran said, at a loss for what else to say. "Maybe someday, you can go back, or it will be safe to send a messenger. But right now, trying to contact them, if anyone suspected, it would only put them in more danger."

"I know," Mir said, his voice hitching. "But I still think about it." He looked back at Corran, sorrow and longing etched in his features. His gray eyes shone with the tears he refused to shed, and his mussed black hair looked like a storm cloud. His shoulders and arms flexed as he fought the despair inside, still strong and toned from years of heavy, hard work. "If I'd never gone after the monsters, would I still be safe and with them? Or would it all have gone to the Abyss some other way?"

Corran shrugged. "No way to tell. Even the seers probably couldn't answer that." He paused. "Look, tomorrow why don't you spend some time in the forge here. You always like that, and the horses probably need re-shod."

"Not a good idea to be putting up smoke if someone's looking for us," Mir replied. "Though you're right, beating the shit out of an iron rod does wonders for my mood," he added with a wry smile.

"We'll get through this," Corran said with a confidence he didn't completely share but hoped to be true. "We have to stick together. Maybe the worst is already behind us."

"Corran Valmonde, you're full of shit," Mir replied, but his tone lacked any bite. "Not on the sticking together part. I'm in it for the long haul. But I can't help feeling that we haven't seen the worst of it."

By the time Corran had gotten downstairs, Ross was back, heaving for breath and surrounded by the others.

"There's a dozen men on their way," Ross reported. Sweat dripped from his hair and beaded on his face, soaking the back of his shirt as if he had ridden hard, or run the whole way.

"Who?" Calfon demanded.

Ross bent over, resting his hands on his thighs, trying to get his breath. "I didn't get a real close look, but the man in charge looked familiar—I think he had something to do with Machison. He was definitely from the city. He had two witches—at least they wore robes like fancy witches—and the rest were soldiers."

"How far away?" Trent questioned.

"Beyond what anyone could see from the tower. I rode as fast as I could. We've got to get the horses out and get down to the caves," Ross replied breathlessly.

Polly appeared with a basket full of everything ripe from the small garden she tended behind the ruins. Elinor and Aiden had helped her plan the plantings so that the patch would look overgrown and untended should anyone come prying. "No point in wasting food," she said in a huff, setting the basket down on the table.

She went to warn Mir, and once he was safe below, bolted the secret trap door from inside. Trent, Ross, and Calfon went to move the horses and their few chickens and goats from the rickety stable down a narrow path to a large cave under the bluff. Aiden, Elinor, Corran, and Rigan frantically collected their belongings and shoved them into satchels, handing them in a relay down the steep steps to the caves below. With luck, the heavy bolt and hidden door would keep intruders out of their haven. If not, they would wait it out in the caves. Either way, it meant that they would move on as soon as the road was clear.

The natural levels of salt in the rock of the cliff side would hinder any attempts for the attackers to detect them with magic. Aiden and Rigan had debated the benefits of deflection spells against the chance that the spells themselves might be noticed by a witch with nuanced power. In the end, they had placed a glamour over the cave where the livestock was penned and kept the magic to a minimum unless needed.

Caves pockmarked the cliff side, so the openings themselves should not attract attention, Corran told himself as they waited in the dark. Aiden and Rigan and Elinor had not left them defenseless; if the intruders found their hiding place, traps awaited the unwary, and the rest of the fugitives were well-armed and ready for a fight.

"The building's good stone. There's not much to burn," Polly murmured. "At least, not that wasn't burned when the king's guard ran the monks off in the first place." Corran could not see her face in the darkness, but her hushed voice sounded small and frightened, stripped of her usual bravado.

"We knew we'd have to move on soon," Elinor whispered. "We'll be all right."

Rigan and Aiden insisted on being closest to the front, with the others packed in behind them. If everything went completely to shit, a maze of tunnels led deeper into the cliff, passageways Corran supposed had been made use of by smugglers over the years. He did not relish the idea of fleeing farther into the darkness, though the thought of being hauled back to the city in chains to be hanged had even less appeal.

While they were out of sight of the cave's mouth, they could hear the rush of the river below, and the sound carried through the rock chambers. A loud scraping noise made them freeze, barely daring to breathe, and Corran's hand tightened around the grip of his knife.

"Valmonde! You can't run forever! I'll find you. You know it's true. Give yourselves up."

The man's voice echoed strangely from above, and Corran's heart skipped a beat as he recognized it from back in Ravenwood City. Hant Jorgeson, the Lord Mayor's head of security, a hated man who was only seen in public for hangings or floggings.

Corran had no desire to surrender, but he itched for a fight. He'd thought Jorgeson dead in the riots the night they overthrew Machison and Blackholt, then suspected the man had survived and had come looking for them when villagers warned them and described their pursuers. If he ever did have the chance to fight Jorgeson one on one, Corran had plenty of reasons to mete out his own rough justice.

Instead, Corran willed himself to remain still. The pursuers hadn't found the trapdoor or made their way into the tunnels, but the darkness that protected Corran and the others now felt suffocating, as they froze in their places, quieting their shallow breaths and fearing someone might hear the rapid beating of their hearts.

A sudden curse and a surprised yelp from above told Corran that Rigan had unleashed his grave magic on the intruders. In the next minute, mournful, ghostly moans and ear-splitting shrieks filled the ruins above and echoed through the caves, and the temperature dropped below the cave's cool norm. Footsteps shuffled against the rock, and in the distance, Corran caught a glimpse of a faint, foxfire glow.

"Be gone!" Jorgeson shouted. "I've no business with the dead."

The shrieks grew louder and closer, and the low mutter of men's voices sounded as the footsteps continued their spectral march. Corran feared that the men had made their way into the caves and tried to be as still as possible.

"Dispel!" Jorgeson's command echoed. "I command you—leave this place!"

When Trent and Ross had first explored the cliff side and its caves, they found the bones and scattered belongings of men they guessed had been pirates. How they came to die here and be left behind in the caves, no one could be sure, but Rigan and Corran had confirmed that the caverns were home to a number of restless and angry spirits.

The two undertakers had promised the ghosts help in crossing to the After, in exchange for their willingness to stand guard until the outlaws moved on. Now, the pirates sounded like they were eager to take out their long-denied vengeance on Jorgeson and his uninvited guards.

Corran closed his eyes, silently lending Rigan his grave magic, hoping that Jorgeson and his witches would assume the ghosts manifested on their own. He heard the clatter of steel against rock, as if Jorgeson or his guards had tried to slash the revenants with their swords. The din of rocks hurled against the stone walls answered as the spirits used the borrowed strength from the grave magic to drive back the assault.

A man screamed, and Jorgeson cursed. The ghosts wailed even louder, and Corran heard the clatter of running footsteps followed by another hail of stones. Then, silence.

After what felt like forever, a faint white glow formed in front of where Rigan and Aiden kept watch. A short, bearded man with broad shoulders and a wide chest appeared, wearing clothing that looked to be long out of date.

We did as ye bid, the pirate's spirit said, and as he spoke, the figures of six more ghosts took shape behind him. *Now keep your word.*

"Are they gone? The men who tried to enter the cave. Are they still above?" Rigan asked.

The ghostly captain shook his head. *No. They've taken their horses and gone. We gave them a fair chase, just to be certain. Aye, you should have heard them screamin'!*

"Thank you," Rigan said, and even though Corran couldn't see his brother, he knew the ragged tone in his voice all too well. Corran felt worn from augmenting Rigan's magic, and he could only guess how much harder it had gone on his brother, bearing the focus on the power. "We will keep our word."

Corran rose to find his way next to Rigan, and together they chanted the words to the ritual that would bless the spirits of the departed and open the portal through which they could find rest in the After. One by one, the ghosts winked out, until the captain gave them a nod of farewell and followed his crew to where Doharmu awaited.

Aiden called a flicker of witch light to his palm, and the others blinked to adjust to even its faint flame.

"That was too damn close," Trent muttered, voicing something Corran guessed they were all thinking.

"Back in the city, Jorgeson was obsessed with hunting down the Wanderers," Corran said, loathing thick in his voice. "What little I heard about him said he was cruel and relentless. He's likely the one who killed Bant, Jott, and Pav—and all the other hunters who got caught. He won't give up until we're caught or he's dead."

"Well, that's easy," Ross said in a cold, dangerous tone. "He's going to have to die, because we aren't going to."

CHAPTER FOUR

POLLY WHISTLED AS she sauntered down the street of the small town, taking her time although every instinct urged her to run. Circumstances had forced her to learn how to look out for herself at a young age, and her skill with a knife came hard-won. After all, she had done murder to protect her honor and maimed men who had threatened her. Parading down the street at night tarted up like a trollop rankled.

Then again, on this hunt, she was the bait.

Two weeks had passed since Corran and the others fought the *nokk*, fourteen tense days looking over their shoulder for bounty hunters and Jorgeson as they traveled to another monastery Polly had identified as a good location and settled in to still another new set of lightless, underground rooms.

Once they finished moving in, Elinor, Rigan, and Aiden brought up the possibility of another hunt. Their new way of searching for monsters, looking for ripples in the magic, had turned up an oddity near the village of Eilertown, a town of little note except for its location at a busy crossroads where a peddler's market gathered to sell to travelers.

"Come on, be a good monster," Polly muttered under her breath.

"Don't make me wander around here like a whore with the pox. What's wrong with you? I'm tasty, dammit!"

Earlier that day, Trent and Ross had gone to nose around Eilertown and returned with confirmation that their suspicions were correct. Young women began disappearing from Eilertown and several nearby villages a few months ago. There had been reports that some travelers —mostly merchants or peddlers—had also gone missing. As far as anyone could tell, none of the victims knew each other or had reason to leave on their own. No one had found any bodies, either.

A sound made Polly freeze and look behind her, but she saw nothing. She forced down her fear and broadened her swagger, a trick she had mastered long ago. While the others might feel more exposed and endangered than back in the city, Polly found herself surrounded by people she trusted for the first time in her life. Knowing that they would all fight to the last to protect each other constantly amazed her, winning out over her cynicism until she dared to believe it.

Best keep your mind on your mission, Polly warned herself. One hand slipped to the blade hidden in the folds of her skirt. Drunks and lechers she could handle; she had been declining their advances since before her moon days began. Monsters might require a little help.

She hesitated a moment before heading on, moving slowly so that Trent and Ross could keep her in sight. She knew they trailed her in the shadows, keeping enough distance so as not to frighten off their quarry, but staying close enough to intervene and make the kill. At least, that was the plan.

Polly whistled again, a tune she remembered hearing at The Lame Dragon back in Ravenwood City. Night had fallen though the evening was still young. The peddlers and tinkers had packed up their wagons until the next day, and few travelers would risk continuing their journey by night when an inn presented the opportunity for a meal and a night's rest.

Lanterns from the windows of the inn and the living quarters over the shops cast a dim glow into the street. Polly kept to the light, aware of how quickly monsters could move in the shadows. She had fought off ghouls and outmaneuvered the creatures that pursued them when they fled the city. Since then, Polly had insisted that the hunters teach her to fight, arguing that she was as much an outlaw as they were. She could hold her own, now more than ever.

Still, no sense in tempting fate, more than she was already doing by trying to attract the attention of a monster that had already killed over a dozen people.

"Lovely night, isn't it?" The voice came from a darkened doorway, and Polly startled despite herself.

"Nice enough, I guess."

A man stepped from the doorway but remained half-hidden in the shadows. "A lady shouldn't be out at night alone. Are you in need of an escort?"

Every survival instinct Polly had honed over the years buzzed a warning.

"I don't know," she resisted, buying time for Trent and Ross to close in on her position and trying to get a better feel for exactly what type of creature they faced. "You might not be a nice man." Polly felt certain he was not. After all, even with the rouge and powder, the tint to her lips and the socks she had shoved into the front of her dress to increase her bosom, she still looked young, and no one could doubt the nature of the agreement forged by accepting his company.

"It's dangerous out here in the dark," the man replied, moving a step closer. "I can keep you safe."

The closer he came to her, the more Polly could feel the stranger's allure. Dark hair and eyes, pale skin, and a handsome face offered only part of the attraction. He had a slim, well-built body and his clothing looked too expensive for this small town. A strange compulsion grew stronger as he neared, and Polly fell back a step and then two, struggling to keep her mind firmly on her mission. The dark-haired man's presence made her feel drugged, or perhaps drunk on potent wine.

He's not a man. Not a man. A monster. Keep your head, girl! Polly chastised herself. But before she had moved another step, the man closed his hand around her wrist. He did not hurt her, nor did his fingers dig into her skin, but all the same, Polly knew she could not break his grip.

"Come with me," he said quietly, and his voice sent a thrill through her that burned low in her belly. "I'll take care of you."

Polly pushed back on the compulsion in her mind, fighting his sway over her. She screamed, alerting Trent and Ross, and in one move, pulled her knife free from its hiding place and dug the point deep into the man's shoulder. Startled, he released her wrist, and she ran, spotting Trent and Ross heading toward her from the side street.

One moment, she stood on a deserted street in Eilertown, and in the next, Polly woke up on a dirty mattress in a darkened room.

"You tried to set a trap for me." The dark-haired man pushed away from the wall where he had been concealed in the shadows.

"Go screw a pig."

Her captor backhanded her. Polly pivoted, grabbed his wrist, and bit down with all her strength. He shook her off, tearing his wrist from her mouth, throwing her halfway across the room for good measure. "Why did you come to Eilertown? How many are in your hunting party?"

"I've got questions of my own," Polly snapped. "Who are you? And where am I?"

The man regarded her, and a cold smile touched his lips. "Of late, I'm called Garrod. It's one of many names, but it will do. And I have brought you to my house."

"*What* are you?" Polly asked, glaring at him.

"You didn't answer my questions. What were you trying to catch?"

Polly regarded him for a moment. She let out her breath in a huff. "Someone's been snatching girls from the village. Figured we'd set a trap."

Garrod chuckled. "I take it that part didn't go well?"

Polly fixed him with an uncompromising stare. "What are you?"

Garrod shrugged. "A businessman. My clients hunger. I supply fodder for their desires—and I feed very well from all that lovely pain and fear and lust."

Polly's lip curled. "I know your kind. Get your hooks into girls when they're hungry and don't have a place to lay their head, drug them up on opium and send them out to sell themselves in the taverns.

You're a monster all right, but nothing special." She spat, barely missing his boot.

Garrod smiled. "Oh, but there you're wrong. I'm a very special kind of... monster. I really do feed on emotions. So I'm not in it for money or blood. I devour desperation." He moved closer as she crab-walked backward, drawing herself up into as small a space as possible, wrapping her hands around her ankles.

"You're a vampire."

"A *ganwau*. Something much more civilized than a common blood drinker."

"Oh aren't you the fancy one? Is that another word for procurer?" Polly's sharp tone hid her fear, and worse; she knew this monster could see right through her defenses, that he savored her panic.

Trent and Ross are coming. They'll be here. I just have to hold him off. Keep him talking. Fight him. Anything to buy time.

"All that anger," Garrod murmured, dropping to his hands and knees and backing her up toward the mattress. "You've been at this point before, haven't you? Such a fighter. You are going to be delicious. Quite the feast." His smile slipped into a leer Polly had seen many times at the inn on drunken men who grabbed at her skirts or pulled at her arm.

"Then eat this." Polly lunged at him; silver knife pulled from her sock. The blade sank into Garrod's belly, and the *ganwau* shrieked in pain. Polly dove on top of the creature, pulling out the knife with her right hand and plunging a handful of the salt-amanita-aconite mixture into the wound from a pouch in her other sock.

"You stupid little cur," Garrod hissed, as his body bucked and writhed. Polly held on for her life, wrapping herself tightly around him with her arms and legs to trap him, mindful to avoid his teeth.

She had no more tricks if this did not work. It was never supposed to get this far; Trent and Ross were supposed to be right behind her. Polly remembered meeting Garrod in the street and breaking loose, running toward Trent and Ross, then her recollections blurred. *That son of a bitch messed with my memory.*

Fear drove her anger; anger gave her strength. Aiden had assured them that if the creature had a vampiric nature, then the salt mixture and silver would poison it. The mix wouldn't kill it, only taking off its head would do that, but it would weaken the creature, even the odds for the fight.

Now what do I do? Polly thought as she hung on so tight her shoulders and thighs cramped. She still clutched the knife in her right hand, though Garrod twisted so violently in her grip that she feared he would break loose if she tried to shift for an angle to stab him again.

He flexed and jerked up, rolling them over, trapping her beneath him and nearly crushing the air from her lungs. For a moment, another time and another place flashed through her memory, and in the remembering of that long ago violation, she felt Garrod draw strength from her pain.

"Oh no," she muttered. "Fuck no you don't." With her hands free of his weight, Polly grabbed on tight as she could with her left arm and both legs, then plunged the knife into the *ganwau's* neck and sawed with the blade.

His mouth opened, but no sound came from his savaged throat. Black blood welled in the vampire's mouth, falling onto her in cold splatters. Polly never stopped her tirade of curses. Focusing on the curses kept her mind off her fear and the utter terror of what was happening.

She kept sawing, ripping through flesh and sinew, tearing at the tough gristle of Garrod's windpipe. *He's a vampire. A dead thing. He doesn't need to breathe and he damn sure doesn't need to talk.*

Her curses grew more creative, blasphemous, and obscene, and she combined them in ever-changing ways, twisting her face to keep from getting any of the cold ichor in her mouth. Garrod gripped her tight as rictus, and she knew that if she survived, she would be able to see the imprints of his fingers on her arms.

The edge of her blade caught on bone, and she realized she had reached the vampire's spine. She stabbed at it, dug at the tendons and soft parts between the bones, but she knew her blade was not sharp enough to behead the creature, and without that final blow, the lore books said he could heal even grievous wounds.

She heard a loud crash and then heavy footsteps.

"Polly, move your hand!"

In the next breath, Polly heard the swish of a sword close enough that it passed over her like the breath of Doharmu. Garrod's body seized once, hands clamping on so tightly Polly thought they might snap bone, and then with a final tremor, the *ganwau* collapsed into a rotting pile of flesh.

"Polly!"

Trent fell to his knees beside her as Ross stood guard at the door. Trent scraped off the decaying skin and viscera as Polly fought back bile. "Did he bite you? Are you hurt? Drugged?"

Polly scrambled free, frantically raking her hands down over her crimson-soaked, ruined dress as if she could sluice more of the blood and offal off her clothing and skin. Her heaving breath seemed loud, though the pounding of her heart nearly drowned out the sound.

"Burn him," she ordered, wrapping her arms around herself in horror as she stared down at the remains. "Salt him and burn him and scatter him and use the vitriol to make sure he never comes back."

Trent reached out a hand, but Polly flinched back. "Don't," she said sharply. "Not now. Please, don't."

Trent nodded. "Polly, we followed as quickly as we could. He moved so fast—"

"I know," she whispered, never taking her gaze from the dead vampire. "I know." She forced herself to look at Trent. "Did you find the others? The ones he took?"

Ross muttered curses, and Trent swallowed hard. "Yes," he said in a choked voice. "And the ones the vampire sold them to. We killed his 'customers' on the way in. We'll get the victims back to Eilertown, but Polly, you've got to understand, there isn't much left of most of them. There are a few survivors, but not many. I'm sorry."

Polly tightened her arms around herself, cold as the blood that sank through her clothing. "He fed on the lust, on the fear. Not on blood."

"Come on," Trent said, moving to stand beside Polly without touching her. "Let's get out of here."

THE VILLAGERS RECEIVED their wounded children with tight-lipped stoicism. Ross collected their fee, and they moved on before too many questions could be asked. Polly refused help to swing up to her saddle, squaring her shoulders and lifting her head. She had scrubbed the blood off the night before, at a horse trough on the outskirts of the village as Ross and Trent took the handful of survivors back where they belonged.

Go ahead. I'll be fine. The monster's dead—remember? She urged them to go, and Polly thought she saw a flicker of understanding in Trent's eyes, that she needed some time alone.

She cried as she scrubbed at her skin; hot, wild, desperate tears on the edge of sanity. The cold water in the trough numbed her, kept the pain away as she rubbed hard enough to raise bright red streaks of her own blood in her attempts to wash away the *ganwau's* black ichor.

Polly's shoulders heaved and her breath caught in her swollen throat. She wanted to rip away the clothes Garrod had touched and that had been soiled by his blood and burn them like they burned what was left of his corpse. She wanted to light candles and press her face into fresh flowers to remove the stench from her nose. The stink of the room where she had been held, the filthy mattress, and the odd, sickly sweet odor of Garrod himself lingered as both smell and taste. Polly would have willingly eaten a whole bulb of garlic to wipe it all away.

"Polly."

When she finally heard Trent, she guessed that he had called her several times already. "I'm here."

"We can go," Trent said in a quiet voice, as if she were a skittish horse, not to be spooked.

"All right." Even to her own ears, her voice sounded dull and monotone.

Garrod's threats, the knowledge of what he used his victims to do, hit too close. She had nearly fallen prey to Garrod's mortal counterparts, and it had taken all her wits and cunning to evade the fate of his victims.

Along the way, there had been too many close calls, too many near misses, and far too many friends lost. She only realized that her skin was cold as ice when she wrapped her arms around herself once more.

"Here." Trent laid a cloak over her shoulders without touching her, and she drew it close.

"Thank you."

"You were… amazing back there," Trent said, standing a respectful distance away. "We thought—well, we feared the worst. It took us so damn long to catch up."

"I'm just that awesome," Polly replied, falling back on her long-time jest, but the words held no humor tonight.

"You did something none of the others were able to do," Trent continued, quiet and persistent. "You fought back. You kept him from getting you completely under his control. And Polly, you nearly cut off that bastard's head with a *throwing knife*." Trent did not try to hide the admiration in his tone.

"I didn't think you'd find me," Polly admitted, barely audible. "I knew he was fast, that he did something weird when he took me. The longer it went on, the more I was sure you couldn't follow us."

"It was damn hard," Trent replied. "But he left a trail. I don't think he was used to being tracked, or he thought we couldn't find him. And then when we got there, his 'customers' panicked and we had to fight our way in." He snorted in derision. "Didn't mind breaking a few bones and smacking some heads together. Those sons of bitches deserved that and more for what they did to those—" He cut off what he was saying abruptly.

"I know," Polly replied. "I know… what he did to the ones he took. What he was going to do to me. I've seen his kind before. Human or vampire, they're monsters."

"He's dead. Destroyed. We saved as many as we could. But now it's time to go home."

Polly took a step toward Trent and looked back at the trough. "I didn't get clean."

Trent's gaze grew worried. "Polly, you scrubbed hard enough to raise blood. I saw you. Come on. You've been through a lot today. Aiden can fix—"

Polly tore away from his outstretched hand. "Nothing can fix this," she said, her tone filled with anger and sorrow. "I don't want to forget what I saw, because he's not the only monster out there. And I have to remember. It dishonors the ones we left behind if we don't remember."

Trent raised both hands, palms out, in surrender and acquiescence. "I'm sorry," he said carefully. "I didn't mean anything by it. But Ross is waiting with the horses, and it's not going to be good for any of us to still be here when someone shakes off the shock and decides to start asking too many questions." He dropped his voice. "Polly, they could call the guards."

Polly sniffed back the last of her tears and nodded. Her throat burned, her eyes felt like they were filled with sand, and her head throbbed. Everything hurt, and she took that as proof that she was still alive.

"All right. Let's go."

They passed few travelers, but at one point they glimpsed a cluster of Wanderers and their wagons in an empty field and spotted some of the nomadic clan's sigils marked on stone walls and fence posts. They always seemed to be camped somewhere near where Aiden and Rigan found the ripples of magic, as if perhaps they, too, were drawn to the places where the veil between realms thinned. Polly wondered if any of these Wanderers had been among those driven out of Ravenwood City the night Kell died, or whether they had always made the farmland their home.

Polly rode in silence between Trent and Ross. The villagers of Eilertown had offered them food and lodging but staying felt too exposed, too dangerous. Their narrow escape from Jorgeson and his guards still loomed large in memories and nightmares, and it did not take much imagination to suspect that their pursuers might still be in the area.

"Do you think they've set a big bounty on us?" Trent asked after they were long gone from Eilertown.

"Probably," Ross replied. "I hope it's big. Wouldn't want to go through all of this for a cheap reward! We're worth more than that!"

Trent gave him a hard glare. "Do you know how much more dangerous this gets if there is a huge bounty on our heads? A big bounty means more bounty hunters, not just Jorgeson and his soldiers. And while townsfolk might not give us up to the Lord Mayor's guards on account of not much liking the Lord Mayor, it's hard to argue against a pouch of gold."

"You worry too much," Ross replied. "Don't forget, we're also saving those townsfolk's hides from the monsters that the guards can't be bothered to fight. That's got to count for something."

"The bounty hunters could take hostages, force the villagers to call for help against a monster that doesn't exist in order to lure us in," Trent said, not ready to let the issue drop. Polly said nothing, content to let them argue and provide a distraction.

"They could. Maybe they will. And we'll deal with it when it happens—if it does," Ross said. "Don't forget, Aiden and the others can sense the way monsters ripple the magic. So if we have a village ask for our help and there's no ripple, then either it isn't a monster at all, or we need to be very careful."

"We don't know for sure that all monsters cause ripples," Trent replied.

"That's true," Ross agreed. "But I'm just saying it's a way to protect ourselves as much as it is to find new hunts."

"And that's another thing: I don't like giving people a way to get a message to us," Trent said. "Sooner or later, the wrong people will catch on and either watch for us or use it against us."

Ross shrugged. "It's not like we've given out our address. And we aren't the ones who started it. People began leaving messages for the 'monster hunters' at the inns and taverns on the off chance we might find out. We don't make regular stops anywhere. We take different routes back to wherever we're staying, and we switch from place to place every few weeks, but not on a schedule. That's about as well as you can hide nine people plus horses and a wagon."

"We're tempting fate."

Ross snorted. "Of course we are! A bit late to have second thoughts about it. If we settled down tomorrow and went back to our trades, we'd still be wanted men. At least this way, we're doing some real good. There's no one else to protect these people, Trent, and you know it. The guards won't, and too many of their own folks will get hurt or killed trying. If we do this, hunt monsters, it almost makes everything we've lost worth it."

Polly swallowed a lump in her throat. She looked down, unwilling for either of the men to see tears burn in her eyes. It had only been three months since Kell's death, and with so much else going on, Polly felt a little guilty to indulge her grief. Especially since Corran and Rigan had lost a brother, and she and Kell had not even had the chance to do more than flirt.

They had stolen kisses at the kitchen door when Cook's back was turned. Now and again, Kell brought her flowers, picked from the roadside, or snatched from a garden. And when she needed someone she could trust, when she had done murder and needed to get rid of the body, Kell had come through and assured Polly that her attacker would be buried under a curse.

And if covering up murder isn't love, I don't know what is, Polly thought, and that forced a hiccup of a laugh through her tears.

She used to daydream what it might be like to marry Kell. Certainly being the wife of a Guild undertaker was far more secure than the life of a runaway working in a tavern. Polly was too matter-of-fact to be bothered by work that required preparing the bodies of the dead. She could be a bit cold-blooded and thought it suited that type of job. Now that she knew Corran and Rigan much better, she wondered how they might have all gotten on together, Rigan with Elinor and Corran with Jora.

Just never meant to be, I guess. Polly cleared her throat and raised her head, letting the cool breeze dry her tears.

"Are you up to giving everyone a report on the vampire, since you're the only one who got a good look?" Ross asked hesitantly as if Polly might shatter, and she hated it.

"I'll be fine," she snapped, and regretted her tone a moment later, knowing his intentions were good. "I mean, it won't bother me. I'm all right," she added, with less bite to her voice. "And you're right—I talked to him, a little before I went after him with the knife. You came in and—whack."

Trent chuckled. "It doesn't sound as good when you put it that way."

"That blade of yours nearly took off my eyebrows!" Polly retorted in mock indignation.

"Better your eyebrows than your throat, which is what the bastard looked like he was aiming for."

"I had it under control," Polly said with the ghost of a smile.

"Hard to cut through a spine with that little shiv of yours," Ross teased. "You'd have been there all night."

"Huh. I'd have managed." Retreating into humor, making a joke out of the horror of the situation eased the tension. They were all quite aware of how close a call it had been.

"I think you two need to learn to run faster," Polly continued.

"And here I was thinking we should put a bell around your neck so we could find you when you go wandering off," Ross jibed.

"I was wondering whether Rigan or Aiden could make some sort of tracking amulet," Trent said, sounding serious. "It could come in handy —and it won't be the only time one of us has to be the bait. That way, if the... lure... gets snatched, we don't have to waste time."

"That's better than a bell, at least," Polly replied.

They rode in silence for a few minutes as the humor wore off, leaving only the horror behind. "Do you think there's a reason that out here, some of the monsters seem to be natural, not conjured?" Trent asked.

"You mean like the vampire tonight, and that water monster the others went up against?" Ross asked.

Trent nodded. "Yeah. Some of what's out here, beyond the city walls, seems to either have been here for a while or happened on its own—vengeful ghosts, that sort of thing," Trent mused. "Not like the monsters we hunted back in the city, the ones the Lord Mayor's witch called."

"Aiden said the lore books told of monsters for as long as there's been history," Ross replied. "There were natural monsters too, back in the city. Rigan and Corran used to have to banish dangerous ghosts from time to time. I imagine some of the other creatures occasionally found their way in, over the walls or in the drains."

"The non-conjured monsters are smarter," Polly spoke up. "Garrod, the vampire, he made his own plans. He didn't need to be sent, or have his prey picked out for him."

"Remember when Corran and Rigan fought that strix, back before the battle? She was smart, too," Trent said.

"The monsters the blood witch conjured weren't exactly stupid," Ross argued. "The ghouls knew how to stalk a victim and surround their prey."

"But all those monsters—the ghouls and those big slug-like things—"

"*Lida*," Ross supplied.

"And the *azrikks* and those creatures that looked like a cross between a bat, a boar, and a really ugly dog, those monsters were just beasts," Trent said. "I imagine they'd be easier to conjure up and send where the witch wanted them to go. The things we're fighting now, they're smart enough to argue about it, maybe defy orders."

"That makes sense," Polly agreed. "And think about it—with people more spread out here in the countryside, there's not enough food for big packs of them to go roaming around. They'd die back, like deer in a sparse winter. But in the city, there's all the food they can eat—until the hunters got to them."

"The smarter monsters would have had more trouble in the city," Ross said, adding his theory. "More of a chance to get caught, harder to fit in. They'd like it out here, and maybe they've even worked out territories like wolves do. Less chance that way to overhunt the food supply or push the villagers into going looking for them."

"Until we came along," Polly said.

"Yeah," Trent replied. "Sooner or later, they're going to notice. And when they do, we'll have more to worry about than guards and bounty hunters."

CHAPTER FIVE

"I CAN GIVE you a chance to be useful," Aliyev added. "To win your freedom and your life. I will supply the weapons, men, mages, and money you need. You'll have to leave the city, but if you achieve your goal, I'll know."

Jorgeson bit the inside of his lip, willing himself to stay still, afraid to look too hopeful or too desperate. Prince Aliyev deserved his reputation as a hard son of a bitch, not known for second chances. Whatever might be offered would come because it suited the Crown Prince's needs, not out of any sort of mercy. And Jorgeson would accept whatever Aliyev gave him, because dead men did not get to be choosy.

"How may I be of service, m'lord?"

"I need to know what Itara and Sarolinia are up to," Aliyev said, and Jorgeson looked up with surprise.

"M'lord?"

"Our spies suggest that they're plotting, planning a move against us, but we don't know what. Maybe you can learn something they couldn't."

"I will not fail you."

Aliyev's bitter grimace suggested that Jorgeson's promise was already too little, too late. "Find the hunters who broke into the *palace. We know two of them were Valmondes. Shouldn't be hard to identify the others by who's gone missing. We need to make an example of the hunters, keep the commoners out in the village from joining up. Hunt them. Punish them. Kill them."*

"And if I am successful, m'lord? What then?"

"If you succeed, I will not do the same to you."

Hant Jorgeson shook off his memories and finished the whiskey in his glass, tossing it back in one gulp. The memory of his dishonorable discharge from his position at the head of the Lord Mayor's security still sent a burn of shame through him. He knew it could have been worse, that Crown Prince Aliyev would have been well within his rights to have had him executed on the spot for the consummate debacle that ended in the death of Lord Mayor Machison and his blood witch, Blackholt.

Killing me would have been kinder. Of course that's why he let me live.

Jorgeson passed a hand over the rough stubble of his battle-shorn hair. He doubted anyone would ever see him as anything other than hired muscle. Even the scar that cut down over his left eyebrow and onto his cheek marked him as a soldier, an enforcer, a killer. And he lived up to all of those titles, especially the last.

Tonight, the meeting place was a stable, out behind the Drunken Shepherd tavern. Easy entrance and exit, and a spot no one would notice or remember a stranger. Jorgeson made sure to reach the stable first. He had checked out the building and the territory around it days ago, assured himself it was suitable, before arranging to meet with his contact.

Jorgeson positioned himself where he had a clear view of the stable doors but would not be immediately visible himself, and waited with a throwing knife balanced in his hand.

He did not know his contact by sight, only by reputation, but the hard-bitten man wearing a worn leather cuirass certainly looked like a bounty hunter. Jorgeson observed the man for a moment before he was ready to make himself known. The bounty hunter's short dark hair had a liberal sprinkling of gray, suggesting he was proficient enough to live past his early thirties. He moved like a predator, with a spare, wiry frame. A long knife hung from a sheath on his belt, and Jorgeson guessed the man had other concealed weapons. Tanned skin and wrinkles at the corners of his eyes suggested a life lived outdoors. He appeared to be exactly what he claimed to be.

"Tell me what you've heard." Jorgeson stepped out from behind the post, and to his credit, the other man did not startle.

"Show me your payment, then I give you the information," the bounty hunter, Shandin, replied in a voice roughened by whiskey and smoke. If he was half as good, half as ruthless, as his reputation, Jorgeson would get his money's worth.

Jorgeson withdrew a small purse of coins from beneath his jacket and held it up, jostling it to let the clink of coins carry through the stable. "I've brought the coins. Now tell me what you've heard."

Shandin eyed the coin purse for a moment before he spat to one side and lifted his head, meeting Jorgeson's gaze, not quite a challenge, but clearly not subservient. "Wherever your fugitives are, they were smart enough to put distance between themselves and the city. I picked up a story from a peddler who said men came to one of the villages off to the West, a couple of days' ride from here, and said they could get rid of a monster in a lake."

"And?"

Shandin chewed something he popped out of a bulge in his cheek, then turned and spat again. "And they did," he replied, matter-of-factly. "Then we chased their sorry asses and nearly got them before their hocus called down the spirits of the damned on us."

"Always an excuse."

Shandin looked daggers at him. "The mayor of the next town was plenty ready to sell them out for the reward, and we almost had them, and their bloody witch dropped a tree on us."

"Did they say how the men found out about the monster?"

Shandin shook his head. "I asked. They said the two showed up and started asking questions, wanting to know if anything strange had been going on. Like they knew, somehow, that there was something wrong."

Jorgeson let out a curse and fought the urge to punch something. "Dammit! Did you at least get a description of them?"

"One was taller with blond hair, the other shorter with dark hair. Didn't look much alike, except for the eyes."

"The Valmonde brothers," Jorgeson muttered. "It's them, all right."

"Except that I heard from other villages that they've seen the dark-haired man with another, different light-haired man, and that two other men and a young girl have also been out in the villages."

"Doing what?"

"Killing monsters," Shandin replied, eyeing him levelly. "Been busy. Vengeful ghosts. A werewolf, and a nest of ghouls, if the stories can be believed. The townsfolk say they're heroes."

"What did the peddler say?"

Shandin cave a cold laugh. "All he wanted to know was how much I'd pay for the information. He doesn't live there; no matter to him who dies."

"I'm paying for results. Have you found a pattern to their hunts?" Jorgeson pressed. "I want to know where they've gone to ground. They've got to have made a base somewhere; if they were camping out, my men would have found them by now." The sting of the last failed assault on a deserted old monastery still felt bitter on his tongue. From the look of the grounds, he had missed his quarry by days, or perhaps mere candlemarks. The failure only deepened his resolve.

Shandin regarded him for a moment before he spoke. "No offense, but I sleep rough, and none of your men have ever found me." He raised an eyebrow to make his point. "If they know what they're doing, they've found shelter. And if any of them have magic, or they're clever, they've hidden their tracks."

"Figure out the radius," Jorgeson snapped. "They might not go back to their base each night, but they won't ride too many days out."

"I would."

"What?"

Shandin spat again and ground the wad of tobacco under his heel into the dust. "There's a lot of forest out there and plenty of fields. Safer for them to go several days out and camp in between than keep going back, especially if they've found a good base. They'll suspect someone's looking for them. Since you haven't caught them, that tells me they're plenty smart."

"I'm paying you to be smarter."

An unpleasant smile tilted Shandin's lips. "Oh, I will be. I've been doin' my own kind of hunting longer than they've been on the run. They'll slip up, sooner or later."

"You'd better find them."

Shandin seemed unfazed by the implied threat. "Did your guards search the kinds of places I told you?"

Jorgeson let out a potent curse. "Do you have any idea how many abandoned buildings there are within a three-month ride of the city walls in every direction? I couldn't search them all if I had an army!"

"They'll slip up... leave a clue," Shandin assured him. "We just have to find it."

"Maybe they've split up, the brothers gone their own way from the rest of them. Harder to hide a big group."

Shandin frowned. "No. I don't think so. They'll want to keep their witches close. They might go hunting in separate teams, but from what you've told me, I think these brigands have got some sort of outlaw family." His smile broadened. "That's going to be their weak point. They won't leave each other behind, and that's going to get them all captured."

"I don't care how you do it, just do it," Jorgeson snapped. "I want results."

"You'll have them," Shandin replied, maddeningly unperturbed. "Now if you'll excuse me, if there's nothing else, I've got men to hunt."

Jorgeson watched him go, fighting the urge to send his knife flying past Shandin's shoulder and into the wall to make a statement. All his sources had told him that Shandin was the bounty hunter with the best kill record in Darkhurst. And as frustrated as Jorgeson was with the man, the truth was, he needed his help—and he was certain Shandin sensed it.

Crown Prince Aliyev had kept his word, giving Jorgeson charge over six guards, two middling witches, a wagon full of weapons and supplies, horses, and enough money to last for another month or two if he was careful. But Aliyev had also made it clear that he expected a quick resolution to the mission. Jorgeson doubted that his master would be as generous if what had been provided was not sufficient.

Then again, if it were easy, Aliyev wouldn't need me. He'd have sent out a garrison, brought the criminals back in chains, and hanged them in the square months ago.

———

ONE NIGHT LATER, Jorgeson slouched at the corner of a building in a crossroads town on the main road from Ravenwood City into the countryside, the road all the merchants and money lenders followed. If he was going to get news out in this gods-forsaken wilderness without backtracking for weeks, it would be here. Even so, he wondered if the outcome would be worth the effort.

Not far from the crossroads, the fanciest building in Debonton loomed against the night sky, three floors tall and made of brick. Nothing else in town—nothing else nearby—looked remotely like it, an outpost of the Bakaran League and the Crown Prince, with some borrowed authority from King Rellan himself.

Word traveled painfully slow out here, which Jorgeson found to be one of the worst parts of his exile. Being banished from the city meant being cut off from news, and since part of winning a stay of execution depended on helping Crown Prince Aliyev regain the status quo, a lack of news amounted to a significant disadvantage.

He had heard through his sources that a delegation from the exchequer's office in Ravenwood City would be making at stop at the tariff house in Debonton to look over the books. He knew the sort that would be sent; minor functionaries who were not personally acquainted with or known to the Crown Prince, but who lingered on the edges of his circle.

No one who would be missed, but potentially someone who could fill Jorgeson in on the essentials he needed in order to keep his bloody bargain with Aliyev.

If he had not already been exiled, banished, and under a reluctant stay of execution, Jorgeson might have felt put out at doing the dirty work himself. *Then again,* he thought, *perhaps it's a sign of the times. Everything seems off-balance since those damned gravediggers and their brigand friends ruined everything.*

Jorgeson knew his job. Before he had risen in the ranks to head the Lord Mayor's security at the mayor's palace, he had been a soldier, and more than once, that job entailed tracking and capturing a witness, a contact—someone his superiors believed to be of interest. Years had passed, but old skills never truly faded. Now that everything else about his world had gone belly up, Jorgeson found cold comfort in that fact. He was still good at this.

His quarry emerged from the tariff building and gave a quick, nervous glance up and down the street. At this time, several candlemarks after dark, businesses and peddlers alike had closed their doors and packed up their wagons to go home. The streets stretched empty in both directions, the darkness broken only by the light from the upstairs apartments over merchant's shops or the two torches on either side of the tariff house steps.

Jorgeson guessed the nervous little man worked late because he had other errands for his masters, other crossroads towns and tariff houses to audit, filled with endless, dusty ledgers. Jorgeson's lips quirked upward with a secret smile. He might be doing the man a favor, ending his boredom. Tonight would certainly be far more interesting than the exchequer's assistant ever dreamed.

Taking him proved pathetically easy. The skinny little bureaucrat had not even looked behind him once he left the building, other than a few furtive glances that were too quick for him to see much. Jorgeson moved quickly, soundlessly, slipping up behind the man when he crossed a darkened street, pressing a hand across nose and mouth while the other arm clenched over his prey's shoulders.

"Make a noise, fight me, and I'll snap your scrawny neck," Jorgeson murmured, his lips close to the man's ear. He did not move his hand from covering his captive's mouth, so the only reply was a high, nervous whine Jorgeson took to be assent.

He had learned a choke hold in his army days, a way to make a man unconscious without killing him. He pressed just so, and the bureaucrat slumped in his grip. Jorgeson paused to make certain that his quarry was still breathing, that he could feel a pulse beneath his fingers. Once he had confirmed those essentials, Jorgeson hefted the man over his shoulder and slipped down the alley.

He did not have to go far. Jorgeson had scouted the area beforehand, and the back room of an abandoned store was well suited to the night's work. Jorgeson dragged the functionary through a door and lit a lantern, then arranged the man in a chair, tying him in securely before he woke.

"What happened?" The prisoner came around slowly, taking in his surroundings with bleary eyes.

"I thought we needed to have a chat," Jorgeson replied, leaning against a scarred wooden table.

Only then did the man seem to realize that he had been bound. "I don't have much money. Take it—it's beneath my vest. Just let me go."

"I don't want your money," Jorgeson said. "I want information."

The thin man licked his lips nervously. "What type of information?"

Jorgeson gave him a cold smile. "Let's start with your name."

"Weston," the man replied. "Garth Weston."

Jorgeson nodded. "Good. All right, Garth, tell me how things are in Ravenwood City. Inside the walls."

Garth licked his lips again. "What 'things'?"

Jorgeson's smile slipped a little. "Start talking. Describe how things are since the fire. The guards, the monsters, the Guilds, trade with the rest of the League—all of it."

Garth looked at Jorgeson, fearful and confused. "Only that?"

"Only... that."

Garth flinched, not mistaking the menace in Jorgeson's voice. "All right then," he began with a nervous swallow, "since the fire. Well, things don't work quite right anymore. You know the Lord Mayor is dead?"

Jorgeson nodded, and the look on his face flustered Garth, who glanced away. "The Crown Prince himself came to Ravenwood to sort things out. I don't see much of him, but I've heard he's quite cross." He glanced up hurriedly. "Not criticizing, just saying what I've heard."

"Go on."

"The Guilds are nearly in revolt. They're upset about the Garenoth agreement; it's not going well. We—Ravenwood—might still lose our most-favored status because we're not delivering. There've been problems. Everything we import costs more 'cause everyone's afraid the agreement will fall apart soon. The Guilds have to pay more and charge more, but they're selling less." He made himself slow down and breathe. "They come to the tariff house every day to complain to the Crown Prince about one thing or another. I work down the hallway. I can't always hear what they say, but voices are raised."

"Say more."

Garth took a deep breath. "When I go to the market, everyone's out of sorts. With the Garenoth agreement being rocky, everyone's edgy. The Guild trades, the merchants in the markets, even the peddlers— everyone's unhappy because, with doubt about that agreement, the trading ships aren't as keen to buy Ravenwood's exports."

"What about the monsters—and the hunters?"

Garth looked down. "I don't know much about that. Just rumors. Everyone says the hunters set the fires the night Lord Mayor Machison died. There've been arguments—fights, even—down at the pub about whether the hunters are heroes or criminals. But since that night, the night of the fires, the monsters don't come around as much, seems like. Not as often and not as many, so some folks say that it was the hunters who fixed things."

"Interesting. What else?"

"Merchant Prince Gorog killed himself, or so they say," Garth continued. He seemed unsure whether repeating gossip would extend his life or shorten it, so the words continued in a torrent. "The Crown Prince appointed Gorog's son to the role. Haven't heard much about him, but there's some gossip suggesting the elder Gorog didn't have much of a choice about killing himself, if you know what I mean."

"That should keep his son on his toes," Jorgeson replied.

Garth nodded in agreement, anxious to keep Jorgeson appeased. "The Crown Prince worries about money. Revenue and taxes, since exports are down." He cleared his throat. "That's my area, that's why I'm here. The king won't take kindly to Ravenwood not bringing in as much to the coffers, regardless of the circumstances, so Crown Prince Aliyev is looking for every copper. Sent a dozen of us out to the countryside, making sure revenues are collected."

"Predictable," Jorgeson muttered, more to himself than to Garth.

"But the good news is, the fires are out. Got the wreckage cleared away, and it's not as bad as you might think, considering how it all looked like it would go up at once," Garth babbled on.

"What of the other city-states? What have you heard?"

Ravenwood was both a walled city and an independent city-state within the kingdom of Darkhurst. Ten such city-states made up a loose —and competitive—alliance known as the Bakaran League. Each city-state was ruled by a Crown Prince, who in turn reported to the king. Merchant Princes owned the land outside the city walls and controlled the commodities yielded from that land—crops, ore, timber, livestock. Within the cities, Guilds oversaw each hereditary profession.

Jorgeson knew first-hand how nasty the politics could get. The Guild Masters vied with each other for pricing and favors. The Merchant Princes cut deals and competed for favoritism when the trade agreements between each city-state and its neighbors came due. A few percentage points one way or the other in a deal made or lost fortunes for the Merchant Princes and the members of the nobility that served as their financiers, underwriting their expenses and the building and maintenance of the trading fleet, paying for its voyages.

Before the fire, Ravenwood and Garenoth had been the two wealthiest city-states in the League. Favors their carefully-crafted trade agreements gave to one another not only guaranteed a certain level— and profitability—of commerce, but also assured that the favored partner would receive the best commodities, whether food or raw materials. Losing that status would affect everyone in Ravenwood on some level, from the profits of the Merchant Princes and the Guild members to the quantity, price, and quality of food available in the market.

"What do you hear about the rest of the League?" Jorgeson repeated when Garth paused.

"Just bits," he said, smacking his lips as if he feared this would not be enough to satisfy his captor. "I'm nobody important, so I don't hear much of anything officially. But people talk, you know? And voices carry."

And there, Jorgeson knew, lay the most important truth of spy craft. *Voices carry.* People who should know nothing often heard everything, because the important people forgot that servants were in the room, that functionaries had their door open, and that whores and mistresses were smarter than they pretended to be.

"After things fell apart in Kasten the other city-states all went scrabbling for the pieces," Garth said. "Especially their neighbors. There's talk Kasten might be partitioned, no longer be independent. And I think people in Ravenwood—important people—are afraid the same might happen to us if the Garenoth agreement fails and Aliyev isn't careful, and tricky."

"Oh?"

Garth's head bobbed in agreement. "Yeah. Sarolinia and Itara seem to be getting bolder, pushing for a bigger piece of the trade Ravenwood's on the verge of losing. I heard the Ravenwood ambassador talking with one of the Crown Prince's men in the corridor—they didn't know I was still at my desk—and the ambassador said he thought Sarolinia might be looking to 'help' Ravenwood fail any way they could."

"I don't doubt that," Jorgeson said. "Did the ambassador offer any proof?"

Garth shook his head. "No. At least, not that I heard. Only rumors. The Crown Prince's man didn't speak as loudly—I couldn't hear everything he said—but I got the impression that he agreed about the threat, and thought Sarolinia might send in troublemakers to stir things up, cause problems with the shipping, that sort of thing. And then there are the pirates—"

"Pirates?" Jorgeson's eyebrows rose. This was real news.

"Apparently, there have been problems. I had to go down to collect revenues at the wharf side tariff office. Two of the ship captains were waiting for their money, talking about pirates. One said they'd fought back a group that tried to board their ship. The other agreed like he knew firsthand, and said there had been talk about shipments being stolen and sold on the black market. Said that was why there'd been shortages on a few things because the pirates and smugglers stole them from the warehouses and sold them off illegally."

Jorgeson's thoughts raced. *It's worse than I thought if pirates and smugglers have gotten a foothold. Aliyev's really lost control, and Ravenwood's going to be bleeding revenue. Sooner or later, the king will notice. Sarolinia's probably meddling to make Ravenwood's problems even worse. Shit. And Aliyev is expecting me to feed him fresh information about Sarolinia and Itara. Now I know why he seemed so interested.*

"What of the Merchant Princes?" Jorgeson pressed. He suspected his captive's usefulness approached its end, but he did not intend to waste a resource if it might still yield one more unexpected nugget of information.

"I heard Merchant Prince Kadar in the corridor, demanding an audience with Crown Prince Aliyev," Garth replied. Sweat beaded on his brow, as if he, too, guessed his time was running out. "That's not uncommon, since the older Gorog's death. Merchant Prince Tamar is fairly quiet when he bothers to come to the tariff house, although he's often quite short with the staff, as if he has a lot on his mind. But Kadar is much more... assertive... than he was before the fire. Not that Kadar didn't make his opinions known," Garth added in a tone that suggested there was quite a story behind that comment if Jorgeson cared to ask. "But now, I get the impression he sees an opportunity and nothing is going to get in his way."

No, Kadar isn't going to let anyone put him in second place, not again, Jorgeson thought. *Clever bastard, rushing to fill the gap.*

Gorog's son will be timid, coming in on the heels of a dead man. Tamas has always been a follower. If Aliyev's attention is elsewhere, Kadar can slip his leash and by the time Aliyev has his house in order—if that happens—Kadar will have grabbed up everything he can.

"Is there more?" Jorgeson regarded his captive, noted the slight tremor that ran through the man's body. He pushed away from the table and slowly walked a circle around the bound man, stopping behind his chair.

"I'm well situated to hear things," Garth offered. "I could be your man on the inside, bring you news every few weeks. I won't breathe a word to anyone."

"No, you won't." Jorgeson brought his knife across Garth's neck in one swift, brutal arc. He wiped the blood that spattered his hand on the dead man's jacket.

"Good talking with you," he murmured, shuttering his lantern.

———

"WE HAD A deal," the bearded man said, stalking across the room to stand too close to Jorgeson, intentionally challenging him. "Your guards were to keep their distance."

"And my guards have kept their part of the bargain," Jorgeson snapped. He kept his hands down at his sides, though his fingers itched for the handle of his knife. Any other man would have been thrown backward with a solid punch to the jaw, taught manners with fists and blades.

Renvar was not just any man.

Jorgeson himself stood slightly under six feet tall and strongly built, but Renvar loomed over Jorgeson by several inches and had at least twenty or thirty pounds more muscle. Thick dark hair, long enough to reach his collar, framed an angular face with a close-trimmed black beard. Startlingly blue eyes peered from beneath storm cloud brows. Everything about Renvar radiated danger, even to a man like Jorgeson, who was no stranger to intimidating others.

"Back away, or so help me, I'll make you move," Jorgeson growled.

"That would not go well," Renvar replied, his voice equally low and dangerous. Still, he took a half step back with a derisive smile that told Jorgeson he was being humored.

"Whose guards are bothering your people?" Jorgeson asked.

"Not guards—hunters. Four of them came after the pack a fortnight ago. They had a witch with them. Two of my family died," Renvar replied. "I've relocated the pack, but that should not have happened."

"Four hunters, and a witch?"

Renvar nodded. "The witch also had weapons."

"Where were you attacked?"

Renvar gave him the location, a stretch of forest dotted with caves along a side road between farming villages. "We covered our tracks well. No one had disturbed us before. I still don't know how they found us."

"Blame the witches," Jorgeson replied. "That's true more often than not." He frowned, considering Renvar's story. "Did you see where they went, where they came from?"

"We were too busy shielding our young and our elders, getting them to safety," Renvar snapped back.

"Have your people been sloppy? Been eating travelers who happen past on the full moon? Snatching some sheep or cattle for a snack?" Jorgeson could see that his comments annoyed the shape-shifter—what some called a *thrope*—and while baiting a werewolf might not be wise, Jorgeson would be damned if he would allow the other man to get the upper hand.

"No. We were careful. We've lived in this area for generations. If we were... 'sloppy'... the farmers would have come after us with torches long ago."

"The Valmondes and their outlaw band aren't thrill-seekers," Jorgeson replied. "They know they're fugitives, so they have a lot to lose if they're turned in to the guards or my bounty hunters." He shook his head. "No, it's more likely that they heeded a call for help. Maybe your pack haven't all been honest with you," he goaded.

"Ridiculous! I would know if my people were lying. I would smell the lie on them." Renvar looked up, and everything in his posture suddenly seemed more wolf than human.

"Unless they're very, very good," Jorgeson replied. "Is there anyone you haven't seen in a while? Anyone prone to causing trouble? Because the problem with the Valmondes is they don't want attention. They aren't playacting being heroes. If they're risking their lives to hunt your pack, then someone put them onto you."

Renvar looked as if he might spring at Jorgeson. His body tensed, hands clenched into fists, muscles taut. With an effort of will, the pack leader took a deep breath and tempered his reaction. "Your suggestion... worries me. My kind needs to kill to eat. We've survived this long by being... judicious... in the victims we choose. Lone travelers, runaways, brigands no one will miss. Stray cattle or sheep—or those encouraged to stray," he added with a dangerous smile. "Always sparingly, no evidence left behind. If someone has violated my orders, it is a grave infraction. If they have lied to me—it is worthy of death."

"Then see to your own house," Jorgeson retorted. "And I will see to these hunters. But if you have a rogue in your pack, this will happen again. Even when I've taken care of the Valmondes, the farmers and villagers will involve themselves if you give them cause. We saw enough of that in the city," he added with distaste.

"We have an agreement," Renvar repeated. "My people and those like us keep the roads reasonably free of highwaymen and cutpurses in the places you lack guards to patrol. In exchange, you leave us alone."

"And my men have left you and yours alone," Jorgeson snapped. "If you want to be of service, sniff out the Valmondes, and I'll kill them for you. That's what I'm trying to do."

Renvar regarded him for a moment. "I had wondered what brought you so far from the comforts of the city," he replied, his voice a low rumble. "Even out here, stories travel—even to such as I."

Jorgeson scowled at the implication that Renvar knew about his disgrace and dismissal. It gave Jorgeson less leverage with the pack leader. *How like a monster to make it clear that he knows where I'm vulnerable.*

"We have common cause in this." Jorgeson took a step forward, refusing to be put on the defensive. He might be willing to work with monsters, but only, always, with himself holding the upper hand.

"There are benefits to our working together," Renvar rephrased the statement. "If my pack could have traced their trail, we would have handled the problem ourselves. Their witches removed the scent. In the interest of discretion, I decided to bring the matter to you. But rest assured, if necessary my people can and will settle the issue. If it comes to that, I cannot assure that it won't be messy."

"If it involves the Valmondes, it will undoubtedly be messy," Jorgeson muttered. "Don't worry; I take your meaning. And you know, I'm sure, that if there's a slaughter, your pack won't be able to stop running until they're far from settled territory, maybe outside of Dark-hurst itself. So," he said, fixing Renvar with a glare, "Some solutions are better than others."

"What do you intend to do?"

"Track the hunters, kill them, and keep the villagers from getting ideas."

"Because trying to stop hunters from looking like heroes for killing monsters worked so well back in the city," Renvar replied.

"Different place, different circumstances," Jorgeson dismissed his rebuttal. "I have witches of my own. We found the Valmondes when they went Below. We can find them out here."

"If you found them once, why are they still alive?"

Jorgeson smiled, baring his teeth. "Sometimes, the sweetest kill is of a worthy opponent."

CHAPTER SIX

"I THOUGHT WE were done with this shit." Corran swung his sword, slicing through flesh, catching for an instant as it hit bone before the ghoul's head went rolling.

"Apparently not," Trent replied, pivoting to keep the two ghouls he fought from scoring a hit.

Corran heard scrabbling overhead and dove to one side an instant before a ghoul dropped from the ceiling, landing on all fours and lunging a second later. Teeth snapped so close to his neck that Corran feared he had run out of luck. Sharp claws dragged down his bicep, and he forced his knee up and between himself and his attacker, buying himself time. Warm blood soaked through his torn shirt and welled at the shallow bite on his shoulder.

The ghoul pressed down, unnaturally strong, and Corran knew he could not keep it clear for long. His undead opponent never tired, but Corran had killed three of the nest already and felt the battle in every gash and aching muscle. The ghoul's claws sank deep into Corran's right arm, and he bit back a cry, trying not to retch at the stench from the creature only inches from his face. He wriggled beneath it, and freed his left arm, bringing his knife down into the ghoul's back with all the force he could muster at such an awkward angle.

The blade slipped between ribs, and the ghoul bucked, arching back with a shriek as its claws tightened, ripping deeper into Corran's skin. The knife's point protruded from the creature's chest, and Corran twisted the blade, pulling back just enough so that if the ghoul collapsed, he would not be stuck by his own weapon.

The ghoul shuddered, and for an instant, its hold on Corran's arm eased. Corran seized the chance, rolling them until he pinned the creature with his weight, driving the blade deeper as he slammed the ghoul back on the floor. Cold, black ichor sprayed him from the chest wound where the blade poked through. He brought one knee down hard on the ghoul's thigh, immobilizing it while he leaned back and brought his sword across the creature's scrawny neck, severing its head, then retrieved his knife. Corran staggered to his feet, bleeding, and gave the head a kick.

"Behind you!" Ross yelled as Corran heard the scuffle of the ghoul's feet on the worn wooden floor of the winery. He wheeled as the ghoul swung at him, its filthy claws catching in the meat of his shoulder even as he avoided the worst of the blow. Ghoul wounds went bad quick, and infection was a certainty. Already, he could feel the older gashes growing swollen, warm, and painful, and he knew that getting back to their safe house would be an ordeal once the adrenaline of the fight left him.

The nest of ghouls had been a surprise, despite the fact that Rigan, Aiden, and Elinor had pinpointed the location by noting a disturbance in the currents of magic. They had grown used to fighting the more sentient monsters that seemed far more common out here, away from the city walls. A different sort of hunting, tracking, and trapping was required for prey that possessed the guile and awareness of a human being, like the pack of werewolves they had recently decimated.

Ghouls, on the other hand, were tenacious, ravenous, and difficult to kill. Stupid, but dangerous, and with the predator instinct of wolves. Corran had forgotten how much he hated them, though he had several scars to remind him of previous encounters.

"Trent!" Corran saw another ghoul crawling across the high ceiling, maneuvering to drop into the middle of the fight going on between

Trent and two other ghouls. Corran ran forward, sheathing his knife and gripping his sword two-handed. He pitched into Trent with his shoulder, shoving him out of the way, and brought the sword around with all his strength, cutting the falling ghoul in half.

Trent thrust his knife deep into the neck of one of the ghouls and pivoted, kicking high. The kick sent the second ghoul stumbling back into the heavy barrels, and Trent went after him, taking advantage of the ghoul's lack of balance to take its head off with one clean swing.

"Damn!" Corran stabbed at the top half of the ghoul he had cut in two. Foul, dark liquid pooled on the floor mixing with the spilled wine, making the floor slippery. His head throbbed, and his arm ached as the poison from the ghouls' cuts made its way into his blood. The ghoul's hand grabbed his ankle, and he went down hard, sliding on the creature's blood. Corran rolled before the ghoul could shift its grip, unsheathing his knife and bringing it across the ghoul's neck.

Its bony grip loosened, releasing his ankle. Corran heaved for breath, as sweat and blood stung his eyes. He rolled to one side, pushing himself up, gripping his weapons in bloody hands. Bodies littered the floor of the building, but thankfully, none of the hunters had fallen. As Corran started forward, intending to rejoin the fray, Trent finished his last opponent. Ross ran his attacker through, keeping him skewered and upright on his sword as he cut off the head with a swing of his knife. Grunting in disgust, Ross tilted his blade and let the ghoul slide to the floor.

Corran went for their gear bag and dug out the bottles of green vitriol and the canisters of the salt, amanita, and aconite mixture. His hands shook, and a growing fever brought a flush to his face.

"Come on," he urged, "let's finish this."

Ross wiped his sword and knife clean on the nearest ghoul's ragged clothing and came to help, taking one of the canisters and sprinkling the mixture over the ghouls' corpses. Corran and Trent followed him, pouring the green vitriol and standing back as it burned through the quickly rotting flesh, sending up noxious smoke.

"We could just torch the whole thing," Ross muttered.

"Rather not if we can help it," Trent replied. "They might be able to salvage some of the barrels, and it's been pretty dry out here. Don't need to destroy their stores and set a wildfire. Can't imagine the villagers would thank us."

The vineyard belonged to Merchant Prince Kadar, as did all of the winemaking in Ravenwood. It looked like a blight had struck many of the vines. Row upon row of dead plants stretched out around the warehouse, the grapevines blackened and shriveled. The gnarled plants still stretched along the wires that supported them like crucified corpses.

Together, the three hunters stumbled outside, coughing and gasping, as the smell of burning flesh and green vitriol filled the winery. They were all bleeding, shirts cut and ragged, covered in blood and ichor. For a moment, they leaned on each other, trying to catch their breath, amazed that once again, they'd emerged from battle alive.

"Not looking forward to the ride back," Trent muttered as they made it down the steps. They had tethered their horses some distance away, protected by a circle of salt, iron filings, and warded stakes that hid them from the notice of most creatures.

"If I know Aiden, he'll have bandages and poultices ready," Corran said. Rigan was still recovering from a hunt a few days before that had badly taxed his magic. Mir had been seriously injured as well, so Aiden stayed back at the monastery to care for both men and await the incoming casualties.

"I'm hoping Polly has dinner for us. I'm pretty sure that once I get the smell of those damn ghouls out of my nose, I'm going to be starving," Trent replied.

Ross took point on the way back, with Trent and Corran walking together behind him. Corran knew he needed to make conversation to keep himself conscious.

"How do you manage?" he asked Trent, as the distance between them and Ross lengthened a bit to give a semblance of privacy. "All of this—being outlaws, leaving the city—you seem to take it in stride."

Trent gave a bitter chuckle and grimaced. "Looks can be deceiving," he replied. "But honestly, I'm all right with it. Oh, I'd rather not have lost everything I had, and I'd prefer not to be hunted, but part of me always dreamed of leaving the city and never coming back."

Corran frowned, looking at him. "Why?"

Trent shrugged. "Not everyone who's born into a Guild trade is suited to it. I'm a good butcher. But I never had the interest in it that my father and brothers have. Although what I learned comes in handy hacking up monsters."

"You don't miss the work or the city?"

Trent shook his head. "I miss my family. I hope they're all right. But I hated the Guild and dealing with customers, and while I don't mind eating meat, I don't like butchering," he laughed. "See? The gods put me in the wrong Guild. But I always wanted excitement. So in a way, although there's a lot about being out here that's horrible, I'm almost enjoying parts of this."

Corran focused on talking to avoid thinking about the injuries that burned. "It never crossed my mind to be anything but an undertaker," he said. "I just accepted that's how it would be, like my father and mother and uncles. Then they died before their time, and I had to take over to keep a roof over our head and feed Rigan and Kell, and it all came naturally. I didn't mind the gore, and I could do the hard work of digging the graves. Rigan and Kell were better with the families. We did all right. Rigan took to the work, but I think if Kell had lived, he might have wanted something different. Something more."

The half-moon shone enough light across the vineyard for them to travel without a lantern. They hadn't gone far beyond the buildings when the evidence of the blight ended, and they traveled along rows of healthy vines. Long shadows stretched from the posts that supported the plants, and vines cast strange skeletal silhouettes.

Corran felt the hair on the back of his neck prickle. Then he realized: the night was far too quiet.

Ghouls rose from the shadows beneath the vines, half a dozen of them, maybe more. Corran bit back a groan. They were in no condition to start a new fight.

"Got any ideas?" Corran muttered.

"Set the grass on fire and hope they run slower than we can?" Ross replied.

"That was my thought," Trent added.

"We won't make it." Corran knew how fast ghouls could move. "Either the fire will get us, or the ghouls will."

"If I have to pick, I'll take the fire," Ross answered.

Corran eyed the distance between where they stood and the trees where they had left their horses. Just getting there would tax their strength, without battling ghouls along the way. "Maybe if we lay down a line of salt and vitriol between us and them, it will hold them off." He didn't believe it himself, but the suggestion was the best he had.

"Even a bad idea is better than none," Trent agreed. "Let's do it."

A flash of light sailed through the air from the shadows at the edge of the vineyard, followed by another and another. They crashed in between the ghouls and the trapped hunters, bursting into flames when they hit.

"Run, you idiots!" Polly shouted. More flaming missiles smashed into the dry grass and vines, sending up a wall of flame.

"Here goes nothing." Trent slung an arm over Ross's shoulder. Corran led the way, keeping his knife and sword at the ready in case more ghouls rose from the darkness. They ran as fast as they could, tripping and stumbling, as the ghouls behind them shrieked in frustration.

"Oil bombs," Corran panted, "That'll buy us some time."

Ross dared a glance over his shoulder. "The ghouls," he shouted. "They're… disintegrating."

Corran spared a look. The creatures rotted as they moved, flesh sloughing off until nothing remained except bone.

"Aiden," he panted. "He must be using his healer's magic against them."

"There shouldn't even be ghouls out here." Trent's labored breath made him difficult to understand. "Thought we were done with conjured monsters when we killed Blackholt."

"Maybe they got loose," Ross suggested. They weren't far from the trees now. Thanks to Polly and Aiden, the ghouls no longer pursued them. The vineyard blazed, sending flames high into the night sky.

"Maybe Blackholt sent them out here before he died, to keep someone in line," Trent said.

"Or maybe Blackholt and Machison weren't the only ones who knew how to summon monsters," Corran said, feeling a chill despite the sweat that ran down his back and the roaring fire behind them.

"Shit," Ross muttered. "I really hope you're wrong."

"So do I," Corran replied fervently, although a sinking suspicion in his gut made him doubt they could be so lucky.

Corran and Ross helped Trent onto his horse and dragged themselves onto their mounts with much cursing and difficulty. Polly and Aiden awaited them on the vineyard road. "Thanks," Corran said. "It looked pretty bad, there for a moment."

Polly grinned. "Why should you have all the fun?"

"What happened to the ghouls, there at the end? Was that your doing?" Ross asked.

Aiden nodded. "Yeah. Sorry, I didn't think of it sooner, but I'm still getting used to using healing magic as a weapon." He grimaced, making it clear that he remained conflicted about going against his vows. "I realized that whatever makes the ghouls able to move, it's not life energy. So I wondered if I could disrupt it, and let the natural decay take over, even speed it up a little."

"You're brilliant," Trent said, unable to hide how ragged his voice sounded.

"And if it eases your conscience," Corran added, "think of how many injuries you prevent in the living by using your magic against the undead."

Aiden nodded, although he did not look fully convinced. "I know. That's what I tell myself, anyhow. But I've been known to lie."

"Did you see them catch fire?" Polly's grin lit up her face. "Doesn't bother me at all to light those undead bastards up. They burn real pretty."

Corran gave Polly a skeptical look. "Sometimes you scare me a little, Polly."

Her grin widened. "Then I'm doing things right," she retorted. "I'm the one you have to thank for the oil lamp bombs. Found some empty lamps around the monastery that would work."

"How did you know to come after us?" Ross asked.

Aiden and Polly shared a look. "I had a vision," Aiden confessed. "Elinor said she could handle Mir, and Rigan seemed to be doing better, so we grabbed what we could and followed you. Calfon stayed behind to protect them, just in case."

"You saved our asses," Corran replied. "Thanks."

Aiden shrugged. "Happy to help."

Ross glanced at Aiden. "When we're all patched back together, is there any way for your magic to tell whether someone is still summoning monsters? We didn't think that out here we'd run into more of the things we fought in the city. It's one thing if they're left over from what was done before. But if Blackholt wasn't the only one—"

Aiden's expression turned grim. "I've never tried to detect blood magic," he replied. "Even thinking about it makes me feel like I need a bath." He shivered. "I can see what the old books and manuscripts have to say. But yes—theoretically—it should be possible." The set of his jaw made it clear to the others that Aiden did not relish the task.

They rode back in silence, worried that guards would come or others in response to the fire. When they put a good distance between them and the burning vineyard, thoughts turned to brigands or monsters lurking in the shadows, awaiting unwary travelers. Fortunately, the only travelers they saw were a small group of Wanderers with horses and wagons, and Corran wondered if the nomads were equally desperate as they were to escape attention.

They had seen little of the secretive group since they fled the city, fleeting glimpses now and again on the road, or of a camp in a field on the outskirts of town or down along the banks of the river. They chalked their sigils on trees and stone fences, and on the wooden posts that marked the distance to faraway villages. Corran had no way of knowing whether these Wanderers had also been among those driven out of Ravenwood City, or whether they hailed from other parts of the kingdom. Rigan still believed that the Wanderers had a part to play in defeating the monsters, but so far, Corran remained unconvinced of the strength of their magic, or their willingness to lend their aid.

Relief surged through Corran as they reached the monastery. But his satisfaction at having made it back in one piece faded when Elinor waited for them inside the hidden stairwell.

"Come quickly," she urged. "It's Rigan. He's having nightmares, and I can't get him to wake up."

Aiden turned to Polly and Elinor. "They're hurt," he said, with a jerk of his head to indicate the hunters. "Why don't you two do what you can to patch them up? I'll see to Rigan."

"I'm coming with you." Corran knew he looked as bad as Trent and Ross. He felt dizzy with blood loss, his head pounded, and he had turned his ankle badly running through the vineyard. None of that mattered, not when he could hear Rigan's strangled cries echoing down the corridor.

"Come on then," Aiden snapped, clearly unhappy but not willing to fight about it. He took off at a run for Rigan's room, with Corran limping behind as quickly as he could push his battered body.

By the time Corran reached the room, Aiden was already kneeling beside Rigan's bed. A sheen of sweat covered Rigan's forehead, and his damp shirt clung to his body. His face looked pale, and his eyes tracked frantically beneath closed lids.

"Come on Rigan, wake up!" Aiden urged, taking one of Rigan's wrists to feel for his pulse. "His heart is practically beating out of his chest," he muttered. "Feels like he ran a mile at full speed."

Rigan's arms flailed, tearing loose from Aiden's grip, and he arched up, crying out in distress. His eyes snapped open, wide, frantic, and unseeing.

"Is it a curse?" Corran asked. He clung to the doorframe to keep himself on his feet.

Aiden shook his head. "No; at least, I don't think so. The monasteries were warded against dark magic, and from everything we could find, the protections still hold."

"Then what's going on and how do we stop it, dammit?"

Rigan's whole body went rigid, straining so hard against an unseen threat that the cords stood out on his neck and his hands clawed at the bedding. A low moan rose to a full-throated scream, reverberating in the small stone room. The sound coupled with a splitting headache nearly drove Corran to his knees.

"Something's hurting him. How do we stop it?" Corran grated.

Aiden chanted quietly as he traced invisible sigils on Rigan's skin. At first, nothing changed, but after a few minutes, Rigan collapsed onto the bed, panting for breath, eyes closed. Not long after that, he drew a deep breath, and his whole body went limp. His head lolled to one side, and the hands that had drawn up fistfuls of blanket relaxed.

"What's wrong?" Corran staggered across the room and fell more than knelt next to the bed. He wrapped his fingers around Rigan's wrist, reassured when he felt the steady beat of his brother's heart.

"He's through it now. I imagine he'll sleep for quite a while. I suspect that may have started as a nightmare, but it became something else. A vision—perhaps even a sending." Aiden reached for the pulse point in Rigan's neck, and a satisfied smile touched his lips.

"Sending?"

Aiden gave him a look. "Don't ask me—you two are the ones who are on speaking terms with an Elder God."

Corran caught his breath. "You think that might have been Eshtamon giving him a message?"

Aiden shrugged. "We'll have to wait for Rigan to wake up and tell us. But it's possible. That would explain why we couldn't wake him. I don't imagine gods like to be interrupted."

When their brother Kell was murdered by guards and monsters, Rigan and Corran had prayed to Eshtamon, an Elder God, the patron of vengeance. Eshtamon appeared to them and agreed to help them avenge Kell, and in return, they were to be his champions. He made them stronger, harder to kill. Only later did they discover that most who prayed to the Elder Gods were not addressed by name and given a quest. Corran and Rigan got their vengeance the night Machison and Blackholt died, but it appeared that Eshtamon had further use of their services.

Corran sat hard on the stone floor, feeling the crash after the adrenaline of the night's activities. "I'll sit with him."

Aiden glared. "He's out cold. Probably will stay that way until morning—or longer. You need food, healing, and some whiskey—not necessarily in that order."

Corran cast a worried glance at Rigan and then nodded. "All right," he agreed reluctantly. "But I'm coming back once we're done."

"I'll send Elinor back when I take over with the others," Aiden said.

"I'm too tired to argue with you," Corran replied.

Aiden stood and offered Corran a hand up. Corran winced as he got to his feet, painfully aware of how much he needed Aiden's help.

"Let's see to you, so you're not passed out when Rigan comes around," the healer said.

Two candlemarks later, Corran returned to Rigan's room. Elinor had set out a pallet and blankets on the floor beside Rigan's bed. She sat on the side of Rigan's cot and twined her fingers with his.

"He hasn't stirred," she told Corran, looking up. "But it seems to help if I talk to him. He didn't wake up, but he stilled like he could hear what I was saying, even if he couldn't respond." She reached over to press a kiss to Rigan's forehead. "You're probably exhausted," she added, looking up at Corran as she gathered her skirts and stood. "I'll let you get some rest."

Corran eased himself down to kneel, and pushed Rigan's hair out of his face, feeling for a fever out of old habit, like he had when his brother was younger. To his relief, Rigan's skin felt cool, and he looked peaceful, breath regular and heartbeat strong.

"Don't scare me like that," Corran murmured. "I can fight monsters, but magic..." He let his voice trail off. He knew how to protect his brother against physical threats, but aside from the grave magic that came with being an undertaker, he possessed no special powers of his own. When Rigan first struggled to control his magic, he had worried Corran would fear him. It had taken Corran some time to make Rigan believe that while he might be afraid *for* his brother, not fully understanding the burden that magic placed on him, he was never afraid *of* him.

Assured that Rigan slept peacefully, Corran let himself down gingerly onto his pallet, wincing at every movement. He had accepted Aiden's help with the gashes inflicted by the ghouls; those would have gone sour. Food and whiskey eased his headache, while sleep and time would take care of his aching muscles. Corran stretched out, gathered the blankets around him, and slept.

When he woke, the candle in the lantern by Rigan's bedside had burned out, leaving the room dark. Corran lit the wick from the banked embers in the fireplace. He passed a hand over his face, uncertain how long he had slept. The hidden underground rooms beneath the monastery were safe but lightless. Corran glanced at the fireplace. From the amount of ash in the embers, he guessed he had slept several candlemarks, possibly through until morning. With a weary sigh, he put a log on the fire and blew on the embers until flames danced, licking at the wood.

Flames. Fire. Unbidden, memories of the fight at the vineyard came back to Corran, and he rocked onto his heels, remembering the narrow escape. In the next breath, he recalled Rigan's nightmares, and turned, lifting the lantern to get a better look at his brother.

Rigan lay tangled in the bedclothes, sound asleep. He turned on his side and made a quiet snuffle, reassuring Corran that all was well. Corran let out a sigh of relief and startled when his stomach growled. With a backward glance at Rigan, Corran left the room and went in search of breakfast.

He found the others in the small room they used as their kitchen. None of them looked very awake, as they waited for the pot of coffee to boil in the fireplace. Bread, smoked meat, and hard boiled eggs lay on the table for them, along with some fresh fruit harvested from the trees behind the monastery. Corran was hungry enough to consider it a feast.

"Feeling better?" Polly asked, arching a brow at Corran as he sat.

"Much," Corran replied, surprised to realize that was actually true.

"How's Rigan?" Elinor asked. She looked tired, still in her night-dress with a thin robe pulled around herself, hair askew.

"Still sleeping," Corran reported. "But he didn't wake me last night, so no more nightmares, or whatever they were."

Aiden looked up, blearily-eyed. "Good. Very good. Mir slept as well. With luck, they'll both be up and around soon."

"Trent said you think we might not have seen the end of conjured monsters." Calfon sat at the end of the table, annoyingly awake.

Polly brought over the pot of coffee and Corran reached for it, earning him a slap on the wrist. "Don't rush me," she reproved, but her expression softened her tone. She set the pot in the middle of the table. "Leave some for the others. I've got another brewing. Figured it was a two-pot morning." She dusted off her hands on her apron and sat down beside Aiden.

"Ghouls," Corran said in reply to Calfon and recounted what had taken place at the vineyard since neither Trent nor Ross had come to breakfast. When he finished, Calfon rocked back in his chair, his expression thoughtful.

"It would make sense if there were more," he said slowly, thinking about his response. "Not only ones that might have gotten out of the city by accident, but others conjured here, to keep the villagers cooper-ative," he added, distaste clear in his voice. "And maybe we were fooling ourselves, but why would Machison be the only one with a pet witch who could summon and control monsters? I mean, the Lord Mayor has power, but there are a lot of others with plenty of money to hire a witch to do their bidding. The Crown Prince, the nobles—even the king himself."

The room fell silent as the implications of Calfon's statement sank in. They looked at each other in horror.

"Do you really think that they might all have blood witches of their own?" Corran managed when he could find his voice.

Calfon shrugged. "Why not? We weren't used to worrying about anyone higher up than the Lord Mayor—or maybe the Merchant Princes—back in the city. But I've been thinking about it, and it would make sense. They all want the upper hand. And they're accustomed to getting what they want."

Corran felt numb. "Where does it all end, then? Machison and Blackholt—they were within our reach. But if this goes higher, how can we possibly stop it?"

"Is it ours to stop?" Calfon countered. "We wanted justice for the people we lost to the guards and monsters, and we got that. We're tradesmen. Maybe it's not our fight."

"No, we're outlaws, and we're monster hunters," Elinor replied, raising her head. Resolve glinted in her eyes. "And the people out here who are dying have families, too."

"We can't save everyone," Aiden said quietly. "Though, gods know, I wish it were otherwise."

"No, but we can kick the arses of the monsters we can find, and kill the sons of bitches that sent them," Polly declared, crossing her arms over her chest. "It's not like we can settle down and go about our business. We're wanted criminals," she added with pride, lifting her chin.

"We don't have to do it alone," Corran mused aloud. "If it turns out to be true, then we can recruit from the villages, train their people to hunt. *We* might not be able to save everyone, but if we teach others— then maybe together we can stop the slaughter."

Calfon regarded him for a second before speaking. "Sounds reasonable. I'm in."

"Me too," Polly said with a grin.

Aiden and Elinor nodded assent. Corran felt a twist in the pit of his stomach. *Gods above and below, for all we know this could set us against the king himself. It's suicidal. But how can we do otherwise?*

Corran cleared his throat. "I'd better go check on Rigan," he said, finding an excuse to make his exit. He hurried to put together a plate of food for his brother and grabbed a cup of coffee, and then gratefully left the others to their discussion.

"Are you awake?" Corran asked quietly when Rigan stirred as he entered the room

Rigan groaned, then nodded, not bothering to open his eyes. "Yeah. What day is it?"

Corran chuckled, opening the shutters on the lamp to provide more light. He got a good look at Rigan and breathed a sigh of relief. Sleep had done wonders. The dark shadows beneath Rigan's eyes were fading, and he looked less haggard. "Not sure. I slept hard, too. Damned difficult to tell day from night down here."

Rigan chuckled at that. Corran sat on the edge of his bed, and handed over the plate of food, putting the cup of coffee on the nightstand. Rigan tore into the breakfast like a starving man. Corran watched him eat, hoping that a healthy appetite was a good sign.

"How did the hunt go?" Rigan asked with a mouthful of bread.

"Not as well as we hoped," Corran said with a sigh. "Ghouls."

Rigan wrinkled his nose. "Ugh."

Corran shrugged. "We did all right, killing the ones inside the winery. But we all got beaten up pretty badly, and then there were more ghouls waiting outside."

Rigan's eyes widened as Corran recounted the rest of the adventure. "And then I came home to see you thrashing and wailing," he added, passing a hand over his face and running it through his hair. "Honestly, some days, there isn't enough whiskey in the world to cope with what we have to put up with."

Rigan finished his breakfast and laid his plate aside. He still looked pale, but his eyes were clear.

"Tell me about the dreams," Corran urged. "Nightmares. Visions. Whatever they were, they really knocked your feet out from under you."

Rigan sighed and closed his eyes. "It started out as a nightmare. I was back in Ravenwood, the night everything went to shit. Bringing Kell back from the warehouse. Cleaning him up for burial." His voice caught, and he swallowed hard. "Seeing the shop burn. But in the nightmare, the guards were right on our heels, and then when we got Below, Damian was standing in the witches' house in the middle of all the bodies, he'd just killed them, and—"

"What?" Corran prompted.

Rigan opened his eyes and looked at Corran with such naked grief that his brother struggled to hold his gaze. "He killed you," Rigan whispered. "Right in front of me. Told me that was what my magic could do, to watch and learn."

Corran reached out and took Rigan's wrist, wrapping his fingers around the bone in an unbreakable grip. "But he didn't, Rigan. I'm still here. That didn't happen."

"It seemed real in the dream," Rigan replied, looking down. Corran squeezed his wrist one more time and leaned back, dropping his grip.

"What else?"

Rigan licked his lips, frowning. "I can see everything in my mind, but it's hard to put into words, some of it. The old Wanderer woman I saw in the city, she's there. And those sigils they drew. I can see the sigil, but I don't recognize it."

Corran grabbed a piece of parchment and a quill from the bedside table. "Can you draw it?"

Rigan concentrated, closing his eyes again, and then looked up and began to copy what he saw in his memories. "There," he said finally, handing the paper back to Corran. "That's it."

The rune meant nothing to Corran. He put the drawing aside carefully. "If we ever meet up with some Wanderers again, we'll have to ask them," he said tiredly, passing a hand over his face.

"They're out here," Rigan replied. "The guards ran the Wanderers out of the city, so they must be somewhere in the countryside. And in a while, they'll be back inside the walls, once things settle down. That's their way."

"Well, we won't be going back," Corran replied. "So if we find them, it'll have to be here in the countryside. What else?"

Rigan's brows furrowed in concentration. "The old woman was trying to tell me something, warn me. She looked worried, but I couldn't make out what she said. And then she was gone, and I saw Eshtamon."

Corran caught his breath. "Do you think it was really him?"

Rigan shrugged. "I doubt it. Nothing else was real. Although, he's an Elder God. If he wanted to get into my dreams, I suppose he could do it."

"What did he want?"

"He stood in the middle of the road, out here beyond the walls, nothing around in sight except fields and fences. And he looked straight at me—remember how that felt?"

Corran nodded. No one ever forgot being the subject of a deity's focus.

"He didn't say anything, but the way he stared at me like he was saying, 'you, boy. I'm talking to you.'" Rigan wet his lips. "And then he spread his arms like he meant everything around us and he *looked* at me. No words. But I *knew*."

"Knew what?" The words barely made it out of Corran's dry mouth.

Rigan met his gaze. "We're not done. Someone's still summoning monsters. We have to stop them. We swore to Eshtamon we would."

"Son of a bitch," Corran muttered under his breath. "That's what we figured on our way back from fighting the ghouls. That some of them might have wandered out of the city, but not all of them. Not the smart ones—the strix and the shape-shifters, the *nokk*—they belong out here, been here for a long time. There aren't that many of them. But the other things, the ones that come in packs, that don't do anything but kill, I think they're the conjured ones. And they can't all be left over from Blackholt."

"Pretty sure that's what Eshtamon tried to tell me. So now we've got to start over again, figure out who's behind it, and how to stop them."

"The Merchant Princes? Some local wealthy landowner? I don't even know where to begin," Corran confessed. "This—it's bigger than what a handful of outlaws can do."

A bitter smile touched Rigan's lips. "Then let's make more outlaws."

"What do you mean?"

Rigan fidgeted as if worried about Corran's reaction. "I've been thinking about this for a while now. What if we made more hunters? Told the townspeople the truth about the conjured monsters, and showed them how to fight back? I mean, they're used to fighting off wolves that want to take their sheep. This is just a different kind of predator. Tell them about salt and iron, show them how to make the salt mix and draw the circles. That way, when we move on, they can still protect themselves."

Corran nodded and smiled thinking of their recent conversation. "And if someone else out here is calling the monsters, we can keep it contained, with more help. Find out who it is with more ears to the ground."

"Do you think the others will go for it?"

Corran laughed. "Pretty sure they will. Polly's already suggested training townsfolk. We haven't exactly hidden what we do. And if the villagers knew how to fight the creatures, they wouldn't have needed our help. It wouldn't take long to give them the basics. That's the key —we can't afford to be out in the open, in one place, for too long. That's asking for trouble, if not the guards than the bounty hunters. But yeah, I think it could work."

Rigan swayed, and Corran caught him by the shoulders, easing him back on the bed. His brother had paled, and a thin sheen of sweat covered his forehead. "I think you overdid it there," Corran said. "You need to rest."

"Send Aiden in," Rigan replied, eyes wide. He could not hide a flicker of fear. "I don't want to dream again."

CHAPTER SEVEN

"What have the Ravenwood spies reported?" Sarolinian Crown Prince Neven stood at the stone railing of the walkway outside his villa, overlooking the sea.

"The city remains in chaos. Aliyev has taken over for now and says nothing about naming a new Lord Mayor. The fires are out, but there's still too much of a mess for them to begin rebuilding," Brice Tagar replied. The Sarolinian spymaster kept his voice low, while his eyes constantly scanned the horizon for threats.

Ingrained habit. Useful. Neven thought. "Yet the Garenoth agreement stands," Neven mused. "Despite the debacle that fool Machison created."

"For now, my lord. Signing the trade agreement is only a formality. Ravenwood may still lose its advantages if it defaults on its obligations." Brice Tagar presented a study in contradictions. His unremarkable appearance and slight build made him forgettable, all the better to pass unnoticed. Tagar was adept at hiding a sharp intellect behind an utterly bland appearance, a fiction he cultivated. He did not vie for dominance; he recorded all slights received in an indelible memory and accumulated the means for payback.

"Then we must assure that default," Neven said, clasping his hands behind his back.

"Our ambassador has returned from Ravenwood," Tagar replied. "I've let him know you'll want to speak with him."

"Tell him I'll expect him at dinner. Let my servants know."

"Of course, m'lord." Tagar stood a respectful distance from his employer, joining him in gazing out over the sea. Ravenwood lay to the south, out of sight but never far out of mind. "I have news about Kadar."

Neven did not bother to turn toward him. "Tell me."

"Kadar's quite upset that he did not gain more advantages in the new Garenoth agreement," Tagar reported. "Machison was Gorog's creature, so he made sure Gorog got most of the spoils. Aliyev doesn't care who ekes out an extra percentage of profit so long as the overall revenues remain unchanged. Merchant Prince Tamar stays largely out of politics, playing bookkeeper to his lands unless Kadar drags him into a scheme. He's likely to be wary, what with Gorog's example."

Merchant Prince Gorog, the wealthiest and most powerful of his three Ravenwood peers, died shortly after the riots. Officially, Gorog was said to have committed suicide, distraught over a personal crisis. Few believed that story. After Machison's spectacular failure, Gorog could not hope to regain Aliyev's trust, and even the usually-pliant Guild Masters disdained him. Gorog might have had cause to kill himself, but all indications suggested murder. His son reluctantly took over the title and responsibilities.

"I don't doubt that Aliyev had a hand in the elder Gorog's death," Neven replied. "It's what I would have done if I were him. But I don't think it will deter Kadar for long."

"Doubtful," Tagar replied. "The man's too greedy to show restraint for long. And he's been most receptive to the possibilities suggested by our go-between."

"Oh?"

Tagar paused for a moment, lifting his face to the wind. "My man is very good at what he does. Made several coincidental meetings before striking up a conversation of any importance. Kadar's bitter about how the agreement turned out, and he's got no love for Aliyev, either. Seemed most intrigued at the thought of using smuggled goods to pad his profits."

"Good. Very good."

Tagar chuckled. "My man said he had the feeling that Kadar had thought about the possibility before, but lacked the connections to bring it off. Or perhaps it was merely a backup plan, in case he didn't get his way with the negotiations."

"How interested is he? Willing to actually do something?" Neven pressed.

"Indeed, m'lord. The fool gave my man money to buy the first load of goods. It'll come ashore on the third night this week, on a back bay not too far from one of Kadar's vineyards. Barrel planking from some of the oak trees in Itara that are so highly prized, delivered without tariff or import fees."

"Excellent," Neven replied. "Make sure he receives the best quality, even if you augment the value of what he paid for a bit. This must be a solid win for him, easy money. He won't be able to resist doing it again, either to line his pockets or to spite Aliyev. Kadar will be pleased with himself for his cleverness. It shouldn't take long before he's begging to expand. And all the while, he's cutting away the very foundation of the League that made his fortune."

"My sources tell me that Kadar might have overextended himself, expecting to reap the benefits of a Garenoth agreement more to his liking," Tagar continued. "He's anxious to make up the shortfall, so backing smugglers to keep his costs down suits him very well."

"Do you see any indications the other Ravenwood Merchant Princes will cause us problems?"

Tagar shook his head. "Gorog's son is hesitant, too unsure of himself. And coming in on the heels of his father's disgrace, he's going to be cautious—too careful. Tamar should have been a monk. The man has little ambition. I think he bores Aliyev nearly as much as he bores everyone else."

"Where are King Rellan's attentions these days?" Before he received the appointment as Crown Prince, Neven had held a position much like Tagar's, feeding information and scenarios to the previous Crown Prince. When the time was right, and the trust he enjoyed was inviolate, Neven had helped his elderly mentor go to the After a bit earlier than the gods might have planned. To assure that history did not repeat itself, Neven arranged for very comfortable house arrest for Tagar's family, contingent on his own longevity and good health. *Negotiations, I've found, work best, when both parties fully understand what the other wants.*

"Outside of his bedchamber?" Tagar smirked. "I'm told the king tears himself away from his courtesans long enough to meet with the exchequer regularly, to make sure that taxes are paid, and revenues don't slip. He doesn't care how the money comes in, only that the flow never falters. It will take more than a few fires in Ravenwood to pull him out of the arms of his mistresses."

"Don't underestimate the king," Neven warned. "He may be preoccupied, but his survival instincts are as sharp as ever, and he won't hesitate to send assassins against anyone who poses a threat. I've heard you get one proxy warning, and then you die."

Tagar turned around, leaning against the railing. "We're a long way from the palace. You've done well, picking the flesh off the bones when Kasten defaulted. That should give us some room to maneuver. And if you can add Ravenwood to your trophies—"

"Let's not start spending gold before it's in hand," Neven said. "What of the hunters that killed Machison?"

Tagar crossed his arms. "My spies tell me they fled the city the night of the fires. Aliyev has men looking for him—rumor is Hant Jorgeson is one of those doing the searching."

"I'm surprised Jorgeson kept his head, after what happened."

"Crown Prince Aliyev has a dry sense of humor, I suppose. Jorgeson's been given a small team and sent out to redeem himself." Tagar snorted. "Or rather, to keep his head out of a noose."

"Knowing Aliyev, he's sent Jorgeson to clean up his own mess, but the noose is still waiting for him."

"I'd expect nothing less," Tagar replied. "It's a danger for Aliyev, having the hunters loose. Inside Ravenwood's walls, they can be contained. But out in the countryside—they could skew the Balance, or worse, let slip about the Cull."

"Let's hope Jorgeson keeps them running too hard to confide in the locals," Neven replied. He turned away from the view and walked to a cart that held a decanter of whiskey and a glass. He poured himself a drink and offered one to Tagar, who declined.

"Even if the king doesn't notice a drop in revenue, his witches will certainly pay attention if the Balance isn't kept," Tagar said. "Having hunters killing off his monsters won't help that."

Blood magic required a price, and on a small scale, the practitioner could pay the debt in his own blood. Physical limits tended to keep the dark magic in check. Then ambitious blood witches discovered that the price of magic could be paid by proxy, enabling larger spells and workings that would have required enough blood to kill a single person. Once the witches learned how to summon monsters from the Rift and sent them to kill, they were free to use blood magic on a scale rarely before attempted. The cost came in the Cull, the death toll caused by the conjured monsters.

"I'm sure that's occurred to Aliyev. He's got to clean up Blackholt's unfinished business, as well as Machison's," Neven said, sipping his whiskey.

"Surely Aliyev has a blood witch. He's wealthy enough to afford more than one."

Neven savored the burn of the exquisite liquor. "Oh, he has his witch. Pretentious little prick that goes by the name of Adder Shadowsworn. He's powerful—better than Blackholt, from what I've heard."

"Talent and strength are only part of the equation," Tagar said, straightening.

"Shadowsworn is also ruthless as the Pit. You would do well to remember that."

"Oh, yes m'lord, I shan't forget it for a moment," Tagar replied with a cold smile. "It makes the game that much more interesting.

———

"To what do I owe the honor of this dinner?" Ambassador Lorenz asked once they had finished the main course. Servants cleared away the dishes, and Neven signaled to the wine steward to refill their goblets.

"You have been in Ravenwood recently, for the signing of the Garenoth agreement," Neven said, leaning back in his chair and observing his guest. Lorenz had the jowls and paunch to suggest he ate well and frequently. As befitting his position, his waistcoat was excellently tailored, of fabric only slightly less opulent than what Neven himself wore. Gemstones glittered in the candlelight in the rings on Lorena's pudgy fingers. One look at the man's eyes revealed him to be anything but soft.

"Just before the... recent unpleasantness," Lorenz replied. "What is it you'd like to know?"

"How was Machison regarded by those closest to him?" Neven asked. *Aside from the fact that I always thought of him as a self-serving rodent.*

Lorenz set his goblet aside and tented his fingers. "May I speak plainly, my lord?"

Neven nodded. "You're of little use to me if you speak only in the veiled pleasantries and nuanced lies of your profession."

Lorenz tilted his head, acknowledging the truth of Neven's statement. "Machison was a street fighter, a brawler who made good. He did not come from a particularly wealthy or influential family. He scrapped for every break he got, and he held on to what was his like a starving cur with a bone." He paused for a sip of his wine.

"I didn't like the man. Few people did. He was brutal and vulgar," Lorenz continued. "But even his enemies respected his tenacity, and his ability to bull his way through to get what he wanted. Only a fool underestimated him. He was productive, in a bare-knuckles sort of way."

Neven chuckled. "I appreciate your candor. Your opinion matches my own. How, then, did Machison make such grave errors?"

Lorenz raised an eyebrow. "He forgot that appearances matter as much as results," he replied. "Yes, he and his blood witch kept the

Cull. But they were sloppy about it, clumsy in their execution. Started setting the monsters against his political enemies' proxies instead of making the strikes random. Those of us knew the truth of the matter could see that he went too far provoking the tradespeople."

"How so?" Neven leaned forward, listening intently.

"He let his side agreement with Gorog drive his choices," Lorenz replied. "Started having Blackholt send the monsters against the neighborhoods with Guilds that owed their loyalty to Kadar or Tamas or that earned his ire. He forgot that tradesmen are not rabble. Send the monsters against the vagrants and the dispossessed; no one will notice or mourn them. But tradesmen are fighters; have to be to earn their living. It was only a matter of time before they fought back, and once they did, he had a rebellion on his hands."

"Surely 'rebellion' is a strong word for a street riot—"

Lorenz shook his head. "I saw what happened, my lord. I was in the city that night. Aliyev may spin the tale that it was a few ruffians and Jorgeson's poor judgment, but how did 'ruffians' defeat a blood witch like Blackholt? How did mere brigands pull off a plot to get inside the Lord Mayor's palace and take down the most guarded man in the city?" He finished his goblet of wine.

"No, my prince. Rabble did not kill Machison or Blackholt. The tradesmen rose up to protect their own, and in the end, even the Guilds had more than they could stomach... with the monsters and the hostages Machison took to assure their cooperation in the negotiations." He folded his hands on the table. "Now Aliyev must work out a truce of sorts with the Guilds because even if the Guild Masters do not understand the Balance or the Cull, they know Machison worked against them. The fires damaged much of the city. And while some of those fires were likely set by the hunters, I am equally certain that the guards set some themselves, on Machison's orders, to implicate the Wanderers."

Neven's eyes narrowed. "Why did he care so much about those dirty vermin?"

Lorenz sighed. "If I had to guess, I'd say he feared them for some reason. His hatred was... irrational."

"Does Aliyev have the support necessary to fix what's broken and fulfill the agreement with Garenoth—or with any of Ravenwood's trading partners, for that matter?" Neven watched the ambassador, looking for tells that he might be shading his answers, anticipating what his master wanted to hear. So far, he had seen nothing to suggest Lorenz had been dishonest.

"Crown Prince Aliyev is a smart man, and also sometimes, clever," Lorenz replied carefully. "He has the family, wealth, and position Machison lacked, as well as the polish of someone born to nobility. He is also a meticulous organizer—single-minded and thorough. All that speaks well to his ability to bring order out of chaos. And yet—"

"What?"

Lorenz frowned. "Aliyev lacks charisma. He is an uninspiring speaker and appears to be uncomfortable in social gatherings. People listened to Machison because they feared him. Aliyev is an able administrator, but he will have difficulty rallying others to his cause. I suspect that the physical mess Machison left behind will be cleaned up long before he has mended fences with the Guilds or their members."

Neven nodded, processing what Lorenz had said. "Which should mean that Aliyev will be far too busy to worry about us," he replied. "He's looking for internal threats. He'll expect the other League states to try to nibble away at Ravenwood's advantages, but if we're careful, he won't realize what we're doing until it's done."

Lorenz smiled, knowing and treacherous. "I believe fate favors us. Aliyev will be distracted for quite some time."

"Good," Neven said. "Do everything in your power to see to it." He paused. "What's being said about Kadar?"

Lorenz signaled for the steward to refill his wine. "Kadar is a cockroach. He survives no matter how many times someone tries to step on him. He complained to Aliyev about Gorog's preferred treatment to the point where I once caught the Crown Prince attempting to sneak out of his own villa to avoid a discussion." Lorenz chuckled. "He was right— Gorog did get preferred treatment, but Gorog brought in more than his share of revenue to begin with, and he built an alliance with Machison to strengthen his position. As opposed to Kadar, who wanted to be given special favors without earning them."

Released from his ambassadorial duties, Lorenz spoke with remarkable frankness. "Tamas follows Kadar—up to a point. If you mean to maneuver Kadar to undercut the League, you'll have to handle Tamas carefully. He's quiet, but he's also smart and stubborn. If you're not careful, he'll figure out your game and hold your balls for ransom."

That matched Neven's assessment and dovetailed with what he had heard from Tagar. "Keep me informed," he replied. "When you return to Ravenwood, make sure you watch Kadar. I think he can be played, but I don't want us to find out he's not quite the fool we believe him to be."

"I don't think he'll exceed your expectations, my lord," Lorenz replied, finishing the rest of his wine with a satisfied exhale.

"You're in a position to hear and see things most of my other spies cannot," Neven said. "If we can bring about Ravenwood's downfall, we all stand to reap the benefits, as we did with Kasten. But I must not allow Kadar enough room to slip our leash. Do you understand me?"

Lorenz set his goblet aside and gave Neven a foxlike smile. "Absolutely, my lord. I'll handle it."

———

"I THOUGHT YOU might visit earlier. Lovely day, isn't it?" The thin blond man looked up from where he gathered clippings from the plants that surrounded him. Monkshood, yew, and hemlock vied for space with other equally lethal plants and fungi.

Argus Nightshade set his harvesting knife in his basket and reached out to lift up the flower on a nearby belladonna stalk. "Beautiful, and so potent. The garden's doing very well this year."

Neven did his best not to dwell on the fact that human bones doubled as plant stakes to hold Nightshade's prized specimens aloft. The ground to his right had been newly turned, and if Nightshade's garden produced exceptional growth, the bodies buried in its beds supplied plenty of fertilizer, as did the blood-soaked rituals he liked to hold at midnight amid the mazes and follies.

"We need to discuss the Balance."

Nightshade rolled his eyes and came away from the plantings, laying his basket on the path. He gave a vague wave toward a nearby gazebo that offered shade, an unspoken invitation to join him at the table and chairs inside. "There's a fresh pot of tea," he said. "I had an extra setting put out for you."

Neven did not remember this particular gazebo before. Nightshade's tastes ran to the macabre, and his garden of poisonous and magical plants proved the perfect setting for his dark whimsy. Bleached skeletons dressed in rags kept scarecrows' vigil throughout the grounds. Mosaics of skulls, vertebrae, and small bones decorated the planting beds and embellished the open-air follies scattered among the flowers and trees. Several evergreen mazes of varying heights sprawled over portions of the gardens and each was ringed by an intricate fence made from human bones.

"Have you built on to the garden since the last time?" He would be damned if he would let Nightshade's sick decorations affect him.

The blood witch sank down into a chair on the other side of the small table and poured himself a cup of tea. "I'm always building on. Daren't stop—it's part of a spell. Price I had to pay for a powerful working. Bad things would happen—can't have that." He added honey to his tea and took a long sip.

"Does the Balance hold?" Neven asked, unwilling to get drawn off topic. He understood the source of Nightshade's power and had no illusions about the fate of the wretches taken for the Cull, either by monsters or by the guards that brought them to the witch's garden workshop. Perhaps the bone decorations and the carefully posed, mummified corpses were tied up in rituals and spell work—or they were simply a testimony to a man who was seriously unbalanced. Maybe both.

"In Sarolinia? Yes. The Cull has been steady—and as you have requested, we've kept the ones we target to the useless and those who won't be missed." With his shoulder-length blond hair, piercing blue eyes, and handsome features, Argus Nightshade looked like he should be a herald of the Elder Gods. Even his pristine white robes gave him an otherworldly appearance. Nothing about him spoke of the abattoir or the torturer's craft. But Neven had seen Nightshade at work, drenched in blood like a vengeful spirit, muttering in long-dead languages and reveling in carnage. Like his garden, Nightshade possessed a haunting, hideous beauty.

"And outside the borders? What of Ravenwood and Kasten?"

Nightshade smiled. "Kasten remains a killing field. I've been playing with something new, calling monsters through the Rifts at greater distances than before. Practicing in Kasten, in case you wanted me to do the same in Ravenwood. Think of it! We can draw power for the magic and conjure beasts to run our enemy to ground, all in a single working."

The blood witch's enthusiasm for his work made bile rise in Neven's throat. "Very good," he replied, hiding his revulsion. "That may indeed be useful. But isn't such a working putting strain on the Rifts?"

Nightshade put his cup aside. "Like most without magic, you don't really comprehend the Rifts or the Balance," he said, condescension clear in his voice.

"I know enough to realize that the Rifts are dangerous, and the Balance might be thrown badly enough askew that even the Cull can't satisfy it," Neven snapped.

"The Rifts are a natural phenomenon," Nightshade countered.

"Are they? Or did blood magic manage to tear a hole in the world so the monsters could crawl through from the Pit?"

"The sources aren't entirely clear," Nightshade replied. "And besides, no single Rift is very large. And it's not as if blood mages leave them open."

"Can you guarantee that you will always be able to get them closed?"

"That hasn't been a problem thus far."

"Thus far," Neven echoed.

"I don't know what you're complaining about," Nightshade sulked. "You benefit from my magic, richly."

Neven fought the urge to rub the back of his neck. "Yes, I do. It's not a complaint—it's a caution. Once torn, few things stitch back up good as new. And what's to say you—or your brother witches—will always be able to control the situation? You've got to open the Rift, summon the monsters—but only so many of them or we'll all die—and then seal the Rift once more. It could go wrong so easily—"

"But it hasn't." Nightshade dropped his sulk to ease into the insincere reasonability he used to "handle" Neven when he pushed for more than the witch willingly supplied. "In all these years."

"How many blood witches can be sustained before it overwhelms the Balance?"

Nightshade laughed, a cold sound like the ringing of a death knell. "There has always been death enough to sustain the Balance. Always enough no-accounts to feed Colduraan's maw. Beyond the Rifts— that's Colduraan's realm, with his First Creatures, like He Who Watches. It's a primal force, chaos. The strongest in the universe, since in the end chaos is all that's left."

"Elder Gods? Really? Leave the children's tales for another time," Neven grated, impatient with Nightshade's embroidered tales of god-monsters. "Perhaps mastering chaos is a bit beyond mortal reach." Neven was unwilling to think too hard on what Nightshade had revealed. He hoped his overly dramatic blood witch had spoken metaphorically, poetically, but the chill he felt warned him otherwise. "What can you sense of Aliyev's mage?"

"Shadowsworn? That old pretender?" Nightshade made a dismissive gesture. "He's long past his best years. Quite a reputation—and he deserved it in his day—but he's hung on too long. Should have quit the game at his peak." He leaned forward conspiratorially. "I don't doubt Aliyev thinks Shadowsworn is a prestigious catch. But he's really too old for the game."

"Humor me," Neven said, straining to keep his tone civil. "What is Aliyev's blood witch doing with his power these days?"

He knew Nightshade used divination and scrying to keep watch on all of his rival witches, though he also suspected that those of real power had ways to block or obscure such efforts. Still, even bits and pieces gleaned around the edges could prove useful in finding the weaknesses of an enemy.

"He's still conjuring monsters, opening the Rift, but not as often as Blackholt. He might not need to if Aliyev's guards are killing rioters in sufficient numbers." Nightshade reached out and plucked a cluster of foxglove from a plant growing near the edge of the gazebo's stone floor, and toyed with the lethal flowers as he spoke. "I suspect Aliyev has him working small magics—protection charms and warnings, coercion spells, that sort of thing. Trying to get his house in order." He wrinkled his nose. "Nasty business, what happened with Blackholt. Though I can't say I'm sorry he's gone."

"If Shadowsworn is busy doing his master's bidding, then we may have an opportunity," Neven mused. "You told me once that Blackholt conjured some monsters to keep the peasants beyond the wall in line, make sure they didn't get any rebellious notions in their heads."

"That's right. We do the same here, to make sure the townspeople know their place. Reducing their numbers lets the strongest survive."

"Can your ability to open Rifts at a distance let you add to the Ravenwood Cull?"

Nightshade smiled. "Oh, yes."

"Then do it," Neven replied. "Start slowly, and stay away from the rivers—I have plans for those. Don't do anything too noticeable—we don't want to draw Shadowsworn's attention."

Nightshade snorted. "That won't be difficult."

"Confidence is admirable; overconfidence is not," Neven reproved. "I don't want this mucked up. Stagger the locations and the kinds of monsters, not too many at once or too close together. The villagers beyond the city walls aren't ready to riot like the tradespeople and the Guild members. They still feel beholden, maybe even loyal, to their Merchant Princes. Kill enough of them while the guards do nothing, and that will change."

"I like the way you think," Nightshade replied. "Given the unrest in the city, it could take a while before Aliyev even notices anything's gone wrong."

"I'm counting on it. And when he does, he'll have to decide what's more important—getting the city back on its feet to meet the finished goods export contracts, or putting down problems in the countryside that threaten his commodity shipments," Neven said. "Throw him enough plates to juggle, and something will crash. And once Ravenwood's in default, Garenoth has the right to renegotiate its agreement. We'll swoop in and pick up the pieces at a bargain rate. For a tidy profit."

"This will take some time if we're not to be noticed, my lord," Nightshade said, though his attention focused on the foxglove in his hand. "I can begin immediately, of course. But aren't you concerned about those hunters that escaped from Ravenwood, the ones that were bold enough to kill Machison—and Blackholt?"

"Certainly not!" Neven's head came up sharply. "They got lucky, and Machison was sloppy. Blackholt's arrogance was his comeuppance. They're nothing but outlaws—and I'm certain Aliyev has his guards running them to ground. Don't worry about them. They'll be dealt with, and we already know Aliyev's guards are spread thin in the countryside. You'll have blood aplenty."

"Of that, I'm sure," Nightshade replied with an enigmatic smile that sent a shiver down Neven's spine.

CHAPTER EIGHT

THE CREATURE MOVED across a moonlit stretch of ground not far in front of them. Rigan could not see the monster clearly, but what he made out gave him chills. It looked like a woman until it raised its arms and revealed long talons instead of hands and feet. The being walked with a hunch, like a crone, and as the clouds parted and the moonlight streamed down, he saw its face. Black eyes and pinched features gave it a weirdly bird-like appearance, oddly human and yet definitely... not.

"It's called a piyanin," Aiden had told them, reading from a lore book. "It prefers to snatch children or young women who come too close to the edge of the forest, but if it's hungry enough, it'll take anything—men, sheep, even full-grown cows. "Some people say it's a death omen to dream of one, that it can ride your soul and drain your life."

"How do we kill it?" Trent had asked.

"Use an iron sword to cut off the vestiges of wings it hides in its hunched back," Aiden had told them. "Stab it with steel and silver, and then dismember it and burn it with salt."

Rigan did not recall anyone mentioning those long, sharp talons.

"You ready?" Corran glanced at Rigan.

Rigan stared in horrified fascination at the monster. Corran elbowed him and glared.

"Yeah. Ready." Rigan realized that he must have sounded spooked since Corran's eyes narrowed as he made a quick assessment to assure his younger brother had not already somehow been injured. Rigan shook his head, and managed a wan smile, hoping Corran would dismiss it as pre-battle jitters.

Across the clearing, he spotted a flicker of lantern light, Trent's signal to engage. Rigan and Corran ran from cover toward the creature, focusing its attention on them while Trent closed in from the other side.

Corran wielded an iron sword in his right hand, a steel knife in his left. Rigan carried a steel sword, but it was a secondary weapon to his magic. He sent a bolt of blue-white energy crackling toward the *piyanin*, but it moved aside too quickly, and the bolt singed past its shoulder.

With a hiss, the *piyanin* leaped high into the air. It came at Rigan with its hind talons, like a falcon about to snatch its prey. Corran lunged, slashing with his iron blade, and connected hard with the *piyanin's* left leg.

The flesh smoked at the touch of iron, and the *piyanin* gave a deafening shriek. Rigan scrambled back, out of range, and summoned his magic again, this time blasting the monster with a burst of flames that caught in its ragged clothing, burning them to ash as the *piyanin* screamed and snapped.

Trent and Corran dove forward, one from either side and while Corran slashed the monster's shoulder, Trent stabbed his iron sword through the *piyanin's* hunched back. Rigan sank his sword deep into the creature's gut before scrambling back, trying to avoid its vicious talons.

The claws caught on Rigan's sleeve, opening up a deep gash on his forearm. Rigan plunged his sword in again, this time through the *piyanin's* ribs. Dark blood flowed from the monster's wounds, injuries that would have felled anything human. Despite their wounds, the *piyanin* kept fighting, snarling, and shrieking as it snatched at its tormentors with long, sharp claws.

"The wings!" Corran yelled. "Get the wings!"

"What in the name of the gods do you think I'm trying to do?" Trent snapped. Rigan's fiery torrent had burned away the bird-thing's meager clothing and charred its flesh. Without the camouflage of its garments, Corran could see a mound of bone and leathery skin gathered between the monster's shoulder blades. Blood streamed from where Trent had cut into the wings but mantled as they were, Corran saw no way to cut them from where they joined the thing's spine.

"Rigan! Hit the wings!"

Rigan scrambled to shift his position to get a clear shot at the *piyanin's* back without endangering Corran or Trent. He loosed a short charge of energy like harnessed lightning that struck the *piyanin's* wings and sizzled.

The *piyanin* shrieked, loud and piercing enough that Corran felt amazed that his ears were not bleeding. The leathery, stubbed wings shook free, and both Corran and Trent threw themselves at the monster, hacking at the bony joints that fastened the bat-like appendages to its back.

With a sharp twist, the *piyanin* turned back and forth, throwing Corran and Trent clear before they could finish their task. The damaged wings hung from broken frames, unable to furl, slashed and bleeding. Before Corran got to his feet to try again, the *piyanin* leaped into the air once more with the strength of its powerful legs and hurtled toward Rigan. Rigan raised his hand to send fire once again, but the *piyanin* moved faster, slamming him down to the ground and pinning him with its long, powerful talons.

"Rigan!" Corran shouted, panic for his brother's safety clear in his voice. He ran at the *piyanin*, tucking his head and lowering his shoulder, and hit the creature with his full weight and the momentum of a dead run. Rigan bent his knees and kicked, and the combined force toppled the *piyanin*. Trent leaped onto the monster's back, sawing with all his might on its tattered wings as Corran stabbed into its flesh again and again; side, belly, and back.

The *piyanin* shrieked again, but this time, the cry lacked strength. It grabbed at the air with its front talons and dug up the ground with its hind claws, but Trent held it down with his legs, and Corran grappled to keep it turned so that Trent could complete his task.

With a cry of victory, Trent hacked through the last of the bone and sinew holding the ragged wings in place. As soon as the wings dropped away, the *piyanin* collapsed. Trent ran it through the heart with his iron sword, for good measure, and then he and Corran began the grisly work of cutting it to pieces.

"Hey Rigan, how about some help?" Corran called to his brother as his steel knife cut through the monster's shoulder, severing an arm. Trent wasted no time bringing his blade down to cut off the creature's head. "Rigan?"

A groan answered him, but Rigan did not get up. "Rigan!" Corran left the *piyanin's* corpse and ran to where Rigan lay where the monster had left him. Blood covered his torn shirt, soaking through one sleeve and plastering the cloth to his shoulder.

"I'm all right," Rigan said, though the timbre of his voice suggested otherwise. "Got the wind knocked out of me."

"It's dead," Corran said, kneeling beside his brother and checking for injuries as well as he could by moonlight. "Just have to cut up and burn the son of a bitch. Did it get you deep with those claws?"

Rigan shook his head. "I don't think so. Still hurts."

Corran helped Rigan sit enough to ease him out of the tatters of his shirt, which Corran ripped into strips that would suffice for bandages until they could get back to the monastery. He looked relieved when he found no puncture wounds, although the gashes were deep and would require Aiden's help to heal. Even then, they might scar.

"Can you walk?"

Rigan set his jaw but nodded. "Yeah. Just don't ask me to swing a sword." Corran helped him to his feet, then went back to where Trent had already cut off the *piyanin's* remaining limbs.

"I've got the salt." Corran dug through the bag Rigan had dropped at the edge of the clearing. He came back a moment later carrying a bag of the salt-aconite-amanita mixture and a bottle of oil. He drenched the *piyanin's* corpse with oil and poured the salt over it as Trent reclaimed the lantern he had left shuttered on the other side of the open space. Corran returned with sticks for kindling, and they watched with grim satisfaction as the flames took hold, forming a pyre.

"Come on," Corran said to Rigan, who swayed on his feet and looked like he might drop at any moment. Blood soaked through the make-shift bandages, and Corran frowned in concern at Rigan's pallor. "Let's get you back to the healer."

Rigan let Corran get a shoulder under his arm, helping him make the walk back to where they left the horses. "It might not be enough," Rigan mumbled.

"What?"

"What Aiden can do. Might not stop it."

"Are you hurt somewhere else? Did it bite you?"

Rigan shook his head. "You don't… understand. I saw it, Corran."

"We all saw it. What do you—"

"In my dreams." Rigan met Corran's gaze. "I saw the *piyanin* in my *dreams*, Corran."

Corran blanched, and Rigan could tell his brother understood. *It's a death omen.*

Corran swallowed hard and straightened his shoulders. "Yeah, well, that *piyanin* isn't going to be hurting anyone. We handled it. The stuff about omens is a bunch of superstitious nonsense, Rigan. Aiden's going to get you fixed up just fine." He gave Rigan a boost into his saddle and kept a hand on his side until he felt certain Rigan would not topple off.

"You think so?"

"Positive. Aiden and Elinor will find some amulets if that's what it takes. But not before they keep more blood from leaking out of you."

Rigan gave a barely audible chuckle in response. Corran let Trent take the lead on the ride back to their base, putting Rigan in the middle where Corran could keep an eye on him, even as he hung back to assure no other predators came up on them from behind.

Rigan's memories of the ride back jumbled together. Corran and Trent helped ease him down from his horse, and he stumbled, barely able to keep his feet under him. He woke in his bed, wounds bandaged, and a cool compress on his forehead.

"There you are," Aiden said with a tired smile. "Been waiting for you to rejoin us."

Rigan considered trying to sit up, then thought better of it. "How long was I out?"

Aiden shrugged. "Not counting you fading in and out on the ride back? A couple of candlemarks. You lost a lot of blood. I've healed the wounds and done what I could to help you replenish, but some things can't be rushed."

"The others?"

"Corran and Trent got some bruises and cuts, but nothing like yours. Elinor took care of them. Corran's been poking his nose in now and again to see how you are."

"Then I imagine he's been bored because I don't remember a thing." Rigan hesitated. "Aiden—are omens real?"

Aiden gave him an inquisitive look. "It depends. Sometimes they are. And sometimes, it's a person's imagination making things mean more than they really do. You have something specific in mind?"

"I've had bad dreams lately," Rigan confessed. "And I've seen the *piyanin* in them."

Aiden frowned. "Maybe you're mistaken?"

Rigan shook his head. "I didn't know what it was before we fought one, but now that I've seen it, that's what was in my dreams."

Aiden had drawn a chair up beside Rigan's bed. He leaned back, frowning. "I was hoping you were thinking more along having seen a black cat. *Piyanin* are trouble, and because they're supernatural, there's some truth to them being a harbinger of bad fortune. But beyond that is just superstition, Rigan," he said.

"Are you sure?"

Aiden sighed. "It's not the type of thing anyone can be *sure* of. But I do know that people tend to make things happen if they believe hard enough that those things *will* happen—good or bad. So if you feel lucky enough—really certain you're having a good day—good things seem to come your way. Go into a fight thinking you're going to lose, and you will. It's not magic; it's belief. And I'm certain that some—maybe most—of the things people blame on omens happen because they've talked themselves into it."

Rigan wanted to accept Aiden's reassurance, but he remained unconvinced. "That's good to know," he said and closed his eyes to end the conversation. He'd see what the lore books had to say about warding off bad omens and take it upon himself to remain safe. *Corran's already lost Kell; I won't leave him, too.*

————

A WEEK PASSED after the fight with the *piyanin*. Rigan hunched over manuscripts in the room they had set aside as a library to store the books they had scavenged. His wounds were almost fully healed; Corran and Trent already chafed to find another hunt.

He scoured the old tomes looking for protection symbols, anything he could find to ward off the bad luck of having seen the *piyanin* in his dreams. With Elinor's help, he had fashioned a wristlet and an amulet, and he had slipped away to work more than one ritual the books promised afforded safety. The dreams had not come again, but Rigan remained unconvinced that he was entirely safe.

"Find something interesting?" he asked Aiden when the healer looked up from the book he studied.

Aiden shrugged. "Always looking for new wardings, rituals we can use. And anything I can find about the Rifts. Some of the old lore is... strange. Like stories people might tell around a campfire to scare children, full of monsters from the Realms Beyond. Except these aren't children's tales. I think some of the old practitioners actually believed them—and if what I've read is true, worshipped them."

"Worshipped monsters?" Rigan echoed. "How crazy do you have to be to do that?"

"Crazy is relative," Aiden replied, rubbing a hand across his temples. "If you want a champion to defeat a bigger, stronger enemy, a pet monster you think you can tame with spells and worship doesn't look so bad when you're out of other options."

"I thought we had enough gods to keep straight, between the Elder Gods and the Guild gods," Rigan replied, pushing away the manuscript he had been reading as his tired eyes burned and his vision blurred.

"These are really old gods. He Who Watches. She Who Waits. First Creatures made by Colduraan. Chaos personified."

"Did the rest of the Elder Gods have their own First Creatures?" Rigan asked. "What about Eshtamon?"

Aiden shook his head. "I haven't found anything about that if they did. Then again, most of what I'm reading has to do with countering blood magic and twisting healing magic for battle. Gods, I'm tired of this."

Rigan regarded his friend in silence. "Surely defending others is a permitted use of your magic."

The pain of his internal conflict showed in Aiden's gaze. "Is it? I guess it depends on who you listen to. The witches who taught me to be a healer made me swear an oath never to use my power to maim or kill. Keeping that oath was supposed to be worth more than my life, or the lives of people around me. For the principle of the thing. But in the thick of the fight, I broke my vow—and I've kept on breaking it."

"We'd all be dead if you hadn't," Rigan pointed out quietly. "And so would the people we've saved, if we hadn't been there to protect them. Doesn't that count for something?"

Aiden turned away, but Rigan could see the strain in his shoulders and the tight cords of the healer's neck. "It does for me. I don't know how the gods reckon things. I wonder sometimes whether the stain on my soul is too much to let me pass to the Golden Shores, because of what I've done."

"If it is, then you'll have plenty of company," Rigan joked bitterly. "Because we'll all be there with you." He sighed. "Amazing how things can go to shit so quickly, isn't it? Not half a year ago, we had our old lives, and never dreamed anything would change. And now, look at us. Walking wounded, torn up inside and out like the old men who came home from the wars and were never right again."

"We're still here," Aiden said. "That's got to count for something.

Still fighting. That's what keeps me going, having a purpose. Be useful. Stop the slaughter. And maybe someday, we can rest."

Footsteps in the corridor made them look up. Rigan expected to see his brother, but instead, Mir loomed in the opening, holding a jug of the rough whiskey the local farmers distilled. From the glazed look in his eyes, Mir was well into the jug's contents.

"Have you tried any of this?" he asked, holding the jug aloft. "It's not too bad."

Rigan wrinkled his nose at the smell, even though he sat several feet away from the door. "Gods, Mir that smells like rotten fruit left in the sun."

Mir uncorked the jug and sniffed deeply, then stoppered it once more. "Yep. Probably what it's made of. But it works—better than your potions," he said with a nod toward Aiden. "They never stopped me from dreaming. This," he said, patting the jug with his other hand, "I can sleep right through the night and not remember. That's the thing that gets you," he added. "Remembering. Need to stop doing that."

"Right now, I think you need to go to bed," Aiden said, starting to rise in case Mir needed help, but Mir waved off his assistance.

"I don't need your pity or your help," he snapped, with more clarity in his eyes than Rigan had expected. "Gods, I wish I were as drunk as you think I am. Maybe then, I wouldn't feel anything at all."

"Only the dead don't feel," Aiden said, worry clear in his voice.

Mir raised the jug in a sardonic toast and took a slug. "Then here's to the dead. Lucky bastards." He headed down the hallway toward his room. Rigan moved silently to look out the door after him, making sure he reached his destination without passing out in the corridor.

"He'll have a shitty headache when he wakes up," Rigan said when he returned to the table.

"There's a price for everything," Aiden replied. "He's sober on the hunts, and he's not picking fights. Not like any of the rest of us look likely to reach old age by abstaining. If it gets him through the night, well, it's the oldest medicine there is."

Still, Rigan thought he saw a twinge of guilt in Aiden's expression and wondered whether the healer could stop feeling personally responsible for wounds too deep for him to fix. "I'll look in on him later," Rigan promised. "Try to roll him on his side, so he doesn't drown in his own puke."

"I'd appreciate that."

Rigan put a marker in the manuscript he had been reading and closed the cover, setting it aside. "I'm going to get some sleep. Damned underground tunnels—can't tell whether it's day or night."

Aiden nodded. "I'm heading to the kitchen for some tea. Thought I might help Polly with dinner. It's a nice change, and I feel useful— when she isn't threatening to wallop me with that spoon of hers."

Rigan chuckled. "Beware the spoon. She's wicked with that thing. I thought I'd take a cup of tea to Elinor. She's pushing herself too hard."

Aiden quirked an eyebrow. "And the rest of us aren't? She misses Parah and worries about how the old lady's getting on without her. I don't doubt that Elinor's intent on finding new ways to use her magic, but I suspect hiding in the library is her way of shutting out the world for a little while."

Rigan thought about Aiden's comment as he fixed the tea, and walked to the room where they stored the books and manuscripts they had found or stolen. The "library" held crates of books, a rickety table with two chairs and an oil lamp. Elinor leaned over a parchment scroll that kept trying to roll back up every time she moved.

"Brought you something," Rigan said, holding out the tea enticingly. "Thought you might want a little company."

Elinor favored him with a tired smile and pushed her dark hair back behind one ear. "So many reasons why I love you, Rigan Valmonde."

Rigan brought her the tea as she pushed the precious scroll to one side, and dipped down to kiss her lightly on the lips. "I missed you."

She returned the kiss with a playful nip, but her eyes suggested exhaustion might preempt the promise of anything more. "I missed you, too. Just trying to do my part."

"You do plenty," Rigan said, settling into the second chair and taking her left hand in his. "You've learned a lot from Aiden about healing, and he swears by the poultices and powders you mix with the plants. Not to mention that you've saved our asses more than once in a fight."

Back in Ravenwood City, when Elinor worked for Parah, the dyer, she had always been slender, with high cheekbones and a sharp nose in a heart-shaped face. Now, Rigan worried that shadows darkened her blue eyes and the hollows of her cheeks made her appear ill-fed. They did not have food to spare, but from what they could steal, hunt, scavenge, or barter, they rarely went hungry. Even so, the bones in Elinor's slim wrists seemed too prominent, and the loose dress she wore hung on her thin frame.

"I wish I could do more. I feel so... useless." Elinor ducked her head to avoid his gaze, suddenly finding her tea worthy of focus.

"You're not, for all the reasons I just gave. And more. You and Aiden and Polly can hold your own in a fight—and you have, plenty of times. But you can do things besides fighting that no one else can, and that's not useless, that's important."

She sipped the hot drink and shrugged. "I tell myself that. But there is always more I wish I could do."

Rigan stood and drew her up into an embrace. "I can think of more things to do," he said with a grin, kissing her again. She returned the kiss, with a sleepy passion.

"I like the way you think," she replied, reaching up to run a hand through his dark, silky hair, tangling her fingers in the long strands.

"I wish you'd reconsider taking a room with me," Rigan murmured, resting his cheek against the top of her head. "We wouldn't have to worry about Polly or Corran walking in on us."

"I'd prefer that, but we've been over this before," Elinor said, leaning against him and bringing her arms up around him, holding him close. "It's too soon. Polly wakes in the night screaming, and I need to be there for her. No one else was, for far too many years. Of all of us, she's been fighting monsters the longest. She'd cut off her hand before she'd admit to needing me, and she'd push me out the door if I brought up the idea of moving into a room with you, but it wouldn't be good for her." Elinor pushed up onto her toes to kiss him again. "It's only for a little while. I promise."

Rigan sighed. "I understand. Well, some parts of me understand better than others," he added, rocking his hips against her as if she might mistake his meaning.

"Besides," she said, as a blush tinged her cheeks, "I don't think Corran's ready to let you out of his sight. He watches you like a mother hen. Or maybe a street cur that won't let anyone near her pups."

"Are you calling me a dog?" Rigan joked, gently rubbing the knots out of her back and shoulders.

She batted at his arm playfully. "You know what I mean. He worries about you, and he blames himself for what happened to Kell."

"That wasn't his fault," Rigan defended quickly.

"I don't think it is, but he does. And be honest—until we stop fighting monsters every few days, one or the other—or both—of you end up battered enough to need someone sitting up to make sure you keep breathing."

"If we'd stayed in the city and had been courting, I might have asked you to marry me by now," Rigan said, liking the way Elinor arched her back as his fingers dug into the tense muscles.

She snorted. "Do you think Parah would have allowed that so soon? Huh. She liked you, I'll grant that, but she didn't think much of rushing into things. Gave me more than one lecture about girls not taking their time. Parah would have wanted us courting at least half a year before she would give her blessing."

"Well then, I've only got three more months to wait," Rigan teased.

Elinor leaned against his shoulder, and he pulled her close. "I'll lie with you, Rigan Valmonde, when we can steal a few moments here and there, hiding in basements and running from the law. But when we marry, I want a proper handfasting and a real house, and a shop where we can make our living, instead of being vagabonds." Her tone was light, but Rigan knew the sentiment was real. "I'd like to be *respectable* again."

Rigan tipped her chin up until he could look in her eyes. "I'll give you that handfasting and a house, although I'm not sure I can promise *respectable*. I'm an outlaw, you know. And a witch."

"That'll do," she replied, and the warm glint in her eyes told Rigan

other thoughts had driven away the lure of sleep. "Let's find somewhere we won't be bothered, and you can *court* me some more."

———

"You up for doing a little exploring?" Corran leaned against the doorframe, barely within the circle of light cast by the lantern on the table.
The hidden underground rooms beneath the monastery ruins were
always dark, like it had been when they fled into the tunnels beneath
Ravenwood. Rigan grudgingly adapted to the perpetual darkness,
though he found that the ventures outside in the sun dramatically
improved his mood, despite the risk of being caught.

"Turn up another monster?" Rigan looked up from his manuscript.
"Did Aiden sense some more ripples?"

Corran shook his head. "Aiden's picked up on something, but he
isn't sure what. Have you—felt—anything strange lately?"

Other than having dreams about the piyanin? "No. What's
going on?"

Corran moved into the room and leaned against the wall, crossing
his arms over his chest. "Aiden says he can sense something that's not
right, concentrated in a few places near where we've fought monsters
before. But it isn't like the ripples when there are creatures. He thought
we should look into it. Polly, Mir, and Ross headed to check out some
new ripples, so Trent and I wanted to go take a look at this 'not right'
thing—and figured it'd be good to have a witch with us. That leaves
Aiden and Elinor to hold down the base."

Rigan nodded. "Sounds good. Yeah, let's go. I could use a little
fresh air."

They rode for several candlemarks, and Rigan gradually recognized
the location. "This is close to where we fought those black dog-things
with the red eyes, isn't it?"

"Real close," Trent replied. "Aiden said he started to pick up his
'not right' sensation after we handled the dog-monsters."

"Was it off before the monsters, or only afterward?" Rigan asked.

"He wasn't sure," Trent said. "The ripples might have drowned out any other impressions. Or they might not have anything to do with each other."

Rigan gave him a skeptical look. "When do things *ever* not have something to do with each other when it comes to magic?"

"Can you pick up anything?" Corran asked.

Rigan reined in his horse and shut his eyes. He sent tendrils of power down into the ground and recoiled, nearly losing his balance.

"What's wrong?" Corran asked.

Rigan shook his head to clear it. "The land is sick... tainted. I reached down to anchor my power and—it was like sinking my hand into a week-old corpse." He shuddered. "Let me try again, something different." This time, Rigan focused on the air, and while he still felt an echo of *wrongness*, the connection was not too uncomfortable to maintain—at least for a while. He reached out with his senses. "Over there," he said, pointing to a clearing not far off the road.

They tethered their horses and walked cautiously toward the meadow. "Everything looks wrong," Trent said as they grew closer. The tall grass lay flattened as if a force from the center of the clearing had pushed outward. The ground and plants were blackened and dead.

"It *feels* wrong," Rigan said in a voice barely above a whisper. "Not just dead, but like everything's been leeched out of it." He looked at the withered plants as words failed to convey what his magic told him. "If you burn ground, crops can come back. There's still life in the soil. But this... the land has been fouled so completely; I don't think anything will grow here again. It's... cursed." He glanced down. Unconsciously, they had all stopped several feet short of the edge of the dead zone, as if instinct warned them to go no closer.

"Why would someone place a curse on a meadow?" Trent asked, utterly confused.

Rigan shook his head. "It's really hard to explain. I don't mean someone truly hexed the land, but something not only killed what's here now, it poisoned the ground."

"So—why?" Trent repeated.

Rigan frowned. "Destroying the ground might not be the main intent, maybe a consequence. We found monsters near here. Beast-like monsters, more like what you fought in the city. Maybe this is where someone conjured the monsters."

"Seems like a strange place for it," Corran said.

Rigan shrugged. "Not really. We don't know how the conjuring is done—only that blood magic is involved. That's shunned by most people, so a practitioner would want to be somewhere he—or she—wouldn't be likely to get caught. But summoning monsters doesn't do any good if there's no one to kill, and there are some villages close by."

"I don't understand," Trent said, looking out over the ruined land. "Back in the city, it made sense, in a sick sort of way, for the Lord Mayor to want to keep the people afraid, keep them obedient. But out here?"

"The villages serve the needs of the Merchant Princes, working in the fields and vineyards," Corran replied. "Why would someone in power need to send monsters against them?"

"We're missing something important," Rigan said. "We still don't have all the pieces. Do you remember what I said, back before the fight in the city? That I thought maybe blood magic *unbalanced* a natural force, and the monsters had something to do with fixing that—the *real* Balance? Aiden and I—"

Rigan's heightened senses from the magic still active and grounded through his body gave him the last-second warning he needed to dive out of the way of a crossbow bolt. "Watch out!" he shouted to the others as he rolled away, drawing his long knife. He raised himself up on his elbows, hidden by the tall grass outside the flattened circle, and peered toward where the shot had been fired.

With reflexes honed from hunting monsters, they fell back to their training. Corran belly-crawled left, Trent went right, and Rigan breathed in, called his magic to him, and strengthened his connection to the air. He listened with his power, seeking their attackers. The taint from the land behind him interfered with his focus, making it difficult to get a clean read. Rigan stretched out his senses, verifying that Corran and Trent were in position.

He rose from cover only as far as necessary to aim. Two men

armed with crossbows ventured into the clearing from the treeline. They held their bows angled toward the ground, looking for motion in the high grass, anything that would give away their quarry's position. Rigan called to the wind, and the grass stirred to one side, far away from his brother or Trent. Both of the men turned to fire toward the motion.

Rigan stretched out his hand and sent a thin bolt of energy crackling toward the nearest bowman. He dared not use fire lest he set the whole field aflame, but the lightning would do. The bolt struck the man in the chest, sending him to the ground, where he lay still.

Before the man's companion could get a new fix on his target, Rigan sent a blast of wind to send all of the grass bending and dropped down, crawling to a new position. A few moments later he heard another quarrel discharge and strike the dirt, then a strangled cry that turned into a pained grunt.

When he raised his head, he saw that Trent had tackled the stranger and disarmed him, holding a knife against the man's throat. Rigan reached out again with his magic, searching to assure there were no other attackers lurking in the forest.

"Clear!" he shouted, rising to his feet. Corran also rose and put the point of his sword to the chest of the injured bowman, in case he had any intention to come to his comrade's aid. The man lay still, eyes closed, and looked to have lost consciousness. A seeping burn covered his left shoulder and upper arm. Rigan walked over to join the others, standing next to Corran.

"You want to tell us what you and your friend meant, shooting at us?" Trent demanded from the man he held pinned.

"There's a handsome price on your heads," the man replied in a strangled voice, careful not to press against the blade. "We've been watching the roads. Had your descriptions. Figured if caught the three of you, we could find the rest."

"You figured wrong, mate," Trent growled.

"Who hired you?" Corran asked.

Even in defeat, the bounty hunter barked out a laugh. "With a bounty like that, didn't need no one to hire us. And the bounty comes from the Crown Prince himself."

Rigan wondered if he looked as shocked as the others. His mind reeled. *The Crown Prince?*

Motion and a glint of silver broke through their surprise. Rigan glimpsed a blur, and then Corran knocked him to the ground, covering him with his body. Rigan heard Trent curse and heard a scuffle, then silence.

"They're dead," Trent called.

Rigan grabbed Corran by the shoulders to roll him away and gasped as his left hand came away wet with blood. Corran groaned and flinched away from the contact.

"Corran?" Rigan wriggled out from under and sat up. A knife stuck out of Corran's upper arm, and blood soaked his sleeve.

"Son of a bitch threw his knife," Corran rasped.

At me, Rigan realized, pressing his hand against the wound and pulled the knife free. Corran gasped in pain, and Rigan tore his own shirt over his head, wadding it up to staunch the flow of blood. "He was aiming for me, wasn't he? And you—"

"I had to," Corran said through gritted teeth.

"If that knife had caught you a little more to the side, he might have had you through the heart!"

Corran looked up at him, resolute, though his eyes were bright with pain. "You saw it, Rigan. I couldn't take that chance."

"Saw what?" Rigan looked around, noting that Trent had dispatched both the bounty hunter he had captured and the injured man with a slice to the throat. *They were just another kind of monster, I suppose.*

"The *piyanin*. You saw... the omen."

Horror accompanied comprehension. "You got between me and the knife because of my dream?"

Corran closed his eyes. "I couldn't risk losing you. Already lost Kell, Jora, Mama, Papa. Can't lose you, too."

Rigan swallowed hard, anger and gratitude warring inside him.

"And you thought I'd be all right with you getting hurt instead? Dammit, Corran! It's no different for me than it is for you."

"Not taking any chances," Corran groaned.

Rigan muttered a curse and helped Corran to his feet. Trent had already searched the bodies of the two bounty hunters, relieved them of anything useful, and rolled the corpses closer to the dead zone.

"If anyone finds them—and I don't think the local folks come near that circle—it'll look like they were beset by thieves," Trent said, wiping his hands on one of the men's cloaks. "Unfortunately, if the bounty's that high, they won't be the only ones who come looking for us."

They made their way back to the horses, with Trent keeping watch and Rigan occasionally casting out with his magic to see if anyone else was nearby. "I guess this means we'd better move on for a while, to one of the other ruins," Rigan said ruefully as he made sure Corran got up to his saddle. "Damn. I'd gotten to like this one."

Trent shrugged. "We can always come back after some time's passed. And from the maps you've found, there are plenty more monasteries to hide in, enough that it'll keep quite a few bounty hunters busy trying to search them all, if they even get it into their heads to look there."

"I don't want to be the one to tell Polly," Rigan said, swinging up to his horse. "She throws things when she's out of sorts, and she just got the kitchen the way she likes it."

CHAPTER NINE

"WE DON'T LIKE strangers nosing around the village." The speaker glared at the three outsiders who stood on the darkened road.

"We came to help," Ross replied, meeting the man's gaze.

"We handle things ourselves, always have." The man who spoke looked to be about ten years older than Ross, perhaps in his mid-thirties. He had the broad shoulders and strong arms of someone who had worked outside all his life. A medium-sized, well-behaved dog with speckled fur sat quietly beside him.

"And yet, your cows are still dying," Polly snapped. "We can stop the monsters."

Two other men flanked the leader, both strong and fit, farmers or farmhands, Polly guessed. "What do you know about monsters?" the man on the left of the leader asked. He resembled the speaker, but his hair was light instead of dark, and a few years younger. *Brother,* Polly thought.

"We do this for a living," Polly replied, ignoring Mir's warning glare. "Hunt monsters. We're good at it, which you can see because we're still alive. Now—about your cows—"

"How did you know about the cows?" The man to the leader's right regarded them suspiciously. His thinning hair and the squint lines around his eyes made him look much older.

"Because we're just that good," Polly snapped. The three men looked confused at Polly's take-charge manner, and Mir chuckled.

"She's telling the truth," Mir said. "We do hunt monsters, and we're good at it. And I bet, you've tried to kill the things that are coming after your cows, and it hasn't gone well. Am I right?"

The leader hesitated for a moment, then finally nodded. "We've set traps, moved the cows to different pastures, and shot it with arrows. Nothing works."

"What does 'it' look like?" Ross asked. The three men remained blocking the road that led to the village, but their stance had shifted. They were still skeptical and defensive, but Polly sensed real curiosity and maybe a glimmer of hope in the men's expression. Best of all, they no longer appeared to be looking for a fight.

"It's as solid as a sow, but faster and taller, and the face is all wrong," the leader said. "All squashed in like a bat, with a crumpled nose and ears that lay flat back." He shook his head. "Don't look like nothing natural."

"That's because it isn't," Polly replied.

"Look, we can tell you more about the monsters later," Mir said. "But I'm betting you're out here for the same reason we are—to get rid of that thing. So why not let us do our job, and we'll explain later."

"What's it to you? Why do you care about our cows?" the blond man asked.

"Like she said, it's what we do. The fewer monsters out there, the better we all sleep," Ross replied.

"Can you do it?" The bald man gave them an evaluating once-over. "You're an odd set. That girl's no more than a—"

"That 'girl' knows what she's doing," Polly said, her voice dropping to a deadly growl.

"She's much more dangerous than she looks," Mir said. "Don't make her mad, if you value your balls."

"I think you're all crazy," the bald man retorted.

"Then what's the harm in letting us get ourselves killed?" Polly shot back.

The three men turned to speak to each other in low tones. Mir and Trent exchanged a glance, while Polly stood with her hands on her hips and wished she had brought her long-handled wooden spoon in addition to her hunting knives. She would have enjoyed smacking all three of the village men upside the head.

"All right," the leader said. "Hans and I will go with you. Belan will go back to the village and round up the rest of the men."

"No." Ross shook his head. "No one else. Too many people to get in the way. Frankly, you'll be targets, and you'll get one of us killed. If you could have handled this yourself, you wouldn't still have the problem. So we do this our way, or we leave you to it and go help someone else."

Once again, the three men conferred, and then the leader turned back to them. "I don't like it, but I've seen too many of our friends get hurt trying to kill this thing. Taken a few blows myself," he added, pushing up the hem of his shirt to reveal four long parallel gashes, recently healed, across his chest.

"You were lucky," Mir said. "I've seen one of these rip out a man's ribs."

The leader paled at that. "Didn't feel lucky when I was bleeding out. I'm Stev, by the way."

Polly's group gave their names but offered nothing else. "What about Belan?" she asked, indicating the dark-haired man. "Is he coming with us? Because if not, we need to make sure he isn't going to cause problems."

Stev shook his head. "No. Not tonight. He's got a wife and newborn at home."

"I can—"

Stev turned on Belan. "This isn't about what you can and can't do," he said. "They need you more, and with... reinforcements, you don't have to take the risk." Belan glowered at Stev, and the leader's expression softened. "You know Sofia would have my head if I let you take risks right now."

Belan ducked his head. "This time," he muttered. "But you'd both better come back in one piece," he added.

Stev clapped a hand on his shoulder. "We will. If these newcomers are any good, we all will."

Belan turned and walked back toward the lights of the village. Stev watched him go until he was lost in the darkness, then turned back to them. "How is it you came to hunt monsters?"

"After we succeed, how about we trade stories over pints in the pub," Polly replied, eyes narrowing. "Better that than standing here in the road, waiting for the monster to find us."

"Do you know what type of creature it is?" Hans asked.

Mir nodded. "They're called *vestir*. Mean sons of bitches, and they've got a taste of human flesh as well as cattle. So all things considered, I'd say your village has gotten off lucky so far."

Stev paled. "They eat people?"

Polly remembered the night they had fled the city, riding down one of the creatures in her wagon, while a second monster killed Tomor, and feasted on the bodies of their dead companions. "Yeah," she replied in a flat voice.

"What's your plan?" Stev asked.

"How good are you with a knife?" Mir asked, with a predatory smile.

———

"This is a bad idea," Polly muttered as she and Trent crouched on the edge of a dark pasture. The cows were quiet and still, some standing, others lying down, dark shadows against the moonlight field.

"Hunting the *vestir* or bringing the village men?"

"Both," she replied.

Mir waited along the edge of the field, his crossbow at the ready. Polly held an iron poker with a sharpened tip in one hand and a steel knife with a curved, wicked blade in the other. Trent had a long knife and an iron rod. Stev and Hans both had farm knives and sturdy wooden staves. Behind them, a bag dropped at the edge of the clearing held the rest of the items they would need, along with the shuttered tin lantern that had lit their way.

"How do we know when it's going to show up?" Polly muttered. A frightened cow gave a startled cry, waking the other animals.

"Like that," Trent replied. "Here we go."

The *vestir* bounded from the far edge of the clearing, closing the distance with its intended prey. But the cow was faster than Polly had expected, taking off running. The rest of the cows, perhaps a dozen or more, started to their hooves or woke and began to move. Instinct drove the herd to gather together, while the *vestir* lunged at those cows on the outside of the group, trying to separate one from the rest for an easy kill.

Mir ran for a position where he could take his shot. A moment later, they heard the twang-thud of a crossbow, and the *vestir* howled in pain, turning away from the cows to search for its tormentor.

"Hey ugly!" Mir yelled and waved his arms. "Come and get me!"

The *vestir* snarled and rushed forward.

"Shit!" Mir yelped, but he held his position and waited for his shot. The first quarrel had taken the *vestir* in the shoulder, slowing its advance but not by much. Mir let the creature bear down on him and then threw himself to one side at the last minute and shot the iron-tipped arrow into the creature's ribs where the heart should be.

The *vestir* kept coming, but its gait was all wrong. That's what Polly and Trent counted on. "Now!" Trent hissed from where he and Polly had gotten themselves into position.

Trent threw his knife, and it sank deep into the belly of the *vestir*. Black blood flowed out of the wound, soaking the ground. Polly took advantage of the distraction to run in from the opposite side, landing a bone-shattering blow with the iron rod to the creature's head. Before it could get its bearings, she sank the tip of the curved knife into its belly on the other side and ripped the razor-sharp blade through the tough flesh and matted, coarse hair, opening the monster's abdomen and spilling out its guts.

Trent lunged, bringing his iron rod down two-handed on the *vestir's* skull and thick, powerful neck until he heard the satisfying crunch of bone and the creature slumped to the ground.

"Cover me," he told Polly as he pulled his knife from the *vestir's* ribs and drove it into the monster's neck, sawing through the crushed vertebrae and sinew until the head toppled from the body in a flood of stinking, black blood.

But before Mir could join them to congratulate his friends on the kill, a howl split the night from the far side of the clearing.

"Shit! There are two of them!" Trent groaned.

"And it's closer to Stev and Hans—son of a bitch!" Mir muttered.

"Come on!" Polly ran toward the place they had heard the howl. The cattle smelled blood and knew the danger. They *mooed* and began to run, and suddenly the whole herd was heading right for Polly.

"Stampede!" Stev shouted.

Polly changed direction, running for the edge of the herd. The sound of thundering hooves nearly drowned out the angry howls of the *vestir*. She had never realized how terrifying cows were before, or how large and solid. She ran fast, but the cows were gaining on her. Polly knew she could not get to safety before they would trample her under those hooves.

A streak of brown and white came from where Stev and Hans had stood, barking like it had lost its mind. It ran at the cows, and suddenly the herd shifted its direction, veering off as the dog barked and nipped at the cows' hooves. Stev shouted directions as he and Hans moved to close ranks with Mir and Trent where they had repositioned themselves to attack the second monster.

The *vestir* chased the herd, then scented human prey and hesitated. With the cows driven off by the dog, Polly found herself in the monster's direct line of sight.

Obviously it did not expect her to let loose a loud shriek and run right at it, brandishing the iron poker.

If I'm going to die, they're going to tell stories about me, Polly thought, running straight for the *vestir*. The closer she got, the uglier it looked. She had never seen one of the monsters full in the face. The night they fled the city, she had only seen its rump and glanced at it in profile. The creature answered her shriek with a bellow of its own, and Polly got a good look at its mad red eyes and long, sharp teeth.

Save me a spot in the After, Kell. I'm coming your way, Polly thought, resolved to go down swinging.

Mir's crossbow thudded once more, and a shot hit the *vestir* in the neck. It reared and gave a terrible, angry cry, pawing at the dirt with its deadly claws. Trent ran at the creature as well, but Stev and Hans were closer, and as Polly braced herself to swing at the *vestir* when it came in reach, Hans leaped onto the monster's back, bringing his staff down hard on its head and stabbing his knife deep into its side.

In the next breath, Hans rolled off, and Stev took a flying leap, cracking the monster soundly on the skull with his staff and sinking his knife into the juncture where the monster's neck met its shoulders. The dog was back, and this time it turned its fury on the *vestir*, barking non-stop and snapping at the creature's hind legs as it had the cattle.

Beset on all sides, the *vestir* stopped running to fight its tormentors. Polly seized the chance and ran forward, shoving her knife into her belt and raising the iron rod in both hands over her head. She brought it down on the *vestir's* face, crunching through the bone of its snout and sinking into the skull between the monster's red eyes. Trent closed in from the right, slamming his rod down on the *vestir's* neck.

The monster listed and began to sink to the ground. Polly dove forward, and this time she wielded the iron rod like a lance, driving it deep into the monster's throat. Blood spilled from the *vestir's* mouth, and with a shudder and a gurgle, the creature lay still.

Stev called out a command, and the dog fell silent and returned to his side. He and Hans walked up to stand beside Polly and Trent as Mir sawed through the neck of the second beast to sever its head.

"Is it over?" Stev asked. Polly glanced at him. Both village men looked pale and shaken, but they had held their own.

"All but the burning," Polly replied. Trent took off at a run and returned moments later with the bag.

"Now what?" Hans asked, managing to look both fascinated and appalled.

"Now we set them on fire," Mir said. He tossed a bag of the salt-

153

aconite-amanita mixture to Trent and another to Polly, who began to liberally cover both carcasses. Mir pulled out a wineskin of oil and tossed the second container to Stev.

"Make yourself useful," he said. He turned to Hans. "Go find some dry branches. Anything will do."

Stev's dog watched them, never moving from where his master had ordered him to stay. Polly thought he looked insufferably proud of himself for his part in the fight.

Hans returned with an armful of wood from the trees at the edge of the clearing and helped Mir pile them around the dead *vestir*. "Go get some for the other one," he said with a jerk of his head toward the second monster's body. Hans obliged, and Mir soaked the creature with oil, then opened the lantern and lit a sturdy twig from the candle inside.

"Burn, you son of a bitch," he muttered as he tossed the flaming wood onto the pyre and watched the fire catch in the oil.

When both of the monsters' bodies were burning, Stev turned to look at Polly and the other hunters. "That was—not what I expected. I guess you were telling the truth, about having done this before."

Ross nodded. "More than we like to think about. But we can teach you how—so you can protect your people when we're not here to do it."

"You mean you're not going to demand payment?" Hans asked, surprise in his voice.

Polly grinned. "We won't turn down a good meal, some beer, and a horse trough to wash up in—not necessarily in that order. You want to throw a few bronzes or silvers our way or a few bags of vegetables and a couple of chickens, won't turn those down, either. Good crossbow bolts cost money, you know."

Stev regarded her in astonishment for a moment, then threw back his head and laughed. "I think both can be accomplished, m'lady brave."

Polly blushed. "And tell your dog I owe him a nice piece of meat for saving my hide. How did he know what to do?" She glanced over her shoulder at the cows. They had retreated to the far corner of the meadow, and once the herd was no longer in danger, they watched the trespassers in their meadow with indifference.

"Fitz is my herding dog," Stev said. "The cows know him, and they're used to doing what he tells them to do. Habit took over, and it was stronger than their fear of the monster."

Polly bent down and looked into Fitz's brown eyes. "Who's a good dog?" she crooned. She reached into a pouch on her belt and withdrew a piece of dried meat, which she tossed to Fitz. The dog grabbed it out of the air and swallowed it, then looked guiltily at his master as if belatedly realizing he should have asked permission.

Stev laughed and patted the dog's head. "That's all right, boy. You're a hero tonight." He looked at Polly, Mir, and Ross and gave a wan smile. "I misjudged you. I'm sorry. What you did tonight was... amazing."

Ross shrugged. "For civilians, you did pretty well for yourselves," he said. "Never expected you to try to ride the damn thing."

Hans chuckled. "We have to rope the calves and colts. That was familiar territory—except for the stabbing part."

"Let's go back to the village," Stev said. "I assume you have horses somewhere?"

Mir nodded. "They're tethered back near where we met you."

"Then come with us. There's plenty of food for you and your horses, and perhaps if you're willing, you'll share some of the tricks of your trade."

Polly insisted that they stop outside the stable to wash up in the horse trough before going anywhere they might be seen. "I'm covered with blood and monster guts, and unlike the two of you, I've got a reputation to uphold," Polly sniffed, then shot her companions a mischievous grin.

"No complaints from me, though I gave up on any kind of reputation a long time ago," Ross replied. "At least, any good kind."

Polly knew the light banter covered the crash of emotion after a battle in which they all could have died horribly. Her mind would process that later when nightmares woke her trembling and crying.

"This had better be good beer," she groused as she dried off with the edge of her cloak. "Not just good, amazing. No, damned fine and amazing."

"There's plenty of it, and it'll be on the house once you tell your story," Stev assured her. "With food as well. Let's go."

Only a few tables had patrons when they walked into the worn tavern in the center of the farming village. Those men looked up and frowned at the sight of three strangers, their clothing stained with blood and worse, shepherded by Stev and Hans. Belan rose from the bar and went to greet them, clasping first Stev and Hans into a fierce embrace.

"Thank the gods! We were worried."

"If you hadn't figured it out, Belan is my brother," Stev said. He clapped Belan on the shoulder. "We've got a tale to tell, so gather around." Stev glanced at the bartender. "Bring out some ale, and three meals. We owe these hunters our gratitude for saving the herd."

At Stev's prodding, Polly and the others recounted the fight with the *vestir*. As they talked, more and more people crowded into the tavern. A serving girl brought out a tray of tankards, a pitcher of ale, and three trenches of stew that Polly swore was the best thing she had ever smelled. Polly, Mir, and Ross took turns eating and telling their story, obliged to retell the tale three times for the sake of those who came late to the tavern.

"It's all true," Stev attested, happily downing a whiskey the bartender slid across the counter to him. Hans sat at the bar nursing a drink and looking like he'd seen a ghost.

"Why do you care?" one of the onlookers asked. "What's in this for you, besides nearly getting killed and all?"

Ross looked up, his eyes haunted. "A *vestir* killed my cousin," he replied. His voice was thick with remembered pain, even after all his time. "That's when I started hunting. I couldn't bring him back, but I could kill the things that killed him, and keep it from happening to someone else."

Mir nodded. "I lost my sister to the monsters. Not *vestir*—ghouls. It's my way of honoring her memory—and getting my vengeance."

Polly laid aside her fork and took a long draw on her tankard. "One of those ugly sons of bitches killed a boy I fancied," she said, managing a sad smile she doubted looked entirely sane. "I like making the monsters pay for what they took from us."

"You said you could teach us," Stev said. "What do we need to know?"

Polly exchanged a glance with Mir and Ross. Wordlessly, they reached consensus. "We can tell you how to kill different types of monsters, and how to protect yourselves and your homes. That's the easy part," Polly said and heard the disbelieving snorts of the crowd.

"Back in the city, beasts like the two we killed tonight didn't show up by accident," Mir picked up the story. "They were called— summoned—by a powerful blood witch that worked for the Lord Mayor. There's been chaos in the city, and the blood witch and Lord Mayor are dead," he continued, leaving out their part in causing that outcome. "We thought that when we came out to the country, there would only be the monsters that happen naturally—like the strixes and the shape-shifters. Then we started running into ghouls and *vestir* again, and some of the other monsters that were summoned by magic."

"That accounts maybe for the *vestir* and the ghouls," one of the men said, "but what about the *guin* that live in the far forest, where the lumbermen won't go."

"*Guin?*" Mir echoed, puzzled.

"I heard my daddy tell of them," the man replied. "Thin, pale things that live on blood. They've been in that forest forever, but ain't no one seen them in maybe a hundred years."

Polly suspected that if no one had seen these mysterious blood-drinking *guin* in that long, they had either died off or were nothing but legend. For once, she kept her opinion to herself. "If they've been there that long," she said, "they're natural monsters—like the strix. Doesn't sound like they're hurting anyone who doesn't go blundering into their part of the forest, so we don't care about them. We kill the conjured monsters, the ones that try to kill you."

"The damage those creatures have done to your livestock and your loved ones—it didn't happen by accident." Ross's tone was grim.

"Someone powerful conjured them and sent them, intending for them to kill and destroy."

"Why?" one of the women asked, shaking her head. "Why would anyone do that?"

"To keep you frightened," Polly replied. "Obedient. If you're busy fighting monsters and grieving your dead, you don't notice what else is going on."

"That's part of it," Mir said. "But the sort of magic these blood witches work needs to draw extra power from somewhere. That's why they need the deaths. *Your* deaths."

"Are you tellin' us that someone in the higher-ups is not only magicking up monsters but meaning for them to kill us for their witch-es?" a man nearby echoed, torn between incredulity and outrage.

"That's exactly what we're saying," Mir replied. "You don't have to believe it. That's what those higher-ups are counting on, that you won't. Because if you did, if you really thought about them sending monsters to slaughter your livestock and murder your sons, daughters, brothers, sisters, parents, mates—you might decide to do something about it."

"That's treason you're talking." The crowd turned to look at a stooped old man who leaned heavily on the bar and his cane.

"Maybe," Ross said, refusing to look ashamed. "But those above us are supposed to protect us, not serve us up as fodder to their witches for their power. So who betrayed whom?"

The old man nodded. "Aye, boy—didn't say I disagreed with you, only named it for what it is. Because if you're telling the truth, and these monsters are sent by men with money and power, they won't let it stand if we get in their way, even if it's to save our own skins."

"That's true," Ross replied. "But fighting back beats laying down and waiting to be eaten."

"Do you know who's sending the monsters now?" a voice called from the crowd.

"No," Mir admitted. "We're trying to figure it out. And maybe it doesn't matter. If we kill enough of the monsters, the blood witch is weakened, and the magic fails."

Or something worse happens, Polly thought, recalling the debates between Rigan and Aiden over the nature of the Balance and what might happen if it was not maintained. *What a choice! Do nothing and get eaten and die horribly, or rid ourselves of the monsters and have magic go awry and kill us all.*

CHAPTER TEN

"Now that there's been a change in power, perhaps we might re-think our relationship." Merchant Prince Kadar leaned back and watched his guest's expression. A servant filled their wine goblets, set a full carafe on the table between them, and left the room, closing the doors behind him.

"I'm not sure what you mean my lord." Guild Master Stanton fingered the stem of his goblet nervously.

"Come now," Kadar chided. "Everyone knew you favored the late Merchant Prince Gorog, and that he supported you as the choice to replace Guild Master Vrioni after his unfortunate death." *Vrioni's poisoning was no accident, nor was the evidence left to suggest my involvement. I had nothing to do with it, but most certainly Machison and Gorog did.*

"I do my best to represent the interests of Ravenwood," Stanton replied. "If the city-state does well, we all prosper."

"A very pretty sentiment," Kadar replied. He took a sip of his wine, wishing it were whiskey. "And yet, not altogether true. I had close ties with the challenger for your new position, Inton Throck. In fact, he was favored to become Guild Master until he, too, died most unexpectedly." *Another murder I blame Machison for, and a complication that persists beyond the grave.*

"I'd heard rumors to that effect," Stanton said. "I hope I've demonstrated fairness to all parties."

"You didn't have much opportunity to demonstrate unfairness, since the elder Gorog killed himself not long after you came into your position, and his son fears assassins so much he barely leaves his rooms."

Stanton shrugged, wisely making no comment.

"That's why I wanted to meet with you," Kadar said, giving his best facsimile of a warm smile. Stanton did not appear to be fooled. "I don't think that young Gorog is going to leave the kind of mark his sire did. And especially with the... fragility... of the new agreement with Garenoth, I wanted to offer you a chance to start things over between us. After all, the vintners and distillers are doing quite well in these uncertain times, which I'm pleased to see since those are my vineyards and grain fields they're using to make their wares. And as you're heading up the Coopers' and Carpenters' Guild, well, there's a natural affinity to be explored."

"The challenge of being a Guild Master lies in doing right by our members, and the three Merchant Princes, all of whom we serve to some extent," Stanton replied.

His guest was either dense about the possibility of collusion or entirely too honest. Kadar found his dislike of the man growing.

"Of course," Kadar replied. "But there's nothing that says you can't do well by them and come out ahead yourself. After all, that's what the others do."

"I'm still learning my role, my lord. I couldn't say."

Kadar chuckled. "Oh, I assure you, all of your fellow Guild Masters have figured out where their interests lie. The Smith's Guild is betting against the Garenoth agreement succeeding. If that happens, there'll be unrest, and that means more weapons—for the guards, and for the average person worried about trouble. More money in their pockets than they'd make sending wrought iron gates and fancy tools to Garenoth."

When Stanton did not reply, Kadar forged on. "And the Potters and Glassmakers' Guild has been experimenting with better ways to store wine once it's aged. Barrels are so heavy. They've scheduled time to meet with me to show me their newest creations. And I have to say; I'm intrigued."

Stanton's expression made it clear that he registered the threat. "I assure you, my lord, nothing can compare to well-made barrels for either storage or the flavor imparted to the contents—wine or spirits." He leaned forward, leaving his goblet untouched. "What is it you want from me?"

Kadar's smile was genuine, if not warm. "That's more like it. I want you to keep an ear out on my behalf. Nothing difficult. But you go places I don't, hear things that people might not say in front of a Merchant Prince, things I need to know to do business. I need an inside man among the Guild Masters, and in return, I assure you, I'll see to your rewards."

Stanton licked his lips nervously. "That's it? Information?"

Kadar nodded. "That's all. I want to see you succeed, Hess," he said, mirroring the man's posture to gain his trust. "That's why I'm passing along my concern about what some of the other Guild Masters are doing. I'd hate to see them gain an unfair advantage."

Kadar could almost see the thoughts churning in the earnest Guild Master's mind. Ravenwood's politics was a cesspool of alliances and betrayals, assassinations, and near-misses. Honesty created a serious liability. *And having all of the Guild Masters worrying about how their counterparts are trying to undercut them means their attention is not focused on me.*

"I appreciate your consideration," Stanton said. "And I find your offer a worthy one. You can count on my support."

Kadar reserved his triumph for later after Stanton was out of sight. He lifted his goblet in a toast. "To prosperity," he said, as their glasses clinked.

A servant escorted Stanton out, leaving Kadar alone in the room. After a moment's pause, a quiet *snick* sounded as a latch opened, and a segment of paneling swung away from the wall, revealing a listening post.

"Did you hear?" Kadar asked, refilling his goblet.

Joth Hanson stepped out of the cramped alcove. "Yes. He wasn't quite as difficult to persuade as you feared."

Kadar held his wine glass up, regarding the glow of the lantern through the dark red liquid. "Find a man's self-interest, and persuasion becomes near-certainty."

"And your meeting later today with the Guild Master of the Potters and Glassmakers' Guild?"

Kadar smiled. "I'll make the same argument to them—against Stanton. We are strongest when the Guilds work against each other."

Hanson nodded. "Very well." He cleared his throat. "I also have news from the harbor."

Kadar raised an eyebrow. "Oh?"

Hanson's lips quirked in a satisfied smile. "I've set up a shipment —through intermediaries—that will come into Talerth Bay. It's a small, shallow river port the large trading ships can't use. Most of the traffic comes from fishermen. In fact, the shipment's coming in on a fishing boat, to get around the tariff inspectors," Hanson reported. "Our man on the boat will offload the crates with the smuggled goods, and take them to a market where peddlers and merchants buy their wares. Within a few days of landfall, the pieces will be sold throughout the rural areas—and no one in the counting house will be the wiser."

Kadar leaned back, savoring a sip of the fine wine in his goblet. Since he began considering the possibilities of working with smugglers and pirates, opportunities had opened up. The Guilds being undercut were not those that owed their allegiance to him; anything that weakened their position strengthened his. Most of the gains came at young Gorog's expense, driving the son of the disgraced Merchant Prince further into financial distress.

"Keep an eye on things—discreetly," he replied. "Take it slow. We don't want to flood the market; that's a sure way to draw Aliyev's attention. Have you inspected the quality of the goods?"

Hanson nodded. "Yes, m'lord. They are as well-made as the regular items. There should be no way for anyone to tell that these did not pass through customs. All markings are per regulation."

Kadar nodded. "Good. Very good. Nicely done. And our profit?'

Hanson's smile broadened. "Handsome indeed. I have the paperwork here," he added and withdrew a folded parchment from his pocket. At Kadar's raised eyebrow, he shook his head. "Merely figures, m'lord. Nothing to indicate the subject, if it were lost or seen by others. Easily burned once you've reviewed it."

Once again, Kadar indicated his approval. "This is going to set us ahead, create a lead the other Merchant Princes can't close."

"If I may say so, a shrewd move on your part, m'lord," Hanson replied. "Fortune favors the aggressive."

Kadar felt a flush of satisfaction. "We're going to come out of this stronger, regardless of whether or not Aliyev manages to salvage the Garenoth agreement. Some of the other city-states are hungry to advance, ready to show what they can do. I admire that. Yes, we gained ground over the previous agreement and Machison's favoritism of Gorog," he added, contempt clear in his tone, "but there's still so much money being left on the table."

"New ways, for leadership of a younger, more vital generation," Hanson said. "The League has grown hide-bound."

"Keep an eye on the smugglers—and the go-betweens who sell to the merchants. We can't afford any slip-ups," Kadar said, setting his empty goblet aside.

"Yes, m'lord," Hanson assured him. "Do you wish me to listen in on your next appointment?"

Kadar nodded. "Yes. There's a candlemark until the next Guild Master arrives. Time for you to stop in on my witch and let him know I'll be by for a chat after my appointment."

"As you wish, m'lord," Hanson said with a bow and left the room.

The meeting with the Master of the Potters and Glassblowers' Guild went much as Kadar expected. So many old resentments and jealousies festered among the Guilds that it didn't take much to nudge the players into action. Just the hint of an opportunity for revenge, or the chance to secure an advantage, and they took the bait so willingly, each anxious to outdo the others.

The elder Gorog had prospered by making the Lord Mayor his creature. Aliyev was unlikely to allow a repeat of that, whenever he got around to naming a replacement for Machison. And while Aliyev had approved terms to the agreement with Garenoth that bettered Kadar's and Tamas's percentages at the expense of Gorog, the Crown Prince clung to the ideal of impartiality—as much as anyone could in the sewer of League politics.

Ambition was expensive. Spies and assassins cost money, as did provisioning his blood witch, Wraithwind. Maintaining his palace and staff in the manner expected for a Merchant Prince was not cheap, and Kadar favored fine things. *And when I've achieved my goals, and taken Aliyev's position for myself, I will spare no expense.*

Kadar dined alone, glad for the quiet after a day of conversations. A hedge witch had assured that his food and wine was not poisoned, on pain of death if wrong, but Kadar ran a spelled charm over his meal to be certain. Advancing one's fortunes in Ravenwood had the drawback of making oneself a more appealing target for other, equally ambitious players.

Thus far, the day had gone well. His conversation with both Guild Masters satisfied his interests and assured mutual suspicion. Stanton and his counterpart had both agreed to spy for Kadar, with very little arm twisting required. Kadar preferred when he could achieve his ends with minimal fuss, unlike Machison who had enjoyed the game far too much. Still, when getting results required taking a hard stance, Kadar did not shy away. Such as with Wraithwind.

With a sigh, Kadar finished his wine and pushed his empty plate aside. He disliked interacting with his blood witch and did so as little as possible. Still, it would not be good to give Wraithwind any illusions of lacking supervision, nor to have him think Kadar stayed away out of fear. No, Kadar found the entire matter of blood magic to be distasteful. *I value a good butcher, but I don't go out of my way to visit the abattoir.*

He debated waiting longer to allow his food to settle, and cursed himself for putting off the appointment until after he had eaten. Then again, there was no *good* time to seek out his witch. No matter when he entered the witch's workshop, one meal or another was bound to attempt to come back up, given the smell alone.

Unlike Machison, Kadar had never served in the army. Any killing came at the hands of others, whose services were well compensated. He was a businessman, and while it could be argued that in the League that was hardly a less sanguinary profession, it had the advantage of being less hands-on. Meeting with Wraithwind reminded him of that reality. Aesthetics, not moral squeamishness, lay behind his reluctance. Blood and bodies were what he paid others to handle.

Resigned, he pinched a few leaves of mint from the bowl on his table and crushed them between his fingers, bringing them with him to hide the smell of Wraithwind's rooms. He would make certain to have tea and anise afterward, to settle his stomach.

Kadar's palace lacked a dungeon, an architectural oversight he had never bothered to remedy. Hanson dealt with problems and prisoners elsewhere, which suited Kadar just fine. That meant Wraithwind could not be relegated to a lair underground, and instead set up his workshop in an old carriage house within the walls of Kadar's compound.

No one but Kadar and Hanson were permitted to visit the blood witch, nor did anyone else have the key or combination to the complicated locks. Wraithwind no doubt had the power to magic those locks open, but his best interests were served by obedience.

"What have you learned?" Kadar asked, striding into the workshop. He held up the handful of crushed mint to his nose and took a deep inhale to mask the smell.

The blood witch who styled himself as "Wraithwind" looked up, his expression a mix of annoyance and momentary confusion. Slender and bespectacled, with a mane of graying hair, he looked every bit the cut-rate mage that he was.

"Oh, it's you," he said. "I think I've got the answer to that weather charm you wanted, the one to set storms on a particular ship? Nasty bit of work, no guarantee it won't break the ship apart, but I've got what I need to do it if you want it done."

Kadar nodded. "Keep it handy; I'll let you know when I have a suitable target. How about the monsters?"

Wraithwind chuckled. "I've sent them where you bid me to. I'll warn you that the Rift feels unstable; we may want to sate the Cull a bit before drawing on it—"

"I care nothing about *how* your magic works, only that it *does* work," Kadar snapped. "We can't let up on the pressure now. If you're worried about bringing more of them through from wherever they come from, move the ones you've got around from place to place."

Wraithwind sighed as if he longed to try to explain that it didn't quite work that way, but he would know from experience that Kadar hated explanations.

"Or do I need to withdraw privileges from your partner," Kadar said, and the blood witch's head snapped up. For a second, before he schooled his expression, Kadar saw raw fear in the man's eyes.

"No, please. Leave her alone. I'll do whatever you want. Just leave Micella alone."

"Her continued comfort is entirely up to you," Kadar replied. "When you please me, she has extra wine, new books, clothes to replace what's worn through. Fail to deliver as you've promised, and her existence can become quite bleak—and your visits extremely rare." He took another sniff of the crushed mint, and while it helped to cover the smell of old blood, it could not completely hide the nauseating odor.

Wraithwind blanched. "That won't be necessary," he replied sullenly.

Kadar brightened. "Good. So glad that we understand each other. Now—I need deflection charms, something that will divert attention from boxes of cargo. Doesn't have to make them invisible, just unimportant, easily forgotten."

Wraithwind nodded, regaining his composure. "Not usually too difficult, although obviously the larger the item is, the harder it becomes—even with magic—to convince people not to notice it."

"I'm not a fool," Kadar snapped, and the blood witch winced at his tone. "I'm not asking you to hide the whole sailing ship, merely the boxes of cargo. I need twenty such charms by three days hence, and there should be no way anyone can trace them back to you—or me."

The blood witch looked as if he wanted to argue, then he glanced down with a resigned sigh and nodded. "Yes, m'lord. That can be accomplished—but I'll need more blood to do it, especially if I'm to keep drawing monsters from the Rift."

"I'll send Hanson—tell him what you need. Be specific, if there's a type that works best—male, female, young, old. He can't be expected to know, and I don't want to hear you complain later that you don't have the proper materials."

Kadar glanced around the witch's workshop with disdain. He disliked the dirty magic in the same way he found it difficult to abide anything untidy, and its particulars bored him. Wraithwind's workplace was a mess, littered with vials and flasks; rafters hung with dried plants, weathered bones, and desiccated carcasses. The witch himself smelled as bad as his blood-soaked shop, and Kadar made a note to himself to have Hanson drag the man out to the stable and dump a few buckets of water over his head to keep down the odor.

"Whatever it takes; spare me the details. Just make sure it gets done and done right. Or you'll regret it." Kadar paused. "Anything else?"

"I'm picking up echoes of other blood magic, powerful workings, but it's faint—possibly outside of Ravenwood. I can't tell what's being done, only that there's a strong witch working the magic, and another witch—closer to us, countering."

Aliyev and one of his Crown Prince counterparts in another city-state, having a duel of sorts between their blood witches? To what end? Is one doing and the other undoing, or is it more subtle than that, putting things in motion and then diverting them? I'll have Hanson see what he can learn.

"Keep your eye on it," he ordered. He held up a hand to forestall Wraithwind's objections. "I know you say that you all cloak yourselves to keep other witches from seeing your magic clearly. Spare me the details. Find out what's being done and by whom, and I might allow you an extra night with your lover."

"As you wish, m'lord," the blood witch replied, with an expression suggesting he had been given an impossible task. "I'll handle it."

"See that you do." *Or else.*

CHAPTER ELEVEN

"Shit. Those are *hancha*," Corran muttered as he, Rigan, Trent, and Mir eyed the creatures heading their way.

"At least it's not ghouls," Trent replied.

Corran hated *hancha* and ghouls the most out of all the infernal creatures they hunted. *Hancha* had the saving grace of being dumber than ghouls, since they were corpses possessed by vengeful spirits, and their decomposing brains did them no favors. With blackened skin like a rotting corpse and yellow eyes, fingers drawn up into claws and an insatiable hunger for flesh, *hancha* made up for in ruthlessness what they lacked in intelligence.

And they never hunted alone.

"How many?" Mir asked quietly.

Rigan concentrated, casting out with his grave magic, trying to sense the spirits that animated the creatures. "At least a dozen."

"Are you sure?" Corran asked, giving Rigan a worried look. Rigan had proposed some changes in their fighting style should they come up against *hancha* again. Aiden and Elinor could not read from the ripples in the magic what type of monster plagued an area, only that creatures of some kind had been summoned nearby. Rigan's magic had made him suspect *hancha*, and seeing his hunch proven correct emboldened him.

"Yeah. I think it'll work—and if it doesn't, we fall back on the tried-and-true."

Corran gripped his arm warningly. "It's not worth a thread of your soul." Neither Aiden nor Rigan had determined exactly how much pulling hard on the magic cost a witch, but the poetic description sounded too dire to Corran for his liking.

"It won't come to that," Rigan reassured him. "I can ground myself better. And if it works, the rest of you are in a lot less danger."

"They're getting closer," Trent warned. "Make up your minds!"

"I've got it," Rigan said, and stepped forward. "Cover me."

The old graveyard sat on a hill overlooking the Talerth River, on the outskirts of the fishing village of Cold Rock. At this hour of the night, few lights glimmered in the village, and the ships in the port lay still at anchor. But the dark shapes that advanced on the hunters were anything but peaceful.

Rigan unfurled a piece of oilcloth on which he had already drawn the banishing sigils. It took less than a minute to lay down a protective circle with the salt mixture, with Rigan standing in the center of the cloth. A "portable" banishing circle was one of the new things Rigan and Aiden had been toying with, and while it had worked well in tests, this was its first use under fire.

Rigan pushed doubt from his mind as he sank his power down into the ground and called to the energies around him.

As he called his power, he felt Corran's grave magic in the background, ready to join with his if need be. But Rigan knew that Corran's real strength lay in fighting off physical threats, and he resolved not to draw on his brother's reserves unless he had no other choice.

The *hancha* closed on the hunters, hungry for fresh meat. Rigan chanted under his breath and focused his attention on the spirits that had locked themselves within the walking corpses. Usually, he and Rigan dispelled angry or trapped ghosts that refused to move on or lacked the ability to go to the After on their own. These spirits had elected to remain for vengeance's sake, and as his magic touched their essence, it felt as putrid and decayed as the rotting flesh they inhabited.

"You are no longer of this world," Rigan murmured, willing his power toward the approaching creatures, suffusing his words with intention. "You do not belong here."

He expected the violent response, an outpouring of anger and bitterness that washed over him, scalding in its intensity. "You have no claim on these bodies. Your time here is at an end."

Rigan anticipated resistance. In all the haunted homes and grave-yards he and Corran had cleansed over the years, none of the angry ghosts had gone willingly to their rest. This felt different. In those other cases, Rigan had no doubt that the spirits that remained behind either chose to do so or got lost, somehow, on their way to the next realm. Now, part of the anger that pushed these souls to madness and violence lay in the sordid power that bound them, unwilling, to their mortifying hosts.

"It's not working," Corran warned as he and the other hunters stepped forward, weapons ready for a fight.

Rigan dared not stop his chant, though his mind searched for reasons why the *hancha* seemed resistant to his magic.

"Rigan, do something or get out of the way!" Mir said.

"Spread out," Corran ordered. He might not know what, exactly, stymied Rigan's magic, but he knew his brother well enough to understand that Rigan had no intention of giving up until he had exhausted all his options. Even if this time, it didn't completely keep them out of a bloody hand-to-hand battle.

Rigan struggled to regain his focus, convinced that his magic could wrest the spirits from their bodies. *Most of the spirits we banished before remained by their own will. Pretty sure* hancha *are conjured monsters, so they're not... natural. Whatever magic brought them here is keeping them tethered, and driving their madness.*

The *hancha* surged forward, and Rigan narrowed his focus. Twelve *hancha*, four hunters. As Corran and the others ran with swords raised to meet the onslaught, Rigan bit his lip, willing his magic to force the spirit free from the *hancha* running for him with clawed, outstretched hands.

His magic always did work best when his life hung in the balance.

Rigan's power swelled, and he brought it all to bear on the wretch scrambling toward him. He searched for what did not belong and found a strand of tainted magic, whisper thin, that fettered the cursed soul to the decaying body. Rigan stretched out his power and snapped that strand, recoiling as he felt the foul brush of blood magic.

The *hancha's* body dropped to the ground as the imprisoned ghost tore free. Rigan did not offer it a choice; he thrust the sullied essence into the After. It took all of his self-control not to flinch away from the filthy residue of the blood magic that clung to the spirit. Later, he might have time to ponder the ramifications, to wonder whether the ghost's soul would be denied its rest by evil thrust upon it. The thick of battle afforded him no such luxury.

Now that he figured out their secret, sundering the blood bond felt like slipping a sharp blade beneath taut string. Rigan took down the next two *hancha* one after another. Three more of the monsters lay headless on the ground, their bodies decaying rapidly now that the animating magic had fled. Corran, Mir, and Trent each battled two of the creatures.

Rigan turned toward Corran, who had set about with his sword two-handed. He saw the blade bite into the dead flesh easily, and heard the cracking bone within. The *hancha* felt no pain, so losing a hand or an arm did not slow their advance, although it did hinder their options for attack. Rigan narrowed his eyes, called to his power, reached for the filthy wisp of blood-soaked magic that tethered the *hancha's* souls, and felt it part like cobwebs.

Both of Corran's opponents fell, mere corpses once more, and Rigan focused his attention on those near Mir just as the hunter managed to get in a beheading strike, eliminating one of his attackers. Rigan clenched his outstretched hand, and the other *hancha* dropped into a stinking heap.

He thought he heard Corran shouting his name, but the voice seemed faint and far away. Rigan took a step toward Trent and staggered. Mir and Corran ran toward the two remaining *hancha*, as Rigan raised his arm. Trent's blade sank deep into the chest of one of the *hancha*, and Rigan ripped its soul from its body as the monster slumped to the bloody grass.

"Rigan, stop!" Corran shouted. Mir and Corran teamed up on the last of the *hancha*. Corran's sword took off the creature's head while Mir's blade cleaved it shoulder to hip.

Rigan swayed as he released the power he called. The magic flowed out of him, and pain replaced it.

"Rigan!" Corran yelled, running toward him in time to catch him by the shoulders as his knees gave way and he sank to the ground.

"You're bleeding," Corran said, wiping a hand beneath Rigan's nose and at the corner of his mouth. His fingers came away bright with Rigan's blood.

He tried to answer Corran but managed nothing but a croak as Corran shook him, desperate for a response.

"We've got to burn the bodies and get out of here," Trent said, as he and Mir bent to the task, leaving Corran to support Rigan, keeping him upright. Rigan's vision blurred, and his soul felt loose within his body as if it might float free and vanish into the night.

"Don't you let go," Corran growled, fingers digging into Rigan's biceps as if he sensed the struggle to hang on. "Don't you leave us. Hang on. We'll fix this. Just please, Rigan, hang on."

Fear and anger colored Corran's voice, along with grief fresh from Kell's death. Rigan clung to Corran's presence, willing himself to keep body and soul together, but he felt his control slipping, and feared his will would not be sufficient.

"I will not lose you," Corran grated. "If I have to follow you into the After and drag your sorry ass back, I will not lose you. Do you hear me? Fight, Rigan!"

The stench of burning flesh woke Rigan from his stupor. He still felt the filth of the *hancha's* soul-tethers, but at least he could also feel his own body and his senses more clearly as well.

"We've got to get out of here," Corran said, getting a shoulder under Rigan's arm. "Someone's likely to see the fire and investigate."

They nearly made it to their horses before half a dozen rough-looking men blocked their way.

"Step aside," Trent said, bloodied sword still in hand.

"What have we here?" A tall, broad-shouldered man with a scruffy brown bearded stepped forward. He held a wide sword with a wicked-looking blade in one hand, and his stance told the hunters that he knew how to use it. His belt and bandolier bristled with knives. The men behind him were equally well-armed, though their stained and worn clothing suggested that what money they had went into weapons.

Brigands, Rigan thought, cursing himself for putting his friends at a disadvantage.

"We mean you no harm," Mir said. "Unless you try to stop us."

The leader gave a cold smile. "Can't let witnesses get away."

The comment made no sense to Rigan. If anyone had witnessed anything, it might have been the brigands being privy to the sight of hunters fighting *hancha*. Then his gaze slid to the darkened harbor, and he saw a ship that had not been at anchor before, and the dim lights of lanterns guiding landing boats ashore.

"Distract them," Corran murmured quietly enough for only Rigan to hear.

Sure he was worth little else in another fight, Rigan let out an agonized groan and dropped like a stone to his knees. Corran swung to his left, Trent to his right, while Mir gave an angry roar and ran up the middle.

The newcomers met the attack, engaging with the cold, practiced moves of men who had seen more than their share of fighting. Four hunters against six brigands might have been almost fair; but with Rigan out of the fight, Corran and the others were at a serious disadvantage.

The strangers—smugglers, Rigan thought—clearly had no intention of letting them leave alive. Corran and his friends must have sensed that, whether or not they noted the stealthy ship in the river's port. They threw themselves into the fight with everything they had, and while their skill was evenly matched, the attackers were fresh and rested.

Mir lamed one of the strangers with a deep wound to the leg that put the man on the ground and might have had him bleeding out. That enraged the others, who doubled the ferocity of their onslaught. The hunters had avoided serious injury in the fight with the *hancha*—thanks mostly to Rigan's magic—but nothing spared them bloody gashes as they circled and parried.

No one noticed Rigan, hiding in the darkness.

Rigan knew he had overtaxed his magic, grounded or not, in the fight with the *hancha*. The remaining magic felt sullied by the noxious power that trapped the creatures' souls inside their bodies. Drawing on more magic might kill him, but Rigan had no illusions about his prospects should the brigands win.

He dug his fingers into the damp soil, as he plunged his magic deep into the ground. Rigan marshaled his strength, and felt the tug of grave magic, as his power touched the spirits of those villagers buried in the cemetery behind them. He doubted he had it in him to harness his newer abilities, but grave magic intertwined with his essence, his by blood and birth.

He had no time to second-guess himself. Corran and the others were losing, fast.

Come to me, Rigan called to the spirits in the graveyard. *I will hear your confession. But first, I ask of you one favor—*

It might be blasphemy to require service of the dead before hearing their confession; if so, Rigan would face Doharmu himself for judgment. Right now, all he cared about was saving his brother and his friends, even if he forfeited his life and his soul.

He called, and the spirits of the dead answered him. The temperature plummeted, growing so cold that their breath misted. Rigan felt the hair on the back of his neck rise, and even though the spirits came to his request, he sensed their anger. These were not vengeful ghosts, but they lingered, unwilling to move on. The unresolved issues that caused them to remain fed their frustration, and left unshriven, some of them would eventually become a danger.

Rigan did not have to speak to direct the spirits. They roiled in from the graveyard like a wave of fog, cold and clammy, smelling of dirt. Faces appeared and vanished in the mist, stretched and distorted. Wind swept through the trees, clacking branches like bare bones, howling with barely contained fury.

"What in the names of the gods is that?" the leader of the ruffians exclaimed as he saw the tide of revenants roll toward them.

Corran, Trent, and Mir went on the offensive, as their attackers fell back in terror. One of the men bled badly from a deep gash on his belly, and another's shirt clung to him, soaked with blood, where Trent's blade had opened his flesh across his ribs.

"They're not here for us," Corran said with a dangerous smile. "They've come for you."

A heartbeat later, the ghostly fog parted around the hunters only to coalesce once more as it bore down on the smugglers. The strangers cried out in fright. As the four uninjured men ran for their lives down the path and toward the bay, the spirits overtook the two gravely wounded brigands, obscuring them from view.

Rigan heard a terrified man's scream, and then the night fell silent.

"You have my thanks and gratitude," Rigan murmured to the ghosts that returned to surround him. "And now I will grant you your confession."

"What's he doing?" Trent asked, fear coloring his tone. Corran caught him by the arm as Trent made to move forward.

"Paying a debt," Corran said. "Confessing the dead."

"*Rigan* did that?" Mir's voice was awestruck.

"That's my brother," Corran said, pride clear in his voice.

The ghosts swirled around Rigan, making their last confessions, admitting the sordid secrets that followed them beyond the grave. Their cold touch sent Rigan's teeth chattering, and his skin felt clammy. He found it hard to get enough air, and he wondered if there was truth to the rumors about ghosts stealing the breath of the living.

... did not pay the full dowry I owed...

... stole a calf from the neighbor's farm...

... the son I bore was not my husband's...

... drowned my faithless husband's bastard...

On and on the voices droned, sapping the last of Rigan's strength. Finally, they grew silent.

"Enter into the halls of Doharmu," he whispered, "and may your journey in the After bring you peace." Rigan watched as the restless dead filed toward a darker space in the night, a portal that had not been there seconds before. When the last of the ghosts passed inside, the portal closed, and Rigan fell forward into the dirt, utterly spent.

RIGAN WOKE SLOWLY and groaned as his aching head reminded him of how much energy he had expended.

"It's about time you woke up." Corran's gravelly voice came from near his shoulder, and Rigan turned his head to see his brother sitting on the floor beside his cot, head pillowed on his arms. "You scared the shit out of me."

"Scared the shit out of the smugglers, too."

Corran raised his head. "Smugglers?"

Rigan closed his eyes and sank back into the cot, trying not to worsen the pounding in his brain. "Saw a ship... in the bay. Wasn't there before. Why come... by night if not smuggling?"

Corran sat up and ran a hand through his hair. "Why'd they bother with us?" He sighed, guessing at the answer. "They saw the fires. Probably thought we set them as some sort of signal that we were on to them."

"Maybe." Rigan knew that if they were back in the hidden rooms beneath the monastery that Aiden had to have treated the worst of his injuries, which frightened him given how utterly spent he felt.

"What are smugglers doing here, and why are they this far upriver?" Corran wondered aloud. "We're a long way from the sea. How did they get past the patrols, and what are they bringing ashore?"

"Not our problem," Rigan murmured.

Corran gave a snort. "It becomes our problem when they attack us. And since we didn't kill them all, there'll be trouble if they ever recognize us."

"Worry later."

Corran leaned against the cot and stretched out his legs. "I'll worry now, thank you, if I feel like it. After all, I've been worrying about your sorry ass all night."

"Magic... worked."

Even though Rigan had his eyes shut, he could sense Corran stiffen against the edge of the cot. "Which time? The time you nearly killed yourself banishing the souls out of the *hancha*, or the time you almost died calling the ghosts from the burying ground?"

"Both." Rigan's whisper barely carried far enough for Corran to hear.

"Not again, Rigan. Do you hear me? Not until you and Aiden figure out a better way." Corran shifted, tense with anger. "In the cemetery, when you were pulling the ghosts out of the *hancha*, you started bleeding from your nose, the corner of your mouth—gods, from your ears. And then when you pulled that stunt with the ruffians—"

"Smugglers."

"—you were cold as a corpse when the spirits finally let you go. Your lips were blue, Rigan. Your heartbeat was slow, and I didn't think you were still breathing. And then, by the time we brought you back here, you'd spiked a fever so bad I thought your blood would boil. Two days of watching you rave out of your head, burning up. Two days." Corran's tirade ended in a croak as his throat tightened. "You cut it too close."

"Not going to let you die."

Corran rounded on him. "That goes both ways, Rigan. Where does it leave me if you sacrifice yourself to save me? I won't... I won't survive that. Not after everyone we've lost. So you've got to find a different way. Do you hear me?"

"Fever?" Rigan's brain felt like it had been stuffed with cotton, but the word tugged at the edge of a memory from the night of the battle.

"Yeah," Corran said, swallowing hard. "Aiden and Elinor stayed with you the whole time, doing what they could with their potions and magic."

"The taint..." Rigan whispered. "Blood magic leaves a residue when Rifts open. I felt it... in the *hancha*. When I broke the tie that bound the soul to the corpse, I felt it touch me."

"Shit," Corran murmured. "That's even worse than we thought. Dammit, Rigan!"

"Not sorry," Rigan slurred. "Do it again to save you."

Corran growled in frustration. "I'll have a chat with Aiden. It's one thing to take risks, but taking on something like that without knowing what you're dealing with is suicide."

"No... I gambled. And won."

"This time," Corran snapped. "But sooner or later, every gambler loses. And that's not acceptable. So once you're better, we'll work with Aiden and Elinor, see what you can find in those old books. If this has something to do with the blood magic and the monsters being conjured, then there's got to be a way to deal with it that doesn't almost get you killed. There has to be."

"We'll figure it out." Rigan's voice was hardly more than an exhale. He had exhausted himself again, and sleep threatened to over-whelm him. "Promise."

CHAPTER TWELVE

"I DON'T LIKE leaving when Rigan needs me," Corran said as he and Ross rode for town. Two days had passed since the fight at the cemetery, and while Rigan was healing, he was still tired and weak.

"It's not like he's alone," Ross chided. "Aiden and Elinor are with him."

"They're working on some type of scrying," Corran replied. "If they get caught up in it, they might not think to check on him."

"By the gods! You're such a mother hen. Have you seen the way Elinor tends him? Your brother won't lack for attention," Ross said with a smirk. "In fact, he's got every reason to stay sick as long as possible."

Corran grinned and shook his head. "You're just jealous."

Ross shrugged. "Can't say that I'd mind a night out with a pretty girl. But considering the situation we're in, it's not likely to happen any time soon. Lucky bastard brought his lass with us."

"You know that was completely accidental." Elinor had fled Ravenwood City days before Kell's death, and Rigan believed her to be gone for good. Then the Lord Mayor's guards came looking for hunters. When Rigan led them Below to his witch-tutors, only Aiden and Elinor had survived the treachery of a witch who had sold out to Machison.

"Still a lucky bastard," Ross said, but his tone held no malice.

"Maybe things will settle down sometime. And then we can give up hunting and go back to doing what we used to do."

Ross turned to look at him. "You think, after all we've been through, you could go back to being undertakers?"

Corran watched the road ahead of them in silence for a few minutes. "I never questioned becoming an undertaker. Mama and Papa spoke of the profession like a calling as if it were a priesthood of sorts. And, in a way, it is. To tell you the truth, I appreciate it more than I used to, now that I know something of magic. It didn't occur to me that the grave magic we do to set the spirits at rest was really 'magic,' not until I saw the extra things Rigan could do, like confessing the dead. I doubt the priests can do what he does."

"Well, there will always be dead people, and horses," Ross said with a sigh.

"We can hear you," Polly called back to them from where she rode with Trent. "And I am *not* going back to serving ale to sloppy drunks."

"How about neat drunks?" Trent joked, earning himself a slap on the shoulder.

"Them, either. You know, we get good enough, we could all be assassins," Polly said. "I bet they make good money, and I bet drunks don't try to grab themselves a handful when an assassin walks by."

Corran knew for a fact that Polly had killed one of those grabby drunks when he tried to force the issue. Kell had brought back the body with instructions to curse the spirit. At the time, Kell claimed to have been paid extra to bury the man wrong, but Corran and Rigan both figured the "fee" had come out of their grocery money, for Polly's sake. He did not begrudge Polly her vengeance.

"You want to kill people whenever some scum like the Lord Mayor has a grudge?" Trent asked.

"Gods, no! I'd only kill guilty scum, people who had it coming to them but weren't likely to get what they deserved." She sniffed. "I'd be an assassin for all the right reasons."

"Oh is that so?" Ross teased.

"Watch it, or I'll add you to my list of people who need assassinating," Polly warned, her eyes dancing. "It's a very long list. Been working on it for a while now. Of course, if there's someone you'd want done-for, I'd give you a discount, since we're friends and all."

"Oj and Ren save us!" Ross muttered, and Corran laughed.

Just before dark, the frantic bleating of a sheep drew Corran's attention. "Wait," he said, dismounting and walking over to the low stone fence where he peered into the twilight. "Someone's staked a sheep out in the middle of a field. There's no good reason to do that."

"Not unless it's meant as an offering—or a sacrifice," Ross replied. "What was the name of the village we passed?

"Milton," Trent said. "Sleepy little place—didn't even have a decent inn."

Corran glanced at his companions. "It's still relatively early. Want to stick around and see what shows up? If the villagers are leaving an offering to keep a monster at bay, we might be able to solve their problem."

The others nodded, and they found a shadowed copse of trees where they could tether their horses. Then they moved as close as they dared to the frightened, captive sheep and waited.

"There!" Ross hissed. Just after nightfall, a huge animal slunk from the woods. The sheep's cries grew more frantic, but the beast never slowed, moving with the grace of a large wolf.

The creature leaped forward, the sheep bleated in terror, and then everything fell silent. They made out the shadow of the beast, rising with the body of the sheep in its jaws. Corran and the others ran toward it, circling to cut off its escape. The predator tensed, realizing it was trapped.

As the hunters raised their weapons, a short man in the work pants and boots of a farmer came running from behind a hill, shouting and waving his arms. "Don't hurt him! Leave him alone!"

Corran stared at the man, stunned. "Get back! This thing is dangerous. We can get rid of it for you, keep you and your flocks safe."

To Corran's utter astonishment, the man placed himself between the creature and the hunters, shielding him with his body. Even more surprising was the fact that the wolf-creature made no move to harm the man. Corran saw a faint glow behind the newcomer, and then the wolf was gone, replaced by a naked man, skin streaked with blood, holding the dead sheep.

"A shape-shifter?" Trent murmured. "But that doesn't explain—"

"He doesn't hurt us—he protects us," the farmer told them, still keeping himself between the shifter and their weapons. "We have a deal. He keeps the bad monsters away, and we pay him. In sheep."

"He's your pet?" Polly asked incredulously.

The naked shifter glared. "I'm no one's pet. But it seemed to make a lot more sense to protect the farmers from those abominations and earn a regular meal than to poach sheep and always be on the run."

Corran looked back to the farmer. "You made a deal. With a monster."

The farmer looked pained. "George here ain't the bad kind of creature. Before he came, we had all kinds of trouble with those big damn black hairy dogs—the ones with the red eyes—"

"*Vestir*," Corran said.

"Don't care what you call them, they were a bloody pain—carrying away our livestock, and a child or two as well. Couldn't go do our night chores for fear of getting eaten. And then George came."

"George?" Polly asked.

The naked man blushed slightly. "It's what they decided to call me. My real name is rather unpronounceable for humans. 'George' will do."

"So everyone's fine with this?" Corran was still trying to imagine the farming village taking a shape-shifter under its protection. Then again, perhaps it wasn't all that different from buying a large, well-trained attack dog.

"They are now," the farmer said. "Took a few people a while to get used to it, but once they quit losing their cows and their sheep and their children to the real monsters, we ain't had any trouble about it." His eyes narrowed. "Until you came and butted into our business."

Corran raised his hands in appeasement and sheathed his sword, nodding for the others to put away their weapons as well. "I'm sorry," he said. "It's just that, usually, the monster is a problem and the village wants us to take care of it. That's what we do," he added.

"Well, don't do it here," the farmer snapped. "We like our George the way he is. And don't go tellin' other people about him or us. Don't need any more busybodies poking their noses in and causing problems." He put his hands on his hips. "Now get off my land, and don't come back."

Corran led the hunters back to where they left the horses, unsure whether to feel humiliated or vaguely insulted. Polly waited until they reached the shelter of the trees to break into laughter that doubled her over, tears running down her face.

"That was... amazing!" she panted, trying to catch her breath. "We go charging in like heroes, and the monster wasn't even really a monster. And his name was George!" she added as if that was the punchline of the joke.

Trent chuckled, braving Corran's glare. "You've got to admit, if it hadn't happened to us, it would be funny," he said, grinning. "Makes me wonder if there aren't more smart monsters out there, natural ones that can reckon that regular meals are worth behaving."

Corran sighed, not willing to see the humor in their debacle. "We don't know that he'll stay 'tame.'"

Ross shrugged. "I've known people who got mauled by their own dog or kicked to death by their mule. George sounded like he knew what he was doing. He's got a good deal. I don't think we need to worry about them."

Polly wiped her cheeks with the back of her hand and grew serious as she loosed the reins of her horse. "If the farmer hadn't stopped us, we'd have killed George and put the village at risk for nothing. So we need to be more careful."

"In all the creatures we've fought, Polly, this is the first time we've seen anything remotely like this," Corran argued. "No one strikes a deal with a ghoul, or a *vestir*—or a strix."

She shook her head. "No, of course not. But George in his human form didn't look or sound like a savage. I wonder if he spent time among people before he went into the woods. Maybe he still does, with the villagers."

"The wolf gets invited to dinner?" Ross asked.

"Maybe," Polly said, swinging up to her saddle. "Just saying, we don't need more enemies. If we get a chance to find some allies, even if they're not quite human, it's worth considering. We could use the help."

Corran bit back a reply, unsure he could feel comfortable trusting a shifter. *Then again, the people in Ravenwood would have burned Rigan, Elinor, and Aiden as witches without a second thought, because they were afraid. So much as I hate to admit it, maybe Polly has a point.*

"We can discuss it when we get back," he said, mounting up. "Let's keep going. We've still got work to do tonight."

When they reached the outskirts of Fenton, Corran and Ross veered off, while Polly and Trent headed for the pub. If all went according to plan, Polly and Trent would spend the next few candlemarks chatting up the locals and eavesdropping on conversations. Corran and Ross would check along the riverfront and the bay and see what they could turn up about smugglers.

"You know, I sometimes think Polly's the most dangerous of all of us, Rigan included," Ross said as he and Corran rode for the bay.

Corran snorted in agreement. "I won't argue that. I intend to stay on her good side." He grew quiet for a few minutes. "She and Kell would have made quite a pair."

"Well, with an assassin in the family, you'd have never wanted for business," Ross joked, trying to lighten the mood.

"Do you ever wonder how in the name of the gods the bunch of us ever ended up like this?"

Ross frowned. "Well, you and Rigan *did* sell your souls to the god of vengeance. The rest of us couldn't sit by and do nothing when our neighbors kept dying."

Corran hadn't been expecting a literal response. Even so, the reality of their lives now as outlaws with a price on their heads took his breath away from time to time. "I hope Kell would have been proud of us," he murmured.

"I think you know the answer to that," Ross replied quietly.

The afternoon sun sent long shadows stretching down the wharves along the river by the time Corran and Ross reached their destination. They tethered the horses and walked down the wooden quayside. Men transferred boxes of cargo from the holds of ships into the warehouses that lined the waterfront, which would supply merchants, traders, and peddlers.

The ships that delivered to a river town like Fenton were smaller and with much shallower drafts than the sea-going trading vessels in Ravenwood's main harbor. Those massive ships with their tall masts and banks of sails traveled back and forth across the Sea of Bakara, and sometimes beyond, to the Unaligned Kingdoms, in search of treasures to sell.

Most of the watercraft along the riverfront were fishing vessels, tied up for the evening. Their crews would go out before first light and return early in the morning with a fresh catch for the fishmongers and shoppers. Corran scanned the wharves for any sight of the ruffians they had fought a few days before, casting a glance toward the hillside overlooking the bay where they had burned the bodies of the *hancha*.

"I don't see them," Ross said quietly as they walked along the docks.

Corran shook his head. "Me, neither. Maybe they're not from here."

"We're a long way from the ocean harbor," Ross pointed out. Quite a trip to make upriver and for what? This is a fishing village, not a merchant crossroads."

"That's my thought," Corran murmured. He looked around at the town. None of the shops sold fancy goods, just the necessities of everyday life. Such items usually came by wagon. Corran remembered seeing many such a load prepared in Ravenwood expressly for the purpose of being sold out in the rural areas. Few items would warrant the effort of going by boat instead. *Few legal items,* Corran mentally corrected himself.

The wharf smelled of fish and river water. A glance at the nearest warehouses told Corran that much of the catch was probably salted and packed into barrels if it didn't supply the townspeople their dinner. This far out from the city, the people living in a town like Fenton either plied a trade with minimal supervision from the Guilds or worked on the lands of one of the Merchant Princes.

Which brought Corran back to the question of who had summoned the *hancha*.

Ross cleared his throat, warning Corran that he had been lost in thought. "There's a gent selling fried fish and ale," he said. "Can't get fresher than this. What say we have a bite and see if anyone's in the mood to talk?"

Several of the dockworkers gathered around the man selling fish from a pushcart. Corran felt his stomach rumble as they approached.

"That'll be a bronze each," the fish vendor said. "Gets you fish, bread, and ale."

Corran put down two coins. "Looks good," he said, collecting his meal and holding out his tankard to be filled.

"You come in from the city?" the vendor asked, never raising his gaze from the hot planks of fish. Corran moved aside so Ross could get his food.

"No. Rode in from Brattlesford," Corran replied smoothly. "A friend of mine said there'd been boats in lately with some good bargains. Came down to see what you had."

"Don't know nothin' about that," the man replied. "I catch fish, clean them, cook 'em and sell 'em. Don't pay to stick my nose into other goings-on."

"This is good," Corran said, chewing a bite of the crisp, flaky fish.

The man gave him a look. "Wouldn't still be selling fish on the docks after twenty years if it weren't."

"Do you know who handles the shipments that aren't fish?" Ross asked, talking around a mouthful of bread. He washed the bite down with a mouthful of ale.

The vendor snorted. "Not much comes in that isn't fish. Hardly nothin' at all by boat. Think your friend told you wrong." He resolutely refused to meet their gaze.

"Well," Corran said, "it's not a total loss. Got some fine fish out of the trip," he said, nudging Ross with his elbow and heading back the way they came. They walked along the wharf, finding seats on two crates, and ate in companionable silence, looking out over the water.

"Do you believe him?" Ross asked, changing a look over his shoulder at the fish vendor, who had a new crowd of customers.

"No," Corran replied. "But I think he's too scared to talk about it."

"Why do you think the smugglers are connected to the *hancha*? It could be a coincidence."

Corran gave him a look. "That's what you really think?"

Ross looked down and shook his head. "No. But we don't seem to be able to prove differently."

"Suppose those smugglers had a rich buyer. Someone who didn't want anyone paying attention to what was coming in at night. A few monsters could be a good distraction."

"And what if the monsters ate the smugglers?" Ross challenged.

"Maybe the smugglers came up to the cemetery to see why the monsters weren't where they were supposed to be," Corran replied. "The smugglers showed up pretty quickly after we lit the pyre—too fast to not have started up the hill before they could have seen the fire."

Ross nodded. "Yeah, I thought of that, too. So now what?"

Corran shrugged. "Let's go back to the pub. Maybe there'll be someone who'll talk about what they've seen. People here are too sober."

No one on the wharves paid them any attention as they made their way back to their horses. Corran let out a breath he didn't realize he had been holding, fearful that they might encounter the smugglers again. He and Ross kept checking over their shoulders but saw no one shadowing them.

"Maybe Trent and Polly have had better luck," Corran grumbled as they headed into the pub.

"Pay up! I beat you fair and square!" Polly's voice carried across the common room. Corran looked toward the crowd gathered at the far end of the open space to see a flash of red hair near the back.

"You must have cheated," a man shot back.

"Because I'm a girl? And half your size? You weren't afraid of playing fair when you took my bet."

Corran and Ross pushed through the crowd. Polly stood toe-to-toe with a burly man. Behind them, a kitchen knife pinned a hat to one of the wooden beams of the wall. Trent stood off to one side with a long-suffering expression, one hand near the grip of his knife in case things went wrong.

"She's got you dead to rights, Tom," one of the men said with a guffaw. "Thought you'd found yourself an easy mark."

"Bad enough you got beaten by a girl—now you wiggle out on the bet?" one of the men called from the back of the crowd.

Polly lifted her chin triumphantly and held out her hand. With a grunt, the loser of the competition slapped several coins into her palm. Polly grinned. "Never let it be said that I'm not a generous winner. Let me buy you a drink, kind sir." She held up a hand and waved the serving girl over. "One for me, and two for my friend here."

Corran and Ross exchanged a look. They had both seen Polly drink back in their quarters. Her size and age were deceptive. Several of the hunters had learned that, to their sorrow, after she drank them under the table.

"Let's find a place to sit and see what we hear from the crowd. A few rounds of drinks and Polly'll have him singing like a bird," Corran said under his breath to Ross, who gave an answering chuckle.

Trent stuck close to Polly, but feigned indifference like an indulgent older brother. Corran wasn't hungry after the fish they had eaten down at the docks, but he waved the girl over anyway and ordered them both ale and a plate of cheese, bread, and sausage. He leaned back in his chair, and as the crowd dispersed and went back to their tables, he kept an ear open to the conversations around them.

They were too far away to hear Polly's comments to the man she had suckered into drinking with her, but even from a distance, watching Polly work her mark was fascinating. Polly joked and flirted, insulted and took potshots at her companion's expense, playing to the crowd. Her drinking partner was so sure of his superiority, while Polly played him at every turn, pretending to be as well into her cups as he was.

Corran felt certain Polly was stone cold sober.

"... that fire up on the hillside. Heard someone was burning virgins."

"... I heard it was children. Some dark witch ate their hearts."

"... those damn monsters. Something burned them down to bone. You think it might be dragons?"

The last one had Corran nearly snorting ale from his nose. Ross pounded him on the back, so he didn't choke.

The tower bells tolled midnight by the time Polly had finally wrangled all she could from her unsuspecting informant. Though she looked a little glazed, she still walked a straight line and possessed enough wits to slap the face of a man who let his hands roam as she made her way through the last group of stragglers at the bar. She and Trent met Corran and the others outside, near the stables.

"Let's get out of here," Polly said, and if her consonants blurred a bit, none of her three companions pointed that out.

Corran and the others had barely left the stable when an arrow thudded into the wood of the barn door, barely missing Trent's shoulder.

"Halt! Surrender yourselves in the name of the Lord Mayor!"

The hunters spurred their horses and took off at breakneck speed down the dark road, with pursuers on their heels. Another arrow zipped past Corran, slicing into the skin of his bicep but otherwise missing its mark.

That's assuming they meant to kill. Maybe the bounty's higher if we're alive for them to torture.

The thought of capture urged Corran onward, bending low over his horse. At the next crossroads, Polly and Trent went left, while Corran and Ross headed right, forcing the guards to split up if they meant to follow all of the fugitives.

For the first time, Corran regretted not bringing one of the witches with them. Aiden's magic was less dramatic than Rigan's, using his healer's knowledge of the body to inflict boils or stop a heartbeat, but it could be lethal nonetheless. Elinor could work powerful sympathetic magic, but it was best suited to premeditation, not combat.

Another arrow sang through the air, this time catching Ross in the shoulder. He cried out in pain but kept his seat, dropping even lower over his horse's neck to make himself less of a target.

Corran's mind raced as he tried to remember the roads in this area. Hunting wherever the ripples in the magic showed up had brought them all over the farmlands, down many back roads and wagon trails. But in the dark, everything looked different, and Corran glanced around for any recognizable landmark.

The sight of an old stone barn with half of its roof gone reminded him of something he had seen the previous day. A desperate plan formed, and Corran dug his heels in to urge his horse ahead, moving in front of Ross. He gestured for Ross to follow, indicating that he had an idea.

If they survived, Rigan would rage at him for recklessness. Corran decided he would gladly bear the brunt of his brother's anger if he could live long enough to experience the dressing down. He and Ross had pulled far enough ahead of their pursuers to make bow shots less accurate, and the guards seemed unwilling to risk killing one of their prizes.

Corran's horse could not keep up this pace much longer. Sweat covered the gelding's neck, and Corran heard its breath, fast from exertion. "Not much farther," he murmured, crouched low.

Up ahead, he saw the bend in the river and the stone abutments of a bridge. He guided his horse straight for the bridge, hoping he remembered correctly.

The guards rode close behind them now, close enough that if they cared to shoot, their arrows could not miss. Corran watched the entrance to the bridge grow nearer and hoped Ross could follow his thinking or had exceptional reflexes.

At the last minute, Corran jerked hard on the reins, turning aside from the bridge and down the embankment. Ross thundered after him.

At least one of their pursuers headed up onto the bridge, then screamed in panic as rider and mount fell to the river below where the bridge lay in disrepair.

That left one guard behind them. Ross turned his horse with a hard pull on the reins and rode toward the stunned attacker, never breaking stride as he pulled a knife from beneath his jacket and hurled it with his full strength. His aim was true, and the blade sank hilt-deep into the man's chest before he could gather his wits to draw his bow. Without a word, he toppled, blood bubbling from his mouth, and fell to the ground.

Corran scanned the dark water of the river, but he saw no signs of the other guard or his horse.

"Come on," he said to Ross. "Let's go before any more of them show up."

"Trent and Polly—"

"Will find their way home," Corran replied. "Or they won't. But if we try to backtrack to catch up now, we'll either get ourselves caught or put them in more danger. If they've been captured, we'll deal with it. But there's nothing more we can do tonight."

Even as he spoke the words, Corran hated the truth of it. Polly and Trent could be down any number of farm lanes and cow tracks, and searching for them in the dark was only likely to lame their horses or get them all killed. *They're smart and sneaky. They'll find a way to hide—or they'll kill the bastards that are after them. I've got to trust them, but damn, I wish I knew where they were.*

Corran and Ross rode cautiously the rest of the way back to the monastery, staying to the shadows and lesser-used roadways. Worry weighed on Corran's heart with every step, but he knew they had made the right decision to return rather than spend candlemarks searching in the dark. One look at Ross's face told Corran his friend was equally worried.

They stabled their horses in a barn behind the monastery, owned by a farmer whose gratitude for banishing the vengeful ghosts from his property earned them his loyalty and silence. Corran rode into the stable, feeling the hard ride in every bone and muscle.

"Took you long enough."

Corran's head snapped up to see Polly sitting on a bale of straw, grinning broadly. Trent emerged from one of the stalls. "Glad you made it—we were getting worried."

Corran swung down from his horse and stood staring at the two of them, hands on his hips, shaking his head in amazement. "How—"

"Polly rides like a madwoman," Trent replied, though a touch of pride tinged his voice despite the report of his words. "It took everything I had to keep up. The horses will be spent for days. I couldn't retrace our path if you offered me my weight in gold, but somehow, we lost the bastards who were following us, and came back here, hoping you'd have beaten us home."

"It's all in how you look at things," Polly said, leaning against the rough wood of the stall. "I was a lot more scared of being caught than of getting thrown from the horse. The guards didn't want us badly enough to ride full out." She dusted her hands together. "And here we are."

"I need a drink," Corran said, leading his horse into its stall. Once the horses had been taken care of and the tack stowed, the four of them headed into the ruins of the monastery. They dared not light a lantern in case they had been followed, but moonlight sufficed. Calfon greeted them from where he stood watch, and Corran promised to give him a full account of the night's events after Calfon's shift ended.

Once inside the secret underground levels, they found Aiden, Elinor, and Rigan waiting for them in the small kitchen.

"Thank Eshtamon you're all right," Rigan breathed, rising to clap Corran into a tight hug. "Aiden had a premonition of an ambush, but we had no way to warn you. We've been worried sick."

"Guards got the jump on us as we were leaving the town," Ross replied. "It took a hard ride and some utterly mad risks, but we're here, mostly in one piece."

Rigan stepped back, realizing that Corran's sleeve was wet with blood. Trent had broken off part of the shaft of the arrow that was still lodged in Ross's shoulder, but the wound bled sluggishly, soaking his shirt.

"You're hurt," Aiden said, guiding Ross to a chair while Rigan forced Corran to a seat. Elinor ran to grab supplies. Aiden looked up at Polly and Trent. "What about you two?"

Polly shook her head. "We're fine, although I'll probably be saddle sore for a week!"

Corran started to get up from his chair. "You need something to eat. And some whiskey to go with it." Aiden pushed him down with a firm hand on his shoulder.

"Sit before you fall down and give me more to worry about," the healer said.

"We're not hurt, and we're hungry too, so let us take care of it," Trent said as he and Polly rummaged for easy edibles. They came back with dried fruit, cheese, sausages, bread, and honey, plus a bottle of whiskey.

"I thought you ate at the pub?" Corran asked as Polly took a bite of sausage.

"We did," she replied with a full mouth. "But running for your life gives you an appetite."

Corran gritted his teeth as Aiden cleaned the gash on his arm and closed the wound. "So after you drank the men at the bar under the table and cheated them at your game, what did you learn?" Ross asked.

Polly poured herself a glass of whiskey and leaned back in her chair, grinning widely. "I learned that most men are too busy staring at my bosom to pay attention to how much I'm really drinking," she confided.

"They were doomed from the moment Polly walked into the pub," Trent confirmed. "She really could have done well with a life of crime, if she'd wanted to."

Polly smiled up at him. "That's the nicest thing anyone's said in a long time." She returned her attention to the others. "No one would talk about the smuggling sober, but after we worked through most of a bottle of whiskey, I got them to admit that there were boats coming into the wharves—no particular schedule that anyone can figure—and bringing in cargo at odd times of the night. In the morning, there's no trace of the boats or their crates. One of the men said that whenever the boats come in, there are wagons waiting to take the crates away. One of the others thought that some of the cargo stays in town, but whoever's receiving it hasn't let on to what it is."

"That makes no sense," Corran said, sipping his whiskey as Aiden worked on the wound in Ross's shoulder. "Smuggling undercuts the trade agreements. It undermines the entire League."

"Maybe that's the point," Rigan said. He looked haggard, and his voice sounded raspier than usual, but his eyes were alight with the challenge of a good puzzle. "Maybe whoever's behind the smuggling wasn't happy with that big trade agreement everyone was talking about. Or maybe they merely found a market for cheap goods without the tariff."

"Corran's right," Trent said, leaning against the wall as he nursed his drink. "Bringing in contraband is a threat to the League itself."

"There's more," Polly said, making them wait as she chewed and swallowed the rest of her piece of bread. "One of the men started to say something about pirates before his mates shut him up."

"Pirates and smugglers," Trent mused. "Do you think one of the other city-states is trying to force Ravenwood into defaulting on its agreement?"

Elinor shrugged. "Could be. Parah was ranting about the trade negotiations before I ran away. Apparently Ravenwood and Garenoth have had a really favorable agreement for quite a while, giving each other their best prices and the best of their wares. The other city-states get what's left over, down the line according to how good of an agreement they can broker with partners that have something to offer. The weakest city-states get what's left. Parah said that she'd heard other city-states, like Kasten and Sarolinia, were jealous of Ravenwood. If Ravenwood lost its favored status, someone else would move up."

"This is the type of thing the Guild Masters fret about, not the likes of us," Ross grumbled.

"And so are monsters, but we saw how well it worked when we left it up to them," Trent noted. "Pirates and smugglers become our business if they're going to attack us. And if they think we're out there spying on them, they won't want to leave loose ends. We need to protect ourselves."

Corran shook his head. "This is different. We have our hands full just staying ahead of the guards and trying to kill whatever monsters are roaming around—and now, teaching the villagers how to be hunters. Policing the riverfront isn't our job. Leave it to the guards—it might give them something to do besides chase us."

"I agree," Rigan replied. "But look at what happened out at the cemetery, when we were there to do a job, and the smugglers thought we were after them. We may not be able to avoid clashes, and every time it happens, they'll think it was intentional."

"Shit," Ross muttered. "Maybe we should move farther inland, away from the river. No river, no boats, no smugglers."

"Except that it isn't just a riverside problem," Polly said. "Someone is taking what's brought in on those midnight ships and carting it away to sell somewhere else. There's probably a whole secret market for it, the way people used to take what they stole down Below or to The Muddy Goat to find buyers."

"The kinds of people who are tangled up in smuggling and piracy survive by being suspicious bastards," Trent added. "It'll be impossible to convince them that we aren't a threat."

Corran muttered a curse. "Wonderful. Now we've got smugglers to worry about on top of monsters, guards, and bounty hunters. Maybe the guards and bounty hunters will go after them and leave us alone."

"We should be so lucky," Rigan said with a sigh. "But I wouldn't count on it. What do you want to bet that whoever's behind the smuggling and pirates has paid off all the right people, maybe cut them in on the deal?"

"Not much of a bargain if it violates the trade agreement and brings the League down," Aiden pointed out.

Rigan shrugged. "You're thinking about the long run. Thieves don't. They're all about the profit for them today. They bet that by the time things fall apart, they'll have taken their money and be long gone."

"Just like Machison didn't care if his monsters killed off the

Guild's members who were making the items Ravenwood needs for its trade obligations, so long as he kept control," Trent said.

"We're going to have to watch our step," Corran warned. "Otherwise, we'll find ourselves caught between the Crown Prince and the criminals. I hate to say it, but we've got to let this go. Let's do what we came out here to do—hunt monsters, protect the villagers, teach them how to protect themselves. Ravenwood is going to have to look out for itself, without our help."

CHAPTER THIRTEEN

"HOW IN THE name of the gods do we even kill those?" Rigan swung his sword two-handed at the nearest of the creatures that had overrun the farm. The monsters stood about as tall as a large dog, with six spidery, jointed legs and a hard white carapace. They looked like a cross between an insect and a crab, only much, much larger. In the moonlight, their shells looked like bleached bones and corpse flesh, and they smelled like dead fish.

"Try an axe," Trent shouted, wading in between two of the monsters, setting about himself with a two-sided axe.

Aiden had called the thing a *higani* when they had found the body of one of the creatures after it had been trampled by a herd of cows. The long serrated legs ended in sharp tips as wicked as any blade. The mouth had a beak like a falcon, sharp and strong enough to rip and rend.

Worse, they attacked in swarms.

Corran, Ross, and Calfon hacked their way through a steady onslaught of the *higani* on one side of the field, while Rigan, Mir, and Trent took on more of them a few yards over. Rigan had brought his heaviest sword, but even so, it took his full strength to sever the creatures' limbs at the joints. Mir set to with a sledgehammer, which cracked the hard bodies and splintered the long, arachnid limbs.

Ross wielded an iron bar, which stunned the *higani* but required more strikes to damage them than the sledgehammer. Swords worked best on the joints, which were the weakest spot.

"Are there more of them?" Trent asked, working his way through the clicking, clattering horde. Like the rest of them, his arms and legs were bloodied where the sharp legs had sliced through clothing and skin.

"Gods, I hope not. They're relentless," Corran replied, his expression grim.

Aiden had alerted them to the ripples a candlemarks ago. It was the soonest they had ever managed to confront the monsters after noting the disturbance in the energies. Rigan wondered if the anomaly that brought the monsters through from wherever they had been summoned had really ended. His magic felt... off, like a headache building before a storm, and his nerves were raw.

Are there more of these things waiting to come through? Or something worse?

Calfon signaled from where he had been laying a trap for the creatures, giving a loud, shrill whistle. Few monsters, regardless of their type, survived fire. While Corran, Rigan, and the others kept the *higani* occupied, Calfon had unloaded the bundles of corn stalks they had brought with them for this very purpose. He stacked the sheaves in a waist-high circle open in one section, and liberally doused the dry stalks with oil and moonshine, then stood back and lit a torch, waiting to spring the trap.

Fewer of the *higani* clicked and clattered across the field than when the hunters arrived, and the dismembered bodies of their fallen comrades distracted some of the monsters, which stopped to pull fresh meat from the broken carapaces. Rigan and the others warily lit torches they had brought with them and formed a line, jabbing at the creatures with the torches to force them into Calfon's trap.

The pain in Rigan's head spiked sharply, causing him to stumble and bite back a groan. Corran shot him a worried look, but Rigan waved him off, intent on finishing the hunt. *Let's get rid of these things and go home. Aiden can give me something for the pain.*

Rigan blinked, trying to clear his blurred vision. Colors seemed more vivid, sounds were louder, and the smell of wet, decaying plant matter suddenly overwhelmed him so much that he feared he might retch.

What's wrong with me? Rigan wondered, trying hard to keep his mind on the objective, forcing himself forward one step at a time. His headache throbbed and a distant squealing noise rapidly amplified to an ear-splitting intensity.

The hunters had nearly reached the trap, jabbing and goading the *higani* with their torches, forcing them into the circle of corn stalks. When the last of the creatures skittered inside, Corran and Ross threw down sheaves to close off the entrance.

"Go!" Corran shouted. Calfon and the hunters threw their torches onto the wall of oil-soaked stalks, which caught fire with a rush, sending flames high into the sky. Inside the burning ring, the *higani* shrieked and clattered as the heat caused their shells to sizzle and crack.

Rigan fell back a few steps, putting one hand to his temples. Mir and Trent were closest to him, and they followed, concerned. Rigan saw Corran turn and start toward him. The pressure inside Rigan's head grew unbearable, and he cried out in pain. In the same instant, a shimmering translucent curtain of energy appeared in the air between where Rigan, Mir, and Trent stood and the other hunters.

For a split second, it looked to Rigan as if something had torn the air and ground apart. A gaping hole appeared when the coruscating light curtain parted, engulfing Rigan and his friends.

One minute, they stood in a fire lit clearing. The next, they tumbled into darkness. Rigan's headache vanished, and he realized that the unusual sounds and odors were gone as well.

"What in the name of the gods just happened?" Trent murmured, getting to his feet. Mir and Rigan stood, dusting themselves off, and looked around.

"What do you see?" Rigan asked, not daring to trust his senses.

"Everything bright and dark—no colors," Trent said, carefully turning to look around them, his knife gripped white-knuckled in one hand.

"Yeah," Mir echoed, sounding like he was close to panic. "Nothing looks right. Something's drained away all the colors. And where's the fire? Where are Corran and the others?"

"The trees are wrong," Trent added, his stance ready for a fight. "We aren't in the same place we were a moment ago."

Mir looked at Rigan. "Why? Do you see something different?"

Rigan nodded, and his stomach gave a flip as cold fear gripped him. "Sometimes, I can see the energy around someone or something that's got a lot of magic. It's like a glow, and sometimes it's different colors. Now, all the colors are wrong, and I see the energy like shadows—like the magic is polluted" He wondered if they also smelled the wet dirt-rotted plant stench and if they could hear the maddening squeal that swirled almost at the upper range of his hearing.

"Where are we?" Trent's eyes were wide with fear, and he looked as if he was barely keeping his composure.

"I think we've been pulled through a Rift," Rigan replied.

Mir and Trent turned to him, horrified. "You mean the holes the monsters come through?" Mir gasped.

Rigan nodded, feeling as if he was barely hanging on to sanity. "Yeah. When we were driving the *higani* into the fire, I thought I was getting a vision or having a seizure. My head hurt, my eyes didn't seem to be working right. I could hear and smell strange things—"

"You mean the way this place smells like a swamp and that sound that's like a rusty hinge only way, way worse?" Mir replied.

"Uh huh."

"So if we're through the Rift, where are we? And how did we get here?" Trent asked. He kept scanning the horizon for threat, and Rigan felt the same need on a basic, primal level. Old, deep instinct warned him that they had become the prey.

"Who cares," Mir snapped. "How in the name of the Dark Ones do we get home?"

They stood in a forest of trees the likes of which Rigan had never seen. The trunks were tall and slender, and the leaves hung in long ribbon-like tendrils, which to his eyes appeared blood red. The light that filtered down took on a reddish cast, and the loamy scent in the air smelled of blood and decay. Beneath the trees, the forest floor was fairly open of underbrush, but hilly and littered with enough boulders and large, fallen trunks to provide plenty of hiding places for predators.

"We need to find a place we can defend," Rigan said, "until I can figure things out."

"The Rift goes to someplace else, someplace that isn't our... world?" Trent said, and for the first time since he had known the hunter, Rigan heard fear in the man's voice.

"That's what the old texts say," Rigan replied. "We've never gotten to a place where the monsters came through so soon after they appeared. I think that's what I felt back there—the passage hadn't really closed, not all the way."

"Why did it suck us through? We're not monsters?" Mir protested.

"Probably an accident," Rigan said. "Like getting pulled under with the current when the tide goes out. Nothing personal, but you can drown all the same."

"Up there." Trent pointed to a shallow cave on a steep hillside. "If there's nothing already living in it, we could hole up there. It's high enough we could see anything coming from three sides."

"And we'd be safe from whatever's out there—unless it can scale a cliff," Mir finished. He did not have to mention that ghouls and some of the other creatures they had fought could do exactly that.

"Come on," Rigan said, setting out at a stiff pace. "We don't want to be out here in the dark longer than necessary."

Even the moonlight seemed wrong, casting shadows as if it were noon but without the warmth of the sun's rays. Whatever the source of the light, it enabled them to see, and they climbed the hillside without incident.

"Did you hear that?" Trent asked, freezing in place.

A howl echoed in the distance, and a few seconds later, the answering calls sounded all around them. Overhead in the branches,

Rigan heard scurrying and scraping. They were not alone, and he had no desire to find out what made those noises.

Trent entered the cave first, holding aloft a candle he took from the pouch on his belt, lit with flint and steel from his pocket. He had his sword in his other hand, ready should something already have made the cave its hiding place. Rigan and Mir turned outward, making sure they were not attacked from behind.

"It's clear," Trent called out to them. "It goes back a dozen feet or so and ends. Pretty dry; doesn't look like anything's been living here for a while."

Rigan collected the dead leaves and branches that littered the cave floor. "Gather what you can. I'm betting the things here don't like fire any more than they do back home."

Before long, they had a fire burning across the mouth of the cave and had laid in enough wood from pieces strewn across the hillside to last them through the night. They pooled the meager provisions from their belt pouches and shared water from their wineskins.

"Now what?" Mir asked as they leaned back against the rough stone.

"I wish Aiden and I had spent more time with the old manuscripts," Rigan admitted. "We were focused more on what might come through the Rifts than on how the Rifts opened. But there's one thing we're fairly certain about—blood magic summons the monsters, so it must be able to open the Rifts."

"So we have to kill someone to get out? That's lovely," Trent muttered.

Rigan shook his head. "Blood magic doesn't always require the taking of life, although some very large workings probably do. As the witches I learned from liked to say, it's all about intent."

"Meaning?" Mir looked at him with an expression torn between hope and terror.

"Meaning I need to think about it," Rigan replied, feeling his headache nag at the back of his skull. "I have some ideas, but I'm too tired to try anything right now. And I think we ought to get the lay of the land a little better, too."

"I don't want to stick around and get eaten," Trent warned.

"Believe me, neither do I," Rigan replied. "But I need to get a better feel for the way magic works here—and where the energy currents run. There might be places where it's easier to… tear open… the fabric between here and there."

"Exploring doesn't sound like a good idea," Mir replied warily. "Those things we hear moving around out there, this is their home. We're definitely at a disadvantage."

"Let's take shifts standing guard, and get some rest," Rigan suggested. "In the morning—if there *is* morning here—I'll start probing with my magic. Don't want to do that now, in case it gets the attention of something nasty."

Rigan knew that his friends disliked waiting, and he could not fault them for their impatience. Even so, they also grudgingly agreed that anything more would be better left until they were rested. Trent volunteered to take the first watch.

"I wonder what's going on back home," Mir said as he stretched out on the uneven floor of the cave and struggled to get comfortable.

"Gods, what do you think it looked like to them?" Rigan replied, wrapping his cloak tight against the chill. "Did we just vanish into thin air?" For the first time since they tumbled through the Rift, Rigan thought about how the men they left behind would react to their disappearance. *Corran will be beside himself, fit to be tied,* he thought. *Aiden might figure out where we've gone, but that's cold comfort unless he can also figure out how to get us home. Corran's not going to take this well—losing Kell, and now me.*

"Do you think Aiden and Elinor might be able to magic something up for us?" Mir asked, settling down to sleep.

"Maybe," Rigan said. "But how will they find us, even if they do figure out how to open the Rift? And what if they try and more of the monsters get out?"

"Then you're going to have to come up with an answer," Trent responded from his post near the mouth of the cave. "Because I don't think we'll last long here on our own."

Despite the circumstances, Rigan fell asleep almost immediately, exhausted from the battle and the hard trek across hostile terrain. He dreamed at first of their home in Ravenwood City, an apartment over the workshop, and of Kell singing off-tune as he cooked dinner. Rigan saw himself at work with Corran busy nearby. He felt a mix of contentment and sorrow that his dream-self did not fully understand.

The scene shifted, and Rigan was in the house he and the others had claimed Below. Despite being underground and in need of repair, the close quarters had given it a feeling of warmth and safety that got him through those early days on the run. He longed to stay, knowing that by comparison to what would come after, they were safe and comfortable.

The scene changed once more, and this time Rigan did not recognize the setting. Darkness surrounded him. He called out, but no answer came, but the sense of being observed, of another presence, remained unmistakable. Rigan knew with gut certainty that whatever watched him was immensely powerful; not human, nor friendly. He sensed the presence a long way off and feared capturing its attention. He caught a glimpse of something blacker than a starless sky, felt its regard for just an instant, and recoiled from the touch of something so utterly terrifying and alien. *It knows we're here.*

Rigan woke gasping, on the cold floor of the cave, and it took him a moment to place himself. "Your watch," Mir said, wearily returning to his spot on the floor. Trent lay snoring a few feet away, bundled in his cloak.

Rigan staggered to his feet and sipped a mouthful of water from the wineskin. The temperature had dropped, making him wonder if this place had day and night or whether it remained forever twilight. When he reached the mouth of the cave, he added wood to the fire and saw that one of his fellow hunters had laid down a line of the salt mixture inside the fire, along with their iron weapons end to end, to ward off spirits. Nothing seemed to have threatened them thus far, and Rigan didn't know whether that was due to their safeguards or because the monsters hadn't noticed them. *Something did. But that was no regular monster. Whatever it is, I don't want to meet it.*

He peered outside into the gloom and saw the glint of red and yellow eyes staring back from the shadows. *The monsters have definitely noticed. Wonderful.*

For the moment, the night was silent, save for the rustling of paws and hooves in the underbrush. The howls had subsided, as had the high-pitched whine. Perhaps not so coincidentally, so had Rigan's headache.

If the fire and the salt lines remained unbroken, Rigan's watch would provide him little to do, something that he desperately hoped remained true. To pass the time, he cast his memory back over everything he could think of from his studies—first with his tutor Damian and then with Aiden and Elinor that might suggest how to get home.

It's not the same as the After, he thought. *We're not dead. Pretty sure my grave magic would tell me if we were. So is the Rift—and what's on the other side of it—natural or a creation of the blood mages?*

The more he thought about it; the more Rigan leaned toward the idea that what lay beyond the Rift was natural, even if the portal between the "real" world and his present location was not. *So if it's natural, why isn't it connected to the regular world?* Then he thought about the monsters that had not been conjured, beings like the strix and the shapeshifter that were "natural" in the sense of not magicked or under the control of a witch.

Did those monsters somehow slip across on their own? Are there places and times when the boundary is thin enough for that to happen without blood magic?

That got him thinking about something Baker, one of his witch tutors Below, had told him early in his training. *"Magic is easiest when the lines between real and 'other' are blurred,"* she had said. *"Dawn and sunset, the equinoxes and the solstices, noon and midnight."* But those weren't the only places that lines between magic and non-magic were thinned, Rigan recalled from the old texts. Boundaries were places where magic worked a little easier, and the gods seemed closer.

Boundaries, like the mouth of a cave, the shore of a river, the edge of the forest. They're all places where those lines blur, he thought.

Maybe that's where to start—go to a boundary place at a boundary time. And then what?

So much for "where" and "when"—the "how" of getting home stymied him.

Rigan stared out into the gloom. *Corran's panicking by now. Elinor's probably not in great shape, either. Maybe Aiden can keep his head and try to figure out where we've gone and how to pull us back. I don't know if I can open the Rift from this side. Gods above! What if we really can't return?*

If they truly were trapped in this place where monsters dwelled, they would not have long to worry about it or to grieve their losses. Humans were never meant to venture beyond the Rift.

And what of the presence I sensed in my dream? Was it real? Am I inventing horrors in a place that certainly doesn't need any additions? The other parts of the dream had faded into fragments of memories. But he had never faced down the sort of *awareness* that he sensed in the dream. *It's not a memory, so is it my imagination? Or something real, here in the rift, that hasn't shown itself?*

Aiden had told him once that ability with magic could be a beacon of sorts for creatures that used—or fed on—such power. Certainly the witches Below and the Wanderers had known him for what he was as soon as they met him, saying that his magic called to them. *Are there creatures here that sense magic that will be drawn to us because of my power, horrors that we haven't seen yet?*

The thought unnerved him. *Whatever that presence was, it seemed much more powerful than the creatures we fought back in Ravenwood, or any that we've seen here. Gods, might we have only seen the small monsters pulled through the Rifts when there are greater threats that haven't made their way to the door?*

By the time his watch ended, Rigan was no closer to having an idea of how to find their way back. He woke Mir for the next shift, and Rigan fell into an unquiet sleep, dreaming of Kell calling to him and Corran waiting for him in the shop back in Ravenwood.

———

WHEN RIGAN WOKE, wan daylight struggled into the cave from an overcast sky. "Plenty of things prowling out there, but nothing came close to the fire," Mir reported as Rigan and Trent rose and stretched.

"We need to find food and water, or this is going to go even worse very quickly," Trent pointed out.

"What do you think we can eat here?" Mir asked. "I never tried to cook a monster before." The dark shadows under his eyes made it plain he had not slept well. Mir took a nip from the flask in his pocket.

"I guess it depends on the monster," Rigan said. "And unless monsters only eat other monsters, then there must be some kind of prey here for them to feed on."

Trent nodded. "I can make some rabbit snares—catch anything that's about the same size, and figure out if it looks edible after we've got it. If there's a stream nearby, we might find water—and fish."

"What's the plan?" Mir leaned back against the cave wall. "I'm not crazy about going out there, but staying here isn't much better. And we'll need more wood if we mean to come back tonight; we're almost out. At least we know there's a day and night here."

Rigan knew both men were counting on him to find a way home. He only hoped he wouldn't disappoint them. "I've got some ideas, but we'll need to scout the area—which we have to do for wood and water anyhow. Unless we find something better, the cave's as good a place as any to spend the night."

"Can you do it? Can you figure out how to get back?" Trent asked.

Rigan had been dreading the question. "I don't know, but I'm going to try with everything I've got," he replied. "And you can bet that Aiden and Elinor will be looking for a way to pull us through from their side." He suspected that Corran would leave them little choice. *He's probably frantic by now and taking it out on everyone's hides. Sweet Oj and Ren! We can't seem to get a break.*

They stepped over the embers and the salt line, leaving it in place to keep anything from moving into the cave while they were gone. The gray daylight gave them a better view of the land beneath them. Rigan found a ledge and raised a hand to shade his eyes, scanning the terrain.

"It looks like there's a break in the trees in that direction," he said, pointing. "If it's a stream, that gets us water, fish, and a good place to lay traps." *And another boundary where the fabric of the worlds might be thinner.*

"Do you see anything moving around out there?" Mir asked, peering into the distance.

Trent shook his head. "No. But the monsters may prefer the dark."

Wary of an attack, Rigan and the others ventured down the slope, looking for landmarks so they could easily find their way back to the shelter. They kept their weapons in hand and Rigan took point, ready to summon his magic if mere steel would not suffice. He could not shake the feeling that they were being watched, though nothing in the shadows caught his eye.

"Something's been busy," Mir noted, pointing to where a carcass lay, its bones picked clean. "I can't even tell what it was."

"Probably something we haven't seen before—and don't want to," Trent replied.

Rigan felt torn between shuttering his magic tightly to avoid drawing attention and using it as an added sense to check for danger. He finally sent out a bit of his power, keeping the touch light and the range limited and hoped it would not be a dinner call to hungry predators.

"This place reeks of magic," he said, reeling from the sensations. "Everything carries a stain of it."

"Stain?" Mir asked. "So it's bad magic?"

Rigan struggled to find words. "Wherever we are, the magic feels tainted. Back home, most of the energy is neutral, and it's all about the intent of what you do with it that makes magic bad or good. Here... it's like the power has been fouled somehow so that it favors the darkness." *Magic back home hums with potential, like all of creation contained in a single glimmer. Here, it feels like decay.*

He debated whether to mention the presence from his dreams and decided against it. He had no specifics, couldn't even be certain it was not simply imagined. *I won't tell them until there's proof it's real. We have enough to handle, without fearing phantoms.*

"What does that do to your power?" Trent tried to keep his voice even, but Rigan could hear the fear beneath his words.

"I don't know until I try to use it. Hopefully, we won't be here long enough for it to have an effect."

By the time they reached the stream, Rigan felt certain he had caught glimpses of movement in the underbrush and suspected they were also being watched from the trees overhead. They reached the wet creek-side, and Trent hunkered down, looking for tracks to indicate where small animals might come to drink while Mir and Rigan kept watch.

"I think I can rig up a few simple traps," Trent said, cannibalizing strings from his jacket to use for twine.

Mir found a few saplings that would do to cut for fishing poles, and within a candlemark, they had some lines set and snares ready.

"Now we come back in a little while and see if we've caught anything." Trent stood and dusted off his hands.

Rigan tried to get a feel for the energy of the boundary between the forest and the shore, the land and water. He probed with his magic and felt a frisson of power he had never noticed back home. *Because I never looked for it, most likely,* he thought. He had picked up something similar the night before at the mouth of their cave. He welcomed any boost to his magic since had no idea what would be required to get them safely back where they belonged.

Just looking out over the landscape gave Rigan a headache as he strained to filter the strange colors and the way energy and magic had become visible. At first, scanning the horizon hurt his eyes and made his head pound. Gradually, the pain eased as he discovered how to use a flicker of magic to temper the new way of seeing. Then he discovered that using a bit more magic snapped the view to normal. By altering how much magic he used and how he concentrated, Rigan could change the way he saw this new world inside the Rift.

That could prove valuable, he mused. Being able to see things as they appeared to his friends and without the confusing colors and auras made it easier to quickly get his bearings. But having the magically-enhanced sight gave him the ability to know more about what was going on at a glance, an insight that might save their lives. *I'm going to have to figure out what it is I'm really seeing with those strange colors, and how to use what I see to keep us alive and get us home again.*

They headed back to the cave, and the prickle at the back of Rigan's neck warning of danger made him jumpy. "I've got a bad feeling," he warned his friends. "Stay sharp."

Barely ten steps farther down the trail, the branches over their heads rattled and shook, and in the next breath, screeching, clawing bodies dropped from the tree canopy. The wiry, scaled creatures were the size of a squirrel but moved more like a monkey, with grasping hands and feet and a tail strong enough to leave a welt when it whipped across bare skin. Worse were the sharp claws that ripped at flesh and clothing, yanked out hair by the roots, and dug deep into skin. Razor-sharp teeth in a wide, vicious maw sank in and ripped away strips of flesh.

Individually, the small monsters were not difficult to dislodge. But when they rained down on the three hunters from above, twenty or more of them at once biting and clawing, the posed a serious danger.

"Get off!" Trent yelled, cursing as he grabbed at the fast-moving beasts, trying to yank one free of his shoulder and giving a hiss of pain as its claws ripped through skin.

Swords were of little use when the attackers clung to arms, legs, and bodies, and even knives were unwieldy. Rigan wished for a dirk, but his smallest knife in his ankle sheath was impossible to reach under the onslaught. One of the creatures clawed at his face, aiming for the eyes, its hind claws digging deep into his chest as its tail lashed across his belly and back, opening slices like a scalpel. Others dug into his legs, their sharp nails easily slicing through cloth. He could feel blood running down his skin.

Long ago, he had heard sailors in the pub tell stories about fish with very sharp teeth that could swarm an unfortunate swimmer and have the flesh off the bones in minutes. Rigan knew that if he went down under the attack, more of the small monsters would join the feeding frenzy and he would not survive.

"They're as bad as those beetles," Mir growled, doing his best to jab and slash at the toothy creatures without cutting himself.

Rigan remembered fighting off the beetles in the workroom with Kell, how they had hissed and popped from the flames in the fireplace, and how he had torn one loose from his brother's shoulder... The memory sparked an idea, and Rigan sank his magic down, hoping he could anchor himself in this alien place. The ground under his feet felt strange to his magic, but he found enough of a tether to suffice, and then he pulled just enough power to draw heat into his body and release it through his hand.

He grabbed for one of the attackers, and it jumped clear and hissed when his palm burned its rough skin. Rigan swatted at the creatures with both hands, first clearing them from his own body and then slapping them away from Mir and Trent.

The small monsters hissed and shrieked, but they learned quickly, scrambling to get out of reach beyond Rigan's grasp. They skittered into the forest and vanished, and the ominous clattering overhead ceased.

"What did you do?" Trent looked between Rigan's reddened hands and a bright pink burn on his arm the shape of a finger where Rigan had brushed against him.

"That night the beetle monsters came, I used my magic to get one off of Kell by making my hands hot enough to force it to let go," Rigan replied. "I thought maybe it would work again, and it did." He eyed the mark on Trent's skin. "Sorry I burned you."

"Your hands aren't blistered," Mir said incredulously.

Rigan shook his head. "No. The magic passed through me, but my skin never felt warm." Trent might have been the only one who had a burn, but all of them were bleeding from dozens of bites and slashes, or from punctures where the sharp claws had dug in and held tight. Rigan felt a little sick, and he remembered the way the fouled magic of the *hancha* had affected him. *Another reason to get home as quick as possible, since we're surrounded by that tainted power. That's sure to take a toll.*

"I'm glad you're on our side," Trent replied, picking up the sword he dropped as the others gathered anything lost in the fray and moved on.

"We need to get back to the cave and see if there's anything we can put on these wounds before they go bad," Rigan replied, watching the plants along their way in the hope of finding some he could mash into a poultice.

"When we come back to check the traps, we're bringing torches," Mir muttered. "See how they like that."

Rigan collected a few leaves along the way from plants that looked like healing herbs from their world. He had no way to know whether the pervasive taint that clung to this place's magic also affected what grew, but he felt certain that the lizard-things' wounds would fester without treatment.

Nothing else attacked on their way back, but Rigan still believed other creatures watched from the brush. He felt nauseous and wondered if it was because of his wounds or the aftereffects of having anchored his magic in the tainted ground. *Maybe a little of both,* he thought.

Trent scanned the horizon, focused intently on their surroundings. Mir grew quiet, doing whatever was asked of him, but volunteering little conversation.

Along the way, they gathered more wood for the fire. Trent and Mir had refilled their wineskins at the creek, which had looked and smelled clean. When they reached the cave and stacked the wood, Trent withdrew a flask of whiskey from inside his jacket.

"Probably ought to wipe down the cuts with this, but go sparingly because it's all we've got," he warned. Rigan experimented with a paste from the plants he had collected on one of his own gashes and breathed a sigh of relief when it caused no unexpected reaction.

"Did you pick up anything on our little trek?" Trent asked, returning to the mouth of the cave to keep watch while Rigan finished tending to cuts on Mir's back.

"There are a lot more creatures in the woods than we've seen," Rigan replied. "None of them feel completely normal. Let's hope any we catch are edible."

"Do you think they're all dangerous?"

From somewhere in the distance, a loud, rumbling growl broke the silence, followed by a sharp, shrill cry of pain. Mir paled.

"I think we assume that to be the case," Rigan replied, wiping the herb paste off his hands and standing. He took a spot on the other side of the opening from Trent and faced outward, then closed his eyes and stretched out his magic. After a moment, he shook himself alert and opened his eyes.

"See anything?" Trent asked.

"I was trying to feel for more ripples in the magic like we do back home to find out where the monsters are coming through," Rigan explained. "Stands to reason that if the shift in the magic when the Rift opens causes ripples on our side, it might on this side as well."

"And?" Mir looked up, with an expression torn between hope and fear.

"It feels different here, but I think I've located one or two."

"That's good, isn't it?" Trent said. "We can get out that way, right?"

Rigan grimaced. "Maybe. And the ones I felt weren't close. I'd hate for us to put ourselves in danger of being eaten to go a long distance and then either not know how to open one if we find it, or have it vanish before we can get there."

Trent turned away. "So, we're stuck here."

Rigan shook his head. "I'm not giving up. But I don't want to take unnecessary risks. Believe me; I'm going to do everything I can to find a way home."

They judged the passing time by the angle of the light, though clouds never cleared enough to see the sun. Rigan attempted small workings with his magic, more to test how his power fared in their present location than to accomplish a particular objective. Mir had gathered thin saplings and spent the afternoon weaving a rough basket, after many failed attempts. If their snares or fishing lines were successful in catching dinner, the basket gave them something to carry the bounty back. Mir and Trent napped, taking turns while the other kept watch, and eventually, Rigan did the same. He was wary of expending too much magic, fearful that it might draw the wrong sort of attention, or hasten any negative effects of the taint.

When they guessed it to be late afternoon, they headed back down to the stream. This time, two *vestir* charged them, and Rigan wondered if the pair had found them by scent. Fortunately, they were only the size of large dogs instead of being the sow-like giants they sometimes became. Trent and Mir fought them off, and Rigan made the killing blows with his sword, taking off the heads.

"Before anyone even asks, I am not keen on finding out whether or not we can eat those things," Mir said, giving one of the carcasses a kick.

"You might change your mind if you get hungry enough," Trent replied. He knelt next to one of the beasts and cut through the tough hide on its side, peeling back skin and coarse hair to reveal muscle. A few slices of his knife yielded a slab of meat. He grinned. "Once a butcher, always a butcher. Smells like pork to me. We'll cook it good and see if it's edible." With that, he put the bloody hunk of flesh in Mir's basket. Mir eyed it with suspicion and wrinkled his nose.

"Look at the bright side," Rigan said as they left the dead *vestir* behind them and headed for the stream. "Two big carcasses nice and bloody might distract a lot of things that would have tried to make us their dinner. Even predators usually take the easy meal."

Nothing else bothered them, and they were pleased to find the snares full and a fish on the line. "Well, at least we'll have choices," Trent said. "Although none of them look like anything I've ever seen before."

After what they had already experienced, Rigan had concluded that all the creatures on this side of the Rift were likely more vicious than anything similar back home. The fish had razor-sharp scales and fins and wickedly-curved nightmarish teeth. The snares held two animals the size of large rabbits, but with wide maws sporting two rows of sharp teeth, powerful hind paws with inch-long claws, and reflexes fast enough to make stabbing them a real challenge.

"Should I let one of them go?" Trent wondered. "I don't know if we can eat all of this, and it won't keep."

"We don't know if we can eat any of it," Mir pointed out. "And I'm starving."

"If we don't need one of the rabbit-monsters, I could use it for some magic I want to try," Rigan replied.

"Can't guarantee how anything will taste," Trent said, improvising a handle for the two snares from his belt to avoid losing a finger to the creatures. The two rabbit-things hissed and snapped at each other, striking out any time the snare-cages got close.

Rigan and Mir lit torches for the return trip. The clouds had thickened, turning the sky darker than expected for the time of day. The sounds and sense of being stalked on the way back confirmed Rigan's suspicion that the larger predators came out in the evening. Carrying raw meat, a fresh fish, and two squabbling prey creatures no doubt enhanced their attractiveness to other monsters that might want to feast on all of them.

Rigan and Mir had knives and swords ready. Trent was hampered by the burden of the awkward basket and snare-cages, but he could get to his weapons in seconds if he dropped what he carried. As a precaution, Rigan stretched out his magic, trying to anchor himself in the air this time instead of the ground. It felt less polluted, though the whole place had the heavy, thick climate of a swamp on a hot summer night. When his magic touched something that sparked in response, Rigan projected a warning, sending an aggressive mental image that might cause an attacker to choose easier prey. Several times he heard snuffling and heavy paws or hooves in the bushes, but felt the creatures turn away.

To Rigan's relief, they reached the cave without incident. Mir and Trent stoked the fire in preparation for dinner. Rigan used magic to pin one of the rabbit-creatures long enough for him to slit its throat without getting a nasty bite from its sharp incisors. Trent skinned and gutted the carcass, then chopped the head and tail from the fish. Mir had fashioned a grid of wood over the fire to keep their food out of the flames. They had nothing to flavor the meat, but by that time, they were all so hungry that Rigan doubted they would notice.

"It doesn't smell bad," Trent noted once the meat began to sear.

"Do you think it's safe to eat?" Mir looked unsure at their bounty.

Trent shrugged. "Most things are if they're cooked well enough.

And we can die of starvation as easily as by poison. The creatures here eat each other, and they eat humans, so maybe it'll all work out."

"Not sure I follow that logic," Mir noted, "but I'm hungry enough to test your theory."

To everyone's relief, the meat proved edible, though tough and gamey. The fish tasted slightly better, though it, too, had a strong after-taste. After going all day on what little they had in their pockets, Rigan thought food had rarely tasted so good. They had no way to boil the water from the stream, but Rigan checked it with his magic, working a purification spell Aiden had taught him.

Night deepened, and the sounds of creatures moving through the underbrush seemed louder and closer despite the fire. Nothing came near enough to test the barrier of salt and flame, but Rigan sensed the presence of several beings he thought might have been ghouls and spotted the reflective eyes of things that reminded him of large cats.

Mir sat with his back against the cave walls and his knees drawn up to his chest. From time to time, he took a sip from his flask. "If we don't make it back, will our souls still go to the After?" he blurted.

Rigan and Trent stopped what they were doing to look at him. Turmoil brewed in Mir's dark eyes. "I don't know," Rigan admitted. "And it's too early to think like that—"

"But if we die here, will we go to Doharmu? Or be stuck in this... nowhere?" The urgency in his voice suggested that the question had tortured him for a while.

"I don't know much about how gods and Rifts work," Rigan replied carefully, "but I would think that Doharmu would be the god of Death no matter where and when something dies. Maybe to the gods, this space on the other side of a Rift is like a spare room, a shed behind the main house, but it would all still be part of the same whole."

Mir chewed his lip. "I wondered, you know?" His voice trembled, and he turned his head so that the others could not see his face. "Just in case."

"I'm going to do everything I can to get us home," Rigan reassured. "And I know Aiden and Elinor are working hard on the other side, too. Don't give up yet. We've barely gotten started."

Mir nodded, but the certainty did not reach his expression, and Rigan wondered if their friend had really heard a word. Mir tightened his arms around his knees and folded in on himself, as Rigan and Trent exchanged a worried glance.

"You said you wanted one of the rabbit-things for magic," Trent said. "What did you have in mind?"

"Blood magic opens the Rift from our side," Rigan replied. "Maybe it works on this side as well."

"I didn't think 'good' witches used blood magic," Trent said.

"We don't," Rigan replied. "I'm not even sure I know how to call it, or what it'll cost when I do. That's why I want to see what I can learn with some grave magic and some scrying, and save the questionable stuff for a last resort."

"We're depending on you to get us out," Trent said, returning to watch over the mouth of the cave. "So whatever you need, we'll back you up."

Rigan appreciated their faith in him, though it made the weight of their expectations that much heavier. He went to the mouth of the cave once more and looked out over the dark valley, letting his magic sense the energies and focusing on the colors and shifts. When he concentrated, he picked up flickers moving in the forest. From their motion, he guessed they were some of the larger monsters.

That's helpful. If I can sense them, we can keep from blundering into them. He wondered whether he would notice smaller creatures at a closer distance. Any help his magic could provide in avoiding confrontation was so much better than risking battles. Finding a way home was only part of the challenge; they had to survive long enough to make their way back.

Once he identified the flickers caused by roving monsters, Rigan parsed through the overwhelming panoply of color and motion. Some areas glowed red. Rigan noted their locations, and from the lack of movement, surmised that they were places where magic might be stronger. *Also good to know. Whether we're fighting a monster or trying to work magic to get home, going to a spot where the magic is naturally amplified can't hurt.*

Finally, Rigan focused on the shimmering streaks that appeared and disappeared without a notable pattern. He had heard one of the sailors tell tales of lights in the sky that he had seen on a sea journey to the most northern tip of the continent, beyond the boundaries of Darkhurst. Rigan had imagined the sailors' lights as broad brush strokes of luminescent colors, folding and unfolding like ribbons. The streaks reminded him of the sailor's story, though he feared these lights had a far more malevolent purpose.

Are they weak spots, between here and home? And if so, are they all caused by blood magic, or did some of them always happen? And the most important question: How long do they stay in one place? If we can find one, and it's what I think it might be, can I open it from this side?

That night, Rigan's dreams were dark. Once again, he and Corran were in the cemetery where they had summoned Eshtamon, but this time, the Elder God stood against the flames of a burning city.

You are my champions. My warrior and my champion mage. Your work is not yet complete.

In his dream, Rigan tried to call out to Eshtamon to beg him to pull them out of the Rift. The words stuck in his throat and he had no voice.

Corran looked haggard, eyes red with grief, features drawn with exhaustion and worry. He moved past Rigan as if he could not see him, and confronted Eshtamon.

Where is my brother? We made a bargain, a contract. We've done everything you've asked, but I need him to come back to us.

Eshtamon regarded Corran for a moment before he spoke. *Your journeys are not always what they seem. The bond between you is strong. Let it guide you, and you may find the answers that you seek.*

Rigan turned toward Corran, shouting his name. He tried to grab his brother by the shoulders, but his hands found only air. Corran did not give any indication that he saw, heard, or sensed Rigan, and he turned away from where Eshtamon vanished, muttering curses, his expression dark with anger and grief.

Abruptly, Rigan stood alone in the dark. The presence he had sensed earlier felt stronger, closer and... curious. It might have barely noted his existence before the first dream, but apparently, recognition went both ways. Rigan sensed the utter wrongness of the presence as if it fell too far beyond the limits of his experience for his mind to comprehend, beyond simple, primal terror. *Not exactly malicious,* he thought, but corrupted, and he realized with a jolt that it stank of the warped energies of the taint. Rigan tried to shield himself; tried to make his presence small and easily overlooked, but he knew he had failed. Though he saw nothing in the darkness, he felt the presence's notice, as if someone stared at him from afar and locked gazes. He shuddered. Nothing good could come of this.

Rigan thrashed his way to wakefulness to find himself tangled in his cloak on the rocky floor in the pre-dawn darkness. Trent watched him with concern from where he stood sentry at the cave mouth. "Are you all right?"

It took a few moments before Rigan's heartbeat slowed and his breath evened before he could answer. Instead, he nodded, forcing himself to take several deep breaths. The panic eased but did not go away completely. Rigan doubted that it ever would, so long as they remained in this godsforsaken place.

"Yeah," he managed, though his dry mouth made it difficult to speak. He felt a little too warm and sluggish, like the beginning of a fever was taking hold, and blamed the taint. "Just bad dreams. I'm fine." Privately, Rigan wondered whether what he sensed was merely a dream or something more.

It would be like Corran to demand that Eshtamon find us. I wouldn't put it past him to go toe-to-toe with an Elder God to get me back. Did Eshtamon have something to do with us being pulled through the Rift? Surely a god would know where I am, and if blood mages can open the Rifts, an Elder God can walk wherever he chooses. Or am I missing something important, something I need to figure out while I'm here? Gods above and below, my head hurts trying to puzzle it out. We don't have time for me to be confused. Mir and Trent are depending on me. Corran and Elinor are counting on me. I've got to get this right because I have the feeling there's more at stake than just our lives.

CHAPTER FOURTEEN

"Rigan!" Corran looked around the field where they had fought the *higani*, desperate to find his brother. "Trent! Mir!"

The shattered white-shelled carcasses of the crab-like monsters littered the ground, and Corran dodged the bodies as he ran toward where he had last seen the missing men. "Rigan!"

They fanned out, lanterns held aloft, caring little that their shouts might attract more of the creatures. Voices grew panicked as they continued to search and no replies came.

"They were right here," Corran said, gesturing to the spot where Rigan, Mir, and Trent had been when they fought the *higani*. "How could they disappear?"

"I couldn't take my eyes of the creatures long enough to get a good look," Ross said, "but out of the corner of my eye, I thought I saw something shimmer and flare. When I did turn, there was nothing."

Corran ran a hand through his hair. "That can't be right. They must be here somewhere. Maybe... maybe while we were focused on the *higani*, something else carried them off."

The three men walked the perimeter of the clearing, growing increasingly frustrated and frightened as it became clear that their missing comrades were not anywhere in the field.

"There aren't any footprints, hoof prints, or claw marks except prints that match the *higani*," Ross pointed out.

"And there's no evidence of anyone being dragged off," Calfon agreed reluctantly.

"Maybe whatever it was carried them—" Corran felt his heart pound and a knot form in his stomach.

"The ground's soft enough that anything carrying three grown men would have left marks," Ross said. "And one of us surely would have noticed if something big enough to make off with an adult man flew in from the sky."

Corran swallowed hard. "That light you saw, the shimmer—could that be one of those 'ripples' Aiden and Rigan talked about?" As he spoke the words, he knew they were true, and he fought hard not to retch at the implications.

"Maybe," Ross replied. "And if so, then a Rift opened—"

"And pulled them into it," Calfon finished.

Corran turned away, feeling dizzy as the implications sank in. "We've got to get them back," he said. "We've got to figure out how to open the Rift and get them out." *What if all Rifts don't go to the same place? How do we find the "door" that leads to Rigan? What's on the other side of a Rift? If that's where monsters come from, can people survive? Oh gods, what if they're already dead?*

Ross laid a hand on Corran's shoulder. "There's nothing else we can do out here tonight."

Corran shook his head. "No. I won't leave him. What if—"

"If it opens again and spits them back out, Rigan and the others will walk home," Calfon replied. "We'll come back in daylight with Aiden and Elinor and see what the witches make of it, and bring the boys home if they've come out on their own. If not, we'll do whatever Aiden and Elinor say we need to do to get them out safely."

"We're nothing but bait out here at night," Ross pointed out. "And getting ourselves killed won't help them. Let's get out of here before something else either picks up our scent or comes to clean up what's left of the *higani*. Calfon's right. We're done for tonight."

Corran wanted to argue and shout and curse, but he knew his

friends were correct. They had been lucky that no other monsters had come along to see what the noise was about. He felt numb, far more than could be blamed on the cold evening air. Before they reached the horses, his stomach rebelled, and he fell to his knees as his supper came back up. He rose on shaky legs but refused help to swing up to his saddle. They each led one of the missing men's horses, and silence stretched awkwardly as the three men made their way home. Everything around Corran seemed blurred and unreal.

Rigan vanished, without a trace. He's gone. They could be fighting for their lives, and there's nothing we can do to help. They could die, and we'll never know it.

Eshtamon! God of Vengeance, Elder God, He to Whom We Swore our Souls—hear me! You promised us your protection. We've held up our side of the bargain—and we'll continue to fight the monsters and protect our people and the Wanderers. But I need my brother. We're in this together, and I can't do what we promised without him.

No answer came. Corran felt no surprise. He did not expect another vision of the cloaked, fearsome deity he and Rigan had seen in the cemetery the night of Kell's death. *Rigan's the one with visions. I just bury the dead.*

A frightening thought occurred to him. *What if Eshtamon's done with us, now that Machison and Blackholt are dead? Maybe that's all he needed us for, and his interests are elsewhere.* Corran pondered that for a moment and reached a conclusion. *No, it can't be. Rigan and Aiden think that others besides Blackholt are conjuring monsters—and we've seen the proof of that in the types of creatures and the Rifts. The Wanderers are still as endangered as ever—they're never welcomed, but they're as much fugitives as we are now. So if they're his sworn people, they're hardly safe. And while the battle back in Ravenwood seemed huge to us, was it really big enough to warrant a god's notice?*

Corran's conclusions frightened him. If they had only uncovered and destroyed part of the problem, then blood witches and their powerful masters still threatened the Balance, and their monsters endangered all of Ravenwood. *How can three witches and a half a dozen hunters possibly set things right? Even with the help of an Elder*

God? Worse was the possibility that if Rigan and the others did not come back, their chances for success fell even more.

"We're nearly home," Ross said, nudging Corran's shoulder to rouse him from his thoughts. Corran nodded in acknowledgment, but his mind spun with possibilities and questions. And beneath everything, a growing level of panic and grief constricted his chest and made him feel as if he were being crushed.

He saw to his horse out of habit, removing the saddle and tack, fetching water and food, wiping him down and giving the gelding a quick curry. Afterward, he tended Rigan's mount, as Calfon and Ross took care of Mir's and Trent's horses. Grooming the horses was a mindless chore so engrained Corran could do it without thinking. Usually, it provided a centering break that calmed him after a fight. Tonight, the tasks passed in such a blur that he questioned later whether he had really done them.

Aiden and the others were waiting when the hunters came down the steps.

"What happened?" Aiden asked.

Elinor registered who did not return and gasped. Polly took her hand and gave it a squeeze, with a look of grim determination.

"You were right about where the monsters were. *Higani.* They weren't the problem," Calfon said. He recounted what happened after the fight, as Corran sank down into a chair in the kitchen and Ross moved to pour him a slug of whiskey.

"You didn't actually see it happen, right?" Elinor challenged. She had gone pale, worry clear in her eyes. "So you can't be sure. We've never heard of someone getting pulled into one of those Rifts."

"We know that people have been going missing more often now," Calfon replied gently. "Some of that is surely the monsters and the guards. But maybe there's more to it than we thought."

"No," Elinor protested, the tears now streaming down her face. Polly took the whiskey bottle from Ross, poured some into a glass for Elinor, and took a liberal swig from the bottle herself.

"Drink this," Polly said, forcing the glass into Elinor's hand. "Come sit down. We'll figure something out."

Aiden and the others joined them, pulling up chairs around the table. Calfon helped Polly lay out a cold dinner of bread, sausage, cheese, dried fruit, and honey. Calfon brought the partly-empty whiskey bottle to the table, and Polly dug another out from the cabinet, setting it down with a *thunk*.

"Seems like that kind of night," she said, taking a chair beside Elinor.

"Go over it again," Aiden said. "I need to know everything, no matter how unimportant. If they did get pulled through a Rift, then we've got a lot of work ahead. We know one way for sure to open it back up—blood magic."

"Don't we become the thing we're fighting, if you do that?" Ross asked.

"I've always been taught that intent matters," Aiden replied. "We became killers to stop Machison and his witch—and the guards—that were controlling the monsters. Killers, soldiers—but not murderers. The intent behind the act makes the difference. I'll see what I can learn of blood magic." He looked to Corran and Elinor. "We'll bring them home."

Corran sat at the table for the next few candlemarks, doing his best to keep his mind on the conversation. Aiden and Elinor brought out old manuscripts and histories, and they all helped search for any mention of Rifts and the Balance. He lost count of how many times his friends refilled his glass of whiskey. He doubted there was enough alcohol in the kingdom to dull the pain of Rigan's absence and his fear for his brother's safety.

I'm the older brother; I was supposed to keep Kell and Rigan safe. Mama and Papa would have expected as much. Now Kell's dead and Rigan's missing. I'm an outlaw and a fugitive. How did things go so wrong? How did I manage to fail so badly?

At some point, late into the night or early morning, they pushed the old books aside, vowing to regroup once they had some sleep. Corran managed to make it to the room he shared with Rigan unassisted, despite the whiskey. He was drunk, but not nearly enough to forget. Without bothering to remove more than his shoes, Corran fell across his bed, turning his head so he did not have to see the empty cot on the other side of the room.

Unquiet dreams made Corran's sleep restless. He relived the fight in the warehouse against the monster and soldiers who killed Kell, only to have the scene shift and become the barn where ghouls killed Jora, his betrothed. The images folded in on themselves, and Corran found himself in the cemetery the night he and Rigan buried Kell, standing over a fresh grave, making an offering to the god of vengeance.

"Magic always has a price, and even with my gift, it is possible for you to draw too heavily upon your power and destroy yourself. If that should happen, your soul will not find its way to the Golden Shores, and it will wander the shadowed places for eternity." Eshtamon said, standing at the foot of Kell's grave. The Elder God had given them his blessing, named them his champions, and bestowed his favor. But he had also given them both warnings, and it was his caution to Rigan that Corran heard again in his dreams.

Bring him back! We can't do your bidding if he's stuck on the other side of a Rift. In his dream, Rigan stood in the distance, able to see him but too far away to hear Corran argue with an ancient god. Rigan's image wavered and blurred as if it might wink out at any second.

I will do whatever you require of me, but give me back my brother, Corran pleaded, no longer certain what separated dream from reality.

"Your bond will lead him home," Eshtamon's voice rang through the darkness, *"if you are able to open the door. You have done well in the quest I set out for you, but there is much left to do."*

If you want me to finish the quest, give me back my brother, Corran demanded. *I need him to complete what you've given us to do. I'm just an undertaker and a hunter. I can't fix the Balance or close Rifts. Rigan's your champion mage. You want your quest finished? Give him back to me!*

Even in his dream, Corran's grief over his brother's absence and fear for Rigan's safety made him bold enough to defy even an Elder God.

"You have all that you require. Remember what binds you togeth-

er." On that cryptic note, Eshtamon's presence vanished. Corran woke, sweating and shaking.

Was that real, or just my imagination? What type of bond? That we're brothers? That we swore our souls to him? Why can't he say what he means?

Corran felt torn between hoping the dream had been an actual communication from Eshtamon, and hoping it was merely his grief and fear taking form. He muttered a curse, pushed his blankets aside, and got up, doubting he would get back to sleep this night. Since he was still in the clothes he had worn all day, Corran took his bedside lantern and padded out to the kitchen, expecting to find it deserted.

Instead, he found Elinor sitting at the table, hunched over a cup of tea, in a room lit only by the banked embers of the fireplace.

"Mind if I join you?" he asked when she startled at his entrance.

"I'm not much company, but sure—have a seat." Elinor gestured to the chair beside her. Corran grabbed a cup. "Better you than our friend the ghost."

"Have you seen him lately?"

Elinor shook her head. "No, but he moves the pens around if I leave the desk in the library. Like he's tidying up after me."

Corran reached for the teapot. "Do I need to make more?"

She shook her head. "There's plenty. Have some. It's a soothing blend, but I'm not sure it can help tonight."

Corran pulled up a chair and poured himself a cup. He stared into the amber liquid for a long time, content to sit in silence.

"I can't imagine what this is like for you," Elinor said after a long pause. "You've lost so much recently."

Corran's lips twitched into a wan smile. "And you haven't? We've all lost everything—that's why we're out here."

Elinor looked up, eyes puffy and red-rimmed with grief. "We've lost our homes and our professions—at least, as far as the Guilds are concerned. Calfon and the others left family behind, but as far as we know, they're still alive. You and Rigan lost Kell and the shop, your home—that's a lot."

Corran ducked his head, not wanting to meet her gaze. "I know Rigan cares about you," he replied, dodging her observation.

She set a hand on his forearm. "Thank you. I care about him, too. It's been about the only good thing, you know? I ran away—with Parah's blessing—when the talk about me being a witch started. And I had nothing to do with what happened, but no one would have believed me. They just wanted someone to burn."

Corran remembered how upset Rigan had been when he had gone to the pigment and dye shop where Elinor had worked, only to find out she had fled in the night. "I couldn't believe it when you and Rigan and the hunters turned up at the witch house Below," Elinor said with a sad smile. "I never thought I'd see any of you again."

"You never did say how you and Polly ended up sharing a house down there."

Elinor chuckled. "We ran away separately. Polly had a bit of trouble at the inn and was afraid someone had seen—she ran away after some men came asking questions and went Below. Then I ran, and I was wandering, still trying to figure out what I was going to do, and spotted a friendly face."

"Polly's 'bit of trouble'—I'm pretty sure we buried the bastard," Corran said. "Kell told us he'd been paid extra for a curse, but I think he made that up."

"Thank you." They looked up to see Polly in the doorway. She had a robe pulled around her nightdress, and her hair was mussed. "I guess I'm not the only one who couldn't sleep."

"There's plenty of tea," Corran said, pulling out a seat for Polly to join them.

Polly settled into the chair and closed her eyes as she sniffed the tea's fragrance. Corran thought she looked young and haggard. "I keep thinking that if monsters can get out, Rigan and the others should be able to, also." She sighed. "Trent and Mir have been especially kind to me—Rigan too, of course—but Trent's gone out of his way to teach me to use the weapons, and he doesn't mind being my hunting partner. I don't want anything to happen to them."

"Aiden's not sleeping either," Elinor said. "His lantern was lit when I came down the hallway—I could see the light under the door."

Corran debated whether to tell them about his dream and decided against it. He would share the information with Aiden, though he was still unsure whether it was a true vision or merely an overstressed imagination. "If there's a way to get them home, we'll find it," Corran vowed, hoping with all his heart that was true.

"Where's everyone else?" Elinor asked. "Are they up, too?"

"Calfon's on watch," Corran replied. "Ross is sleeping. It'll be his turn next."

"You think there are more bounty hunters out there?" Elinor finished her tea in a swallow.

"Pretty sure of it," he said. "Guards, too. And that damned Jorgeson. We'd have to leave Ravenwood to be completely free, and even then, within the kingdom people talk."

"We've outrun soldiers a couple of times," Polly volunteered. "Fought off some bounty hunters, too."

"If there are more monsters, does that mean more blood magic that has to be paid for—more of a Cull needed?" Elinor asked.

"I don't know. If so, that brings us back to the Balance—and the Rifts," Corran said, rubbing a hand over his eyes.

When most people in Darkhurst spoke of the Balance, it was in the sense of a cosmic tit-for-tat, good and evil balancing each other out. The reality, Corran and the others had learned, was far less appealing.

"Aiden said he was looking into the old histories to see if anyone knew what was on the other side of a Rift," Elinor said.

"We didn't even know there *were* bloody Rifts until lately," Polly muttered. "But if they're where the monsters come from, then they must open and close a lot."

"The trick is being able to get a message to Rigan and the others so they'll come to the right opening," Corran replied. "Otherwise, they could get out of the Rift and find themselves anywhere in the kingdom —or beyond." He thought of what Eshtamon had said in his dream and stood. "I'm going to check in on Aiden, and then see if I can finally get to sleep." Corran laid a hand on Elinor's shoulder. "Don't stay up all night. That won't help anyone."

Corran knocked on the door to the room Aiden had claimed as his library. He heard a tired grunt in response and stepped inside. Aiden sat at a table with books and manuscripts piled around him. His hair was wild, as if he had been running his hands through it, and he had a day's growth of beard. A glass of whiskey sat beside his books.

"I see you're still up," Aiden greeted him.

"Couldn't sleep."

"Neither could I." Aiden rubbed his eyes and stretched, but he looked worn and worried. "It's slow going," he added, with a sweep of his hand to indicate the manuscripts. "And I hate small lettering. Damned hard on the eyes."

"Found anything?"

Aiden shrugged. "Witches don't like to say things straightfor-wardly. I guess it's a carryover from being persecuted—if you speak in code and write in riddles, you can deny what something means, and no one can prove you wrong. Damn them."

The healer stood and stretched again, yielding a few loud pops from his spine. He took a sip of whiskey and sighed. "I get the feeling that investigating the Balance—and hence, the Rifts—wasn't a popular or safe field of study. Thank the gods witches are curious by nature and don't listen well. So there are bits and pieces spread through a lot of books, but not all in one place. I have to follow references one book makes to another and put it together for myself."

"Do you think they're still alive?" It hurt Corran to ask, but the question weighed on him to the point where he could barely think clearly.

"Honestly? I don't know. I haven't found any references to people going in and coming out again. What's here stems from people who got a look inside when a Rift opened near them, right before the monsters came through."

"What did they see?" Corran set aside Aiden's disclaimer to process later when he had the luxury of falling apart in private.

"That's where the texts diverge wildly. Some witnesses say the realm inside looked shadowed, with all the colors muted like at twilight. And others say the opposite, that they could see lights and auras and some really strange shit. I don't know what to believe." He paced. "I've got a theory that the people who saw the muted colors might not have been witches, and the ones who saw auras had magic."

"Sounds possible."

"I think I've found some hints on how to open a Rift, although it's complicated magic. I've got to study it more, or the results could be really, really bad." Aiden ran a hand over the stubble on his chin, as if suddenly noticing that he needed a shave. "That might not be the hard part. Other than one legend about a hero making his way through the land of the living, dead, and undead—inside the Rift, by the way, was the land of the undead—there's no map or description of what's on the other side. In addition to the monsters, of course. So how do we know that if we open a Rift, Rigan and the others would be anywhere close or know about it beforehand? We don't want to hold the Rift open long —and it will take enough magic that we couldn't even if there wasn't the danger of setting all sorts of monsters loose."

"I might have an idea about that," Corran said, still leaning against the wall by the door. "I had a dream tonight," he blurted, changing his mind about keeping it to himself. "Eshtamon was in it."

Aiden looked up, fixing him with an intent stare. "Tell me."

Corran recounted his dream, trying to repeat the words the Elder God had spoken as closely as possible. "So if we could figure out what he meant by our 'bond,' maybe we could use that to pull Rigan and the others through."

Aiden nodded. "Not only that, but if the bond is that strong, it might work as a beacon, calling to Rigan so that he's in the right place at the right time." He looked energized, newly animated by the information. Aiden pushed aside the books he had been studying and went to his shelves, plucking new volumes and scrolls and setting them on the table. "I need to look at this more closely. Come back in a few candlemarks. I'll know more then—I hope."

Instead of going back to his room—too empty without Rigan— Corran wandered. The hidden, underground floor of the monastery was surprisingly large. He wondered how the monks had used the area, back before they were forced from their homes when the worship of the Elder Gods fell out of favor, and the king seized their lands. Perhaps the hunters weren't the first fugitives to seek refuge in these secret rooms. The monks left little but their furniture and some books behind, so Corran would never know for sure.

His mind raced, and while his body ached for rest, Corran knew he would end up tossing and turning if he tried to sleep before exhaustion gave him no alternative. He kept coming back to Eshtamon's words—and his insistence that the "bond" would bring Rigan home if they could only figure things out.

"There's the bond of being brothers," Corran reasoned aloud, since no one else was around. "That's both blood and emotions, growing up together. We're close—we've had to be, losing Mama and Papa so early." Corran had seen other families; he knew that many siblings did not get along. He'd always counted it a blessing that he, Rigan, and Kell worked together so well and lived in close quarters with relatively few spats. *Sure, we've argued. Taken a few swings at each other, too. But some brothers can't stand each other. At the end of it, we've always stuck together.*

"We're both undertakers, of course, since we're family. But I guess it's a bond of sorts, what with the Guild and the grave magic," he continued as he paced.

Magic. We both have grave magic because it comes down through the families of undertakers. But what about Mama's Wanderer blood? Rigan got her power, and I didn't, but we share the same mother. The Wanderer woman who found me in the city seemed to be able to tell we had a relation. And what did Rigan tell me the Wanderer he met told him?

"Blood calls to blood."

Corran raced back to Aiden's room and found the healer still staring blearily at his manuscripts. "I think I've got something," Corran said excitedly. He recapped what he had been thinking, and as he talked, Aiden grew more focused and alert.

"Eshtamon called us his champions," Corran said. "We swore our souls to him for vengeance. And the legends say that when Ardevan cursed the Wanderers to be forever reviled and hated, Eshtamon granted them his favor and a measure of protection. So what if the 'bond' isn't just one kind, but bond upon bond? Brother and Wanderer blood and grave magic and hunter—plus the vow to Eshtamon that seems to be larger than life."

"I think you're right," Aiden replied, nodding. "Your vow to an Elder God could transcend life and death—and everything in between. I don't know why Eshtamon can't simply pluck them out of wherever they are and bring them back, but maybe there are rules, even for gods."

"Or maybe it's a test," Corran said. "To see if we're worthy of his favor."

Aiden snorted. "I think you've already proven your worth. But that's my opinion. No, I think your bonds with Rigan might be exactly the beacon we need to call him to where we're going to open a Rift—assuming we can figure out how to do that."

"Is there some way I can use the bond to communicate with him?" Corran asked. Grief and worry tore at him.

"Maybe," Aiden replied. "Gods, you're giving me a series of impossible tasks! If it's possible, it would probably be through dreams. That seems to be the time when your mind is the most open. There are plenty of stories of people dreaming about a loved one far away and seeing something they're doing or warning them of danger. So it certainly wouldn't be unheard of." He scratched the stubble on his chin. "The trick is, doing it on purpose. In the stories I've heard, it's something that just sort of happens. Like my foresight—I can't control it."

He sighed. "All right, we've got a task for tomorrow. But I've reached the point—between the small handwriting on those manuscripts and the whiskey and how late it is—that I can't think anymore. So I'm going to try to sleep. You should, too. Then you and Elinor and I will start looking through books again tomorrow."

"Thank you," Corran replied. "I don't know—"

Aiden laid a hand on his shoulder. "We'll figure this out. I'll do everything I can to get them home safely."

Corran nodded, unable to say anything as his throat tightened. Both men knew that Aiden's promise depended on many things that might be far outside their power to control.

CHAPTER FIFTEEN

"THIS ISN'T THE city. You can't just kill people to get what you want." Viktyr Helton weathered Hant Jorgeson's glare and did not flinch.

"I give the orders," Jorgeson growled.

"I'm responsible for the lives of my soldiers, sir," Helton replied evenly. "And out here, things work differently."

Jorgeson swept the papers from the corner of his desk. "Out here, things don't seem to work at all, from what I can see."

He had to grudgingly admire the fact that Helton stood his ground.

"With all due respect, sir, our mission from the Crown Prince was to assist you in hunting the fugitives and keeping peace in the farmlands. I can assure you that burning out their crops to force them to give you information will do neither." He stood ramrod straight, jaw set to endure Jorgeson's anger.

"I've found that people become more reasonable when they understand the consequences of their actions," Jorgeson replied.

"In my experience, sir, I've learned that people who have nothing to lose will spite you to their dying breath."

Jorgeson paced from corner to corner in his office. "We've been out here for months! We know someone is killing the monsters, but no one seems to ever see anything. More than once, when your soldiers or my bounty hunters thought they caught the outlaws' trail, the villagers found a way to block their path or delay them."

"The hunters mostly work at night, m'lord. If the villagers fear that monsters are about, they won't be out in their fields and forests after dark."

"Do you deny that they've blocked us from going after the fugitives?" Jorgeson's fists clenched at his sides. If it were entirely up to him, he'd have the defiant young captain hauled away in chains. But Helton was both Crown Prince Aliyev's gift and his operative. Aliyev had made it clear that the soldiers and witches he provided were on loan, not Jorgeson's to do with as he saw fit. And always, behind everything, lay the threat that Jorgeson's time was running out.

"No, m'lord—but that is suspicion, not something we can prove. And if the hunters are offering the villagers protection against the monsters, it will be difficult to get them to turn against the outlaws."

Jorgeson's fist came down hard on the wooden desk. "That's why I said to burn their fields. Take hostages. Do something!"

A tic twitched at the corner of Helton's jaw. "M'lord," he said in a reasonable voice. "Our guards and the other patrols of the Crown Prince are vastly outnumbered, should the farmers choose to rise up against us. If our men at least made a pretense of eliminating the monsters, we might gain some favor and supporters—who then might provide information."

"What of the bounty? That's enough gold to let a man live quite well for the rest of his days. Surely one of these farmers would grab the chance to rise from squalor."

"Gold does not mean as much to some people, m'lord," Helton replied. "And if they perceive the hunters as saviors, protecting their families and livelihoods, they might consider that more precious than gold."

"Fools," Jorgeson snarled. "If we can't buy their cooperation or frighten them into it, how are we supposed to get what we want?" He paced the room, wishing he had an outlet for his rage. Helton remained unruffled, though Jorgeson felt certain he saw a flicker of judgment in the other man's eyes.

"We set traps, perhaps," Helton replied. "Cage up a couple of monsters for our use, and then let them out in a place of our choosing. Let it be known that there's a problem. Tempt the hunters into coming to save the day."

"Perhaps," Jorgeson said, unwilling to yield ground.

"Ideally, if we knew when the monsters would show up and where, we could be waiting to catch the hunters, but that's impossible. Those things come and go at the whim of the gods."

Jorgeson knew better, but he dared not say so. Only a few among the higher echelon knew that some of the monsters were called and controlled by magic, wielded for vengeance and profit against enemies or their proxies, sating the Cull. Blackholt's death removed one of the blood witches summoning monsters, but Jorgeson knew that Aliyev and perhaps even some of the other Merchant Princes had their mages who worked death magic that required the Balance, like the two useless blood witches Aliyev had sent into the countryside with Jorgeson.

"If the hunters can hear of monsters, so can you. Get your men in the field and find out where the creatures are, and then wait for the hunters and attack when they arrive," Jorgeson ordered.

Helton's face gave away none of his thoughts, but Jorgeson saw the man square his shoulders and stiffen his spine. "As you wish, m'lord."

———

JORGESON WALKED TO the rundown shack and forced down his fear. Aliyev had given him two blood witches of middling power whose magic, as far as Jorgeson could tell, had little practical application.

The shack had been a compromise. Jorgeson did not want to have the witches living under his roof, but he needed to have them close by, somewhere he could access their abilities and keep an eye on them. *Perhaps Aliyev wished to be rid of them, as well as me. He's given me broken tools and expects me to do a job with them.*

Amulets of bone and hair hung on leather straps from rusted nails around the doorframe. Runes carved into the wood and painted on with blood served notice that unexpected visitors were unwelcome. Freshly turned dirt mounds around the yard signaled that those who entered often did not return. Once he got within a dozen paces of the shack, the air felt oppressive, and a sense of dread slithered up his spine. *Theater, that's all it is. They've probably worked some kind of spell to make people uneasy, scare them off. Nothing but a street performer's tricks,* Jorgeson thought.

He was not afraid. *Aliyev gave me these witches. They're in this just as deep as I am now. They might spy on me, but if I fail, they go down with me. And I'll make sure they never forget that.*

Jorgeson did not bother knocking. He did, however, call out to announce himself. Surprising a witch was dangerous. He strode into the shack, resisting the impulse to wrinkle his nose. The cabin reeked of old blood, tanned hides, and an unpleasant mixture of alchemist potions.

"What have you got for me?" he demanded.

The two witches looked up from the mixture they were concocting. Aliyev had told Jorgeson their names, but Jorgeson knew that witches generally went by an alias, something about keeping enemies from using the "power of their true name" against them. Their witch names were pretentious and ominous, and Jorgeson couldn't be bothered to remember them.

He thought of the thin, twitchy one as "Spider" and the stocky, dark-haired man as "Roach." It amused him to see the dislike of his nicknames whenever he addressed them, but that couldn't possibly match his distaste for them and their infernal magic. They were stuck with each other, and he did not intend to let them forget it.

"We've been scrying," Spider said. He pointed to the wide, shallow bowl of liquid on the table between him and Roach. "Searching for your missing hunters."

"Since your neck is as much on the block as mine over this, I'd suggest you consider them to be 'our' missing fugitives," Jorgeson snapped.

"As you wish, m'lord," Spider said with an unctuous grace that did not fool Jorgeson. "We believe they are being shielded. Their trail is very difficult to trace."

"If it were easy, I'd have a pack of dogs and be done with it," Jorgeson fumed. "What have you found?"

"We catch glimmers of them, m'lord," Roach replied. "Like catching a glimpse of someone out of the corner of your eye. But as soon as we try to fix their location, they vanish."

"How is that possible?"

"We know two of them are witches," Spider said. "They've probably made amulets for the others to hide them."

"What of the witches? Can you track them?"

"Not to a specific location. We've caught the echo of their magic, and we recognize the signature of their power, but by the time we pick something up, it's there and gone."

"You're both useless!" Jorgeson raged. "What *can* you do?"

"I can tell you that witches in Sarolinia—who aren't as good at shielding—have been summoning monsters here in Ravenwood," Spider said with a sly smile. "I don't think those witches expect anyone to be looking for them. Twice now within a week, they've opened a Rift inside our border."

"How can you be certain the magic is coming from Sarolinia?"

"They aren't making any attempt to hide," Roach answered. "We're far from the city, and neither the Crown Prince nor the Merchant Princes would have cause to keep witches out here in the country under normal circumstances. Who else would notice, or realize what they were seeing if they did pick up on the surge?"

"What reason would Sarolinia have to conjure monsters in Ravenwood?" Jorgeson said. But as soon as the words passed his lips, possibilities came to mind. After Machison's debacle with the trade agreement, Ravenwood's competitors within the League no doubt saw them as weakened, compromised, easy prey. Sarolinia had been quick to benefit from the downfall of its northern neighbor, Kasten. *Perhaps they've decided not to wait for fate and step in and benefit from hastening Ravenwood's disgrace.*

"I would think that to be obvious, m'lord," Spider said with an ingratiating smile that looked to Jorgeson more like a cat toying with a mouse it intended to eat. "They're meddling, for their own ends."

"Can you stop them?"

"Not without revealing we've noticed what they're doing." Roach wiped his hands on his work robe. "We'd lose our ability to watch them without them being aware."

Jorgeson swore under his breath. "Can you conjure monsters across their border? Can you summon monsters at all?"

Spider's expression grew hard and calculating. "No, m'lord. As you knew when we were provided to you. The Crown Prince wishes to reserve that power to his own blood witches."

"I want to trap the hunters," Jorgeson growled. "They show up where monsters appear. Can you do something that creates a similar effect?"

Roach looked intrigued by the suggestion. "We can work on it," he said, frowning as he thought. "We can open Rifts; but we aren't permitted to call monsters."

"Out here, I'm your authority, and our task is to do what the Crown Prince requires," Jorgeson replied. "I give you permission to call monsters if that is what it will take to keep Sarolinia at bay."

"And you will explain this if the Crown Prince objects?" Roach asked, his eyes narrowing.

"Gods, yes! Just find me those damn outlaws!"

"There is another... possibility." They turned to look at Spider. "When we work blood magic near where a Rift opens, I've sensed a... presence... like a voice in the distance."

Roach nodded. "I've felt it too, but I wasn't sure it was real."

A cunning expression stole over Spider's hard-featured face. "Oh, I believe it's real. The question is, have we found a more powerful sort of monster, or might we have touched the god of chaos, Colduraan, himself?"

"I don't believe in the gods," Jorgeson said with a snort. "But if this thing you sense is a new monster, I want to know all about it.

Perhaps we've only seen the kinds closest to the 'doorway' when it opens, and there might be other creatures that would better suit our purposes." He glanced from one witch to the other. "Find out what you can, and report back to me."

Spider nodded. "In the meantime, we've created some of the elixir you requested." He reached over to the table behind him and selected a small vial of blue liquid. "This will force a man to tell you the truth. Mind that you use it carefully; it could permanently damage the person who takes it. Forcing the mind never ends well."

"How much does it require?"

"That should be enough to dose three full-grown men. The ingredients are difficult to find and very expensive, so use it carefully—I can't guarantee that we can make more," Spider cautioned.

"I'll use it as I see fit," Jorgeson snapped. "If you can't tell me more about the hunters, what can you report about Sarolinia's other dealings?"

"We scry their coastline every day, but we've seen no ships beyond what is to be expected from League trade. The Crown Prince is tightly shielded; we can't pick up anything from him or his witch—we've tried." Roach's expression practically dared Jorgeson to challenge his assertion.

"Useless," Jorgeson muttered.

"There is one thing," Spider added. "We've picked up traces of magic along the river. Not the same as the glimpses we've seen of the hunters. Different power signature—very different. We mapped where we've sensed the disturbances, and it's always up and down the waterways. Hard to get a fix on it; we think they're using deflection charms, but not particularly good ones."

"Along the river?" Jorgeson echoed. "Could they be boats?"

Roach nodded. "That's our thought. But why those boats would need to deflect magic—or even expect to do so—escapes me."

"Can you tell me anything else about these traces along the river?"

"They only happen at night, and not every night," Roach said. "They don't come all the way up to the headwaters, just move from the mouth of the river through the widest section and back again. And always after midnight."

Smugglers, thieves, pirates, or all three, Jorgeson mused. *Most likely from Sarolinia. Aliyev wanted me to keep an eye on them. This might help me.*

Jorgeson fixed both witches with a glare. "I want everything you can find out about those flickers you're picking up along the river. See if you can find a pattern of the days and times they come, or if you can map their stops. Even better, figure out where they come from. And find those bloody hunters!"

With that, he turned and strode from the cabin, letting the rickety wooden door slam behind him.

Jorgeson slowed his pace before he reached the abandoned house on the other side of the small yard from the witches' shack. He preferred to squat in empty buildings rather than take a room at the inn, both to save on scarce coin and to avoid notice. Often enough, he disguised himself and went into one town or another, nursing a drink in the pub, listening to the locals' gossip, hoping to pick up word about the fugitive hunters. So far, he had overheard little of any use, and nothing that led him to his quarry.

Spider and Roach were like dull knives when he needed a razor-sharp sword. He cursed again, damning Aliyev for sending him on this quest with the promise of redeeming himself only to undercut him at every turn.

It's never been about "redemption." Just a stay of execution. He's given me enough rope to hang myself.

The ramshackle house had stood empty long enough that every night required chasing away the mice and rats which had claimed it as their own. It suited his purposes, with a stable for his guards and their horses, the shack for his witches—he could not bring himself to think of them as "mages" given their limited talents—and a place he could be alone.

Jorgeson walked into the house and lit the lanterns. They made it easier to see the shabby conditions which were now his lot. He only used the one room with the fireplace, not trusting the overhead beams or the wood of the stairs to support him on the second floor. He had no use for the other downstairs room, except to have one guard at all times keeping watch there, out of his sight.

He'd had the guards sweep out the two rooms when they first arrived. Too much damage had been done to make the old place truly livable, but at least it was no longer disgusting. Jorgeson's scant possessions gave him a faint sense of familiarity. His trunk held clothing and essentials and doubled as a chair. The previous owner had left behind a wobbly, scarred table which served for eating and as a desk. The fireplace worked without smoking up too badly, and he had a few tin pots, which sufficed for cooking.

Jorgeson withdrew a flask from beneath his jacket and took a long drink. He had little more to show for the past three months than he'd had when he started this misbegotten quest, and Aliyev's patience would not be limitless. While he could not earn full absolution by succeeding, he would cement his ignominy by failure. Not that there was anyone left to care.

He glanced at the fireplace and sniffed, trying to guess what might be for supper. The guards had the task of hunting small game for their dinner and bartering, buying, or stealing vegetables to go with it. Options were limited by knowledge and ingredients, leaving a choice of roast or stew. When Jorgeson visited the town to canvass the pubs, one soldier always went along to purchase bread, cheese, whiskey, and ale. Rations weren't plentiful, but he had survived on worse during campaigns. And it far surpassed the fare at the prison.

There must be a way to find the Valmondes, he mused.

Later that night, Jorgeson slipped out to The Plow and Ox, a pub on the side of the main road by the river ports. He looked the part of a dockhand or laborer, not rough enough to cause concern, but no one anyone would notice.

"Ale," he replied when the bartender asked. He glanced up when the tankard was put in front of him.

"I'm looking for work," Jorgeson said. "Know if they need anyone down on the river?"

The bartender shrugged. "No idea. Best way to find out is to wander down there, see who needs a hand with the cargo."

"Maybe I'll do that," Jorgeson replied. He sipped his ale and focused his attention on the conversations around him as the bar began to fill with patrons. The rural accent irritated him, and the ale tasted flat and watered. He had grown used to the best Ravenwood had to offer in his capacity serving Machison, but that life was gone forever.

"... they're together—until her husband finds out."

"... won't say it's him, but we all know who the father is."

"... stole those sheep. Of course, he won't admit it, but they were in his pen."

The local gossip bored him as much as the people themselves. He finished nursing his ale and reached for coin to pay the bartender.

"Should be more coming in tonight, if you liked that. I can guarantee a good price. Cut out the extra costs, if you know what I mean."

Jorgeson didn't dare turn to see the speaker. Two men stood behind him, talking in low tones, sure the hubbub around them drowned out their voices. He stilled, listening intently, and hoped he didn't look like he was eavesdropping. He had much more experience as an assassin than as a spy.

"You bring it up the river; I'll have a buyer for you, no questions asked."

"That's what I like to hear."

The men moved on, and Jorgeson thought he had lost them until he saw two strangers go to the other end of the bar to order drinks. He managed to get a look at them, memorizing their faces. Neither stood out in the crowd, though one of the men looked rougher than the other. Jorgeson guessed he was the seller, and the slightly better dressed, somewhat more polished man was the buyer.

When it appeared that the two men intended to stay for a while, Jorgeson paid his tab and slipped out. He rode toward the river, unsurprised to find few people traveling as the evening wore on. Though he had left the guards back at his base, Jorgeson had no fear of cutpurses. He carried enough weapons beneath his cloak to handle ruffians, and he brimmed with frustration, welcoming a fight.

The smell of the docks reached him before he could see the river, and he tied his horse behind a row of shops closed for the evening. Then he headed toward the waterfront. An empty wagon sat with a driver and a horse, waiting for someone. Down by the water, several men stood together, smoking pipes and talking. Jorgeson headed their way.

"Nice night," he said as he approached them. "Mind if I join you?"

Grunts and shrugs answered, but the men yielded a few steps to open their circle. The smoke of their tobacco hung heavy in the air, and Jorgeson withdrew his pipe and filled it, lighting up in camaraderie.

"You're new." The speaker stood to Jorgeson's left, a red-haired, broad-shouldered man who looked like he had spent a lifetime of heavy labor. The carefully neutral tone provided neither invitation nor provocation.

"Heard there might be work." Jorgeson took a long drag on his pipe.

"Maybe," one of the men agreed, a short, thick-set man to Jorgeson's right. "Never know until it happens. Ain't no tellin' 'til the boats show up, if they're gonna show."

They stood and smoked in companionable silence. Jorgeson hung back, listening to the others trade news about sick cows and children with fevers, impugn the questionable honor of a few of the village women, and speculate about when it might rain. The conversation reminded him of his time in the king's army, when men made small talk because boredom became more uncomfortable than finding something to gossip about.

"Looks like we're getting lucky tonight, boys." The red-haired man said, pointing toward the dark waters of the riverside docks.

Jorgeson saw the shuttered lanterns of several small ships drawing closer. He followed the others down to the waterfront and joined in when ropes were thrown to haul the ships to the docks.

The red-haired man moved to speak with a tall man in a dark coat who climbed ashore from the first of the boats to dock. "You need help? I've got men here if you can pay." A few moments later, the negotiating finished and the leader of the dockhands whistled for his crew to get to work.

Jorgeson took his place in a line as crates were handed off the ships and passed from man to man into the wagon. He strained in the moonlight to make out any of the markings on the boxes.

The suspicion that formed back in the pub grew as he watched the unloading process. *Why bring small ships upriver in the middle of the night? Look how impatient the boat captains are to get unloaded— they're worried about staying too long. And the marks on the crates have been burned or altered. They're smuggling. But what sort of goods? And who's behind it?*

He could hear the red-haired man talking with one of the ship captains. The captain had an accent that Jorgeson had heard before. *Sarolinian. I'm sure of it.*

When the ship captain walked away, a stocky man with a worried look on his face jogged up. "Hey Boss, we found the bodies from that crew that said they were attacked—no idea who killed them," he told the red-haired man.

"Find out." The boss snapped. "Did the rest of the crew say anything else?"

"They said they saw lights in the cemetery above the harbor and figured someone was spying on them—maybe guards. Bunch of rough-looking guys jumped them, and killed several of their crew, but didn't chase after them when they ran away."

"I want to know who those men are, why they were there, and who they work for," the boss growled. "And then I want them dead."

Jorgeson melted back into the shadows. *Lights in a cemetery at night... rough-looking men—hunters. I'm sure of it. Maybe the Valmondes. Which means they've got to be based near here, or else they're just wandering around the kingdom, looking for haunts.*

He made certain that he held one of the final crates to be unloaded and walked it to the wagon, then hung back until the others left. While he wouldn't have minded a few extra coins—Aliyev's miserly stipend barely covered essentials—he knew the others would be busy collecting their pay. That bought him a few precious minutes to pry the lid off a box and look inside.

He caught his breath. Bolts of cloth and skeins of dyed yarn filled the box in the colors and patterns that were distinctive to Sarolinia.

"What do you think you're doing?" The driver came around the side of the cart, a big man with the squashed face of a brawler. "Stealing, are you? Got a way to deal with that." A knife appeared in his hand, glinting in the moonlight.

Jorgeson would have preferred to keep his presence unnoticed, but the wagon driver gave him no choice. He went on the offensive, attacking with the practiced moves of an experienced soldier, and had the driver down and his throat slit before the man knew what had happened. Jorgeson dragged the body into the bushes at the side of the road and paused as an idea struck him.

He peeled the cloak and hat off the wagon master's body and rolled the corpse farther from the road, then climbed into the driver's seat and waited.

"Everything loaded?" A man Jorgeson had not seen before climbed up to the seat beside him.

Jorgeson grunted and nodded his head, keeping his hat low on his face. "Where to?" He made his voice as deep and rough as he could, hoping he sounded like he had a cold. His ruse would only work if the stranger did not know the wagon driver well, and the destination was not the same every time. He had a knife ready in one hand in case of trouble.

The man muttered directions, and Jorgeson flicked the reins. His heart hammered in his chest, and he felt sweat on his back although the night was cool. Coming out alone to the pub was already risky. Going down to the docks even more so. And this? This was suicidal. But if he could get through it without discovery, he would have valuable information that might reveal more about the smugglers—and which would buy him more time from Aliyev.

His passenger said nothing during the ride. Jorgeson had a vague familiarity with the roads, but rarely had reason to travel this way. He noted landmarks without appearing too interested and wondered if the drop point changed with each shipment. That would certainly be safer, but more confusing. In his experience, people tended to be lazy and repeat what was familiar.

The stranger directed him to a large barn. The dark approach gave Jorgeson little confidence, but shadowy forms appeared out of the night and opened the doors for them, revealing a dimly lit interior.

Several men approached and began unloading. His passenger climbed down and went to talk with three men who Jorgeson guessed were the buyers. They were too far away for him to hear their conversation, but their dress and manner suggested that while they had the appearance of merchants, they had risen from rough beginnings.

Inside the city walls, the Guilds kept a tight grip on their merchants. Jorgeson did not doubt that a shadow trade existed of goods sold without the appropriate taxes and fees, obtained from dubious sources. But the penalties enforced and the vigilance of the guards kept its impact minimal.

Since he had been outside those walls, Jorgeson discovered a disdain for the Guilds and the city's authorities that surprised him in its bitterness and magnitude. That explained, in no small part, how the Valmondes and their hunter friends had been so successful in eluding capture. Now, Jorgeson felt certain he was witnessing some of that shadow trade in action, as smuggled goods from a neighboring city-state made their way through an inland port and into the hands of merchants he was sure had no Guild affiliation.

"Why don't you take the driver outside and pay him," one of the merchants said to the man who had accompanied Jorgeson.

"Come on," the stranger said. "No need for you to stay. We'll get the rest unloaded."

Jorgeson trailed the man, appearing unawares. When the knife flicked toward Jorgeson's throat, he grabbed the man's wrist, and within seconds pinned the man to the ground, his arm bent painfully behind, the knife digging against the pulse in his neck.

He took a kerchief from the man's pocket and shoved it into his mouth. Then he used the stranger's belt to tie his wrists behind his back. "You'll do as you're told, or I'll kill you," Jorgeson whispered, prodding him with his knife.

Jorgeson steered the man into the dark scrub of trees beyond the barn. He knew they had only minutes before someone noticed that his captive had not returned.

"I'm going to remove the gag, but my blade is against your throat. Scream and you die immediately. Answer my questions; you live longer. What's in the boxes?" he asked with a jab of the knife.

"Fabric. Lace. Spices. Tobacco. Whiskey," the man replied.

Jorgeson poked him again. "Where do the boxes come from?"

His prisoner glared at him but apparently did not consider the information to be worth his life. "Sarolinia. The smugglers get around the tariffs and taxes so the goods are cheaper."

This time, Jorgeson twisted the point of the knife in the muscles of the man's chest. "Spices aren't a Sarolinian export. You're leaving something out."

The prisoner cursed. "All right, all right. Some independent captains bring in cargo from ships that, uh, had problems at sea and needed to unload early."

"You mean, pirates."

"That's a nasty word."

Jorgeson pressed the knife against the man's throat.

"Yes. Yes! Pirates. They work with the smugglers to bring in cargo at low prices."

"Outside of the League treaties."

"Screw the League. What does it do except drive up costs and keep honest men from making a living?" The man kept his voice at a whisper, but Jorgeson could not mistake his bitterness. "Those treaties benefit no one but the city Guilds and the Merchant Princes."

Jorgeson held his tongue, knowing the penalty Kasten and the lesser League partners paid in the Cull. "What else?"

"Let me go. You can take my money. Please, don't kill me," the man begged.

"What else can you tell me about the smugglers?" Jorgeson made a shallow cut against the man's Adam's apple.

"There's no regular schedule to when the boats come—that's why the roustabouts stay near the harbor," the man said, babbling with fear. "When the boats do come, a runner heads out to a location one of the boat captains gives him—different each time—and meets a contact. That contact makes sure there are workers to unload and buyers ready to take the goods."

"Who are the smugglers working with in Ravenwood?" Jorgeson's patience was wearing thin.

"I don't know." Jorgeson dug the point deeper. The man grunted in pain and writhed against Jorgeson's hold. "I don't! I swear by Oj and Ren on my soul! I'm just the go-between. I get the goods from the port to the meeting point."

"How did they know I wasn't the regular driver?"

"They didn't."

"Then why—"

"We kill the driver. Can't leave witnesses."

"Tell me something so important I'll spare your life."

Jorgeson had the man pressed up against him, one arm across his chest, knife blade to his throat. He could feel the man's heaving breath and thudding heart, smell the panicked sweat and the odor of urine as the terrified man pissed himself.

"The smugglers must have a patron," the man said, his words tumbling out in a panic. "Their goods are quality. Someone's putting money into this."

"How long?"

"Months." Another jab. "Three months. At least, that's all I know about."

"How about in Ravenwood? How did this start?"

"I don't know. I don't!" the man squawked when the blade cut him again. "But the harbor master is never on duty when the smugglers come in, and the patrols don't come down the wharf like they usually do."

"Someone's paid them off?"

"Maybe," the man said. "Or someone in town is in on it."

This is bigger than a village scheme. Someone else has to be behind it, a minor noble, a big merchant, maybe even one of the Merchant Princes?

"Who lines up the buyers? Where do the goods go?"

"I don't—I only know what I overhear. I'm not part of it." The man was close to hyperventilating. "Whoever's at the top has some connections. The wagons go out to all the major trading villages on this side of Ravenwood. Probably turns quite a nice coin for whoever it is—the goods cost a third of what the Guilds charge."

"I want names!"

"And if I could, to save my life, don't you think I'd give them to you?"

"What about the Guilds?"

The man in his grip snorted. "Guilds? That's something for city folk. Out here? They take their fees and do nothing in return. We get by. People work their trades. Now and again, the Guilds demand money. Do they give us anything? Do they protect us from the monsters?" He turned and spat on the ground.

"No. They're leeches, the Guilds. That's why nobody minds the smugglers. Cheers for them, really. Cheating the cheaters. Putting one over on the high and mighty," he said, his voice dripping with contempt. "I'm proud of what I do. You can kill me if you like, doesn't change a thing."

"Proud of undercutting the League and undermining the Merchant Princes?" Jorgeson snapped.

"No. Proud of cheating the leeches that profit off us," the man tossed back.

"You have no idea—" Jorgeson began.

"The city takes everything we have," the man said. "Our crops, our grapes, our young people. And what do we get back? Whatever the trade agreements promise never makes it past the city walls. We're on our own out here; always have been. Can't fault a man for trying to do the best he can."

"No, I can't." Jorgeson drew the knife swift and clean. The man fell in a heap at his feet.

All the way home, the dead man's words haunted Jorgeson. *I know one truth. But did the man I kill speak another? It's different out here. The city is so far away. The Guilds dominate inside the walls, but out here, they're nothing, just another tax.*

He could hardly spare sympathy for the rural fools. The only way he would evade the noose and his commuted sentence was to satisfy Aliyev's orders. *Pity is a fool's game. And this is a contest I intend to win. If it's a fight to the death, I'll be the last one standing.*

CHAPTER SIXTEEN

"I'VE ALREADY GIVEN your smugglers protective amulets and taught them sigils to mark their boats. There's nothing else I can do." Nightshade bent to add a few clippings of belladonna to his basket of cuttings. A moan came from one of the scarecrows suspended from a wooden cross in the garden.

"Can't you shut those bloody things up?" Neven snapped.

Nightshade stood and eyed his garden decoration with artistic pride. "Now where would be the fun in that? It's rather like the howl of the wind. Sounds of nature."

As if on cue, chimes rang, a shimmering glissando. The bells hung off the arms and torso of a man impaled on a stake, ringing with every tremor of his body.

Neven eyed the abomination with disgust. "Aren't you burning magic keeping them alive?"

Nightshade shrugged. "I don't expect you to understand. Sometimes art is for its own sake. And before you ask, their pain counts toward the Cull."

"Someone's killing my smugglers—I want it stopped," Neven said, returning to the original conversation.

"I'm busy conjuring monsters to send Ravenwood scrambling,"

Nightshade said dismissively. "I don't have time or energy to waste on your petty thieves."

"Have a care how you speak to me."

Nightshade raised an eyebrow, then turned and looked up at the moaning wretch on the scarecrow's cross and back at Neven, leveling a threat without saying a word.

"Our trade agreement comes due with Morletta in a month," Neven said. "I've promised the Lord Mayor and our Merchant Princes that we'll support them."

"By 'support' you mean I'll send monsters into Morletta as well as Ravenwood, and work up some poisons and curses so your men can intimidate their counterparts into giving them the terms you want?"

"That's how this game is played," Neven said.

"Even with my... indulgences," Nightshade said with a gesture that took in the living "art" scattered throughout the garden and its fencing and decorations made from the bones of past victims, "I can't shore up the Balance indefinitely. Blood magic has a cost, and what you require of me sorely taxes that."

He moved to another garden bed and added foxglove and hemlock to his cuttings. "It's one thing drawing the power necessary to summon monsters nearby, within Sarolinia. But opening Rifts over a distance—like in Ravenwood and Morletta—requires much more magic. I can sense the strain on the energy. The Rifts are growing unstable. If they become erratic and begin to open and close on their own—or worse, if the fabric between our world and what lies beyond the Veil 'rips,' we will all suffer the consequences."

"Then make bloody sure that doesn't happen." Neven moved away from the moaning scarecrow, trying not to get closer to the shuddering man on the pike and his death bells. "Surely the Cull will compensate. I've never heard of Rifts opening by themselves."

"You're not the only one with a blood witch," Nightshade replied. His calm voice seemed at odds with his conviction that a misstep could bring a cataclysm upon them. "And none of you have a care about the amount of blood magic being worked. I've researched the old manuscripts. There's no precedent for this ongoing level of blood magic putting a strain on the Balance. If you're not careful, there won't be anyone left by the time the Cull is satisfied."

"I'm not going to pull back now because of some old wives' tales," Neven countered.

Nightshade shrugged and bent to snip off a few more flowers. "Have you ever heard of He Who Watches?"

"Is this another story told to frighten children?"

A cold, mocking smile touched Nightshade's lips. "Oh, I assure you, it's no idle tale. The Rifts we open to summon monsters lead to a realm different from our own, perhaps the place of the Elder Gods."

"Foolishness. The gods are nothing more than stories told to cow the gullible," Neven snapped.

"Some say that He Who Watches is a creature of Colduraan's, one of his Ancient Ones, a First Being. A practice creature, if you will, before the gods created animal and humans. Others say He Who Watches is Colduraan himself. Though I rather doubt that." Nightshade looked at Neven with an unreadable expression. "I hear his song in my dreams."

A few Death's Angel mushrooms went into his basket, along with yew and monkshood. Neven did not care to know what Nightshade intended to do with the plants; all were deadly poison. He knew that some were used to bring about a "waking death," locking the victims in their failing bodies while slowing their demise. Some of those unfortunates were posed like statuary around the garden, limbs contorted and frozen however Nightshade chose to "sculpt" them.

"Your dreams are your business," Neven retorted. "Spare me the sordid details."

"You also forget that some of my time—and magic—is spent repelling the attacks of my counterparts in Itara and Kasten—as well as Morletta—who would benefit should Sarolinia fail to increase its standing in the League."

"With Ravenwood's fulfillment of their agreement rocky, we're well on our way to taking their place in the rankings," Neven assured him. "And don't think too highly of yourself—my spies and assassins have their own plans in the other city-states to keep the rivals at bay."

"And so do your rivals," Nightshade replied with an indifferent shrug. "Or have you forgotten the warnings and sigils I've placed in your palace to deter their attacks?"

"Of course I haven't forgotten," Neven growled. "Although I'd appreciate it if you could do something to get those vile Wanderers out of Sarolinia for good."

"Anything I might do to the Wanderers will be a stopgap, at best. They've survived the curse of one Elder God by gaining the favor of another. If Ardevan himself couldn't wipe them out, who am I to think I can exterminate Eshtamon's favorites?"

"Lies and children's tales, all of it! They're wily thieves, with dirty magic, and they always seem to be present right before bad things happen."

An ironic smile crossed Nightshade's lips. "Perhaps that's because the bad things happen to those who raise their hand against the Wanderers. Actions have consequences, and with so much in play, you'd be best served by leaving the Wanderers alone."

"I'll be the judge of what best serves my interests." Neven did not fully dismiss Nightshade's caution, but he'd be damned if he intended to let the blood witch rattle his nerves. "Keep your focus on Ravenwood. I don't think it will take much to bring them to their knees, not with their trade agreements faltering."

Twilight set the garden in a deep blue half-light. Nightshade waved his hand, and tall torches flared to light the pathways. Neven could not suppress a shudder when he realized that the "torches" were corpses dipped in wax.

"Of course, my lord," Nightshade replied, as the shimmer of bells sent a chill down Neven's spine. "I live to serve."

———

BRICE TAGAR WAS waiting for Neven when he entered his study.

"News?" Neven snapped, annoyed at the surprise visit.

"Of sorts," his spymaster replied. "I've made enquiries with my sources. No one's heard anything officially—or unofficially—about credit being claimed for killing the smugglers. That supports your suspicion the hunters are to blame."

"Of course they're to blame! They brought down Machison, and now they're trying to undermine me."

"I doubt outlaw hunters have access to that kind of power—or information," Tagar soothed. "Perhaps they happened to run into each other by accident."

Neven snorted in disbelief. "That strains credulity."

"Maybe not," Tagar replied. "The bodies were found outside a cemetery overlooking the harbor. If the smugglers saw lanterns—"

"Do you believe me a fool?" Neven thundered. "There are no coincidences, only well-disguised conspiracies. Maybe the hunters being outlaws was simply an elaborate ruse by Aliyev. I've always suspected he despised Machison and Blackholt. They were never quite up to his standards. So he engineered some unconventional assassins, passed them off as hunters, and then spun the fiction of putting a price on their heads—and sent his chief buffoon of a disgraced head of security after them, ensuring they wouldn't be caught."

"I don't quite follow—"

Neven slapped his hand on the table. "It's obvious! Aliyev got rid of three failures and used them to give cover to his assassins for their real task—countering our efforts in Ravenwood."

Tagar hesitated, choosing his words carefully. "M'lord, I think you give Aliyev—and the hunters—too much credit. Machison and Blackholt were arrogant and dangerous. Half of the League sent assassins against them, all unsuccessfully."

"That's my point! The Lord Mayor and his pet blood witch ably defeated every assassin sent against them—professional killers—only to be destroyed by tradesmen-turned-hunters? It can't be so."

"Never underestimate what men can do when they are fighting for their survival," Tagar warned. "I assume the assassins prized escaping with their lives. From the boldness of the attack that brought down Machison and Blackholt, I suspect the hunters expected to die achieving their goal—and may have been surprised to escape. Even so, several of them were killed."

Neven waved his hand in dismissal. "Can't have checkmate without sacrificing a few pawns." He shook his head. "No, we've read this wrong. Those 'hunters' are shadowing our smugglers, perhaps even aware of our pirates. Probably reporting every move back to Aliyev. They've got at least two witches of their own—powerful enough to destroy Blackholt. They're a threat. I want them eliminated."

"My men are searching the countryside for them as we speak," Tagar assured him. "As are Aliyev's guards and Jorgeson's men."

"*Pfft.* Aliyev is making a pretense, and Jorgeson is incompetent."

"Perhaps," Tagar allowed. "But we are hampered by both distance and the need for our agents to remain hidden. They dare not operate openly without drawing notice, which would lead Aliyev directly back to you."

"Aliyev is too busy trying to salvage his precious agreement with Garenoth to notice."

Tagar shook his head. "Don't be so sure, my lord. Neither Aliyev nor King Rellan is as indifferent as they like to appear. Our spies report that Rellan has a keen eye for ledgers, and tracks the revenue of each city-state meticulously when his advisors report to him. Aliyev is shrewd. He may be focusing his attention on repairing the damage in Ravenwood, but I doubt very much he has lost sight of the larger goal."

Neven paced. "Kadar is finally on board with us, enthusiastic about using the smugglers to undercut the rest of the League and pad his pockets. If word reaches him about the murders—"

"Smuggling is a risky business," Tagar replied. "Bad things happen to bad men. I sincerely doubt Merchant Prince Kadar worries about the personal safety of the smugglers, only about the results to be gained. If he gets those results, he'll be happy—even if it requires a mound of bodies."

Neven warred with himself, torn between his fears and Tagar's reassurances. Nightshade's smug comments did nothing to assuage his concerns. "Need I remind you of the stakes? Sarolinia has always been one of the most unappreciated of the city-states. With Kasten partitioned, we are now among the least powerful of the League partners. We *must* rise. This is our chance, with Ravenwood in chaos and

Garenoth open to advances for the first time in a decade. We can't allow anything to take our eyes off the prize."

All his life, Neven chafed at Sarolinia's poor showing in the League rankings. While Garenoth and Ravenwood took the accolades, the rest of the city-states fought each other for the leavings, and those not blessed with either exceptional resources or the luck to have fore-bears who were canny and ruthless enough to carve out a legacy got left behind. *No more*, he vowed. *I intend to see Sarolinia rise, usher in a golden age, prove those of us right who dared believe that there was more to us than has been acknowledged. This is our time, our chance, and I will be damned if I let some upstart hunters compromise our best hope for ascendancy.*

———

"I'd appreciate a warning, that's all." Ambassador Lorenz cradled his injured arm in a sling, with a bulky bandage covering the knife wound left by an assassin. "I understand the risk of being your proxy—it comes with the job. But at least when I know you're about to make someone angry, I can keep my guards closer at hand."

"These days, it's almost impossible to do anything without annoying someone," Neven said. "We haven't begun the new trade negotiations with Morletta. Itara would probably love to undercut those, as would Kasten. I fear you may always need your guards close by. These are dangerous times."

"That appears to be true, more's the pity. I understand Morletta is also up to renegotiate its terms with Ostero, so their ambassador will be stressed and distracted. I plan to use that to our benefit," Lorenz added and wiped his mouth with his napkin. "Itara might have designs on undercutting our agreement with Morletta, but it needs to see to its own house. The Arlan ambassador told me his Crown Prince is eager to reduce Morletta's trade with them in favor of Torquonia. After all, their exports are similar, and for the past two seasons, Torquonia's quality has been better."

"Interesting."

"I'd consider it to be gossip, even with the Arlan ambassador's comment, but there's been a proxy strike against the Torquonian ambassador to Arlan. I read that as Morletta sending a warning that they won't take a reduction in their terms quietly."

Politics in the Bakaran League was a deadly game of chess. The king, nobility, Crown Princes and Merchant Princes were rarely the victims of direct attacks unless the stakes were unusually high. Instead, assassins sent "messages" in strikes against the proxies of those powerful men, varying in their severity depending on the urgency of the issue. Those determined to advance their status accepted the risk as a necessary evil.

"What do you hear of the League Council?" Neven asked.

Lorenz leaned back in his chair and sipped his whiskey. "You understand, my lord, that anything I hear about the Council is second-hand at best. I have no dealings with them directly."

"People talk."

Lorenz chuckled. "Oh, yes they do. Much of the gossip seems to be centered on the repercussions of the Ravenwood situation. Speculation on what King Rellan thinks of Crown Prince Aliyev and to what degree he holds Aliyev responsible. Guesses about whether Aliyev will be able to meet the terms of agreement given the chaos—bets are against him—and keep his position. The odds are even on that."

The ambassador paused to think. "There's the usual personal tidbits —whose wife might be sleeping with someone else, who may have fathered a bastard, who's gambling far too much and likely to squander his fortune."

"What do you hear from the other city-states about hunters, monsters, and Wanderers?"

Lorenz gave him a look as if he were trying to guess Neven's reasons for asking. "Not much," he replied. "Those are everyone's dirty little secrets. We've all got to deal with them, but it's like lice or the clap—no one wants to admit to having them." He paused. "After what happened in Kasten, everyone is cautious. I personally doubt the hunters could have caused that much chaos, to make the city-state to teeter on the brink of defaulting on its agreements. Seems like an easy way to pass the blame. But everyone's wary, and I think they've cracked down more on the hunters—or at least they claim to."

"And the rest?"

"Monsters are always with us. It does seem as if they've been a bigger problem lately in Morletta and Itara, though that might be exaggerated in the reporting. As for the Wanderers—they also never go away. Always causing problems, can't seem to get rid of them. Like rats, only harder to poison."

Neven nodded. "Anything else?"

"One thing that everyone's complained about... the Guilds... that they're getting above themselves, demanding too much, trying to meddle in negotiations when agreements come due. The Merchant Princes in Ravenwood seem to be having the most problems, but they're not the only ones. No good can come of it."

Neven agreed wholeheartedly, though he could never say so publicly. Given the way the city-states organized, the Guilds posed a threat to the Merchant Princes should they ever stop their infighting and stand together. Without the Guilds' members, the Merchant Princes would have no goods to fulfill their trade obligations. Historically, both the Merchant Princes and the Crown Princes subtly encouraged ill will among the Guilds to keep them mistrustful of each other. But if circumstances were dire enough, Neven could imagine the Guilds finally overcoming their old grudges and working together—which would be very bad news indeed.

"Keep me informed," he said as he finished his whiskey and stood, indicating that the meal was at an end. "I look forward to your next briefing."

"Let's hope, my lord, that I am in better shape to make my report," Lorenz replied, glancing at the sling that held his injured arm. "It would be... inconvenient... for you to have to find a new ambassador at this late date."

CHAPTER SEVENTEEN

"How long do you think we've been gone?" Rigan asked, staring at the cloudy sky that never grew fully light or completely dark. Without being able to see the sun or moon, it was difficult to judge the passage of time—assuming that it passed here in the same way as outside, beyond the Rift.

"Couple of days, maybe three or four," Trent said. "Just a guess, but that's what it feels like."

Mir nodded. "I can't see myself, but from the stubble you two have grown, that would be my guess."

Rigan groaned. "Corran is going to be a wreck. And Elinor—"

Trent laid a hand on his shoulder. "We'll figure it out. If the monsters can get out, so can we."

"Except that when a Rift opens, it must take the monsters closest to it. We haven't seen any of them migrating, and whenever I've sensed a ripple in the energies, it's gone before we can find an actual Rift." Rigan let out a sigh and dropped down to sit on a log. "We don't even know how big this—wherever we are—is."

"Which is why you're going to figure out how to open a Rift from this side," Mir said. "You can do this, Rigan."

Since they had been pulled into the Rift, they had held their own against more monsters than Rigan had dreamed existed. He had seen firsthand evidence that many of the creatures Corran and the hunters fought back in the city had their origins here, in a strange realm he suspected to be more a place of magic than of stone and substance.

They had fashioned a redoubt of sorts in a cliff side cave, reinforcing its protections with rocks and makeshift fencing woven from saplings. Just gathering wood, water, and food proved to be a life-or-death struggle. Rigan was glad that the small prey creatures proved edible, sparing them from trying to choke down meat from most of the monsters they killed.

"There are more of them now." Mir was on watch, looking into the valley beneath them.

Rigan suspected that the longer they were in this realm, the more monsters would sense their presence and be drawn to their scent. It grew harder each day to fight their way down to the stream and to keep back the creatures that hunted them when they went to gather wood for the fire. Soon, they would be outnumbered. Sooner, perhaps, than Rigan could muster the magic to get them home.

"I'd give a lot for some of the books Aiden's got back at the monastery." Rigan sighed. Without texts, he had only the spells and lore in his memory to draw from, and new as he was at magic, he feared it would not be enough.

"Whatever you need, we'll help you get it," Trent promised.

So far, Rigan's attempts at blood magic had been unsuccessful. He had killed a couple of the rabbit-like creatures in a ritual he hoped would create ripples in the ambient energy like those that signaled the opening of a Rift. The exercise left him covered with blood and feeling as if he had tainted his soul, but drew very little energy to him, certainly nothing sufficient to tear the fabric of reality and open a door home.

But it did call the presence in his dreams closer. Before he attempted to work blood magic, he only sensed a vague awareness in the darkness; now he heard murmured words too quiet for him to make out. He still felt the same dread and gut-deep fear of the thing in the darkness, and now that it felt closer and its awareness fixed on him,

Rigan wished he could hide himself, or clean away the residue of corruption that hung about the presence like a cloud of flies.

Rigan strengthened his mental protections as Aiden had taught him, and forced the disturbing memories away. He had work to do. Today, they had stumbled on some plants Rigan recognized, and he needed to try another working. Rigan disliked the feel of the power that came when he killed for magic, and he felt sure that the taint within the Rift was to blame for the persistent fever and headache he fought, like a slow poison. He hoped once they were home he might cleanse the stain, but right now he was resolved to do whatever it took regardless of the cost.

"Cover me," he said to Trent and Mir as he leaped across the fire and climbed over the protective wall of rock. They had argued all afternoon when Rigan had told them that he wanted to work this next magic outside the cave. He knew the risk, but he feared that being inside the rock might hamper the magic. *An experienced blood witch like Blackholt didn't seem to be hindered by being in an underground dungeon. Then again, I've got neither his experience nor his power.*

Rigan slit the small animal's throat, clean and fast. For all that he desperately wanted to get home, he could not bring himself to torture. In the next breath, he brought the blade down across his left palm, letting his blood drip into the same vessel that rapidly filled with that of his prey. *Maybe blood magic requires human blood, especially for a working this powerful.*

Rigan dipped two fingers into the bowl and painted sigils at the quarters of a circle around himself. He remembered the markings that he had seen in Blackholt's workshop, and at least these runes he and Aiden had been able to translate, so he knew something of their intent. Magic was always rooted in intention.

Next, he completed the circle drawing on the stone with bloody fingers, and then he turned back to the bowl. Rigan reached into his pouch with his right hand and withdrew the bits of plants he had gathered earlier. Then he lifted the bowl and closed his eyes, stretching out his power and trying to sense the currents of energy all around them.

He focused on the blood and rooted his magic in it. He had been taught to anchor himself as if magic were one of the core elements. Rigan envisioned the power as red tendrils branching out, like the veins he had seen in bodies they had tended in their undertaker's workshop back home. His mind's eye saw the ritual blood run through these tendrils, stretching farther as they branched. Each tendril and its offshoots were exquisitely sensitive, practically humming with energy that thrummed like a heartbeat, growing attuned to his pulse.

Now he could see the ripples, shimmers where the beat became erratic. He felt a tug, as if the shimmer called to him. Rigan stretched farther, endeavoring to grab hold of those shimmers and draw one to him.

When his power touched the ripple, it felt as if lightning struck, burning through him and throwing him backward. His body broke the circle of blood, and his connection with the tendrils of power vanished.

Strong hands grabbed him and pulled him back over the stone fence as a growl sounded too close for comfort.

"Get back!" Trent shouted, letting go of Rigan's arm and grabbing a torch, then thrusting it into the darkness beyond the wall.

Red eyes glared, and the torchlight revealed the squashed bat-faced maw of a *vestir*, one of the black dog monsters they had hunted back in Ravenwood. Rigan had seen the damage one of those monsters could do, and he had no desire to become its dinner.

"What happened?" Mir asked as they helped Rigan stagger into the cave and find a seat against the rock wall.

Rigan told them what he had seen. "I had it partly right," he said, trying to ignore the headache pounding behind his eyes, a side-effect of working magic without enough food or rest. "I saw the ripples, but as soon as I tried to touch one to bring it closer, the power threw me clear."

"Now what?" Trent asked, ever practical. The look on his face told Rigan that his friend felt the same keen disappointment, but refused to give in to despair. Perhaps it was bravado, but if so, Rigan needed the pretense to hold onto his waning hope.

"I'm going to try something with the plants we gathered," Rigan said, wondering if he sounded as tired as he felt.

"I don't know much about plants and nothing about magic, but I do recognize what you picked—and they're poisons," Mir objected. Since his small flask had run dry, removing his way of dealing with the loss he struggled to accept, Mir's tone grew snappish, and he rarely spoke unless spoken to.

"That's one reason I didn't try this first," Rigan said. "I saw a recipe for an ointment that witches use to 'see beyond.' Some of the old texts claimed it made them fly, but newer books said that was poetic, not real."

Trent raised an eyebrow. "I've seen some of the lads mix up a concoction and smoke it to put them out of their heads for a while. Is that what you're aiming at?"

Rigan frowned. "Not exactly—or at least, not for fun. If I do it right, I should be able to sense the world beyond the limits of my body. That would let me find the ripples and where the Rifts are opening, maybe learn more about how the energy works here."

"When you say 'beyond the limits of your body' do you mean you die?" Mir asked.

"Not exactly," Rigan said, "or at least, not permanently. More like being in a place between life and death, like a trance or a vision. And while I'm there, I'm going to try to see if I can get a message to Corran. Some of the lore suggested that witches who used the ointment could visit people in their dreams."

"None of that is reassuring, Rigan," Mir replied. "And I do not want to be the one to tell Corran we let you get yourself killed."

Trent and Rigan exchanged a look, and Rigan did not need words to know the same thought passed between them. *If I can't get the magic to take us home, you won't have to worry about telling Corran anything.*

"I don't like it, but we don't have a lot of options," Trent said. "Do you have everything you need?"

Rigan nodded. "I'm going to scrape up some fat from the carcass of the animal I used in the ritual. Which you can cook now since nothing I did should have made it bad to eat."

While Mir stood watch, Trent prepared the animals they had snared for dinner, being careful to save the fat. Rigan found a depression in the stone floor that would work for a bowl, and a rock he could use to grind the plants to mash. He wrapped his hand in cloth, careful not to get any of the mixture on his skin, and added the fat.

"There. It's supposed to sit overnight—lets the ingredients mingle, I guess. I'll try it tomorrow when we have fresh blood to go with it."

After dinner, Trent took his turn at watch. Neither of his friends would permit Rigan to take a shift, declaring that he had done enough by working the magic. Much as he wanted to do his share, Rigan felt secretly grateful, doubting he could remain awake or alert.

He fell into a deep, troubled sleep. Rigan saw himself back in the monastery. Corran and the others were there, but when Rigan tried to speak to them, they did not seem to hear.

He could not hear them, either, but he did not need to know what was going on. Corran looked like he had not slept or eaten in days, haggard and hollow-cheeked. By turns, he raged and then withdrew as if he neared the breaking point. Calfon and Ross comforted, advised, and cajoled, but nothing stopped Corran's restless pacing.

Elinor and Aiden worked in the room they had claimed as a library-workshop and looked little better than Corran. Dark circles under their eyes and rumpled clothing suggested they were pushing themselves hard. Where Corran showed his fear with anger, Elinor barely spoke, pausing to blink back tears now and again. Polly drafted Calfon and Ross to fetch food and help with chores since the others would not leave their tasks.

The monastery vanished, and Rigan stood alone in the darkness. The presence had drawn closer, and he imagined he felt cold breath against his skin. It watched him, calculating, ancient, and dangerous. Panicked, Rigan struck out around himself to drive the thing back, but his blows met only air. Perhaps it did not need to be physically nearby to project its awareness. His heart pounded, and sweat slicked his back. Or maybe the presence truly was nothing more than his imagination.

Rigan woke with a start. The fire at the cave mouth had burned down, telling him he had been asleep for a while. Trent glanced at him when he startled awake.

"Vision or dream?"

Rigan shook his head. "Can't tell. I saw the others back in the monastery, but I couldn't communicate with them. They didn't seem to see me. Maybe it was just a dream. Doesn't take magic to guess they're worried sick." He almost told them about the presence, but at the last minute, changed his mind. *If it's my imagination, there's no need to worry them. If I'm going mad, they'll see the proof of that for themselves soon enough. And if it's real... gods, if it's real, there's nothing we can do about it.*

Trent looked back into the night. "This mixture you made, you telling the truth about surviving it? Because not only would Corran kill us if we let you do something stupid, but we won't get home for him to have the chance."

Rigan drew his legs up and wrapped his arms around them. "I have every intention of surviving. The texts Aiden and I read certainly made it sound like many witches had lived to tell the tale. We discussed it quite a bit. Aiden thought that combining the poppies with the belladonna was the key—kept it from being too toxic." He gave a nervous chuckle. "I guess I'll find out."

"Will it really let you do magic, or just make you see things?"

Rigan debated his answer and decided to tell the truth. "I don't know, but if I couple it with the blood magic, I think it will be real. I have to try."

"Tomorrow, as soon as the sky lightens, I'll get Mir to help me move the rocks out, so you don't have to go on the other side of the wall. All the magic in the world won't help if you get eaten."

"You look like you're barely on your feet," Rigan said. "I can take a turn."

Trent snorted. "You look worse. Save your strength and get some sleep. Even if this witch ointment of yours works, I don't imagine it'll go easy on you."

Rigan tried to get comfortable on the rocky floor, surprised that exhausted as he felt, he still had trouble falling asleep. His thoughts raced, replaying his dream. Rigan did not doubt that their friends were searching for them. Nothing Corran could have done would have

273

prevented them being pulled through the Rift, but Rigan knew his brother would blame himself anyhow.

Aiden and Elinor at least could lose themselves in searching old texts and lore, and trying to open the Rift from their side. Corran might help them dig through the books, but he had only his undertaker's magic, which seemed of little use now.

I can't leave Corran, not after we've lost Kell.

Rigan could not forget how wrecked his brother looked in his dream. Whether or not the vision was magic, he doubted it was far from the truth. He fell into a fitful sleep, but the dreams did not return, and for once, neither did the presence.

———

RIGAN WOKE SLOWLY, frustrated by the inability to tell day from night. He shook himself awake, and put out a meager breakfast of berries and nuts, rationing the servings for himself and the others. Trent roused shortly after Rigan, but Mir continued sleeping, tossing and murmuring in his sleep.

"Are you still going to try the ointment?" Trent asked. "Because I can help you move those rocks so you have a bit more room."

Rigan finished the handful of food that was better than nothing and washed it down with a few swallows of water. He glanced again at Mir. "I'm worried about him," he murmured.

Trent nodded. "Me, too. I was, even before we came through the Rift. More, now."

Only a few months had passed since their entire world turned upside down that night in Ravenwood City, and Rigan knew it would take longer—perhaps a lifetime—to fully recover from that kind of loss and grief. Each of them dealt with it in his or her own way, but mostly with hunting and silence and whiskey. Rigan suspected that the pain of what they had lost, or what had been taken from them, would linger like a wound that would not heal. Some of them would find a way to go on, while others went under.

For all that Corran and Calfon argued with Ross about his reckless solo hunts, Rigan didn't feel especially worried. Ross had excellent skills, and while anything could go wrong on any hunt, Rigan did not get the sense that Ross sought suicide by monster. Sometimes, Rigan knew, the pain and fear of a near-death encounter broke through the numbness, a reminder of being still alive, and in those moments, having a target to fight and kill helped to work off the loss.

Mir's silence and his withdrawal into a jug of whiskey worried Rigan far more.

"What did I miss?" Mir sat, rubbing his eyes, damp with sweat from another night terror.

"Nothing yet," Trent replied. "Come eat breakfast, and then we need to help Rigan get ready for his latest magic."

With three of them moving the rocks, preparation for the working did not take long. Rigan had scooped out the "witch ointment" onto a flat bone and brought it with him into the circle he drew with soot and the sigils he had drawn onto the rock.

"If this goes wrong, how will we know?" Trent asked. "What can we do?"

"You'll know something's wrong if I don't wake up, or if something else seems to... take me over," Rigan said, noting the sudden alarm on Trent's face.

"Take you over?"

"I don't know what spirits or entities exist in this realm," Rigan replied, trying not to think about the presence in his dreams. "I'll do my best to stay away from them, but I can't promise. Shit, I don't even know if everything I see and feel will be real. But if it is, this might be our best bet to get a look around without needing to fight off all the monsters."

"How do we wake you?" Trent persisted. Mir said nothing but watched the others with dark, hooded eyes that flickered between despair and terror.

"Throw water in my face. Wipe the ointment off with a rag, but don't get any on yourself. Pinch me or cut me—pain might work. Put something that smells really bad under my nose." He withdrew a small cluster of strangely shaped beans. "If all else fails, put these in my mouth. If they're the plant I think they are; three beans will counter the strongest of the ingredients in the mixture. Don't use more, or you'll kill me even if the ointment didn't."

"I still don't like this," Trent objected.

"I don't either, but we don't have a lot of options." Rigan clapped a hand on Trent's shoulder. "If Eshtamon meant what he said, I'll come back." Neither of them needed to say aloud how little they trusted in the promises of the gods.

Rigan stripped off his shirt, revealing a lean chest with muscles strengthened by hard work and sparring, and seated himself in the middle of the protective circle. He used the flat bone like a trowel to smooth the pungent ointment over the pulse points on his wrists and throat. Then Rigan stretched out on his back, with his arms by his sides, closed his eyes, and waited.

The smell tingled in his nose, strong enough he could taste it on the back of his tongue. Where he spread the paste, his skin burned, but not painfully. He focused on keeping his breathing deep and regular, and within a few minutes, his body felt lighter, as if his consciousness floated out of his physical form.

Unlike in his dreams or his attempt to use blood magic, Rigan felt separate from his body but tethered to it, which eased his fear. The warmth from his pulse points seeped into his blood and bone, giving him a heady feeling as if he had drunk strong wine. His spirit-being stood, then stared down at his still, solid body before stepping out over the edge of the cliff and falling.

He fell—then rose, and in a giddy moment of flight understood the appeal and danger of the forbidden mixture. He dove at the monsters, easily dodging their claws and beaks, not drunk enough with the ointment to forget all caution. Rigan laughed as the creatures that hunted them flinched away at his approach, or ran after him only to be left behind. He looped and rolled, losing the tension that had settled in his back and shoulders, free.

An effort of will brought his focus back to scouting the territory. He soared above the tree canopy, scanning the dark horizon. He confirmed his suspicion that this realm had day and night, but the sun brightened for only a few precious hours, dawn and twilight lingered much longer than in the outside world, and night seemed to last forever.

In the fleeting light of morning, Rigan had difficulty making out the shimmer of new Rifts by sight alone, but his magic pointed him unerringly toward their ever-shifting locations. Several glimmered and darkened not far from their camp, giving him hope of a way home, if only Corran and the others could find those nearby portals.

Gliding over the tall trees or swooping above the ground, Rigan saw many more unfamiliar creatures that had not yet made their way through the Rifts, all of them worthy of the term "monster." Despite the buzz of the ointment, Rigan shuddered, hating the idea of an ever-greater horde of attackers at the command of the blood witches.

He felt the touch of the presence like a cold finger pressed to his beating heart, and Rigan's flight faltered. The entity loomed too large to comprehend, too terrifying for his mind to grasp, and even those brief glimpses threatened his sanity. What he saw, he struggled to map, memorizing anything he knew or recognized. Some things were so alien that it hurt to think about them, or to keep the images in his mind long enough to process. Vast size. A huge, unhinged maw with suckers to draw prey in and rows of sharp teeth to mince it fine. Insatiable hunger, and tendrils of darkness to find and bind. Whip-like antennae and the slick ooze coating smooth black skin to begin digesting anything close enough to touch.

Rigan dropped like a stone, falling through leaves and branches, his shadow-self too immobilized by the horrors he glimpsed to fully register the pain. Worse, the great dark eye of the presence *saw* him, and Rigan felt flayed to the bone, then unwound as the implacable orb stripped his mind away.

Not just one presence; others lingered in the vast shaded moors and fens behind the first. Some rose from the foul water, others fell from the sky, while some assembled themselves out of the dead pieces of things forgotten and left behind, into a new abomination that woke ravenous.

Rigan did not think he could survive if they all noticed him; he had doubts that even now he clung to sanity by more than a shred. As his shadow-self neared the ground, Rigan wrested his gaze away from the primordial horrors in the deepest corners of the Rift and summoned enough presence of mind to pull up, taking flight before he could slam into the loam and rock.

The ointment's power waned, and Rigan looked around, desperate and panicked, trying to find a way home. He searched for landmarks, but everything looked unfamiliar. Rigan had no idea what exactly might become of him if his shadow-self did not return to his body before the ointment lost its hold, but he could not imagine that anything good would come of it. He might die, or worse, be trapped as a wraith, far from his friends and forever lost to his home.

Gathering all his waning strength and resolutely refusing to spare a glance in the direction of the dark entities that called to him in his dreams, Rigan closed his eyes and focused on the cave and the cliff ledge. He willed himself to find his body and sensed a thin, foxfire thread almost too fragile to notice in the gloaming, and he followed it with everything he had left in him.

This time, when he fell, he hit the ground.

Rigan's consciousness crashed back into his body, overwhelming every system as his self, his soul, forced its way back into flesh, sinew, and bone. Muscles seized and his thoughts stuttered, as his jaw went rigid and teeth clacked in a terrible staccato. He could control nothing but felt everything, as his body bucked and twitched and his heart threatened to beat its way past his ribs.

A sharp, foul taste invaded his mouth as his teeth ground down on seeds that popped and dissolved on his tongue. Rigan had a dim aware-ness of hands gripping him on his shoulders and ankles, fingers digging in hard enough to bruise as his body fought them, shuddering and shaking. He gasped for breath, and he felt the throbbing of his heart in his ears and eyes. Everything was too much: sound, color, scent. Distant voices cried out, but their words could not penetrate the fog of pain. Finally, everything went dark.

"… never get home with him dead!"

"… we don't know yet."

"… going to die in this godsforsaken place."

"… not helping anything!"

"… you won't accept it, but we are never going home!"

Voices woke Rigan, and he swam toward them. A part of him felt a twinge of concern over the heated argument, but his blurred thoughts could not grasp why it might have anything to do with him.

What he did know was that he was terribly, painfully thirsty. "Water," he croaked, and everything around him went silent.

"Rigan?" Trent loomed over him, eyes wide with concern. "Oh, gods. Rigan!"

"Water." It took all of Rigan's will to force the word out past a dry tongue and parched lips. Trent vanished from his view for a second, and returned to spill water from the wineskin over his lips, slowing the stream so Rigan could swallow without choking.

Trent turned away. "I told you not to give up so fast," he chided Mir. "Rigan's tougher than you give him credit for."

"He died," Mir argued, sounding petulant and frightened. "We couldn't feel breath or a heartbeat. How do we know it's really him?"

Trent's patience reached a breaking point. "Gods, man—what is your problem? Must you make everything worse? Go take watch, and stop inventing more trouble than we already have."

Rigan heard the reluctant footsteps as Mir trudged to the front of the cave. Trent turned back to him, managing a shaky smile. "We thought we'd lost you," Trent said quietly. "You were in the trance for a day and a half, and then you had a seizure, and everything stopped." He swallowed. "Except apparently, it started back up again while I was arguing with Mir."

"He's afraid," Rigan managed.

Trent muttered a few curses under his breath. "You don't know the half of it. I thought he'd completely unraveled with the idea that if you were dead, we were trapped here for good," he replied in a low tone, glancing toward the cave mouth to make sure Mir wasn't listening.

"I didn't mean to worry you," Rigan said.

Trent dismissed his concern with a wave of his hand. "I'm just glad you made it back. You need to eat something and drink, and get some sleep," Trent said. "Then I want to know what you found out."

"Rifts are close," Rigan murmured as Trent helped him sit, holding a cup to his lips while he drank, and tearing off small bits of cooked meat for him to eat. His entire body ached, and his head throbbed, reminding him of his early training when he had pushed his magic too far without proper anchoring and nearly died.

"Then we have to get them open," Trent replied, supporting him until he waved away more food or drink, then easing him back down to the cold cave floor. "You don't have to tell me now."

Rigan grabbed Trent's arm, clenching tightly with his fingers. "A horror lives in the shadows," he said, as his mind cringed away from the awful glimpses. "It saw me."

Trent frowned, patting his arm and gently removing his hand. "Sleep, then tell me more. There's nothing to do about it tonight."

Rigan wanted to tell him that the presence could find him in his dreams, but as it turned out, he was far too tired to dream.

———

RIGAN FORCED HIMSELF up and about before his protesting body had fully recovered, but the knowledge of what lurked in the recesses of the Rift would have made him rise from his deathbed. Trent had listened intently while Rigan recounted what he had seen. Mir huddled in on himself at the edge of the firelight, head down, arms wrapped around his knees.

"We know more about what's here inside the Rift," Trent said after he had chewed on the information a while, "but not much to help us get out."

"I've got another idea," Rigan said as they headed out to replenish their supplies, something Trent had been loath to do while Rigan lay unconscious. From what little he could gather, Mir had not dealt well with the situation and now seemed utterly convinced that they would never return home. Rigan fought down his temper, grateful for Trent's bloody-minded practicality, even if Mir had all but surrendered.

"I need to find something bluish and something reddish," Rigan told the others as they ventured out to get food, water, and wood.

"Will those work?" Mir asked, pointing to a cluster of orange seeds dangling from a tree.

"With luck," Rigan said, gathering some of the seeds. He picked some red flowers also, just in case, then spotted dark blue berries as they neared the stream and tied them up in his shirt so he could leave a hand free for a weapon. They all had their swords, and Trent carried a lit torch although it was as bright as this realm ever got. Rigan and Mir each had an unlit torch, as a precaution.

"Watch out! We've got company!" Mir shouted moments before half a dozen of the crab-monsters clattered up from the edge of the stream. He dropped the wood he had gathered and lit his torch from Trent's flame, as did Rigan.

"Swords don't work well on those shells," Trent reminded them. "Go for the joints, and finish them off with a big rock."

The three hunters formed a circle to protect their backs, and the *higani* closed the distance. Their carapaces clacked and their strange chittering noise made Rigan's hackles rise. At first, the hunters kept the creatures at a distance with the torches, but soon there were too many, and all Rigan and the others could do was make some back off while they engaged others. The creatures were fast, and Rigan remembered too late how sharp the pointed and barbed ends of their long, jointed legs were when one sliced into his calf.

"Damn things have knives for feet," he swore, getting his vengeance as he brought his sword down hard on the joints of the creature's front legs, slicing two from its body. That slowed the *higani* but did not stop it. A second monster skittered closer, but Rigan wasn't sure whether it was more interested in him or its wounded comrade.

To his relief, the second *higani* set upon its companion as an easy meal, ignoring Rigan until he brought his sword down on it as well, taking out all the legs on one side. He slammed a heavy rock down on the two damaged monsters with all his strength, cracking open their tough shells. The smell that rose from their innards reminded him of fish left out in the sun.

By the time he looked up, Mir and Trent had hobbled or killed their share of the *higani*. All of them were bleeding from where the sharp shells had sliced through cloth and skin.

"We'd better move fast," Trent cautioned. "If the monsters couldn't smell us before, they're sure to scent blood."

Trent hurried to fill the wineskins while Mir and Rigan grabbed wood for the fire, and Rigan snatched up his parcel with the plants.

They heard noises in the brush as they headed for the cave, snuffles and grunts that told them creatures followed, looking for an opportunity. Trent had both hands free with the wineskins on straps slung over his shoulders, so he kept a sword and a torch ready. Mir and Rigan had their hands full carrying wood.

The three men made it back to their shelter, winded and bleeding. Along with what he had gathered for the magic, Rigan had also picked some medicinal plants, and he made a paste out of them to keep their wounds from festering. The only thing worse than being trapped in this nether realm would be for one of them to get dangerously ill.

The *higani* or other predators had raided the snares down by the creek, but the traps Trent set on the rocks yielded three of the small furred animals, enough for each of them to have a decent portion. While Rigan had found plants for magic and medicine, they had found nothing that looked trustworthy to eat.

When they finished their meager supper, Rigan prepared what he needed for the working that night.

"What now?" Trent asked, watching Rigan get ready.

"I'm going to try some grave magic, see if there are any human souls—ghosts—here that I can communicate with," Rigan replied as he gathered his things. "If there are, maybe we can learn something from them."

"You've barely come back from the dead. Do you have the strength to do another working?" Trent challenged.

"Do we have the time for me to wait?" Rigan snapped. Trent sighed and shook his head. "I'll be careful," Rigan added, softening his tone. "But we need to get out of here. Maybe the ghosts can show me how."

Trent raised an eyebrow. "If they're still here, then they aren't going to lead us to the way out."

"Maybe not," Rigan conceded, "but they might tell us what doesn't work."

"Seems like a long shot," Mir said.

Rigan glared at him. "Got a better idea? Getting out of here at all is a long shot. I'll take any help I can find."

He moved to the protected area of the ledge, outside the cave but within their stone wall. He had crushed the plants and hoped that the color of the strange berries and seeds would be close enough to the pigments he had used back in their workshop. As he painted the familiar sigils on the rock, Rigan felt a stab of concern for Corran and Elinor.

I'm doing everything I can to get us back home. Whatever it takes. Gods above! I don't want to die here.

Rigan set his jaw. They were not going to die in this godsforsaken realm. No matter what the cost, he intended to get them home.

When the sigils were drawn and the circle complete, Rigan knelt and closed his eyes, gathering his magic. He drew from the runes and let his power flow along the familiar paths. This magic came as effortlessly as breathing.

Death was no stranger in this realm. Rigan's magic was not attuned to monsters, but the sheer amount of carnage pulled at his power, though there were no souls for him to pass to the After. He let his magic sweep as far as he could cast it, listening for a response. When nothing stirred, he despaired, until finally, something surged toward him in answer.

"Who are you?"

I don't remember.

"How did you get here?"

It was so long ago; I'm not sure.

"You were human?" Rigan pressed.

Yes. At least, I think so.

"How long have you been here?"

How would I know? Who is the king?

"Rellan is King of Darkhurst."

I do not know of Darkhurst, the ghost replied.

Rigan's heart sank, but he pressed on. "How did you get here?"

I walked across a field, and the air changed. I woke here.

"How did you die? How did the other ghosts die?"

So many ways. A growler killed me and ate my flesh.

Rigan tried a different approach. "The big, powerful presence in the darkness. What is it?"

Old and hungry. Flee from it.

Either the ghost died before he could learn much about this realm, or it had faded too far to care. Rigan tried again. "My friends and I were pulled through a Rift. We're trying to get home."

You can't. At least, we couldn't.

Rigan's heart sank. "What did you try?"

We chased the ripples. But we couldn't get pulled into the current.

"Current?"

If you're close enough when one opens, it's like a river moving very fast. It pulls what's nearby into it. I can remember that much.

The connection with the ghost began to fade. It took all of Rigan's concentration to hold it steady for one last question. "Were any of you witches?"

It took so long for a reply Rigan thought the spirit was gone. And then, he heard the reply. *No. And maybe it will help you. But don't count on it.*

Rigan sat lost in thought after the ghost vanished. Talking to the spirit had tired him, but he had enough in him for a second attempt. This time, Rigan sent his anchor down into the rock beneath him, and cast his power into the air, seeking the ripples he suspected were thin spots between this realm and home.

He had no clear idea of how to do this, only a vague sense that he should try. Gathering his grave magic, Rigan pushed out toward the ripples, calling to any lost souls who might hear.

Ghosts often learn things after death that they didn't know when they were alive. Maybe I can make contact with a ghost on the other side of the ripple—back home—and see what I can learn about crossing the threshold.

It occurred to Rigan that opening a door into another realm was something he was intimately familiar with as an undertaker when part of helping "stuck" souls move on involved opening the portal to the After. Rigan had no desire to go to the After any sooner than necessary, and he felt sure any path back to the world of the living that wound through the After would be equally fraught with peril as what they faced here beyond the Rift. *But if my magic can open one door—and such a big one, to Doharmu's kingdom itself—surely I can open a small one to get us home.*

He felt a tug on his magic, faint and tentative, but unquestionably real. Rigan reached out and willed the ghost closer.

Where is this place? The ghost asked. Rigan found himself looking at the spirit of a man in his middle years, bald and pudgy, who glanced about himself in wonder and fear.

"I'm not completely sure. I'm lost, and I hoped you could lead me home."

That might not be a good idea. I'm pretty sure I must be dead.

"You are. I'm an undertaker. That's how I could draw in your spirit." Rigan tried to be as reassuring as he could, though he had no idea how to handle this conversation.

Oh gods, am I stuck here? Send me back!

"I will send you back—and if I can't, I'll send you on, into the After. But show me the path you took to come to me, so I can follow."

The ghost turned, looking behind him. *There. Can you see the lights? Like the insects that fly at night and glow. That's the way I came.*

Rigan strained his vision, but he could not see the twinkling lights. *Maybe I need to be dead to see it, though my grave magic has shown me many things the living can't usually see.* He turned to the ghost. "Can you follow them back? I'll watch your path."

The ghost gave him a skeptical look, then turned and began to move away. Rigan traced his path with magic, maintaining a connection to the ghost's energy until they reached an invisible barrier.

Here, the ghost said. *There's a door.*

"I can't see a door."

Right here, the ghost repeated as if Rigan were blind.

Rigan felt the unstable energy of the ripples, but nothing of the rending power he sensed when the Rift opened around them. "Can you go through it on your own?"

The ghost nodded. *I think so.* He stepped toward the door, and then his image wavered before he vanished.

Rigan kept his power lightly connected to the spirit—like an invisible hand on his shoulder—until the second the ghost disappeared. In that instant, Rigan felt the barrier between realms like a wall of energy, and he tried to force open the door with his magic.

The currents of energy surged, and Rigan felt the connection brutally severed as the power repelled his magic as strenuously as if he had been hurled across the room.

He came to, lying on his back within the warded circle, gasping for breath as his heart hammered in his chest.

"Rigan, are you all right?" Trent knelt outside the circle, watching him worriedly. Rigan could only imagine how hard it was for his friend not to break the warding to help him.

"I think so," Rigan replied, sounding worn and reedy even to himself.

"Find something?"

Rigan swallowed. His dry mouth made talking difficult. "Yeah. I found a door home. But it only works if you're dead."

"Oh."

"I've got some more ideas on how to get it open without dying," Rigan said. "But first, I really need to sleep."

"The warding—"

Rigan nodded, feeling completely drained. "I dispelled the magic. You can break the circle." He chuckled tiredly. "I think you're going to need to, or else I'll be spending the night right here."

Trent rose and moved to help him, getting a shoulder under Rigan's arm to keep him upright. Together, they stumbled toward Rigan's cloak. After Trent eased him to a seat, he went to fetch water. Rigan took a gulp, savoring it.

"I'd bring you food, but there isn't any left," Trent apologized. "You look worn to a frazzle."

"I feel like shit," Rigan admitted. "But I traced a path to one of the thin spots—not a Rift, but a ripple. And there's something else I want to try. But not tonight."

Trent clapped him on the shoulder, helping him settle in on the ground with his cloak wrapped around him. "Definitely not tonight," Trent echoed. "Sleep. Mir and I will keep watch."

Rigan shifted, trying to get comfortable. He knew he needed to rest to regain his strength. As he drifted off, he recalled what had happened at the "door." *If I can open the Gates of Doharmu, surely I can open a Rift. I call on Doharmu to open the portal to the After. If I called on Eshtamon, would he hear me? Would he grant me the power to open a Rift if I can find one? And if I do the blood magic right, will it add to my grave magic to give me enough energy to do what needs to be done?*

He sent out a wisp of magic, seeking the Elder God. *Eshtamon, if you're listening, you said I was your Champion mage. I'm stuck on the other side of a Rift, so I can't be your champion or anyone else's until I get home. Open my eyes so I can see the way, and increase my magic so I can do what needs to be done. I've got to get home to Corran and Elinor. You made Corran and me your champions—that takes both of us, and it can't happen if I'm over here.*

CHAPTER EIGHTEEN

"HE'S NOT DEAD. I'd know if he was dead. Somehow, I'd know."
Corran shook his head. "I won't believe it. We aren't giving up."

Calfon sighed. "We aren't going to give up, Corran. But you have
to be prepared for the possibility—"

Corran came up out of his chair so fast that Calfon barely had time
to step back. Corran's arm was cocked for a punch. "Don't say it. I
don't want to hear it. They're not dead! We just need more time."

Ross stepped up, interposing himself. "Cool down," he ordered.
Corran lowered his arm and looked chagrined, though anger simmered
beneath his embarrassment at losing control. Calfon looked at Corran
in concern.

"No one's giving up," Ross soothed. "Aiden and Elinor are chasing
some new theories. We've all but stopped hunting monsters since
Rigan went missing, trying to find him. If there's an answer, we'll
figure it out. And I know Rigan and the others are doing everything
they can to find a way home."

Polly came to the door, making enough noise that Corran felt
certain she had been eavesdropping and wanted them to know that she
was coming. "Dinner's ready," she announced. "Another amazingly

good meal made from practically nothing, because I'm awesome. So get your asses in here and eat before it goes cold."

Aiden and Elinor joined them a few minutes later, and they sat around the battered table in the room they used for a kitchen. "Do I smell chicken?" Aiden asked as Polly carried bowls over to the cauldron in the fireplace.

"You do," Polly replied. "Chicken stew with dumplings."

"I'm hungry enough to eat a horse," Aiden said, grinning.

"You'll have to make do with chicken," Polly replied breezily. "It's the specialty of the house."

Polly's stew was as good as it smelled, complete with fresh biscuits and homemade jam from the fruit bushes at the back of the monastery. She basked in their compliments as the group cleaned their plates and used the biscuits to mop up the gravy.

"And there's a cask of wine and a barrel of ale, courtesy of grateful villagers," Polly announced, dusting her hands. "I'd say for outlaws; we eat rather well."

"You do us proud, Polly," Ross said, grinning as he wiped his mouth. "I never expected the food in exile to be this good."

Polly beamed. "That's because I cook as well as I fight."

Corran knew he should be hungry, but the food tasted like ash. He glanced at Elinor and saw that she also merely picked at her food, shoving pieces from one side of the plate to the other, eating very little.

"What have you got?" Corran asked after they were finished.

Aiden sighed. "Not as much as I'd like to have, but we're making some headway. There's very little in the lore about Rifts. That makes me think that before now, they weren't as common."

"Is that because of something natural, or are there more blood witches putting a strain on the Balance?" Ross asked.

"I wish it were natural," Aiden replied. "But I'm afraid that's probably not the case. We know Blackholt could summon monsters from somewhere, and control them once they got here. Well, monsters come from the other side of the Rift, so blood witches—at least those of Blackholt's power—must have a way to open Rifts and pull things through."

"Can we find a blood witch and force him to 'summon' Rigan and the others?" Corran met Aiden's gaze, completely serious.

"You were there for the battle against Blackholt," Aiden answered. "Even if we could capture a blood witch without having to kill him, compelling him to do our will would be an entirely different matter."

"We're not sure how the Rifts work," Elinor replied. Her voice sounded raspy and tight, and the dark circles under her eyes testified to her exhaustion. "And we have no idea what the... geography... is like on the other side. What if it's as big on the other side as the world on this side? We don't know for sure where the Rift they went through dumped them out. They might still be close by. But what if we open a Rift here, and they're in a completely different one?"

Corran looked up. "I had a dream last night—about Rigan. It felt more real than usual."

Aiden's focus narrowed immediately. "Tell us."

"It was like Rigan was here, but not here—like a ghost," he admitted, hating what that might mean. "He could see us, but we couldn't hear him. He was trying to tell me something. But I don't know what it was." He glanced at the others. "I know it might be just a dream, but there was something about it that felt like it was... more."

Aiden and Elinor exchanged a glance. "I dreamed last night, too," Elinor said, a blush creeping to her cheeks. "I thought it was because I miss him. But now that you say that, it was the same for me. Not like the usual dreams. Much more real."

"If there was a ripple nearby while we slept, it's possible that Rigan was able to reach out with his magic through the 'thin spot,'" Aiden mused. "Strong emotion can create powerful magic, and he wouldn't be the first witch to discover that he still uses his abilities in his sleep."

"If that's true, then he's alive—or he was as of last night," Corran said, feeling the first spark of hope in days. Elinor raised her head, and he saw some of the weariness and grief fade from her features.

"And if he could see as well as project, then he knows we're trying to find them," Elinor added.

Aiden nodded. "I'm certain Rigan is doing his best to find a way back to us. If you have another dream like that, try to take control of it and let Rigan know that you see him." He pushed back from the table. "In the meantime, I've found a book I need to study. The monks didn't have much on blood magic, but I may have found some lore that could help." He grimaced. "Unfortunately, it's in an old language style that makes it very difficult to read—and spell books are already known for speaking in riddles."

"I'll go with you," Elinor volunteered, more lively than before the conversation. "I've got some ideas of my own." She reached out to touch Corran on the arm. "We'll find him—and the others—and bring them home. Trust us."

Corran watched the witches go, wishing he could trust anything except the certainty that more trouble was on the way.

———

AIDEN WALKED INTO the kitchen in the morning looking as if he hadn't slept all night. Corran hadn't either and was waiting with a pot of coffee already boiling on the fire.

"Anything?" Corran asked.

Aiden scrubbed a hand down over his face and blinked to banish sleep from his eyes. "Elinor is plotting the ripples on a map, trying to find a pattern in timing and location. If we can guess the next occurrence, we could be waiting with a ritual to pry the damn Rift open. And the monastery ghost was in quite a mood last night. Toppled over a stack of books on my table and gave Polly a fright when she came in and found her pots rearranged." He poured himself some coffee and sat next to Corran. Polly had left them a pot of boiled eggs and a loaf of bread, and Aiden helped himself to some of both.

"I'm working on a beacon of sorts—something that acts like a magical lighthouse. It's a crazy idea—if we can find that Rifts open in the same general place over and over again, then we want to help Rigan and the others find the Rift closest to us," Aiden explained. "When the Rift opens, we toss in the beacon—an amulet that pulses with magic. And we hope that Rigan can pick up on the signal, get to the place we tossed the amulet, and stay safe until the Rift opens again."

Corran sipped his coffee, forcing down his fears. "How about being able to open a Rift from this side?"

Aiden sighed. "Still trying to make sense of old lore. For obvious reasons, witches don't like to write things down so that they're easy to understand. Most magic is intended to be passed down from teacher to pupil—manuscripts and grimoires are just to remind you of the details, not to be how you learn from scratch. And since blood magic is dangerous, rare and generally unpopular for obvious reasons, those who practice it are pretty cagey about the notes they leave behind."

"But with all the research, you're making progress?" Corran hated that he could not keep a note of desperate hope from his voice.

"I think so. Elinor is a big help. I'm asking too much of her—she's only a student herself. And I'm not exactly an old sage. I'd give a lot to have the help of some of the witches I knew Below." They fell silent, remembering the treachery that killed Aiden's and Rigan's teachers.

"Of course, the flaw in your plan is that if we have to get close enough to an open Rift to toss in your 'beacon,' we're also close enough for the monsters coming out to make hash out of us," Corran observed.

"I'm trying for something that can be attached to an arrow and shot through the opening. It doesn't have to be large; it simply has to sustain the magic," Aiden replied. "That would at least put you at bow range from the monsters, too."

Corran drained his cup and reached for another one. "It just might work." He left unsaid how many "ifs" were involved.

"Elinor's figuring out how to carve a message into the amulet. We'd stand the best chance if we were using magic on our side while they were doing the same on theirs," Aiden said.

"I'm ready. We need to get them home."

That night, Corran worked with Elinor on mapping the ripples and fashioning an amulet that could attach to an arrow and still fly true. They settled for a small piece of parchment with a message and an amulet of braided hair steeped in blood and plants Elinor selected for their magical enhancement.

"Calfon is our best archer," Corran said. "He's the one who should take the shot."

"If my tracking is right, we should be seeing a Rift open near here," Elinor said, pointing to a spot on the map that had been pinned to the wall.

"That's awfully close to the Sarolinian border," Corran observed.

Elinor shrugged. "We're doing good to find the Rifts when someone else is opening them. So far, we haven't figured out how to rip one open ourselves." Her hands shook, and Corran saw how much Rigan's disappearance weighed on her.

He gave her shoulder a squeeze. "You've done good work. We'll find them," he said with more confidence than he felt. Though he wanted the safe return of his brother and their friends, Corran doubted it would go as smoothly as Aiden's plan suggested. "When is this Rift due to open?"

"Tomorrow, either late in the afternoon or early in the evening— sorry, we can't be more precise than that," Aiden replied.

"We'll be ready," Corran promised.

He left the witches and headed back to his room. On the way, he found himself turning down one of the corridors he had explored when they first moved in, an area they rarely used. This room had been a shrine to the Elder Gods, and while any sacred objects or relics had long ago been taken away, the murals on the walls remained.

Corran was not especially devout, despite his role as an undertaker helping souls find their way to the After. Kell had been the one to make their offerings in the temple to Doharmu, god of Death, the only Guild god that was also an Elder God and the patron of undertakers. Corran had given up on the gods when their parents died, finding no reason to keep praying when no one was listening.

But the night Kell was murdered, Corran and Rigan called on Eshtamon, and the Elder God answered, naming them his champions. Corran slowly walked along the mural until he found Eshtamon's image, a wily old man in a hooded robe with a glint of malice in his eyes, the god of vengeance. The mural looked much as Corran remembered Eshtamon's appearance in the cemetery that night. *Perhaps*, he thought, *Rigan and I weren't the only ones to have seen more than a glimpse of him.*

Corran knelt, and the position felt awkward and unfamiliar. "I don't pray much," he murmured. "But you heard us before, and I hope you're listening now. This isn't for me. It's for my brother and his friends. I know how to open a portal to the After, but I don't know how to pull them back from a Rift. Please." His voice broke. "If we're to be your champions, then bring them back. I can't fight this alone."

He remained still for a few moments, trying to pull himself together, wiping the tears from his eyes with the back of his hand. Nothing stirred in the silent room, and although he had not really expected a response, he felt a pang of despair. Blinking to clear his vision, Corran rose and left the room.

Even whiskey could not help him sleep that night.

———

THE NEXT AFTERNOON, the main rooms of the monastery's hidden basement bustled with tension and activity. Calfon, Corran, and Ross had the bow and the arrow with the amulet and message, along with their usual weapons. Aiden had not been able to give them any idea of what sorts of monsters might come charging through the Rift if it did, indeed, open in the anticipated spot, so they took plenty of the salt mixture, some green vitriol, and an array of swords, knives, and axes capable of killing nearly every type of monster they had encountered.

"I wish we could go with you, for backup," Polly groused, unhappy at the decision to leave some of their team back at the monastery.

"Hush," Elinor said, laying a hand on Polly's shoulder. Polly shrugged it off ill-humoredly.

"I fight well enough. I should go too."

Corran turned back to her. "You do fight well. That's why you're going to be protecting Aiden and Elinor. Not every threat can be magicked away. And you're wicked with a knife."

Polly grinned. "Well, that's true. But I still would rather be out there than in here."

"We all would," Aiden admitted. "But if we stay here, we can keep working on getting Rigan, Mir, and Trent home. It's going to take all of us to make this happen."

Polly gave in reluctantly. Corran could not blame her for her disappointment; she fought well and had proven her courage many times over. But at the same time, they rarely risked their whole team on one fight. If things went wrong, either with the magic, the monsters or the bounty hunters, someone would be able to mount a rescue.

The hunting party rode in silence. Calfon had spent the last day practicing with the weighted arrow, perfecting his aim. Ross and Corran rested, deep in their thoughts. Calfon led the way, following the directions to the place the witches believed a Rift might open.

"Here?" Ross asked. "Nothing looks any different."

"This is where they said to go," Calfon replied. He eyed the terrain. "Let's back up to there," he said, pointing to a slight ridge. I'll have the whole clearing in range, and we'll have the advantage no matter what comes through the Rift."

"I don't like being this close to the border," Ross muttered. "Bad enough to have Ravenwood's guards after us. How are we to know where the bloody border even is? Not like there's a real line."

"Stay on this side of the clearing, if you have the choice," Corran said. "If you can't tell where the border is, neither can the guards so long as you're not too far inside. If they know what's good for them, they'll be far away from here, what with monsters coming through."

They waited, watching for any sign of a Rift forming. Corran tried to remember what had happened immediately before Rigan and the others vanished. But in the thick of the fight, his attention had been on the monster trying to rip out his throat, not on their surroundings until it was too late.

"Aiden said we might feel something—like a storm rolling in," he said as the others watched and paced.

"We aren't even completely certain that this is the spot," Ross muttered. "From what we scouted, it would be the best place to bring through an attack force—which is what the monsters are. But who knows if the witch opening the Rift knows anything about this area to pick a clearing rather than the middle of the woods?"

The witches had also been less than precise about the time the Rift might open. Time dragged on as they waited for something to happen, dreading the battle but hoping for a chance to connect with their lost friends. As the afternoon stretched toward evening, Corran readied lanterns and torches, kindling a small fire so that they could light them easily once darkness fell.

"Nothing," Calfon said with a sigh, looking out over the clearing.

"It would make sense not to bring the monsters through until evening," Ross replied. "Harder to see and fight at night, and if creating fear is part of it, then everything is scarier in the dark."

As the sun set, Corran felt a sudden chill that had little connection to the warmer air. "Did you feel that?"

The others nodded. Ross ran a hand up the back of his neck. "All my hair stood on end."

"I've got gooseflesh," Calfon replied.

They turned toward the clearing, straining to see in the gloaming. Pinpricks of light glittered in the empty field, first a few, then more and more. "There!" Corran hissed, pointing.

Calfon readied his bow, aiming toward where the dancing points of light coalesced. Corran tried not to hold his breath. The temperature in the clearing plummeted, and at the same time, a pervasive uneasiness settled over them, as if they sensed on a primal level that something bad was about to happen.

The night tore in two. Calfon let fly the arrow.

Corpse-pale forms tumbled through the split in the darkness, landing in a tangle of emancipated limbs. A circle of dead and diseased grass spread out from the Rift at its center, shriveling and rotting as they watched.

The arrow soared over the outpouring of monsters, into the void.

The Rift snapped shut and disappeared. The dead zone around it stopped expanding.

"Ghouls," Corran groaned. "I really hate ghouls."

Ross's eyes widened. "There are at least a dozen of them. We can't fight that many."

Calfon readied another arrow. "If I can get in a few good shots, maybe we won't have to."

"There's no use running—they'll smell us," Corran said quietly. "And stay out of the dead grass—we've seen what happened to the cattle that got too close."

Calfon sent off four shots in quick succession, hitting all of his targets before the surging scramble of ghouls forced a change in tactics. Calfon fell back to find a better angle to keep shooting since the bow could take down attackers before the ghouls were close enough to do damage with teeth and claws.

Corran and Ross each grabbed a torch, fending off the ghouls with fire then lunging closer with their swords. Corran kept watch for any sign that the Rift—or the missing men—might reappear, but the tear between realms did not reappear.

"Still too many," Ross grunted as he and Corran waded into the fight. Calfon's targets moved fast with an unsettling, spider-like grace. They could scramble up sheer cliffs, climb boulders like a fly, and scale trees to launch themselves airborne onto their intended victims.

"Watch out!" Ross shouted, grabbing Corran back as one of the ghouls dove from overhead. The crunch of bone as the creature landed face-first on the hard ground would have stopped a person, but the ghoul rose to its feet undeterred, though an arm and shoulder hung at an unnatural angle.

Corran was soaked with ichor to his elbows, splashed with gore from head to foot. Ross looked worse after being caught in the spray of foul liquid that pumped from a ghoul's neck when Ross's sword removed its head from its shoulders.

"We must have counted wrong," Ross panted as they chopped their way through the onslaught. Ghouls never tired, giving them still another advantage on top of unnatural speed and strength.

Corran shoved his torch into the face of a ghoul that dared get too close. The undead creature's hair ignited, but it never slowed its attack, though the skin of its face and scalp blistered and charred. Corran stumbled backward, got his footing, and lunged, this time pushing the torch into the monster's eyes.

The ghoul shrieked and flailed. Corran thrust his sword through its chest, then followed with a swing that took off its head. It raked his arm with its claws as it fell, opening deep, bloody gashes.

Too many of the ghouls swarmed toward Calfon for him to keep on firing with the bow. He took one last shot, skewering an oncoming ghoul through the throat, which slowed it but did not stop it. Calfon dropped the bow and grabbed an axe from his belt, setting about himself with a two-handed grip that channeled all his anger and strength.

We might not make it back, Corran thought as he kicked one ghoul so he could take a swing at a second. Together, they had cut the number of creatures by at least half, though he was certain now that his original estimate had been wrong by quite a few. Even so, that left several ghouls for each of them, and Corran's energy was flagging quickly.

"Got a plan?" Two deep gashes marked Ross's face and a swipe of claws across his chest cut his shirt to ribbons and gouged into his skin.

"Short of setting the forest on fire? Not really," Calfon rasped.

"Gods! Are there more out there?" Corran thought he caught a glimpse of movement in the shadows. The battle had forced them a distance from the clearing where the Rift opened, and Corran felt sure they had traveled far enough to have crossed the border. Right now, he would have welcomed the appearance of guards, so long as they helped beat back the monsters. If they survived, they could elude the guards, but if they went down beneath the ghouls, they would be done for.

"If we could hit them with vitriol, it might push them back," Ross said, out of breath as he cut the legs out from under one of the ghouls, only to have it drag itself forward with its arms, still a potent threat.

"We'll burn ourselves as well if it splashes," Calfon warned. "And that goes down to the bone."

Corran set his jaw and kept swinging, fearing it had finally come down to a choice of how they wished to die: by fire, by acid, or torn to pieces by the ghouls. *I'm sorry, Rigan. I did the best I could.*

The three hunters stood back to back, still badly outnumbered. The ghouls sensed their weariness and pressed forward, teeth bared for fresh meat.

This is it, our last stand, Corran thought.

But before the ghouls could make their last assault, dark forms poured from the woods. At first, Corran feared they were more monsters; then he realized they were people dressed in black, armed much like they were.

Whoever they were and wherever they came from, Corran welcomed the help. With an advantage gained on their attackers, Corran and his friends fought with renewed energy, battling the monsters shoulder-to-shoulder with their rescuers until the last of the creatures lay dismembered on the ground.

"Thanks," Corran said to the newcomers, while Ross and Calfon were already reaching for the salt mixture and green vitriol in their packs.

"Stay where you are." A tall man moved forward from the half-dozen fighters that had emerged from the woods. He and the others had scarves tied to cover their faces except for the eyes. That made it nearly impossible to gauge whether they were friend or foe.

"We mean no harm," Corran said. "We're only here to fight the monsters. Let us finish so they can't return, and we'll leave."

"You're from Ravenwood."

Corran thought he picked up a trace of a Sarolinian accent. All of Darkhurst had a common language, but the different city-states spoke it with subtle differences in words and inflection. "We didn't intend to cross the border," Corran replied. "We were fighting for our lives, and the battle shifted."

"Are you witches?"

Corran and his friends exchanged a glance at that. "No. Are you?"

The man shook his head. "Then explain how it is you were here before us, how you knew where the monsters would show up."

Shit, Corran thought. *That's going to be hard to explain without making this worse.*

"We were on patrol," he said. "This is what we do—hunting monsters. To protect the villages."

"It's illegal to hunt monsters—in Ravenwood and in Sarolinia."

"Yet here you are," Calfon challenged. "Seems to me you came to the same party ready to dance."

The man's laughter surprised Corran. "Well then, perhaps we all hang together," he said. "We also hunt monsters, and we, too, are outlaws."

The newcomers removed their scarves, revealing their faces. The tall man had sharp, angular features and dark hair, bearing a strong enough resemblance to Rigan that Corran had to blink to keep from tearing up. The others, two women and four men, had a wary, determined look to them that gave Corran to suspect they had been fighting this quiet war for a while.

"We need to get back—" Corran began.

"It's late, and you're injured," the tall man said. "At least come to our camp and eat, and let our healer take care of your wounds. I would like very much to hear your stories." He extended a hand. "I'm Brock."

Corran exchanged a glance with Ross and Calfon, whose expressions clearly said it was his call. "Thank you, Brock. We'll take you up on your offer."

CHAPTER NINETEEN

"IT GOT too dangerous inside the walls, so we left," Corran finished a highly edited version of their story. "We'd seen our families and friends die, and the guards wouldn't stop the monsters and wouldn't let us stop them, so we came out here and figured we'd try to do what we could."

Brock and his companions listened intently to Corran's tale. Corran wondered whether they guessed he had censored the details. The bounty on their heads was too high for him to risk that their new "friends" were entirely trustworthy.

"Commendable," Brock replied. "And similar in many ways to our own situation. We've all seen too much death, and now, there's the blight."

"You mean the dead zones, with the tainted grass?" Calfon asked

Brock nodded. "Yes. And more than that. When one of those things appears in a grazing field, the sheep or goats are torn apart. In a crop field, everything either dies or rots."

"It gets worse," one of the women in Brock's team spoke up. "The last time one of those circles showed up, some of the goats that got caught in it were pregnant. Most of them miscarried, but the couple that did give birth—the kids were misshapen, deformed. They didn't survive."

Corran knew what she didn't put into words. It was only a matter of time before the blight caught humans in its taint. Maybe, somewhere, it already had.

"Do you trust witches?" Corran asked, testing the waters before he revealed more.

Brock gave him an appraising look. "Some witches. My wife is a witch. I was raised a Wanderer. So if you're asking, do we fear magic for its own sake, no. We know better than that."

Corran nodded. "Good. We have some witches who help us. They believe the blight is something bad leaking out when a portal opens to a different place and monsters come through." He waited for their reaction.

Brock and the woman shared a glance. "We came to the same conclusion. But we still aren't sure why the portals open, or how to shut them for good."

"We can't shut them—not yet," Corran said abruptly enough that Brock frowned.

"Why not?"

"My brother, Rigan, and two of our friends—hunters—got pulled through one of those Rifts several days ago. We have to find a way to get them back."

"If monsters come from the place on the other side, there's no telling whether your brother and your friends are still alive," the woman said.

"I can't accept that. I won't."

"Please forgive my wife," Brock said. "She sometimes speaks bluntly." He smiled at her. "This is Mina. She is a talented witch—and if there's a way to find your brother, she may be able to help."

"Any help is appreciated," Corran replied. "And I know we're running out of time. They won't be able to last for long on the other side." He met Mina's eyes. "Please. He's the only family I have left, and Mir and Trent are good friends. We need to find a way to bring them home."

"Enough talk for now," Brock said. "Let's get you fixed up, and we'll talk while we eat."

Mina and one of the other men gathered supplies from a rucksack to treat the cuts the ghouls inflicted. Several of the wounds had already started to go bad, so Mina filled a cup with an odd-smelling liquid and insisted the three newcomers drink, as she and her helper cleaned the wounds and applied a medicinal paste before binding up the gashes.

"I'll pour some of this into a flask for you," Mina said, taking back the empty cup. "It's good medicine, and it will keep the infection from spreading."

"Our healer would love to have the recipe," Calfon said.

Mina smiled. "I'm sure he'll be able to figure it out once he tastes it. Simple, but effective."

Two of the men brought out trail rations of dried deer meat, hard cheese, and tough biscuits, and the group shared the provisions equally. "It's not our best cooking," Brock joked. "I'd hate for you to think this is what Sarolinians usually eat."

Ross laughed. "Don't worry. We understand. Can't pack a home-made hot meal in a saddlebag."

A wineskin passed around the circle gathered by the fire, and Corran thought the contents tasted like blackberry wine. When they were finished with their meal, he looked to Brock. "We will need to get back soon. Please, tell us what you know of the Balance and the Rifts. We've got to find Rigan and the others."

"You know of the Wanderers?" Brock asked.

Corran nodded. "My mother's people were Wanderers, though my grandmother left and married outside the clan."

"As have I," Brock said, with a sidelong glance toward Mina, who reached over and placed a hand on his forearm. "I saw a darkness coming, and my people were too stuck in the old ways to do all that they could to stop it. Or, so I thought at the time."

He stared at the fire for a moment before he continued. "The Wanderers help to keep the Balance. It's part of what their magic does, and some of the reason they always keep moving. Blood magic harms the Balance, and the Wanderers do what they can to restore it, but now—the harm is too great."

"How did the Wanderers get tied up in this anyhow?" Calfon asked. "They don't work blood magic, do they?"

Brock shook his head. "No. They were chosen—and cursed." He gave a sad smile. "I'll tell you a story. You can believe it or not, as you like. Long ago, in the days of the Elder Gods, Eshtamon and Colduraan struggled to see which was the greatest. Now, most people think of Eshtamon as the god of vengeance, but he has dominion over many things. Eshtamon favors creation and the Balance. Colduraan grows stronger in chaos. Colduraan taught humans the ways of blood magic, and he thrives on the bloodshed. The more blood magic is practiced, the stronger Colduraan becomes. Eshtamon does not favor blood magic, but so long as Colduraan has sway, Eshtamon must support the Balance. He chose a small group of nomads who had strong magic and made them his priests. That burden has been passed down from generation to generation, and those nomads became the Wanderers."

Brock looked up. "I have some of my people's magic. I had already sensed our blood in you," he said to Corran.

"My brother is a witch," Corran replied. "He also has Wanderer magic."

"Then they might survive," Mina said, her apologetic smile a peace offering for her earlier words. "I have spent years trying to understand my husband's abilities. They are different from other magics. I believe they come from Eshtamon himself, a portion of his power as a god."

Calfon and Ross looked at Corran, who gave a small shake of the head. He wasn't ready to tell these strangers about the night in the cemetery and receiving the blessing of an Elder God.

"We believe that Colduraan is using the blood witches to force a confrontation with Eshtamon, a proxy war of sorts," Brock continued. "The blood witches strain the Balance, opening Rifts that poison the land with the taint. Eshtamon has no choice but to respond or see chaos win."

Brock leaned forward. "This battle has raged for generations, centuries—maybe millennia. Colduraan seduces greedy men with the power of blood magic, knowing they will use too much, push too far. Eshtamon raises up champions to preserve the Balance and fix what is broken, and stop the ones who cause harm."

"And in all this time, neither side has won?" Calfon asked incredulously.

Brock shrugged. "Humans can't settle a score between gods. But each time the battle starts again, we can hold the line. And each time Colduraan fails to destroy us, there is a break—a time of peace—before the cycle starts again." He looked to Mina with a fond smile. "That's what I'm fighting for. Not an end to the war, but for a space in which we can live and raise our children without fear of the monsters and the taint before we pass the sword to the next generation."

"Do either of you know anything that would help us open a Rift and pull Rigan and our friends out?" Corran asked.

"I think so," Mina replied. She went to her rucksack and returned with a scrap of parchment and a bit of charcoal. "Give this to your witches," she said, marking some sigils on the parchment and a few words that meant nothing to Corran. He recognized one of the marks as the same one Rigan saw in a dream.

"Is it Wanderer magic?"

She shook her head. "It's bastardized magic—a little Wanderer and a little other. The Wanderers use their sigils for many things—but one use helps to ward against Rifts opening. This is the reverse. With luck, it will help you open a Rift in the place and time of your choosing."

Corran took the parchment. "If you can stop Rifts from opening—"

"Why don't we?" Brock finished for him. "Because it takes quite a lot of magic—energy—to activate the sigil and keep it active. There aren't enough of us to do that everywhere, and here in Sarolinia, unsanctioned magic is prohibited, as it is in Ravenwood. We dare not draw attention to ourselves too much. So we do what we can, to protect as many as we can."

"If—when—Rigan comes back, can he use his Wanderer magic to work the protection sigil?" Corran asked.

Mina took back the scrap and marked a second, different symbol on the other side. "That is the sigil to keep Rifts from opening. I don't know what your brother will be able to do. But warn him that such magic is visible to those who look for it. Be careful."

"Thank you," Corran said, tucking the parchment into his vest. "We need to head back. It seems we have a common enemy. Maybe we can help each other from time to time. How can we find you again?"

Brock rose to walk them to the edge of the camp. "We are often along the border. If you're near, we will find you. Good hunting."

———

To CORRAN'S RELIEF, the clouds overhead which had threatened rain parted without a storm. He and the others made sure their horses had food and water before starting the journey back to the monastery, but they were all anxious to get home. His body ached in every muscle and joint, and his gashes throbbed despite Mina's healing, making him fear how they might have been without it.

Aiden and Elinor greeted them when they came down the steps. "Thank the gods you're alive. When you didn't return, we worried," Elinor said, taking in the blood and dirt on their clothing and the evident exhaustion.

"Polly said she wasn't waiting up, so she went to bed," Aiden added with a chuckle. "Although I noticed she took a shot of whiskey before she went. We were all worried."

Corran found that between the ghouls' cuts and the ride, he couldn't help limping. "It's been a long night. I'll fill you in tomorrow. But in the meantime, there's this." He pulled out the parchment and handed it to Aiden. "A Sarolinian witch said it might be the key to opening a Rift, to getting Rigan home."

Aiden and Elinor exchanged a glance. "I'll make more coffee," Aiden said. "We'll get on this right away."

The next morning, Corran found Aiden asleep slumped over one of the worktables in their makeshift library. Aiden roused at the sound of footsteps. "I sent Elinor to get some sleep," he said, stretching and rubbing his eyes. He touched the half-empty coffee cup on the other side of the table. "It's still warm, so she hasn't been gone long."

"You didn't have to stay up all night," Corran chided.

Aiden yawned. "New information makes my mind churn. I wouldn't have slept even if I'd tried." He pushed out a chair with his foot. "Sit. Tell me what happened."

Aiden listened intently as Corran recapped the fight and their meeting with the Sarolinian hunters. "And then she gave me the sigils," he said, barely stifling a yawn himself. "Can you make anything of it?"

Ross came in with a tray of hard biscuits, boiled eggs, and salt beef, along with some fruit and a kettle full of coffee. "Polly left breakfast in the kitchen for us, and I figured I'd find you two in here. Elinor and Polly are still sleeping."

"Thanks," Aiden said, reaching immediately to refill his cup.

"Calfon's going to make some more arrows," Ross told Corran. "Right now, he's sharpening the axes, in case there are more *higani* or ghouls."

Ross went to help Calfon, and Corran turned back to Aiden. "What else?"

"Elinor and I went through more of the old texts," Aiden said, running a hand over his eyes. "Damn but some of them are hard to read! We found more about blood magic. I think it's enough for us to try opening a Rift—but then again, we don't know what we don't know. Might work, might kill us all."

"Aren't you cheery in the morning?" Corran muttered.

Aiden waved vaguely in the direction of their basement hideout's ceiling. "If it even is morning. Feels more like midnight."

"Pretty sure it was already after midnight when we got back," Corran replied, pouring some of the coffee for himself.

Aiden leaned back in his chair. "What your Sarolinian friend told you about Colduraan and Eshtamon—I've found legends to that effect in the lore books. Normally, I'd consider them to be just stories, but now that I actually know someone who talked to an Elder God," he cleared his throat with a pointed look at Corran.

"I've reconsidered my appraisal. Maybe there's some truth to the legend. Some of the old sages believed that the realm on the other side of the Rifts belongs to Colduraan, and it's a twisted mirror of our own.

Order and chaos again. Colduraan doesn't seem to have been overly popular with the other Elder Gods. Ardevan and Balledec didn't get involved in the argument, and Oj and Ren seemed to be curious about how it would all end."

"Curious," Corran echoed. "Two gods start a pissing match that could wipe out the world, and the Eternal Mother and Forever Father are merely 'curious'?"

"Maybe they figure if the kids break their toys, they'll make new ones," Aiden observed. "Gods aren't known for compassion."

"Did you find anything other than stories?" Corran felt his patience dissolving. It had already been four days since Rigan's disappearance into a hostile realm. Even with magic, he and the others could only fight for their lives for so long.

"Some of those stories make a lot of sense," Aiden replied, sipping his coffee. "Like the ones about the monsters that come through the Rift—the 'conjured' monsters. Once they come to this side, they can't breed. So if blood witches stop bringing them across, or we could seal the Rifts—after we get Rigan and the others back," he added hurriedly, holding up a hand to stave off Corran's protest, "then they would die out on this side."

"What about the other ones, like the strix?"

"Plenty of stories, nothing authoritative. They seem to belong here, like other predators. Some of them can breed, and others make 'off-spring' by killing and turning humans. But they don't seem to have anything to do with the Rifts or the blood magic," Aiden said. "Which is probably another reason why we never saw any in the city. They wouldn't have been controlled by the Lord Mayor and his pet blood witch."

"Or by whoever's using blood magic now," Corran muttered. "Someone brought those ghouls across last night. And the taint from the Rifts is getting worse."

"The more unstable the Rifts become, and the more skewed the Balance is, the worse that will get," Aiden said with a sigh. "It's all part of the energy trying to find equilibrium. If the Cull doesn't satisfy the Balance and the blood mages don't pay for their power, then the taint kills more and more to even it out."

Corran pointed to the sigil Mina had drawn. "Can you use it to open the Rift?"

"Probably. But before we try, I need a little more information."

"Rigan's running out of time."

Aiden fixed Corran with a look. "I know that. But we've probably got one shot at this, and if we don't do it right, not only do we not get Rigan and the others back, but we could make things worse."

"What do you need?"

Aiden smiled. "I need to see a ghost about some unfinished business."

————

"RIGAN IS THE one who knows how to summon spirits," Corran grumbled. "I'm more experienced at banishing them."

"How do you know this ghost is even going to show?" Polly asked.

"We found some of the old records about this monastery," Elinor replied. "One of the monks who was an original resident here felt so strongly about his duty that he swore his spirit would never leave this place and that he would watch over those who came after and help where he could."

"And you think that's true?" Calfon asked skeptically.

"I do," Elinor said. "Aiden and I have had a lot of strange incidents happen since we've gotten here. We'll be looking for something and not find it, and then turn around, and the book will be pulled out from the shelf, but neither of us did it. Or we'll be searching a manuscript in the middle of the night and close our eyes for a moment, and when we open them, the pages have turned to exactly the right place."

Aiden nodded. "It's always cool down here, but there are times when it suddenly gets cold enough to see my breath, for no good reason. I've seen candles flicker with no breeze, or a draft come out of nowhere. Doors open and shut on their own. Never anything that made me feel threatened—"

"More like having a teacher watching over your shoulder," Elinor finished for him.

"Did Rigan ever have any experiences with this ghost of yours?" Corran asked. "Because I'd have thought he would have summoned him before this, if there really is a ghost."

The door to the workroom slammed shut, without anyone near it.

Aiden raised an eyebrow. "As you were saying?"

"Nothing ever happened when Rigan was around," Elinor jumped in. "We teased him that the ghost was afraid of him. Maybe since Rigan's an undertaker, the ghost was afraid he'd send him to the After."

Corran frowned. "He could do that, but he wouldn't if the spirit objected. There have been many times we've allowed spirits to stay if they weren't hurting anyone."

"We always meant to ask Rigan to see if he could contact the ghost, but then… well," Elinor said. She had to close her eyes for a moment and look away.

"If Rigan scared him off, what makes you think he won't be scared of me?" Corran asked. "I didn't have Rigan's Confessor magic, but I've got the same grave magic."

"We were hoping you could introduce yourself and let him know you don't mean him any harm," Aiden said, a flush rising in his cheeks.

"I'll try," Corran replied. "I usually let Rigan talk to the ghosts. He's the patient one."

"What do you want the rest of us to do?" Polly asked.

Elinor shook her head. "Nothing. Make sure we aren't disturbed, which should be easy enough. And have something ready for us to eat afterward because we're likely to be drained from the magic."

"That I can do," Polly said. She elbowed Ross. "With a little help."

"Anything you need, Polly," Ross chuckled.

"Tell me a little about this ghost," Corran said as he set out the materials he needed, the salt mixture and the pigments to draw the sigils of the summoning circle. Now that he had taken a good look at Mina's rune, he saw similarities to the markings he had made for years to send the dead to their rest. Mina's sigil was similar, but the slight differences were vitally important. They would not be using her mark tonight.

"The only name we have for him is 'Tophen,'" Elinor replied. "He had been with the Order for many years, from the time he was a boy until he died of old age—and if the record is correct, he was ninety when he passed away. He was very smart and memorized a lot of their most important materials."

"Tophen became something of a wise man," Aiden said, preparing for his part of the ritual with a scrying bowl, special candles, and several rune stones which he positioned in a circle at the center of the larger summoning circle which Corran drew on the floor.

"The stories say he refused to let anyone help him pass over," Aiden continued. "He wanted to stay and watch out for those who came later."

"But he couldn't protect them when the Crown Princes drove out the monks," Corran replied quietly.

"No, he couldn't. But he stayed on—whether he's stuck or whether he wanted to remain, I don't know. The stories stop before the time that the monastery was abandoned. I guess up to that time, Tophen moved among the monks like an invisible brother. They talked to him and about him as if he never left."

"I think he's been lonely," Elinor said with a sad smile. "The monastery's been abandoned for a long time. Maybe that's why he's tried to be helpful. He wants us to stay."

"I looked through the journal Rigan brought with us, the one where he found the summoning ritual," Corran said. "So I can call his spirit so you can see and hear him—if he'll come. It's possible to compel a ghost, but in this case, I don't think it's wise."

He remembered what Rigan had told him—after the fact—about interrogating the spirit of someone who had betrayed them. Spirits could get angry and vengeful, and if that happened, it sometimes took all of Rigan's and Corran's magic together to send the ghost on and emerge unscathed. He did not want to take that chance working alone.

"I'm hoping we don't have to," Aiden replied. "And if the stories are true, Tophen might be happy to help us."

Corran marked four sigils on the worn wooden floor at each quarter, one in blue woad, orange ochre, white chalk, and black soot, with a line of the salt-aconite-amanita mixture connecting them to form a circle. Corran, Elinor, and Aiden would be inside the circle, and if all went well, the spirit would remain at a safe distance on the other side of the line.

"I won't be able to hold the connection long," Corran warned. "So don't spend too long chatting. Do you have your questions ready?" Aiden nodded.

"I can help you strengthen your bond with the spirit," Elinor said and withdrew an old string of prayer beads. "We found these with one of the monastery histories. They're said to belong to Tophen. I can do sympathetic magic—taking the properties of one thing and projecting them onto something else."

Elinor held up a small kerchief, and as it fluttered in the air, Corran caught the scenes of several types of plants. "I've steeped it in a 'tea' I made of plants that affect the memory or that support fidelity and loyalty. Once you open the conversation and call Tophen here, I'll put the kerchief over the beads. It won't force him to stay, but I'm counting on it to enhance the characteristics that would cause him to want to help us."

"Let's do it," Corran said. "The sooner you get your answers, the sooner we get Rigan and the rest of them back here with us."

It felt strange and wrong to work the grave magic without Rigan, and Corran fought down a lump in his throat at his brother's absence.

He shook off his fears, knowing that they were doing all they could. Whether it would be enough... remained to be seen.

Corran closed his eyes and began the chant. He and Rigan had done many banishing rituals together, but only Rigan had done the summoning spell. Corran had seen it once, the night of Kell's death when Rigan brought their younger brother's spirit back to them for a final goodbye. Between his memory of that night and Rigan's notes, Corran did his best.

It has been a long time since someone called to me. The ghost of a short, pudgy man with a bald head stood outside the circle, peering at Corran through slightly-askew spectacles. *You don't look like monks.*

Corran sat back on his haunches. "We aren't monks. We're only staying here for a while. We needed a safe place to hide from people who are trying to hurt us." He paused. "Are you Tophen?"

The monk nodded. *Yes. I wondered why strangers had come to the monastery. I tried to let you know I was here.*

Corran did his best to look non-threatening. "We noticed, but we didn't want to disturb you. I'm sorry to bother you now, but we need your help."

Tophen's ghost pushed up his spectacles and peered at Corran. *No bother. It was too quiet around here after everyone left. Nice to see people again. You need help?*

"The monks said you knew a lot of things. We need to find out how to get someone back from beyond a Rift."

Tophen's expression went from curious to cautious. *Why?*

"Someone's been using blood magic to open Rifts and bring monsters through," Corran explained. "Something from the other side of the Rift snatched my brother and our friends. We want to bring them home."

The ghost began to pace. *Oh, dear. That's not good. Not good at all,* he muttered, shaking his head. *I thought people had learned their lesson back in my day about monsters and Rifts and blood magic, but I guess not.*

"As a general rule, people don't learn well from experience," Corran commented.

Tophen gave a nervous chuckle. *They don't, do they? I guess some things never change.* He nodded, as if ending an internal discussion, and turned back to Corran. *What help did you think I could provide?*

"Your fellow monks thought that you knew all the lore."

They were generous with their praise and very young, Tophen deferred.

"Have living people ever gone beyond a Rift—and gotten back

alive?" Corran asked, and found himself holding his breath, waiting for an answer.

Tophen frowned. *The realm beyond the Rift was not made for humans. It belongs to Colduraan, a play yard for his monsters. I have never heard of anyone journeying there on purpose. The last time Rifts opened, there were stories about people who disappeared near them. I never heard that they came back.*

Corran swallowed hard. "Theoretically, could magic find them and bring them home if we could open a Rift near them?"

Tophen considered the statement, silent for so long Corran did not think he would answer. *Perhaps,* he said finally. *But such a working would be dark. I could never condone it for one of my monks, even to save lives.*

"Why?"

Tophen looked at him as if he were slow. *A Rift can't be opened without blood magic. And the amount of blood magic it would take to do that would require death—human death.*

Corran felt like he had been punched in the gut. "Are you sure?" he croaked, his throat suddenly dry.

From what the records suggest, yes, Tophen replied. *I have never worked such infernal magic myself.* The ghost managed to look insulted.

"What about a large animal—a wolf or a cow or a horse?" Corran bargained.

Perhaps, the ghost replied. *But some magic is intentionally repugnant to test the intentions of the one who casts it. Those who work blood magic care little for life of any kind, only power.*

Corran's chest felt tight, and it was hard to breathe. His pulse raced, and he wanted to throw up. *We can't get them back. We can't bring them home.* "But suppose… that it didn't have to be a human sacrifice. How would we reach through the Rift to guide them back?"

Tophen clasped his hands behind his back as he paced, head down, thinking hard. *Your grave magic might be able to make an opening, if you focus on the Rift instead of the After. In both cases, you're pulling apart the fabric of your world to create a doorway to another.*

"That door could open anywhere. How do we make sure Rigan and the others are in the right place at the right time?"

Tophen chewed his lip as he thought. *You are able to communicate with me—a ghost—across the chasm that is death. The Rift is just another sort of chasm. Two possibilities come to mind. Your grave magic may be able to communicate with your brother's spirit—dead or alive—if your power is strong enough. The other road lies through dreams.*

"Dreams?" Aiden echoed.

Tophen nodded. *For those without grave magic, dreams are often a "thin space" where the normal rules of reality don't always apply. If you can dream walk, you might be able to reach them and pass along a plan. It would have to be simple and quick, but it might work.*

"I've heard of dream walking, but I don't know how—"

Before Aiden could finish his sentence, a book wiggled loose from one of the shelves and appeared to topple to the floor entirely on its own. Tophen gave a pleased smile. *That text has what you'll need.* His smile faded. *But beware—dreams can be just as real as the waking world, and some monsters can hunt in dreams. Die in the dream world or beyond the Rift, and you will remain dead.*

Tophen's image flickered as Corran felt fatigue sap his magic. *I will watch over you,* Tophen promised. *I'm not going anywhere.* With that, the monastery's resident ghost winked out of sight.

Corran found himself breathing heavily and fighting a blinding headache. He released the power from his wardings and smudged open the protective circle. As he tried to get to his feet, he stumbled, and both Elinor and Aiden ran to help him into a chair.

"Well, at least we know who's been keeping an eye on the place," Aiden said with forced levity as he fetched a glass of water for Corran.

"Seems like a decent guy," Elinor added. "Although I would have liked it better if he'd announced himself from the start. I feel a bit... exposed."

Corran chuckled. "He didn't seem like the type to misuse his advantage," he assured her. Aiden brought him cheese, dried fruit, bread, and honey, and Corran forced himself to eat, knowing how much a working took out of him. Elinor gave him a cup of medicinal tea, and Corran felt himself begin to rally.

"I can't do much to ease your headache," Aiden said. "It's a consequence of overusing magic. But when you feel better, remind me to give you a lesson on grounding your power. You might not have quite the same amount of magic as Rigan, but knowing how to ground it properly will keep it from taking quite as bad a toll."

"What did you think, about our options?" Corran asked.

Aiden leaned against the wall, while Elinor pulled up a chair. "I guess you already know that I don't like any of them," Aiden said. "They're all risky, and we really don't have good information to know what we're getting into."

"The way I see it, we can do it the easy way or the hard way," Corran said, exhaustion clear in his voice. "The easy way is trying the grave magic again, but focused on the Rift, and if that doesn't work, doing a dream walk. And the hard way—" He looked to Aiden. "If I cut myself, how far can I bleed out and how close to dead can I get and have you still be able to heal me?"

Aiden paled, and Elinor gasped quietly. "You can't be serious," Aiden stammered. "That's suicide."

"I'm not going to leave them in that godsforsaken realm if there's a way to bring them back," Corran replied. "And I'm not going to trade the life of a horse. So that's why I'm asking, if it comes down to it, how close can I get and still have you keep me from dying?"

Aiden ran a hand over his face and shook his head, looking as if words failed him. "What you're asking... I can't be sure... There'd be no way to promise I could fix that type of blood loss in time, especially if I had to work the actual ritual." Aiden paced. "Maybe if we had several strong witches—one to work the ritual and open the Rift while one maintains your life, keeps you from dying... even then, it would be too much of a gamble."

"Elinor?" Corran asked, "could she be the helper?"

Elinor shook her head. "No. I don't have enough training, and my power doesn't work that way. I can do like-calls-to-like magic, maybe ease a headache, but my magic is mainly with plants and poppets. I'd be little help on either side of the working, though I'll do anything that you think would help. I want them back, too."

"Mina," Corran said, meeting Aiden's gaze. "The wife of the Wanderer-hunter we met in Sarolinia. She's a witch, and a powerful one too, I bet. Maybe she'd help."

"Let's hope it doesn't get to that point," Aiden said. "You need to rest, and then tomorrow—"

"Rigan and Mir and Trent are already on borrowed time," Corran snapped. "How long do you think they can hold out? We don't even know if they've got food and water, but we know for sure that there are plenty of monsters."

"Pushing yourself until you collapse—or trying some crazy suicide trick—isn't going to bring them back," Aiden argued.

"Enough," Elinor said, in a tone that shut up both men. "You're both right, but I've got to side with Corran—putting this off might be safer for us, but not for Rigan and the others. So how about you split the magic? Aiden does the dream walk—I think I can come up with a way Corran and I can see what he sees without doing the magic ourselves—and then Corran tries the grave magic to open the Rift."

Aiden looked chagrined. "She's right. There isn't time for 'careful,' although I'd rather not run right past into 'reckless.' I'm in."

Corran nodded. "Yeah. Me too."

It took another two candlemarks to gather everything needed for the dream walk and put together the mixture that would allow Aiden to slip into his trance. A second potion would enable Corran and Elinor to observe, but not participate, in his dream. Corran glanced at the others. They were all tired, but he saw the same resolute set to the jaw on both Aiden and Elinor that he glimpsed in his own reflection. One way or the other, regardless of the outcome, they intended to see this through.

"Don't 'not now, Polly' me!" Polly kicked the workroom door open with such force that Aiden had to jump back or be knocked off his feet. "You can't do good magic on an empty stomach. We've got rabbit stew, courtesy of Ross's traps and some onions and potatoes Calfon found in the garden out back. There's coffee boiling and plenty of whiskey for afterward."

She set down a tray with three bowls and some fresh bread. "Eat," she ordered, hands on hips. "Don't make me get out my wooden spoon!"

Despite everything, Corran and the two witches managed tired smiles and thanked Polly as they ate quickly. Nervousness and grief made Corran's stomach sour, but he realized how long it had been since he'd had a proper meal and forced the food down, though nothing tasted right.

"That's better," Polly said after they finished their meal. "I'll send Ross down with some bread and honey with some cheese and raisins for later, because I get the feeling you're in for a long night." She gathered up the tray and paused. "Do you have a plan? Can you get them back?"

Corran looked away and shrugged. Aiden stepped forward. "I won't say it's a great plan, but we've got some ideas. And we won't know whether they'll work until we try."

Polly nodded. "All right then. The rest of us will do whatever you need to give you the best shot. Try not to leave too much of a mess."

Elinor closed the door behind her. Aiden dragged some bedding into the center of the room, and Corran set down a fresh circle of the salt mixture. Later, if they needed him to do grave magic again, he would draw the sigils. Different magic, different wardings.

Aiden sat on the pile of bedding and Elinor handed him a cup with a decidedly unappetizing slimy green mixture. From the expression on Aiden's face as he drank it, the concoction tasted as bad as it looked. In his right hand, Aiden held something that belonged to Rigan, one of his shirts that Corran had retrieved from Rigan's room. In his left hand, he held a polished focus stone to help ground his magic and anchor him to this side of the Rift. Elinor placed candles at each of the quarters.

"Ready?" Aiden asked.

Corran and Elinor took cups of a different, brownish mixture and drank. It looked awful, but it smelled like flowers and tasted of mead. Aiden lay down on the bedding, stretching out and getting comfortable. Corran and Elinor sat down one at each side of his head and placed their right hands on Aiden's shoulders.

"Here we go," Aiden murmured nervously, closing his eyes.

"It's going to take a few minutes for the potion to work," Elinor explained in a whisper. "He won't begin to dream until he's relaxed enough to slip into a deep trance."

Corran tried not to fidget, reining in his nervousness and impatience. He could feel the drink begin to affect him, softening the tightness in his shoulders and lessening the remainder of his headache. He kept his eyes on the candle as Elinor had instructed, using it to focus, and took deep, regular breaths. When he could not hold his eyes open any longer, Corran let them close, still keeping his contact with Aiden.

For a few moments, everything remained black. Then blurry images began to form, though he kept his eyes closed. Gradually, the vision cleared.

Everything around him had been leeched of its color, leaving only shades of gray. They stood in a forest, but it looked unlike any Corran had seen before, with unfamiliar plants and an eerie sense of being watched. He glanced around, searching the brush and the tree canopy for threats, but could not shake a pervasive, primal fear of being stalked. That was when he realized that even when they hunted monsters, Corran took for granted he was the predator. Here, he and the other humans were clearly prey.

Aiden moved through the tangled brush with confidence as if he knew the way. Perhaps he did, Corran thought, remembering that Aiden held something belonging to Rigan. As Aiden ventured deeper into the woods, Corran felt itchy for the grip of his sword in his hand, something to heft and hold to be able to protect Aiden's back.

The sense of being watched grew stronger, and now that his eyes had adjusted to the shadows, he saw movement everywhere and glimpses of reflected light from the eyes of the things that watched them. Corran had to remind himself that they were not really beyond the Rift, not real. *Then again, maybe there are monsters here that feed on dreams that eat ghosts. Maybe you don't have to be entirely real to die here.*

The terrain changed without them moving through it, proof once more that they were in a dream state. In another heartbeat, the forest was behind them, and Aiden looked up at a cliff side in the twilight. Near the top, a fire lit the entrance to a cave. In the blink of an eye, they stood outside the cave, and Corran saw a barricade of stacked stones with a line of burning wood inside, and beyond that, in the flickering light of the fire, he saw the forms of three men.

Aiden's dream-self passed through the stone wall and the fire without harm. Trent stood watch near the mouth of the cave. As Aiden moved past, Trent frowned, glancing around as if he sensed a presence, then going back to staring into the night after he assured himself nothing had entered.

Mir lay wrapped in his cloak on the left, while Rigan slept huddled on the right. Corran's heart leaped to see the three of them alive. Then he took a closer look and saw the strain on their dirty faces, the blood and mud that streaked their ripped clothing, and how much thinner they looked.

Aiden knelt next to Rigan and placed his hand on Rigan's forehead. Rigan stirred his sleep, mumbling and turning over, but did not wake.

Their surroundings changed again, and this time Corran guessed that they were inside Rigan's dreams. Rigan was running for his life from one of the bat-faced *vestir*, as big as a sow with matted, shaggy hair, sharp teeth, and wicked claws. Corran felt his brother's panic as branches and leaves whipped at him when he ran past, slicing skin. The monster grew closer, and Corran had no way to know whether Rigan was reliving a narrow escape or having a nightmare about possible threats.

Aiden stepped between Rigan and the monster. In a blink, the creature vanished, leaving Aiden and Rigan together in the forest.

"How? How are you here?" Rigan panted. "Is Corran with you?"

"He sees what I see," Aiden replied. "I can't stay long, so listen. Find your way back to the clearing where you were taken, or the place in this world where you came through. We're going to try to open the Rift, but you need to be where we can find you when it does."

"I'll help from this side," Rigan promised. "When?"

"I don't know how you reckon time here," Aiden replied. "Noon tomorrow is the time our magic will be strongest. It's around eighth bells here now. Get to the meeting place and stay safe until we can get you out."

Rigan nodded, and looked as if he were searching behind Aiden for someone he couldn't see. "Tell Corran and Elinor that I miss them. Tell them we're going to make it back."

Corran felt his throat tighten, and he mouthed the words he wished he could say to encourage his brother to hang on.

"I will," Aiden said. "They know. And they're doing everything to bring you back. Just be there and watch your backs, and you'll be home before you know it."

As quickly as the scene had appeared in their minds, it vanished, leaving Corran in the dark once more. He had wondered if they needed to make the return trek in the dream world, but apparently not. Either that, he thought, or Aiden had tired and snapped them out of the vision when his magic failed.

Slowly, Corran came back to himself. His legs were numb, still folded under him where he sat next to Aiden on the floor of the workshop. His shoulder ached from keeping one arm outstretched in contact with the healer. He felt dazed and groggy, but nothing mattered except that he had seen with his own eyes—through Aiden's vision—that Rigan and the others were still alive.

Elinor moaned as she shifted position, stiff muscles protesting after remaining still for so long. Corran opened his eyes and looked at Elinor, who stared back in amazement.

"Did you see that?" they both asked in unison.

On the floor between them, Aiden groaned and then blinked awake. He melted into the bedding in relief to see that the others were also lucid and that they were back where they belonged.

"It worked," Corran said, surprised that after everything he could muster the energy to be excited. He clapped Aiden on the shoulder. "Damn, that was some fine magic."

"I feel like I've been dragged behind a wagon," Aiden mumbled.

Corran and Elinor moved as quickly as they could to help Aiden off the floor and into a chair. Elinor opened the door, and the promised tray of food lay in the hallway outside, along with a flagon of whiskey.

"Polly was as good as her word," she chuckled tiredly, bringing the tray inside and setting it on the table.

She looked at Aiden and Corran. "Eat. There's a reason heroes in the myths are always feasting. Food grounds the body to reality."

"You've been reading the old epic tales again, haven't you?" Aiden replied, chuckling.

Elinor sniffed as if she were offended, although her tired smile suggested otherwise. "And why not? They're fine reading. Imagination wound around bits of truth." She nudged Aiden with her shoulder and elbowed Corran. "So, eat!" She ordered, tearing off a hunk of bread and drizzling it with honey and butter before adding cheese and raisins.

"They're alive," Corran said the words aloud and felt a weight roll off his shoulders. "I can hardly believe it, and they look like shit, but they're alive."

Aiden nodded. "Damn fine to see that. Now they just have to stay that way a little longer."

Corran looked over at him, worried. "Do you think he'll remember?"

Aiden frowned. "Yes. The encounter in his dream was clear and sharp. Stopping the monster attack helped; strong emotion makes dreams more memorable, and Rigan was afraid and then relieved."

"All right then," Corran replied, feeling more confident about the possibility of his brother's and friends' safe return since their disappearance. "Tomorrow, we head for the clearing, and we give it all we've got."

———

"WELL, WE'RE HERE. Let's hope Rigan and the others got the message," Aiden said as they readied themselves for the working.

The empty clearing where the Rift had opened looked as it had the night their friends had been pulled through, with the exception of the circle of dead grass that marked the spread of the taint. Wordlessly, they all kept back from the poisoned area, wary of how it might affect both health and magic.

Corran had anticipated the challenges of attempting grave magic in a field of tall grass. He stomped down a circle and flattened the weeds inside. Then he took out four wooden stakes, each one marked with one of the sigils Mina had sketched for them for his working and hammered them into the ground at the quarters. Finally, he took a rope that had been soaked in the salt/aconite mixture and strung it between the posts to make his warding circle.

"Ready," Corran said, trying to tamp down his nervousness. He stared at the spot the Rift had appeared, hoping in vain it would happen once more on its own. Corran had barely slept, too nervous to relax, fearful of what might happen—or worse, what might not.

Calfon, Ross, and Polly had insisted on coming to stand guard. Now that they were here, Corran felt safer knowing someone was watching out for them. They still had guards and bounty hunters on their trail, and while the clearing was fairly remote, he did not want to bring Rigan and the others home only to land them in the middle of a battle.

Aiden set a larger warded circle, still remaining clear of the tainted ground. Elinor followed, sowing a mixture made from plants that enhanced perception and aided with Sight. They both had pledged their help with boosting Corran's magic, helping him sustain his working for as long as possible.

From what Aiden could find in the old texts, the realm beyond the Rift would be closest—and the barrier between realms the thinnest—at noon or midnight. Since they had lost their companions just after noon, they all agreed that was the best time to attempt the working.

"Let's do it," Aiden said, giving a nod to Corran. Aiden and Elinor came to stand with Corran inside his salt rope circle.

Corran felt his heart thud and wiped his clammy palms on his pants. He was more afraid than before any fight with monsters. Even though he had seen Rigan, Mir, and Trent through Aiden's eyes in the dream walk, he could not silence the voice in his mind that whispered tragic possibilities. *What if something attacked them in the night? What if this doesn't work? What if we can't get them back?*

Corran pushed the fears aside and took a deep breath, then closed his eyes. For a few seconds, he could have almost been back in their workshop in Ravenwood, with bodies to prepare and Kell upstairs making supper, in the home where he and Rigan had grown up. He let the familiarity of that image ground him as he found his center and then he began to chant.

The words were almost the same as the traditional ritual to guide a spirit into the After. Almost, but not quite. With Aiden's help, Corran had made adjustments, and he hoped with all his being that the changes were sufficient and that the magic would follow his intent.

Corran felt the thrum of power rise with his chant, tingling over his skin and through his veins. He had not thought of their undertaking rituals as true magic until Rigan had pointed it out to him; now, he wondered how it ever escaped his notice. He might not be able to cast fire or move objects with his mind like his brother could, but the energies that rose to his summons were unmistakable a force of their own.

Aiden and Elinor murmured chants to mesh their magic with his and amplify his effort. Corran felt the power built around them, crackling in the air like sparks from a fire. The air felt heavy like a storm was brewing, and he tried to repress a shiver and hold his focus on the intention of opening a tear in the sky and bringing his brother home.

Corran opened his eyes, staring at the place where Rigan had vanished. The air shimmered, and he heard Elinor gasp.

"It's working," she breathed.

Corran's chant built to a crescendo, and he pulled all the magic he knew how to command into his invocation. For an instant, he saw a vertical line in the midst of the shimmering air, a cut in the fabric of their world.

And in the next heartbeat, the tear vanished.

Corran's eyes widened, and his heart hammered. He kept on chanting, finishing the ritual, hoping that the glimmer would return.

"It's gone," he moaned when he completed the invocation, and no sign of a Rift appeared. "Did you see? It started and then—"

Tears ran down Elinor's face, and she nodded silently. Aiden looked dumbstruck. Corran's disappointment shifted into anger, and he pulled the knife from his sheath.

"If grave magic won't work, then let's see what blood magic can do," he snarled.

Aiden grabbed his arm. "Corran, wait!"

He shook his head. "I've waited long enough—Rigan, Mir, and Trent can't wait any longer." Corran swallowed hard. "If there's way to do it, bring me back. I don't want to die. I want to bring them home. And if we can't then it doesn't matter anyway…"

Corran brought the knife down on his left forearm, cutting a bloody slit from wrist to elbow, and as the warm blood spilled over his outstretched palm, he chanted the forbidden words he had spent the night committing to memory.

I just want to bring my brother home.

CHAPTER TWENTY

RIGAN TOSSED IN his sleep, at the edge of wakefulness. His cloak offered scant comfort against either the chill night air or the hard rock of the cave floor. The fire that protected them from things that hunted in the dark also filled the cave with smoke, making him cough. His arm cramped, protesting at being used as a pillow.

He shifted, getting as comfortable as he could, and fell back asleep. Once more, Rigan's dreams were dark, filled with memories of Kell's death, the night their home went up in flames, and of battles with monsters and the final fight with Blackholt. The scenes shifted, and he saw the attack at the clearing, the *higani* pouring through the Rift seconds before he and the others were pulled in. But in his dream, one of the *higani* skittered straight for Corran, and before his brother could react to Rigan's warning shout, it sank the sharp tip of a jointed leg through Corran's chest.

"Corran," Rigan yelled in his dream as the Rift pulled at him.

Corran sank to his knees in the clearing, grasping at his chest, tearing away the *higani* too late. The last thing Rigan saw before the Rift closed behind him was Corran, ashen-faced and dying, as he fell forward into the poisoned grass.

Rigan moaned and thrashed, but did not wake. Once more, he felt the attention of the presence focused on him. Each time, he sensed it more clearly, though whether that meant it was closer, he could not tell. It fixed him with the glare of its many eyes, and he felt its appraisal. The presence regarded him curiously as if deciding whether he might be friend or foe, food or ally. Its utter alienness made Rigan's flesh crawl. Instinct overrode conscious thought, and he ran.

The hideous images faded, and Rigan found himself walking in darkness. "Hello? Is anyone here?" he called into the shadows. A *vestir* emerged from the thick brush, charging with its fangs bared. Rigan tried to outrun the creature, then finally turned to fight when he realized he could not escape. The *vestir* attacked with tireless energy, and Rigan knew he would lose the fight.

A new figure appeared from nowhere and stepped between Rigan and the *vestir*. Rigan stared, fearing a greater threat than the monster until Aiden moved into the light, and the *vestir* vanished. Rigan breathed a sigh of relief. "You're here? How? Can you take us home with you?"

He listened as Aiden spoke to him of a desperate plan, and warned that their time together was short. Rigan committed the details of the plan to memory and swore to do everything in his power to help from his side of the Rift. Far too soon, Aiden's image flickered and faded.

Rigan woke, unsurprised to find tears on his face.

"Rigan? Are you all right?" Trent stayed at his post at the front of the cave but turned enough to give him an appraising look.

"I had bad dreams," Rigan said and frowned. "At least, some of them were nightmares." He licked his dry lips and decided once again to say nothing about the presence. "But at the end... I swore that Aiden came to me with a message about a rescue plan." He looked up at Trent, feeling the first flicker of hope in days. "I'm certain that really was Aiden using his magic, somehow, to tell us what to do."

Trent's pained expression mingled doubt and despair. "I want to believe you, Rigan. Gods, do I want to believe you. But... it's so easy to see what we want to see. How could Aiden send you a message, across the Rift?"

Rigan drew his legs up and wrapped his arms around them, pulling himself into a tight ball. "I don't think it's a coincidence that I saw him when I was dreaming," he said slowly, working out his thoughts as he spoke. "We talked about dream magic once. There are stories about witches being able to dream walk—either out of their bodies or into someone else's dreams. It wasn't something I had time to look into, but the idea sounded interesting, and when I asked Aiden, he believed that at least some of the stories were true."

"If he can get to you in a dream, why can't his magic reach you when you're awake?"

Rigan frowned. "I don't know, but I think it's because dreaming is a 'place between' waking and sleeping, the same way ghosts exist in a place between life and death. If someone could learn to travel those between places, it might work like a hidden passageway, taking them to where they otherwise couldn't go."

Mir groaned and turned over, clutching his cloak, but he did not wake. Trent looked out into the darkness, silent for a few minutes.

"If he made the trip—assuming I believe it was real—he must have had a message. What did he say?"

Rigan repeated the instructions he had memorized. "That's it?" Trent asked. "Just, go back to where we came through and wait? With all the monsters out there? How long do you think we'll last?"

"We found the marker," Rigan replied. "And the note on the arrow. So we know they're trying to find us. But if they open the Rift and we aren't near it, they won't be able to come looking for us. We'll miss our chance—and we may not get another."

"How can they open the Rift if you can't?"

Rigan heard the skepticism in Trent's voice and tried not to take it personally. The other hunters had come a long way since that first night when they had fled the guards in Ravenwood and learned his secret. They had accepted and protected him—and Aiden and Elinor—even though magic was strange and frightening for them. Trent was clearly trying to understand something utterly foreign to him, and Rigan struggled to find a way to make it easier to accept Aiden's message.

"Aiden's got the benefit of all those lore books back at the monastery. I'm betting he found something he thinks will work. He's got Elinor to help him, and if it involves grave magic, Corran too.

"But you tried grave magic, and it didn't work."

Rigan shook his head. "I didn't try to use it to open the Rift, just to see if there were spirits of humans here. I've been thinking about what to do next, and I'd decided to try a mixture of grave magic and blood magic." He looked to Trent.

"So here's my plan," he ventured. "Go to where the marker is, where we came through. And as close to noon as we can reckon it, I work a ritual on this side, trying to thin the curtain between realms. If Aiden and Corran and Elinor are on the other side, and we're both tearing at the Rift, maybe we can get it open long enough to get through."

Trent nodded. "I won't lie. I'm not really sure of this. But we're running out of options, and Mir is running out of time."

Rigan and Trent both looked to where Mir lay, shivering and twitching beneath his cloak. Despite Rigan's poultices and teas, Mir's wounds from the previous battle with the monsters had gone sour. Fever came and went. His strength was waning, and his moments of wakefulness grew shorter as the candlemarks passed. Rigan suspected that Mir had given up and that the bleak moods that plagued him since their escape from Ravenwood finally wrested his surrender. Rigan had not told the others, but the sickness he felt from the tainted magic grew worse each day. They needed to make their move soon, while they still could.

"Do you have any idea how to know when it's noon on the other side?" Trent asked. "When it's daylight, with all the clouds, I can't see a bloody thing in the sky."

"I've got a candle in my pouch," Rigan said. "If I mark off the hours, we can light it at dawn and figure it that way. Won't be precise, but it might be close enough."

"You realize how many 'maybes' are strung together in this plan, don't you?" Trent cautioned. He sounded tired and resigned. They had been trapped in the Rift for days, and it had gone hard on all of them.

The prospect of remaining here forever seemed more likely the more time passed.

"Yeah. It's not the best, but it's all we've got."

"If it doesn't work—" Trent licked his lips and looked away. "If it doesn't work, we might not get back to the cave. Magic like that will draw attention. The things out there that feed on it—or on us—will smell dinner. We probably won't have another chance."

Rigan swallowed hard and nodded. "Then we'd better make it count."

———

BETWEEN THE TWO of them, Rigan and Trent got Mir down the cliff side along with the gear they had remaining. Trent held a torch and Rigan had his sword. Mir stumbled between them, drifting in and out of awareness.

Over the days they had been there, they had used most of their precious remaining salt mixture to protect a path down to the stream, so at least they knew they could make it that far without a fight. Rigan had left the marked candle back in the cave, but they had waited until two candlemarks remained before what they guessed was noon. If Rigan had reckoned time correctly, that gave them one candlemark to travel to the beacon, and another to wait for rescue and work magic of their own.

The monsters preferred the dark. Rigan felt no less watched than usual as they made their way toward the place where they had come through the Rift, but fire and steel were warning enough to keep daylight predators at a distance, and the prey creatures that scurried to find food paid them no mind.

"I won't miss roasted rat-thing," Trent mused as they walked. "I like being able to identify what I'm eating."

"Then I guess you never ate at The Muddy Goat back in Raven-wood," Rigan said. "Any animals that went missing near there, people figured they went into the pot."

"There are things about the city I don't miss," Trent replied.

It took longer than Rigan anticipated to reach the rendezvous point, but given that they arrived without being eaten or maimed, he counted it as a win. They eased Mir to the ground.

"We're here," Rigan told him.

Mir stirred, and he looked up at Rigan with lucidity. "You think they can get us home?" he asked, his voice rough.

"Yeah. I think they can. And I'm going to do all I can to help from this side." He clapped a hand on Mir's shoulder. "Sit. I've got this."

Rigan marked sigils on the bare ground with the pigments he made from the plants they gathered and set out a thin line of salt with the last of the mixture he had hoarded. If this didn't work, it wouldn't matter if they ran out.

"What are you planning to use for blood magic?" Trent asked. "I don't see a sacrifice."

Rigan rolled up his sleeve. "I'm hoping it doesn't require one," he said. "I'm hoping what I can supply is enough."

Trent looked at him incredulously. "It's not bad enough that we're stuck in the open, waiting, or that we're going to reek of magic— you're going to add fresh blood? We won't live long enough to get through the Rift even if they can get it to open!"

"I won't work the blood magic until the very end," Rigan said. "But the more I've thought about it, the more I'm convinced that for something this big—a hole between realms—it's got to be human blood. I just hope it doesn't need all of it." *But if that's what it takes to get Mir and Trent home, then that's the price of passage.*

"Corran will skin me if I come back without you."

"With luck, it won't come to that," Rigan said with a thin smile, which didn't reach his eyes. "And if it does, I'll haunt his ass if he gives you grief."

"Won't do me much good if he kills me," Trent muttered.

Rigan watched the light, hoping that the gradual brightening was not merely a trick of the ever-present clouds. When it felt right, he exchanged a glance with Trent. "It's close enough—I'm going to start."

"I hope you know what you're doing," Trent replied. "And if you don't, put in a good word with Doharmu for me."

Trent moved to stand guard over them while Rigan worked his magic. Mir, still shaking with fever, watched with glassy eyes where he sat propped against a log a few feet away from Rigan's circle.

Rigan knelt in the center of the circle, closed his eyes, and drew a deep breath. He sent up a prayer to Doharmu and Eshtamon for protection and success. *Please, if I'm supposed to be your champion, let me get back to my brother. We can't serve your vengeance otherwise.*

He had spent the morning preparing, not simply for the magic, but for the very real possibility of death. It broke his heart to think that the gambit might not be successful, that he might die here in this godsforsaken realm and never see Corran or Elinor or his friends again. But grief had cooled into resignation and a cold resolve.

They were going home today, or they were going on. But they would not be staying here.

Rigan drew on the power that went beyond his grave magic, the legacy of his Wanderer heritage. He laid a hand on each sigil and the pigments stirred with an inner light, as did the salt circle, burning with a pure white fire. He began to chant the incantation that he and Corran and Kell—and his family before them—had used to speed the dead to their rest.

He had made adjustments to the wording, more on gut feel than out of specific knowledge, trying to adapt it to opening the Rift instead of a portal to the After. *Although we might be needing that if this doesn't go well.*

As he chanted, Rigan watched the sky. He had not been entirely truthful when he told Trent his plan. He suspected that a working of the magnitude of opening a Rift would require not only blood magic, but the shedding of lifeblood. The blood witches used the poor wretches they snatched from the street or the criminals they pulled from their jails. Rigan intended to use himself as the source to get his friends home. He hoped Corran would forgive him, eventually.

Rigan felt the magic rise around him. He sensed the interest of creatures lurking in the shadows and saw the reflected light in their eyes. Magic and fresh meat were an irresistible call to the monsters of the Rift, and Rigan knew they were surrounded. Trent had been right; if this didn't work, they would never make it back to the cave.

Rigan continued his chant, taking comfort in the mostly familiar words, imagining that he could hear Corran's voice rising and falling with his own. He anchored his magic in the air around them, unwilling to take a chance on the tainted ground beneath their feet, afraid that the taint that spilled out of the Rift might somehow twist his magic.

The air stirred around them as power rose. Rigan felt it raise the hairs on his arms and make the back of his neck prickle with primal fear. He felt it tighten his stomach and speed his heart. He pulled hard on his anchor, channeling all of his magic into a single focus, willing the air to shimmer and ripple, to open into a portal home.

He saw something begin to sparkle and raised the sharp knife over his forearm. But before he could draw the blade across his flesh, a deep, guttural growl came from the trees.

One of the bat-faced black *vestir* bounded from the shadows. It shouldered Trent aside, ignoring his lit torch and his sword, shoving him toward where the air twisted and bent. Rigan turned the knife he intended for himself, rising from a crouch, expecting to feel the impact of the monster as it bore him to the ground with a crushing weight and tore him to pieces.

"No!" Moving faster than Rigan thought possible, Mir staggered to his feet, placing himself squarely between the charging monster and his friends. The creature swiped a massive paw, throwing Mir out of its way, tearing open his belly with its long, sharp claws.

Mir stumbled toward the circle, holding his entrails in with both hands, gasping in shock and pain. Blood spilled down over his hands, soaking his tattered clothing, pooling on the hard, dry ground. "I knew we wouldn't make it…"

A sound like thunder made the ground quake, a blinding light made them look away, and then a thin, fiery tear opened in the air like a rip in the fabric of the universe, and in the distance, Rigan heard Aiden shouting for them.

"Now!" he yelled. Trent dove through the opening and Rigan pushed Mir through before plunging into the Rift himself.

He landed in a heap on the other side, on the dead, poisoned grass of the clearing. Trent struggled to his knees, and Mir lay sprawled a few feet away.

"Rigan!" Corran shouted.

In the next moment, Rigan felt himself pulled into a bone-crushing embrace, barely able to breathe. "Thank the gods you're back!" Corran said, and Rigan could feel his brother shaking, and the moisture of his tears with his face buried in the crook of Rigan's neck.

"Thank you," Rigan managed, too overwhelmed and stunned to say everything in his mind. Gradually, clarity returned. Rigan leaned against Corran, and felt warm, wet heat soaking through his shirt.

"You're bleeding."

Corran seemed to suddenly remember, and he pulled back, revealing his bloody forearm and the clean slash. "I knew it was going to take blood to bring you home," he said. "I wasn't going to leave you there."

Rigan gave a shaky chuckle, afraid to admit how similar their thoughts had been. If the monster had not attacked and Mir had not been sacrificed, Rigan would have drawn the blade through his own flesh to satisfy the cost of passage.

Aiden laid a hand over Corran's arm, and the cuts healed as they watched.

"Mir—" Rigan began.

Aiden knelt next to the spot where Mir lay on the dry, brown grass. "He's dead. There's nothing I can do."

Rigan's breath caught, and he struggled for composure. "We need to do right by him. We owe him that."

"Someone might notice us riding home with a corpse," Aiden observed.

"We can't leave him here like this," Trent said.

"Plenty of rocks in this field," Calfon said. "We can raise a cairn. I know you don't have your special pigments, but surely two undertakers can send his spirit to the After without fancy paints."

Corran nodded. "Aye. We can do that."

Trent, Ross, and Calfon began fetching rocks, while Polly and

Elinor sidled closer, offering to help with the ritual. Corran and Rigan raised their voices in the chant, but the litany seemed lonelier than ever on this windswept plain.

"Thank you," Rigan said as Mir's spirit hesitated, then moved toward the After, tinged with relief and regret. They finished the chant and stood, then they all helped to stack the rocks over Mir's body.

"We need to get out of here," Calfon said. "All that magic is going to get noticed—the wrong kind of attention. Can you ride?"

Corran looked at Rigan, silently echoing the question. Rigan nodded. "Yeah. I might not be able to walk, but I think I can stay on a horse."

Trent looked as unsteady as Rigan felt. Polly ran to help him, even as Elinor moved toward Rigan. Corran drew back as Elinor reached them, and she wrapped her arms around Rigan, drawing him into a deep kiss.

"Save it until we're safe," Ross ordered. "Let's go home."

CHAPTER TWENTY-ONE

"KEEP THE DAMNED monsters away from my warehouses and vine-yards!" Merchant Prince Kadar raged.

Wraithwind, his blood witch, regarded the tirade impassively. "My lord, you wanted to increase the monsters in the rural areas to draw out the hunters so they would be easier to catch. Those are also the areas where your lands are located. Monsters are not precise."

Kadar balled his fists and tried to rein in his temper. Wraithwind was an idiot, but he also possessed the magic to swat Kadar like a fly. "Can't you send the monsters into Tamas's or Gorog's lands instead?"

Wraithwind shrugged. "I certainly can—but we've had no reports of hunters in those areas. If you wish to capture or kill the Valmondes and their fellow conspirators, then the monsters must go where the hunters have been seen."

"The harvest is coming before long. I need workers for that. I can't run vineyards if my workers are dead or too frightened to show up. The last time you called the monsters, those bloody hunters torched one whole field of vines! And half the winery burned. Do you know how many barrels we lost? I can't just make new to replace them! The wine has to age."

Wraithwind adjusted his spectacles and nodded, as if agreeing that

Kadar's observation was, indeed, a problem. "A very unfortunate loss and a waste of a good nest of monsters," he said. "We barely got a few nights' use out of them. It takes a toll on the Balance to open the Rifts so often."

"Unfortunate? That wine makes the money to keep you supplied, and those vines are our future. And that's another thing," Kadar snapped. "My managers have been telling tales about dead areas in other fields, places where nothing will grow—and those zones are getting bigger. What sort of dark magic is that?"

The witch frowned and tapped his spectacles as he thought. "Oh, the taint. It's an unfortunate result of opening so many Rifts. Part of what's on the other side begins to spill out, and that realm holds more than monsters. It belongs to Colduraan, after all."

"Surely you don't believe the Elder Gods are real," Kadar said, condescension thick in his voice.

"Assuredly, I do," Wraithwind replied. "The Rifts lead to one of the Realms Beyond, where the First Creatures still dwell. Like Colduraan, they favor those who work blood magic. The Ancient Ones have their own magic, torn from the chaos before the worlds were created. He Who Watches, She Who Waits, Shadow of Night—the beings told of in the old lore, they're all quite real, and we have gained their attention through the amount of blood magic being done." He smiled. "They have a taste for blood."

"I care nothing for your fantasies," Kadar snapped. "Can you fix the taint?"

"Fix it? No, at least not without putting a stop to opening the Rifts. I keep telling you," he chided, "magic has a price."

"I depend on those vineyards for my livelihood," Kadar thundered. "I can't have monsters and that bloody taint causing problems." He glared at Wraithwind. "Can your magic increase the production of my vines to make up for the ones we've lost?"

"Yes, but—"

"Do it," Kadar snapped. "I don't care about the Balance, and I don't care about the Cull. Keep the monsters away from my warehouses, my vineyards, and my workers, make my grapes grow, and do what you need to find those damn hunters!"

He slammed the door to the witch's workshop behind him and stalked back to his rooms. Merely talking with Wraithwind was enough these days to put him in a foul mood. *Why is it so hard for everyone to understand? Kill the hunters, eliminate the threat, go back to making a tidy profit. Must that damned witch make everything complicated?*

"I take it that your meeting didn't go well with Wraithwind," Joth Hanson's voice came from the doorway. Kadar realized he had heard and ignored several knocks and that Hanson was indeed due for their briefing.

"Come in and sit," he snarled. "Don't try my patience."

"Wouldn't dream of it," Hanson said smoothly. "Though I'm not surprised that the witch does. He's certainly not the most gifted of his kind, though he was the most affordable."

Kadar scowled at Hanson, who appeared not to notice. "It's not only what we pay him; it's also what his magic costs me. You heard about the warehouse and vineyard?"

Hanson nodded. "Though, to be fair, my lord, that's not exactly the witch's fault. The hunters burned the building and the vines."

"And how is it the hunters are still alive? I thought Aliyev put a bounty on their heads big enough to attract the best rat catchers around. Jorgeson's supposed to be on their trail, and so are your men. How can a handful of outlaw tradesmen elude so many so-called professionals?"

Hanson winced at the dig but recovered quickly. "My lord, we've nearly caught them on several occasions."

"That isn't good enough."

"Agreed. But I have had spies in the countryside, gathering stories of where and when these hunters have come to the rescue, and I've been plotting their movements on a map. We believe they work within several days' ride of wherever they're hiding, and I think we're close to finding them and destroying their base."

"I don't care about their base," Kadar said in a low, deadly voice. "I want them eliminated." He threw his hands in the air. "I have more important things to worry about. The last message I had from my man in Aliyev's court said that the trade agreement with Garenoth is in danger because Ravenwood did not meet its last shipment."

"Did your contact know how it fell short?"

"Raw materials," Kadar replied. "Grapes. Corn, lumber—the kinds of things that are difficult to harvest with monsters running around killing the workers."

"My lord, they're your monsters."

Idiots. I'm surrounded by idiots. How is this so difficult? "I didn't tell Wraithwind to put the monsters in my vineyards and kill my harvesters," he grated. "I told him to lure the hunters so we could get rid of them."

Hanson opened his mouth to reply and shut it again without saying anything.

"I've got no love for the terms of the Garenoth agreement, even if Aliyev tossed Tamas and me a bone with a slightly sweetened percentage," Kadar continued, pacing. "We could have done better, if Machison hadn't been the elder Gorog's lap dog. But not meeting the shipments will damage us all."

"I've brought you a report on the latest smuggling shipments," Hanson said as if he were searching for good news. "Your profit was handsome on these shipments."

"What of the smugglers that were killed? I heard those shipments did not get delivered."

Hanson fidgeted. "There have been incidents, m'lord. We believe hunters are to blame. Several smugglers were killed near a cemetery, and there was an altercation in a warehouse from an intruder. A few of the smuggling captains have expressed concerns. We promised them safe passage and an easy job."

"Hunters, again," Kadar fumed. "I don't think those deaths by the cemetery were an accident at all. They knew. Somehow, they knew about the smugglers, and they're trying to make it look like it had to do with the monsters." He shook his head. "And the intruder—another hunter trying to undermine us?"

"Why would the outlaws care?" Hanson asked, genuinely puzzled.

Kadar cursed. "Because they're Guild men, at the bottom of it. And the Guilds can't stand free trade. It cuts into their inflated prices." He stopped and then turned to Hanson with a wary expression.

"These outlaw hunters, are we certain that's really what they are?"

"I don't understand—"

"It's no secret Aliyev was angry with Machison, and it's been whispered he gave Blackholt to Machison to get rid of them both. And these hunters—untrained, with scavenged weapons—manage to do what paid assassins could not, get into the Lord Mayor's palace, kill Machison and defeat his blood witch?" Kadar shook his head. "Doesn't that seem... unlikely... to you?"

Hanson licked his lips nervously. "I hadn't given it much thought, m'lord. But now that you put it that way, I guess they'd have had to be pretty lucky to do all that and escape."

"Luck had nothing to do with it," Kadar replied. "What if Aliyev hired assassins to do the job and made it look like tradesmen-hunters? No one would suspect he was behind it, and it gave him the perfect excuse to get rid of the elder Gorog and take charge of the Garenoth agreement himself. There'd been proxy attacks to warn Machison before the coup, but that man was so full of himself, he thought they were all from me."

"Some were," Hanson prompted. "I remember."

"But not all," Kadar said, "and certainly not the stroke that killed him. No, now that I think about it, I was blind not to see it before. It has Aliyev's mark—clever, devious, impossible to prove."

"Do you think Aliyev knows about the smugglers?" Hanson asked, and Kadar could hear the worry in his voice.

"He may know that smuggling is going on, but there's nothing in what those damned hunters interrupted to tie it back to me," Kadar answered. "Still another reason we can't let them poke around. Sooner or later, they'll find a link. We can't allow that."

"Despite their interference, your take from the last cargo run was handsome," Hanson said, and Kadar knew the man was doing his best to placate his master's mood.

Even that did not cheer Kadar. "The smuggling profits are supposed to be in addition to the income my wines and grapes earn

343

from the League trade, not a replacement for them. I've already heard from Aliyev about the reduction in the vineyard production. He's worried we won't meet our obligations."

"Have you spoken with Wraithwind—"

"Yes, I've spoken with the witch. I get vague platitudes and muttered lies," Kadar stormed. "What good is a witch if his magic can't do what needs to be done? I've ordered him to increase the yield on the vineyards."

"I'll have my contact arrange for the smugglers to land at a different harbor," Hanson ventured. "One that takes them farther upriver, away from where the monster attacks have been. If the monsters keep the hunters occupied downriver, they won't have time to interfere with the smugglers."

"Do it. And make sure there's nothing to trace the cargo back to me."

"Is there anything else, m'lord?"

"Find those hunters and bring me their heads."

Hanson bowed. "As you wish, m'lord."

Kadar waited until Hanson closed the doors behind him before he poured himself a generous measure of whiskey and sank into a chair by the fireplace. There had been more to his letter from Aliyev, something he did not care to share with either Hanson or Wraithwind.

According to Aliyev, there was talk in the League about Raven-wood becoming undependable, because of the problems meeting the Garenoth agreement. *If we defaulted, we'd lose our ranking, and all our trades and goods would suffer. Even if the other city-states think we might default, the next round of agreements to be negotiated might not go as favorably for us.*

Damn Aliyev! What game is he playing? He steps in to save the Garenoth arrangement, making himself a hero to King Rellan and rids himself of two problematic liegemen at the same time, as well as a pain-in-the-ass Merchant Prince. Aliyev has to be calling monsters of his own; Wraithwind certainly isn't the only one. So why is Aliyev targeting my vineyards and the riverfront? Is he hoping to push me out the way he forced Gorog's failure?

He's a ballsy bastard if that's his game. Foul up my affairs too much, and he can't make the shipments—and the whole thing comes crashing down. Does he have a replacement for me, waiting for me to fail? Is he hoping to seize my lands? There's something in this that I'm missing, either a prize Aliyev's chasing that I don't see or another player who's staying hidden.

Bad enough if Aliyev is behind it, toying with the fortunes of the city-state for his own ends. But if there's another player, then that's even worse. By Colduraan and Balledec, I'll get to the bottom of it! I'll be damned if I'm going to be cut out of the game.

CHAPTER TWENTY-TWO

THE GROUP HEADED back into the ruined monastery, silent and somber. Polly had prepared most of a "welcome home" dinner before they left to open the Rift, hoping they would be successful. Everyone expressed appreciation, but Rigan had little appetite, and to him, the food had no taste.

Usually, the friends passed the time in the evening playing cards, sharpening their weapons, or planning their next hunt. Tonight, conversation lagged, and people turned in early. Corran and Rigan found themselves alone in the sitting room.

"How's the arm?" Rigan asked.

"Better. Almost completely healed."

Rigan gave a wan smile. "I had the same thought, on the other side. I thought it would require human blood to work the spell, and it did. Then we got jumped, and Mir pushed me out of the way before I could—"

"I'm sorry we didn't figure out how to get you back faster," Corran replied. "We tried. Gods, we tried everything, from the moment you disappeared. And each time it didn't work, I got more worried—"

Rigan nodded. "Yeah. We had a few false starts, too. If what we did hadn't worked—I don't know what would have happened." He hesitated. "There was something else... something in the Rift. A presence I don't know how to explain."

"Presence?" Corran asked, leaning forward.

Rigan grimaced and shifted in his seat, uncomfortable with even thinking about the creature he had sensed. "There are stories about the Elder Gods experimenting with creation before the worlds were slung. In those legends, the First Creatures are monsters, and the gods seal them away when they leave our world. I never believed those tales before. But now..." He stared off into the distance, trying to find words to explain.

"You sensed something like that, inside the Rift?" Corran asked.

Rigan nodded. "It's hard to describe, like any of the words I could use aren't big enough or dark enough. Huge—beyond reckoning. Powerful, almost a god itself. And cruel... something that feeds on fear and death and pain, but so much more than just an evil person." He dropped his head. "I'm not explaining this very well."

"You mean those stories about He Who Watches?"

"Yeah," Rigan replied, brushing the back of his hand across his lips in a nervous gesture. "I'm pretty sure he's real, and he knew we were there. And when I tried to use blood magic to open the Rift, the... creature... paid more attention. I saw him in my dreams."

That didn't sound good at all, but Corran knew Rigan needed no new reasons to worry. "You're out of that place. Maybe whatever it was can't follow."

"Maybe," Rigan said, clearly not convinced.

Corran looked up. "What matters is that you and Trent got back. I'm sorry about Mir. He was a good friend and a good hunter, but despite it all, I'm still glad to have you two home." He winked. "And I'm sure Elinor is glad, too."

Rigan blushed. "She's waiting for me."

"Go," Corran said with a laugh, slapping his brother on the shoulder. "We can talk in the morning."

Rigan started down the corridor, and Polly shuffled into the room, heading for the kitchen. "Thought you'd be asleep by now, what with all that magic," she said. "I wanted to get some things ready for the morning. Easier to do while I'm still awake than trying to wake up to do it, if you know what I mean."

"As long as there's coffee, I imagine we'll get by," Corran replied.

Polly gave him a look. "Coffee doesn't solve everything, you know. That's why there's whiskey."

Feeling adrift, Corran found himself following Polly. He should be exhausted from the working in the clearing and the fear and relief of getting Rigan and Trent home, but he felt wide awake, humming with energy that he doubted even a drink would dampen.

"When everyone's ready to go out again, I think I've found a hunt," Polly said, mixing ingredients into a pan that would bake on the coals overnight. "And for what it's worth, I think we should pack up and move on to another hideout for a while. Been here too long, done too much. We get comfortable; we're gonna get caught."

Corran let out a long sigh. "I was thinking the same thing, about finding a new place to stay. We've been lucky to have made it this long."

Polly pushed a lock of red hair behind her ear as she stirred her mix. "I know a little bit about hiding," she said, not looking at him. "Ran away from home, got myself a job in the big city, managed to stay a jump ahead of everyone."

"Who was chasing you?" Corran asked, concerned. Kell had cared for Polly, and if things had gone differently, Corran would have welcomed her as a sister by marriage when the time was right.

Polly shrugged. "People I owed, people I didn't want to get to know better, people who wanted to make me go back where I didn't want to be."

Corran watched her work, noticing for the first time a jagged scar on the inside of one arm. *She's Kell's age, fourteen, maybe fifteen, and been on her own for a while. Had the guts to kill at least one man who tried to take advantage of her, and ran away again before everything went to shit in the city. How bad did it have to be, at home, for this to be better?*

"I have a lead on a haunting," Polly said, rousing Corran from his thoughts. She bent to push the pan into the hot coals and covered it with a lid, then stood and dusted off her hands. Polly returned to the table with a bottle and two cups, pouring them each a finger of whiskey.

"How did you hear about it?" Corran asked, accepting his cup and tipping his head in salute. Polly grinned and mirrored the gesture, raising her cup in a mocking toast.

"Last time Ross and Calfon and I went to the pub, I heard people talking. Then we got so busy with the Rift business and all, it didn't seem important, what with everything else going on," Polly said, taking a sip.

"Seems there's a village that comes and goes. Most of the year, it's nothing but ruins. People keep their distance. But once a year, at midnight on one particular day, the town reappears as it was."

Corran let the whiskey burn down his throat, and considered Polly's tale. "Sounds interesting."

She nodded. "I know. That's why I went over all big-eyed and innocent-like at the pub and got the man to tell the whole story." She widened her eyes and batted her lashes, looking so completely unlike herself that Corran had to laugh.

"And he fell for that?"

Polly lifted her chin. "You know, that's what Ross said after, too. But yes, he got the chance to show off for a pretty girl, and he sang like a lark."

"You're a dangerous woman, Polly."

"Don't you forget it." Polly knocked back the rest of her drink.

"So what did you learn?" Corran asked, finishing his whiskey as well.

"According to the legend, the people in the town all got wiped out in one night. Killed in their beds, murdered where they stood. No one seems to know who did it or why, although I guess folks have been arguing about it since the whole thing happened." Polly leaned back in her chair.

"Not sure we need to get involved if the town simply shows up and then vanishes again," Corran said.

Polly shook her head. "That's not all. According to the stories, the ghosts that haunt the village lure travelers in and then kill them. Next morning, there's nothing but ruins and a few fresh corpses, and when the town shows up again, those poor travelers are part of the village— killing more people."

Corran toyed with his cup. "It's a great story. Sounds like what people tell around a campfire on a dark night to get a shiver. But who went back to find out if the dead travelers returned? And how did that person live to tell about it?"

Polly shrugged. "I'm just repeating what I heard. We don't have to do anything about it. But I did find out where this village was, and it's in the right direction for the next monastery I had figured we'd stay in."

Before they left Ravenwood City, Polly and Elinor had scoured old texts about the monasteries that once dotted the countryside. They had long ago fallen into ruin after being abandoned, but many, like the one in which they had been living, were solidly built. Most people ignored the old structures, and no one had cause to meddle with them.

"I hope we can come back here," Corran said. "For being outlaw exiles, this has been pretty comfortable."

"Those monks had it good," Polly replied. "Everything I read about the new place makes me think we'll find a hidden section like this, maybe more books."

"How will our resident ghost feel about us moving on?" Corran asked.

Polly smiled. "I'm sure he'll keep an eye out for us to come back. I think he was lonely." She ran a hand up her neck. "I have a bad feeling we've used up our luck here."

"So this village," Corran said, beginning to feel the stress of the day as the whiskey hit him. "Did you mention it to Aiden and Elinor and see what they made of it? Maybe it's more than angry ghosts. Might be a curse involved, or some other kind of magic."

"In case you didn't notice, it's been kinda busy around here lately," Polly said with a sniff. "I meant to talk to them, but it wasn't the right time. I figured if it is angry ghosts, you and Rigan know how to put that sort of thing right. Travelers would stop getting killed. The ghosts could move on. Good for everyone. And if it's bad magic, well, maybe our witches could still take care of it."

"How long has it been happening?"

"The man in the bar wasn't sure, but he thought it had been a while. Maybe ten years or so."

"Why haven't the other villages blocked off the road and routed travelers a different way?" Corran enjoyed a tall tale as well as anyone, but before he committed the hunters to taking action, he wanted more information. Especially given the condition Rigan and Trent were in.

"Apparently they tried," Polly replied. "But someone—or something—moved the barricades, stole the signs, undid whatever they put up to stop people."

"There's got to be more to the story," Corran said, intrigued despite himself.

"Rigan can confess the dead, can't he?" Polly challenged. "And the both of you can banish vengeful ghosts. Maybe between the two of you —with Aiden and Elinor to help and the rest of us watching your backs —you can put them to rest and solve the problem."

"Maybe," Corran replied. "I'm just wondering—who killed them? Brigands? A fit of madness? Someone with a grudge against the whole village? Or did a witch put a curse on them? We're missing something, and it could be important."

"Well, if we do this, you'll get your chance to find out. The stories say that the village reappears three days from now, which is barely enough time to pack our things and get where we're going." Polly gave a little smile of triumph.

"Let's talk to Aiden and Elinor in the morning," Corran said, stifling a yawn. "And if they're willing, we'll see what the others think. At the least, we do need to change locations. We've spotted too many patrols lately, and it's only luck we haven't had more run-ins. But now you've got me thinking about the village, and I'm going to have a hard time forgetting."

"I was counting on it," Polly returned with a smile.

———

"THAT'S IT? THAT'S the place?" Rigan looked at the darkened ruins warily. "How long ago were the villagers killed?"

"Ten years," Calfon replied. "At least, according to the version of the story Polly heard."

Oberfeld had not been a large village. Corran and the others walked among the remains of houses and shops and tried to imagine what it once looked like. Some of the buildings had burned or crumbled down to the stone foundations, but others remained remarkably intact, though damaged by weather and neglect.

Here and there, enough remained of the ruins for Corran to see where fire had charred wood, making him wonder about how the villagers met their end. It would not be the first town to suffer great loss due to a fire, but the buildings were spaced too far apart for that to be the whole answer.

If they died from something natural—a fire caused by lightning, for example—or from an accident, then why the vengefulness? Why kill travelers and lure them in?

"It feels... cursed," Rigan said quietly. Ross and Calfon hung back, weapons at the ready, letting the Valmonde brothers get a sense of the place. Before their exile, Corran had never considered using grave magic as a source of information about the dead. Rigan had realized that potential, with his ability to summon ghosts and hear the confessions of the dead.

Corran nodded. The whole area since they entered the ruined village set his hackles rising and gave him the feeling of being watched. He looked at the tumbledown buildings and attempted to guess what might have happened to set the doomed villagers on a quest for revenge so strong that it extended after death.

"Whether or not your ghost story is true, there's got to be some reason people just left the buildings to rot without anyone moving in to take them over," Ross said, coming up to stand with him.

"Can you tell—are there any ghosts?" Aiden asked.

"Not at the moment, although the whole area feels... strange," Corran replied.

Polly, Elinor, and Trent had stayed behind to pack up their things at the monastery. They had agreed to leave the furnishings behind, except for a few books Rigan and Aiden wanted to study, which they asked Tophen's permission to borrow. Still, packing up their personal items would take a while, and they all had the sense they needed to move out quickly.

"How do you intend to banish an entire village?" Calfon asked.

Rigan frowned. "I don't intend to banish them right away. There's got to be a reason they're killing people. I want to confess them and find out what happened. Once they've been heard, they may go to the After willingly."

"And if not, we'll shove them through the door, and make sure they can't return," Corran said.

Whatever tragedy befell the village, it happened far too recently to be noted in any of the histories at the monastery. Wanting to keep a low profile because they feared pursuit, they had decided not to make a stop at the nearest pub to see what they might learn after they spotted other travelers at the inn. Rigan still debated that choice. Walking into a bad situation without enough details had nearly gotten them killed before.

"Are you sure we can't hide on the other side of the village and lure in the bounty hunters for the ghosts to take care of?" Ross asked, only partially in jest. "It might sate the ghosts' hunger for blood so they'd be more polite to us afterward, and we'd get rid of some of the sons of bitches who are after us."

"Tempting," Corran said. "But we've only got tonight, and I don't much fancy playing bait."

Rigan and Trent were mostly recovered from their injuries beyond the Rift, thought Corran knew his brother's nightmares would likely take much longer to fade than his bruises, and whether real or not, Rigan still sensed the presence he had felt in the Rift. They all bore Mir's loss like a heavy weight. Corran had been uncertain about the wisdom in taking this hunt so soon, though Polly and Trent argued vigorously for it. Eventually, the others had come to agree, but with so much going on, everyone seemed on edge.

"I wish we could put the whole village inside a salt circle," Rigan muttered. "Or at least use my salt rope."

"I'd like that, too," Corran agreed. "But it's a little too big for that."

Instead, they had used the salt-aconite-amanita mixture and iron filings to make a large circle for the hunters to stand in. Rigan carefully painted the sigils at the quarters and set out the candles. Separate circles several feet away gave Ross and Calfon defensive positions from which to keep watch. Calfon had a bow and Ross a crossbow in addition to their swords, in case the most dangerous enemies turned out to be human—or flesh and blood monsters.

"How will we know when it's midnight?" Rigan asked.

Corran shrugged. "If the stories are true, we'll know."

He and Rigan both had iron swords as well as steel, and silver knives. Elinor had prepared pouches of dried leaves and plants that would contain evil and decrease its power, and she gave them a wineskin of water steeped with protective herbs. Corran had no illusions that settling an entire village of haunts would be easy.

In the distance, bells rang from a far-away tower.

"Look!" Rigan murmured, eyes fixed on the ruins.

One moment, the moon shone down on the lonely remains of a deserted village. In the next, the damage vanished as if it never was, and the shops, houses, stables, and other buildings stood whole. Lanterns glimmered in the windows, and people moved through the streets.

Corran blinked once, then again, but the scene remained the same. If he had not known the truth, he might have wondered why so many people were up and about at midnight, but at least from this distance, they appeared solid and real.

"What do you make of that?" Rigan asked under his breath.

"I don't know what to think," Corran replied. "They don't seem to take any note of us."

"Then again, we're outside the village boundaries. The stories say bad things happen when a traveler enters."

"I'm not going to test that," Corran said. "Let's bring them to us."

Corran and Rigan both had scars from vengeful ghosts they had faced in the past. Even if the spirit could not manifest a physical body, many of the revenants could muster sufficient energy to throw candlesticks, smash pottery, or hurl knives. Not only did the ghosts have unnatural strength, but they also did not tire, putting mere mortals at a disadvantage in a physical fight.

Magic evened the score.

Rigan and Corran chanted, letting their voices rise and fall in the familiar litany. Rigan had taught Corran the slight variation he used to summon ghosts; they both knew the incantation for banishment by heart.

At first, nothing changed. The ghostly villagers went about their chores, lamplight illuminated windows and spilled out into the street, and the night air filled with the sounds of people winding down their day. Gradually, activity slowed, then stopped, and Corran felt as much as saw the ghosts' attention shift to where the hunters stood.

"They're coming!" he warned, and in the next breath, a blast of frigid air swept around them, raising the dust and swirling leaves into the air. The wardings might hold the restless spirits at bay but did nothing to protect them from the cold. Corran's teeth chattered, and he felt gooseflesh rise on his arms.

Ghastly figures assembled just beyond the protective salt ring, glowing with a green hue. The spirits no longer appeared as they had in life; instead, their ghosts manifested with their death wounds to stare balefully at those within the warded circle. Rigan faced them while Corran stepped back, concentrating on maintaining and strengthening the magic that kept the ghosts outside the sigils and salt.

"Spirits of Oberfeld, hear me! I am a confessor to the dead," Rigan said. "Tell me what happened and why your ghosts remain, and I will ease your passage to Doharmu."

What do you care? A dead woman's ghost stepped close to the shimmering blue-white energy of the protective circle that rose like a curtain between the brothers and the ghosts. *We mean no harm to you. Go away, and leave us to our task.*

"You might not mean us harm, but you kill others," Rigan pressed. "Tell me why, and I can help you find your rest."

Rest? A spectral man roared. *There can be no rest, as long as those who stole our lives go unpunished.*

"Then tell us who they are, and we'll report them to the authorities," Rigan replied, keeping his voice even and reasonable.

A low, bitter chuckle began from somewhere in the throng of spirits that massed around the edge of the salt circle. More of the ghosts echoed the sound until the night rang with the mocking laughter. *Who do you think killed us?* The woman's spirit taunted. *Come outside your circle, and we'll show you.*

"Why did they kill you?" Rigan asked, and took a half-step forward as if he meant to cross the salt line.

Corran gripped Rigan's arm, fingers tight enough to leave a bruise. "Don't," he warned.

Rigan looked from his brother to the spirits beyond the protective warding.

"Rigan, don't be a fool!" Corran hissed. "They kill people, remember?"

Are you guards? Did you come from the Lord Mayor or the Merchant Princes? the woman who spoke for the spirits asked.

"No," Rigan replied. "We hunt monsters."

Then you have nothing to fear from us. You want to confess us? Come across, and see what we saw, what happened here.

Corran kept a tight grip on Rigan's arm. "You can't trust them."

"Swear to me," Rigan said looking out to the ghosts. "I will hear your confession and see your truth, but I want you to swear safe passage for my brother and me. Swear it to Doharmu, on peril of your souls."

The glowing ghosts knelt, one by one, and bowed their heads. *We swear,* their hushed voices replied.

"This can't be a good idea," Corran muttered. He glanced at Aiden, who shared the warded circle with them. "Are you all right with this?"

Aiden looked troubled. "No. But I don't think you have a choice if you want to find out what really happened here—and the ghosts won't go peacefully until they've been heard. I'll stay here, out of their reach, so I can help if things go wrong."

Corran turned back to Rigan. "Let's go." His expression left no doubt as to his thoughts about the decision.

"Remember—you gave your word, all of you," Rigan cautioned as he moved toward the salt line. The ghostly villagers backed away, giving them space. Rigan traded a nervous glance with Corran, and then carefully stepped across the warding. He followed a few seconds later.

Surrounded by ghosts, the night felt as cold as the middle of winter. Corran saw his breath, and he shivered although he wore a jacket. Now that he was beyond the warding, he saw the ghosts more clearly.

A village of about fifty people stood in rows, watching them with dead eyes. Young and old, male and female, they had died together and died horribly. Corran flinched at their death wounds. Rigan led the way, moving slowly among the spirits, and his face was expressionless as he saw what had been inflicted.

Many of the villagers bore deep slashes across their throats. The dying would have been quick, but not the terror of what was about to happen. A woman's ghost held out the baby in her arms, revealing bloodstained blankets and the unmistakable gouge of a sword's blade in the child's belly. Corran gasped and backed up a step, closing his eyes for a moment as he steadied himself.

Old women stood with necks bent at an unnatural angle. Others met Corran's gaze unblinking though their skulls were smashed. Some of the old men clutched gut wounds. No one had tried to make their deaths easy.

By comparison, the women and children received mercy. Some of the boys and young men bore wounds that could only have come from impalement, while it was clear many of the older men had been hanged, crucified, or dismembered.

Corran emerged from the throng of ghosts and fell to his knees, retching. Rigan stood close to him protectively, pale as the revenants, with anger blazing in his eyes.

"Show us who did this to you," Rigan ordered. "And I will see you to your rest,"

Corran blinked, and the night around them changed. He saw a sunny autumn day in a village like many they had passed through since they left the city. Small but well-kept shops lined the main street, with tidy homes and stables behind that. At the edge of town, a pub welcomed travelers. Like the rest of the village, the pub looked worn but cared for, and Corran had the sense that the people in Oberfeld led a quiet, hardworking life.

He glanced around, trying to determine how the villagers made their living. From what Corran noted, they were farmers or the merchants who supplied the farmers. Beyond the village, on the hills that stretched in all directions, were vineyards. He had always paid little attention to matters relating to the Guilds or the League since they had little to do with the concerns of undertakers, but Corran thought he recalled that Merchant Prince Kadar owned the vineyards in Ravenwood and that the Guilds associated with winemaking depended on him for his patronage.

Corran hurried to keep pace with Rigan, who walked slowly through the recreated village, studying the details. How the ghosts managed to project a seamless vision eluded Corran, but he reminded himself that while what they saw might be true, none of it was real. *We are standing in the ruins of a dead village in the middle of the night, surrounded by murderous ghosts.* This time, his shiver had nothing to do with the unnatural cold, and he gripped the pommel of his iron sword more tightly.

"What do you make of it?" he asked Rigan in a low voice, unsure why he felt the need to whisper.

"I think it's probably taking all of their energy to show us this," Rigan replied. "It's not magic, at least not their magic. More of a collective memory they're sharing with us. I wonder if we can see it because of our grave magic? It'll be interesting to find out what Aiden's seen."

"Let's get this over with," Corran urged. "I didn't like this before, and I like it less now."

He studied Rigan's face. His brother had an expression of rapt concentration, and beneath it, seething rage. Corran thought he detected the barest hint of a glow around Rigan and remembered that same, strange light from the night Rigan killed the guards that murdered Kell. This might be his younger brother, but Rigan was also a powerful witch who could be devastatingly dangerous when moved to anger.

"Why aren't we seeing what happened?" Corran asked.

Rigan frowned, as if listening to something only he could hear. "They're showing us who they were, what was taken from them."

The illusion grew more realistic, adding sound and smell. Corran heard the buzz of conversation, of friends calling out to friends and merchants hawking their wares, of children squealing and dogs barking.

Hoof beats made him turn. Twenty riders on horseback rode up to the pub. Before they could dismount, two of the village men stepped out of the pub to block their way.

"We don't get many soldiers this way," one of the villagers said, his friendliness tempered with an edge.

"We'll be the last ones you see," the ranking soldier replied as his men dismounted and drew their swords.

More men poured out of the pub. "What are you doing?" an older man protested. "We've caused no trouble, paid our taxes, delivered our crops."

"Got my orders," the captain replied. "Grew too many grapes, and the price of wine went down. Can't have that. Won't need as many farmers if there's not as many vines to tend."

Corran saw the horrified realization dawn on the faces of a few of the villagers, while others struggled to grasp what was about to happen.

"We can destroy what's been harvested," the elder said. "Or if Merchant Prince Kadar wants, we can abandon the vines."

"That's not in the orders."

Nothing prepared Corran for the shock of seeing soldiers move through the village, setting their swords against unarmed villagers as if they were a tide of monsters. At first, he rushed at the soldiers, unable to remain still, only to have the illusion vanish as he ran through thin air.

They were watching echoes of a massacre a decade past, and nothing could stop what had already happened. *The screams of women and children echoed along with the curses of dying men and the shrieks of those whom the soldiers toyed with before allowing them the release of death.*

Corran thought he had already purged the contents of his stomach, he thought that as an undertaker, little would affect him, but the sound of screaming and the stench of blood and entrails had him heaving again. Rigan stood beside him, rigid and angry, his jaw set and his eyes narrowed.

Corran believed nothing could be worse than the screams of a village dying at the hands of those who should have protected them. But he was wrong. Silence was worse, much worse.

They blinked, and the scene changed. By the angle of the sun, morning had given way to late afternoon. *Smoke rose from the ashes of the homes and shops Corran had seen just moments before, and the pub had burned down to its stone foundation. Bodies littered the streets, lying in bloody pools where they fell. The trees in the village green held the corpses of hanged men, and crosses and pikes with the bodies still impaled dotted the open, grassy area. Beyond the limits of the village, the vineyard still burned.*

Corran felt his heart hammering in his chest. His mouth was dry and tasted of bile. Everything in him wanted a fight, wanted to cut down the soldiers that had done this and make them pay.

"That's the point," Rigan replied, guessing Corran's thoughts. His voice sounded nothing like his own, cold and hard, emotionless. "They can only return one night a year, and they take their vengeance on soldiers they lure into the ruins."

"Those aren't the soldiers that did this," Corran protested, though he could understand why that distinction might not matter, to the remnants of people who had seen their loved ones slaughtered.

"It's as close as they can get to recompense," Rigan said in a strangled tone.

As he turned to look around the savaged village, the illusion blinked out, leaving nothing but overgrown foundation stones and ramshackle ruins.

Do you understand? The ghosts surrounded them, filling the night with a foxfire glow.

"Yes," Rigan replied. "You were badly wronged. Betrayed. But it's time to end the killing. We know your secret. We swore our souls to Eshtamon, and the Elder God himself named us his champions for vengeance. Go to the After, knowing you will be avenged."

Corran stared at Rigan, wide-eyed, wondering when their quest to find justice for Kell and their friends had somehow burgeoned into this. But he could not bring himself to protest. What happened in Oberfeld broke all oaths of lord and liegeman, violating the essence of the agreement between the Merchant Princes and the citizens who served their interests.

No one else knows the truth except us, Corran thought. *If it happened here, where else did it happen? We hunt monsters. Maybe some of them are human.*

"Are you ready to give up your vengeance, let us take on your burden, and go to your rest?" Rigan asked the spirits.

Corran watched the faces of the dead as they spoke quietly among themselves, fearful, angry, and struggling. Finally, the milling crowd stilled, and the ghost that spoke with them first stepped to the forefront.

We are agreed. Give us your word, and we will move on.

Rigan looked to Corran, who nodded, and then back to the ghosts. "You have our word, as the servants of Eshtamon, that your deaths will be avenged. Now, in the name of Oj and Ren, the Eternal Mother and Forever Father, in the names of Doharmu and Eshtamon, I bid you enter the After, and take the rest you deserve."

Corran and Rigan spoke the words of the ritual, and in the distance, Corran saw the doorway open into the After. Always before, Corran had looked into that absolute darkness with trepidation. Now, having seen the worst men could do to other humans, he saw only the rest of peaceful sleep. The villagers moved into the doorway, some alone and some clutching the hands of others, individuals and families, until the last of Oberfeld's ghosts was gone.

Corran felt a rush of power as the doorway to the After closed, the last of the magic dissipated, and the energy the ghosts had summoned for their illusion faded away. Rigan staggered, and Corran caught him, supporting him with a shoulder under his arm when it looked like Rigan's legs might not hold him.

"Do you think it's true, about Kadar?" Rigan asked, his voice tight.

Corran nodded. "Yeah. I do. It fits. If Machison could call monsters on his own people, why not this? You said that when you were inside the other realm, you saw Rifts opening in many places. Someone else must still be calling the monsters, setting them on the people. Damn, Rigan," he said, looking at his brother as cold fear formed a knot in his belly. "This is much bigger than we thought."

"And when they figure out that we know what they did—what they tried to cover up—we become more dangerous to the ones controlling the monsters."

"Shit," Corran swore. "Now the bounty on us is going to go even higher."

Before he could say more, Aiden started scuffing away the circles. "Riders are coming," he said. "Scouts. Trouble." Whether it was his foresight or his magic that warned him, the others knew better than to doubt. "They're not far; less than half a candlemark's ride away. We've got to go."

Corran and the rest of the hunters rode out of the deserted village, intentionally riding away from their base, hoping to circle around. They veered down smaller lanes and side roads, eager to put as many hedges and fences between them and the scouts as they could, tempering the desire to fly at full gallop with the knowledge that the sound of several horses riding at top speed would carry on the wind and attract attention.

After a candlemark of picking their way down muddy paths and farm lanes, they finally reached a road that would bring them back to the monastery. "Too bloody close," Corran muttered.

Rigan laid a hand on his shoulder. "We're home safe. And we're moving the base as soon as the road is clear. We got around the scouts, sent the ghosts to the After, and no one got hurt. That's as good a night as we get."

Corran looked up, a pained expression in his gaze. "Our luck will only hold so long."

Rigan gave him a wan smile. "It held tonight. That's enough."

CHAPTER TWENTY-THREE

"I HATE THESE bat-nosed things," Polly grumbled, swinging her sword to lodge the blade deep in the neck of a *vestir*, sending up a spray of dark blood. The sow-sized monster squealed in pain and fury as blood soaked its black, matted hair. It jerked free of the blade and turned on Polly, forcing her to jump out of its path. She stabbed at it, and the tip of her sword slashed into its side, opening the flesh down to the ribs.

Trent came at the creature from behind as it wheeled to face Polly once more, and sank his sword into its left haunch, severing the muscles and laming it. Polly charged with a mighty swing of her blade to lop the head from its powerful shoulders.

Before they had a chance to catch their breath, another beast thundered toward them. Calfon and Ross teamed up on a *vestir* a few feet away, while Corran and Rigan fought off two of the creatures by alternating magic with great, hacking sword strokes.

"We've got an audience," Polly called to Trent, and spared a shrug of her shoulders and a tilt of her head toward the top of the hill, where they could make out the figures of men, women, and children from the nearby farm village, watching the battle unfold in the valley below.

"They could damn well pick up a weapon and help. We're not entertainment," Trent muttered as he braced for the next onslaught.

A blast of fire from Rigan's hand dropped one *vestir*, and Corran seized on the distraction to gut its companion, then ran his sword through the ribcage and heart. Ross scored a hit through the throat of one of the beasts, giving Calfon the chance to come from behind, leap astride the creature's back and drive his sword down two-handed through its spine.

The last of the *vestir*, too enraged or stupid to run away, charged into their midst. Rigan loosed a blast of white, arcing energy from his palm, catching the creature full in the chest, and with a shriek, the monster fell to the ground, twitched and then lay still.

"I hope they liked the show," Polly quipped, glancing up at the hillside. Her smirk vanished when she realized the villagers were gone. "Shit. Something else is wrong."

The sound of hoof beats echoed in the night air, and the hunters scattered.

"Surrender in the name of Merchant Prince Kadar!" the captain of the soldiers shouted. Six guards, all in the livery colors of their prince, rode into the clearing at full speed, jumping the corpses of the fallen monsters in their haste to ride down the hunters.

"Not bloody likely," Polly shouted back as she ran. She turned, and let fly with a throwing knife that took the captain in the chest. He toppled from his horse, hands clasped around the dagger as a bloody stain spread across his uniform.

"No turning back now," Trent mumbled. He sent his knife flying and caught another of Kadar's soldiers in the shoulder.

"Watch out!" Polly yelled, and dove for Trent, colliding with him and knocking him out of the way of one of the horses that nearly had him under its hooves.

Ross dodged behind the scant cover of a watering trough and unholstered his crossbow, then rose and sent a quarrel through the air, striking one of the guards in his sword arm as he moved to bring his blade down against Calfon. Calfon wheeled and blocked the sword's swing, narrowly keeping the tip from slicing into his throat. The injured soldier jerked on his reins, and the horse reared, kicking at

Calfon's head. Calfon's sword came down across the soldier's thigh, and he threw himself clear of the horse's hooves.

The clatter of rocks distracted the rider, and Polly looked up to see some of the villagers venturing down the hill, arms full of rocks to hurl at the guards. More than one of the missiles hit their marks, striking the soldiers in the head and chest, opening up bloody cuts.

"Stand still, you sons of bitches, and fight like men!" one of the soldiers shouted as he turned his horse straight for Corran. Rigan sent a torrent of fire a few feet in front of the guard's horse, throwing up a spray of dirt and causing the panicked animal to buck its rider clear. He fell hard, and from the snap of breaking bone and the awkward angle of his head, Polly knew he would not be getting up again.

"Go back and tell your master to stop sending monsters against his own people," Corran yelled, standing amidst the carnage covered in the blood of the guard and that of the *vestir* he killed.

One of the remaining soldiers swayed in his seat, pale from blood loss where Trent's knife had lodged in his shoulder. He looked like he could barely sit his horse, in no shape to fight. The other two hesitated, seeing their captain and their comrades easily dispatched by the hunters they expected to rout.

"Leave now, and we let you live," Rigan called, hands held out from his sides, arms straight, palms turned out, fingers splayed, a clear threat.

"Maybe you'd see reason if we made those villagers pay for your insolence. Our orders were to bring you in," a young lieutenant replied, lifting his chin and raising his sword. "And by the gods, that's what we're going to do."

All three of the remaining soldiers rode forward, swinging their blades as they came, intent on capturing or killing their quarry. The lieutenant angled to ride for the villagers on the hillside, who scrambled back toward the crest in fear. Ross readied another shot, and his bolt took the lieutenant in the throat, knocking him from his horse.

Calfon sprang at the uninjured soldier, meeting his blows strike for strike, avoiding the hooves of the horse and the nip of its teeth. While

Calfon kept the soldier's attention trained on him, Trent sent a throwing knife into the man's chest.

The last soldier paled and then slipped bonelessly from his horse. Rigan knelt beside him. "He's alive. And I don't care to kill an unconscious man."

"You think he's worth interrogating?" Calfon asked.

"I think the sooner we're rid of him, the better," Corran replied. "If we take him back with us, you know we'll have to kill him."

Corran hefted the unconscious soldier and heaved him across his saddle, then bound his wrists with the reins and tied the man's ankles with a length of rope from his saddle bag. A sharp slap to the rump of the horse sent it running. "That should send Kadar a message," he said, watching the horse disappear down the road.

"What about them?" Polly asked, directing the attention of the others to the onlookers who had once again come out of hiding on the hilltop. "I wouldn't put it past Kadar to send more soldiers to punish the village, even though they didn't have anything to do with us. We can't leave them defenseless."

"Sure we can," Calfon grumbled. "And they weren't exactly defenseless. We need to get out of here before more soldiers come. I told you that this smelled like a trap."

"You want to have a fist fight over who picks the hunts?" Corran snapped, rounding on Calfon. "Have at it later. We've got bigger problems at the moment."

"What if we teach the villagers how to defend themselves from the beasts?" Polly urged. "Just a few basics, enough that they stand a chance."

"We need to get out of here," Calfon retorted. "You'll get us caught for sure."

Two of the village men, one older and another who looked enough like the other to be his son, were already halfway down the hillside. "You killed the monsters," the older man said, looking at the bodies of the *vestir* that lay still in the moonlight.

"And the guards," the younger of the two added, eying the corpses of the soldiers.

"The monsters are being sent by those in power," Corran said, moving forward with Rigan at his side, placing himself between the newcomers and the rest of the hunters. "They'll keep coming until someone stops the witches from summoning them, but you can defend yourselves if they come again."

"We know something of hunting wolves and wild dogs or the big cats that snatch our sheep," the younger man said. "But nothing of fighting."

"We can't stay long," Corran replied. "But we can tell you what works best with the kinds of creatures the witches call up most often. The soldiers won't defend you if the monsters come back, and we won't always be nearby."

"Come back to the village with us," the older man offered. "We'll bind your wounds, give you food for your journey as our thanks, and you'll tell us what to do. I'll set a watch, and if more soldiers come, they'll send them off the other way. Damn guards never show up when we need help. No love lost there, believe me."

A candlemark later, injuries bandaged, the hunters bid the villagers goodbye. Corran glanced at Rigan as he stretched out his magic, then shook his head. "I'm not sensing anyone on the road ahead. Let's get out of here while we can."

"Do you think we taught them enough to be able to defend themselves if more monsters come back?" Polly asked, casting a glance over her shoulder as the lights of the village receded.

"They know more than they did before," Trent replied. "They'll have to learn on their own, like we did. But maybe what we told them about the weak points will save a few lives."

They kept a wary eye out for more of Kadar's soldiers, and picked up their pace, intent on reaching their latest hiding place before the guards could muster a new attack. After Polly and the others had seen to the horses and left them stabled and fed, Aiden and Elinor awaited them, hungry for news, and Aiden looked them over with a practiced gaze, taking in the hastily bandaged injuries.

"Come on, we've got food ready, and you can tell your tales while we fix you up," Aiden said, as the rest of them filed into the room that served as a kitchen.

"We're going to have to leave again," Corran said with a sigh as he ladled stew into bowls, taking one for himself and passing one to Rigan before he stepped aside and handed the ladle to Ross. "Kadar's guards came right on the heels of fighting the *vestir*. Could have gone badly if luck hadn't been with us tonight."

"Could have, but didn't," Rigan said quietly. "There'll be times enough it doesn't go our way."

Corran shrugged as if he disagreed but didn't feel like arguing. Polly understood both men's perspective. Had the soldiers come upon them when they'd been in the thick of the fight with the monsters or more badly injured, the outcome could have been much different. She said a quiet prayer to the gods in thanks, filled a bowl and grabbed a chunk of bread, and launched into a retelling of the fight that was as enthusiastic as it was embellished.

"The next time she tells that story, it will be a legion of guards and a few dozen *vestir*," Trent said with a laugh as Polly concluded.

"If the stories grow with the telling, maybe soon the likes of Kadar will tremble at the thought of sending guards against us," Polly retorted with a cheeky grin, raising her cup of whiskey in salute.

"Somehow, I doubt that," Ross replied.

"For all we know, Kadar's blood witch called the *vestir*, and we walked right into his trap," Calfon snapped, not bothering to look up from his bowl.

"And what's the answer?" Corran responded. "Stay hidden and let the monsters run loose? We didn't do that in Ravenwood; why would we give in now?"

"We can't save the whole kingdom." Calfon lifted his head to level a glare at Corran.

"Probably not. But we saved those villagers, and their livestock—which means they can harvest their crops, and Ravenwood might keep its agreement with Garenoth. Tell me how that's not winning."

"We need more of a plan than wandering the countryside looking for monsters to fight." Calfon's fist slammed against the table, sending the bowls tottering.

"What did you have in mind? Marching up to Kadar's palace and calling him out for a duel?" Corran's eyes flashed with anger. "Storming King Rellan's palace? This is the only plan we've got right now—doing what we can when the opportunity presents itself and keeping the monsters in check."

"Piss poor excuse for a plan, if you ask me, which you don't." Calfon got up with enough force to send his chair sprawling and stalked out of the room.

"What crawled up his ass and died?" Ross asked, staring after Calfon in the darkened corridor.

"He's still upset he's not calling all the shots," Trent said, leaning back where he sat next to Polly. "He's always been prone to take everything as a challenge. Let him sleep it off."

"Butting heads like that will get someone killed," Corran muttered. "He'd better be out of his mood by morning. We're going to have to pack up and be ready to leave once the sun goes down. Kadar's soldiers are too close."

Polly sighed. "Barely got unpacked. I'll go pull my things together, but don't expect a big breakfast if I've got to pack up the kitchen," she warned, retreating toward the room she shared with Elinor.

Polly looked up a while later when Elinor entered. A slow smile spread across Polly's lips as she took in Elinor's slightly rumpled appearance. "Welcoming your hunter back from the fight?" she joked.

Elinor blushed. "Just letting him know I'm glad he's not hurt."

Polly chuckled. "So when are you and Rigan going to wed?"

Elinor went wide-eyed, then coughed. "Polly!"

"Well?" Polly gave her a cheeky grin, waiting for an answer.

"Now really isn't a good time," Elinor replied, and even in the moonlight, Polly could see her cheeks redden. "Maybe when all of this is over... when things quiet down—"

"And how long will that be?" Polly asked. "Maybe never. For all we know, the high borns' witches have been calling monsters forever, and maybe they always will. Can't put off living for a job that never ends."

Elinor rolled her eyes. "Maybe so, but still, it's too soon. We're all so raw; the losses are too fresh."

Polly guessed that in Rigan's case, she meant Kell's death or maybe Mir's. "Well, you know, it's not like I wouldn't be giving something up," Polly said with a grin. "I lose a roommate when you marry him. It's a sacrifice."

Elinor swatted her. "You wait, Polly. Your turn will come."

Polly turned away, and Elinor froze, realizing what she said.

"I'm sorry," Elinor murmured. "I didn't mean—"

Polly nodded. "I know you didn't. It's all right. I cared for Kell, and maybe in time, it would have been more. I had hoped so, but we didn't get the chance. And I know that I'm young and I'll meet someone. But... it's only been a few months, even though it feels like a lifetime ago. I'm not ready to let him go yet."

"Of course not," Elinor replied. "It's not the same, but I miss Parah and my friends from the city."

"I know we can't go back, but I miss the city sometimes," Polly said wistfully. "All the noise and bustle and people. It's pretty out here, and quiet—sometimes too quiet. There aren't enough people. Back in Ravenwood, if you wanted to not be noticed, you could slouch and pull up your cloak, and no one paid you any mind. Out here, I feel like we've got a big sign that says 'outlaws' hanging over us!"

Elinor laughed at the image that invoked. "Or at least, 'watch out for the strangers.' Gods, they don't care much for people they don't know—at least at first." She shook her head. "They'd never make it a day in the city, full of strangers."

"Some who were definitely *stranger* than others," Polly added, and they both chuckled.

They packed in silence for a while, but this time it did not feel strained. "Do you think you'll go back to being a dyer if we ever get to settle down?" Polly asked.

Elinor shrugged. "Maybe. It's the only trade I know—aside from being a witch. And even if we can stop the monsters and the people who summon them, I can't think that townsfolk will suddenly take a shine to witches."

"Probably not," Polly agreed.

"What about you?" Elinor gave her a sidelong glance. "Would you want to go back to working in a pub kitchen? You could do anything you wanted to."

Polly laughed. "That sounds grand—anything I wanted. I don't know. I don't come from a Guild family—I don't have a trade. Ran away from home. My father was a dockworker and a drunk who beat me, and my mother died when I was a baby. No one missed me when I left, so I kept on going."

"We'd miss you," Elinor replied, and nudged her with an elbow.

Polly blushed and turned away. "As well you should. Because I'm awesome." She stared off into space for a moment. "Truly? I don't know. Not sure what I'm suited for, or who'd teach me. I guess I'm good at killing things. I could be an assassin."

Elinor chuckled. "You know, there's probably a future in that, if you could live with yourself doing that sort of work. I used to hear the women come in and talk to Parah about their faithless husbands and the men who hit them or stole from them or did them wrong. Some of them forgave the louts, but I wager that others would have come up with the coin to have someone make the blighter disappear forever if the price was right." She gave Polly a sidelong glance. "Although I don't think you're the hardened killer type."

"I'll have to think on that," Polly replied with a grin. "I rather like being an outlaw. It's daring and romantic."

Elinor snorted. "Except for the running and hiding and sleeping in cellars and nearly getting killed part."

Polly sighed. "Yes, except for that. Stop ruining my fantasy."

———

THE ROAD WOUND close to the river, taking them farther north. They spotted a dozen or so Wanderer wagons clustered along the edge of a stream, and the glow of a campfire. Polly noted some of their sigils chalked on trees and on the road marker and wondered again what they meant. She looked at the nomads' camp, frowning in thought. *I wish they weren't so damn secretive. We could help each other. I bet they know things Rigan and Aiden and Elinor need to fight the monsters. But there's no use asking. They won't tell.*

Polly led them to another abandoned monastery, in hopes of finding more hidden books as well as seeking shelter. They were still within Ravenwood, and still among the vineyards, but farther than any of them had ever been from the city itself. The group stopped in front of what remained of a large, circular tower overlooking the river. In the distance, farther north, lay the village of Brockridge.

"I figured once we made ourselves at home, we'd wander into town and see what's what," Polly said as she climbed down from the wagon and stared at the tower, hands on hips.

"This is it?" The skepticism was clear in Calfon's voice. "Doesn't look as big as where we were before. Older, too."

"Beggars—and outlaws—can't be choosy," Polly reminded him. "Remember—don't let looks fool you. It's supposed to look like a ruin. That's what keeps the guards away."

"Wish it would have kept the spiders away, too," Corran muttered as they headed inside, batting at cobwebs that covered the entrance where the doors hung broken and askew.

"Are you sure it's got catacombs?" Trent ducked as a bird flew past his head from where it had been disturbed in the rafters. "Because it's bloody awful, otherwise."

Polly glanced at Rigan and Aiden. "Well?"

The two witches moved into the large main room, one going left and one right. Both wore expressions of concentration and walked as if entranced, focused on searching for any indication of where the monks secreted their hiding place. Elinor, whose magic lent itself more to potions and elixirs, began an examination of the next room based on her study of the drawings they had found of the old building.

"There are rapids down in the river below this point," Ross mused, looking out the window and down into the ravine. "I'm guessing this served as a beacon as well as a retreat?"

Polly nodded. "Not that big of a stretch, if you think about it. Lighthouse keepers aren't the most sociable folks. It's the light that matters, not the company of the people who keep the lanterns lit."

"I might have something," Elinor called out from the kitchen. Aiden and Rigan were first to join her.

"I paced off the dimensions, and I think there's something strange. Here," she said, moving to a large cabinet sagging and warped with age, apparently built into the wall. "Even accounting for the thickness of the walls, I think there might be enough space that there could be a thin stairway between this room and the main one."

"I'm willing to take your word for it," Rigan said with a shrug. "We didn't find anything in the other room, and there's something about the stone here that makes it very difficult to use magic to sense what's on the other side."

"The walls here are like trying to see through heavy fog," Aiden added. "Don't know whether it's just part of the type of stone they used, or something the monks built in, but the good part of it is that no one outside should be able to use spellcasting or scrying to see what we do in here—assuming we stay."

Trent and Ross had gone to stand guard outside. Polly and Elinor examined the cabinet, pushing and pulling to no avail. Corran and Calfon put their backs into it, trying and failing to find a way to move the piece of furniture to one side or swing it open.

"Other ideas?" Calfon asked as he stepped back.

Polly frowned, studying the cabinet. Six shelves evenly spaced on the top might have once held dishes or cookware, maybe supplies. Beneath the shelves was a broad wooden counter, now damaged from neglect and weather. The base of the cabinet had two sections of additional storage, each one covered by doors. Polly got down on her hands and knees, pulling open one of the doors. She blinked and choked at the dust and wrinkled her nose at the evidence that generations of mice had lived, bred, and died on the warped wooden shelves.

"Maybe we won't be staying, after all," Corran mused. "There's not enough of a roof left in what's standing for us to be able to live here, and any repairs make it obvious that it's not deserted anymore."

"Don't be in such a hurry," Polly chided. She pulled at the wooden shelves, which came away fairly easily. They rested on boards on either side of the cupboard, instead of being nailed in. Polly batted away mouse nests and a few small, desiccated corpses, and then crawled partially inside the enclosure. It smelled like dust and rodents.

"I think I've got something." Her voice came out muffled, but the click as she pressed a hidden catch was loud enough for them all to hear. The back of the lower cupboard swung away, revealing darkness.

"So the monks didn't take on any new brothers who were overly large, I'm guessing." Corran stared at the opening. He and Ross had the broadest shoulders of the group, and Corran eyed the doorway as if trying to decide whether he could get through. "They could climb through into the tunnel, put the boards back up, and then swing the door shut and bar it on the other side. Clever, but not a quick way out."

"Might have been intentional for the opening to be small," Rigan mused, coming up behind them and squatting down to have a better look. "Soldiers in armor aren't getting in there, and neither is hired muscle."

Polly shimmied backward and sat on her haunches. "I'm guessing there's a narrow staircase through there, going into a cellar. I found it: someone else gets to do the honors and lead the way." She brushed cobwebs and dirt out of her hair and off her shoulders.

"I'll go." Rigan was the slimmest of them other than Polly, and while he was tall, his shoulders were not as broad as his brother's. Polly scooted out of the way, and Rigan crawled forward. The air coming from the opening felt cool and damp, and it smelled musty but not unpleasant.

"I wouldn't be surprised if there were caves underneath, like in that other priory," Rigan said. "Given the river below, I'd almost expect it. Let's see."

"You want a lantern?" Corran held out one he had pulled from his pack.

Rigan shook his head. "Don't know what the air is like in there. Let's let it breathe a bit before we put a flame in there." He conjured handfire, a cold tongue of blue-white light that illuminated without burning.

"Wish me luck," he muttered as he crawled toward the opening. Corran grabbed his ankles.

"Just in case," Corran said. "We didn't come this far for you to fall head-first into a hole because the stairs rotted away."

Polly fidgeted as Rigan wriggled into the opening. "There are steps... and they're stone," he said. "I think I need to go in feet first. And Elinor was right—the steps are very narrow, so some of us are going to have to go down sideways."

Reluctantly, Corran let go of his grip and Rigan moved into position. "There's a decent-sized landing at the top, probably exactly for this purpose," he said as he eased himself into the passageway.

"I'd feel better about it if you had a rope," Corran muttered.

"The stairs go on pretty far; I'm not sure we've got one long enough," Rigan called back. "But the air isn't too bad."

Once Rigan had disappeared into the hole, Corran squirmed in far enough so that his head and shoulders were inside as well. "Tell me what you see," he called to Rigan. Polly and the others crowded close enough to hear.

"The stairs are man-made, but it looks like there's a cave at the bottom," Rigan yelled up. "Give me a few minutes to explore. I won't go far."

The group up above passed the time nervously until Rigan's face appeared in the opening and Corran hastily crawled backward to let him out.

"The stairs get wider—I'd say there are about fifty steps," he reported. "At the bottom, it looks like the monks started with what was a natural cave and 'improved' on it. Much like what we found at the last monastery—several rooms, one which has a fireplace." He coughed and brushed dust and worse from his clothing. "We need to clean it and see where it comes out, but at least we can cook. The air smells pretty fresh, so I'm betting there might be a way out at the bottom down to the river."

"If we all go through the door, how do we put the shelves back in?" Corran mused. "We need to make sure there's another way in and out so we only use this for emergencies. Otherwise, nice as the tower is, we aren't going to be able to stay."

"Too hard to get us all out in a hurry," Rigan agreed. "Maybe the monks thought so too."

Trent poked his head into the room. "We found a place where we can hide the horses and the wagon, at least for tonight," he said. "If we're staying."

"We're staying," Aiden replied. "Can't think of anywhere easier to defend than a solid rock tower."

Trent and Ross drew water from the well outside using the buckets they carried in the wagon. Elinor, Polly, and Calfon formed a relay line to unload their belongings. They handed them through to Corran after he maneuvered himself into the tunnel, and Corran passed them down to Rigan. They traveled light, so it didn't take long to unpack.

"Tomorrow, we'll scout around, set some snares for dinner," Trent said once they were back inside. "I'm betting that there's a tunnel that leads to the basement somewhere between the stable and the river, too."

"If Rigan's right and there's a path to the river, we might be able to do some fishing," Ross said with a grin.

"Always thinking with your belly," Polly teased, but she was tired, and the prospect of even a cold meal and some hot tea made her rumbling stomach settle.

Corran hung lanterns on metal hooks sunk into the rock, lighting the way. At the bottom, they looked around at the long-empty rooms.

"Not the worst place we've been," Polly said, hands on hips. "Trent —you brought in the brooms from the wagon?"

"I wouldn't dare forget them," he said.

Polly leveled a glare, then grinned. "All right everyone—you know what to do. The sooner we whip this place into shape, the sooner we can put our feet up and drink."

It didn't take long for them to find a doorway leading to a rough-hewn rock passageway enlarging into a natural cave tunnel. The tunnel led away from the tower and down past the stables, coming out hidden by carefully-positioned rocks and a tangle of trees and vines. Polly grinned when they reached the opening.

"Damn, that's hard to see," she said, taking several steps back and trying to find the mouth of the tunnel. "Glad we decided to go from the inside—it's a lot less hidden from that direction!"

Ross and Calfon went to clean out the fireplace and make sure the chimney drew. Trent went back outside through the tunnel to gather wood. The others pitched in to make the rooms livable, and scrounged ramshackle furniture, or swept away the dust and cobwebs.

"Rigan and I found another set of steps," Corran announced when they finished. "We're going to see where they lead. If they do go down to the river, we want to make sure we don't get any surprise guests."

"I can help get dinner," Aiden said, and Elinor followed as Polly led the way to the room with the fireplace.

"It won't be much," Polly said with a sigh. "Not until they get the snares up. Fish would be nice for a change, too. But we've got bread and cheese and some sausages, and there's whiskey. So we won't go hungry."

Corran and Rigan reappeared after a candlemark, flushed with the exertion of climbing the steep steps. "The stairs go all the way to a cave on the riverbanks," Corran reported. "The cave is deep, and the steps are in the back, so even if anyone did venture in, the stairs are easy to overlook."

"Handy to know, in case the area around the first tunnel opening isn't safe. Anything else?" Trent asked, stretching to loosen sore muscles after the ride.

"Hard to tell if anyone's been in the cave," Rigan added. "The floor is rock with very little loose dirt to show footprints."

"You're thinking about those smugglers we ran into a few towns back," Calfon said.

Rigan nodded. "We didn't see any evidence that people had been in the cave. And we're a good ways upriver from where we saw the smugglers. But still…"

"We'll be careful." Ross looked up from where he knelt, trying to start a fire. "But for now, let's have someone go outside and make sure the chimney vents far enough away not to give us away. I'd hate to go through all this only to get caught by a smoky flue."

CHAPTER TWENTY-FOUR

"Tell me about the raids." Sarolinian Crown Prince Neven looked out over the vista from the covered walkway that ran along one side of his manor house. Brice Tagar, his spymaster, kept pace with him out of necessity.

"We leave the populated areas to Nightshade's monsters," Tagar said. "My men go under cover of darkness, set a field afire or burn a warehouse, and leave. It's not enough to cripple the towns, but plenty to set them on edge. They have no idea who's behind it or why it's happening."

He smiled coldly. "I've got to say; it's been interesting hearing them speculate at the pub. I've gone back a night or two later, never to the same place twice, to hear what's being said." He shook his head. "Amazing what people will come up with when they've got no information at all to go on. They're quick to blame the Guilds loyal to the other Ravenwood Merchant Princes, or chalk it up to old grudges, local dimwitted boys or roving gangs of troublemakers." He laughed and shook his head. "Anything but the truth."

"Make sure it stays that way," Neven replied. "We can't afford any evidence pointing our direction. Sooner or later the farmers and towns-folk will demand that their Merchant Princes do something, and they'll send out their guards, who are easy enough to evade. Inflict enough losses, do enough damage, and Ravenwood will not only be in chaos; it won't be able to meet its trade obligations."

"I don't believe we're far off from that point, m'lord," Tagar said. "Tempers grow short in the villages, between the increase in monster attacks, and the raiders."

"Good." Neven tented his fingers and leaned back. "What of the smugglers?"

"Kadar's kept his guards away, as he promised."

"And the outlaws? The hunters? What of them?"

Tagar shook his head. "No problems since that one time, although they're still at large. The stories grow with the telling. They're becoming heroes to the farm folk, an unfortunate turn of events."

"Quite," Neven said. "What do you hear?"

"Rubbish, for the most part. Tall tales. It's said they've killed ghouls and *higani*, and those bat-faced black dogs Nightshade is so fond of summoning. Those undertaker brothers are the leaders, and one is said to be a witch of some power."

"And still, Kadar can't find them, when they're practically under his nose. Pathetic."

"I've sent a few of my men across the border to keep an eye out for the Valmondes and their companions," Tagar said. "They're to insinuate themselves into Jorgeson's trust, and steer him toward the outlaws. And report his movements back to me, of course."

"Naturally." Neven fell silent for a moment. "What do you hear of the impact of the smugglers? Kadar is pleased, no doubt, at least for now. Has it affected their League obligations?"

"You'll have to ask Ambassador Lorenz how things are going in the city," Tagar said. "I doubt the Guilds pay a lot of attention to the rural areas, but by now even they must know someone is undercutting their trade." He smirked. "Their own Merchant Prince."

"Who believes he is making quite the clever deal," Neven replied, shifting in his chair to reach for the snifter of brandy on the table. "Light enough fires, and sooner or later, it'll all go down in flames."

He swirled the amber liquid before he spoke. "I received a letter from Lorenz. It was in code, of course. Ravenwood is verging on chaos—and it's not improving, despite Aliyev's efforts. It's bad enough that it's reached the ears of the other League members. There's talk that Ravenwood can't be counted on to fulfill its obligations. The Guilds are still angry about Machison's tactics, Aliyev is trapped being Lord Mayor as well as Crown Prince until he has the city under control, and the ship captains who come into the harbor complain more about pirates every week."

"Aren't you concerned that King Rellan will get involved?" Tagar asked. "He's distracted, but not stupid."

"Aliyev is the immediate problem, still another reason to have so many things on fire he doesn't know where to turn first. Does he worry about the monsters? The Balance? Rumors of smugglers and pirates? Try to keep peace with his Guilds?" Neven shook his head. "No matter what he chooses to focus on, it will be the wrong thing because there is too much going on at once. And when it all comes crashing down, Garenoth will break the agreement for cause, and we all get to move up."

———

THE NEXT MORNING, Neven intentionally lingered over his breakfast, loathe to move on to the first appointment of the day. Having to deal with Nightshade always put him in a bad mood, no matter how useful the blood witch was to his ambitions.

Two bodyguards strode after him as he left his manor and climbed into the waiting carriage. One of the guards would ride with the driver, while the other rode behind, keeping watch. They gave Neven little comfort since he knew that the real danger came from the man who would be waiting for him.

The carriage stopped in the middle of a field deep within Neven's private reserve. Here, they could be assured they were far from the prying eyes of farmers or passersby. Neven looked around as he alighted from the carriage. The blue sky and sunshine amid a clearing of tall grass seemed a strange place to keep an appointment with a blood witch.

"I wasn't sure you'd come," Nightshade said as Neven walked up.

"I said I'd be here," Neven snapped. "What do you want to show me that was important enough to drag me out here?"

With his blond hair and white robes, Nightshade hardly looked like a man whose power rose from blood and death. He led Neven down a worn pathway. All of the land Nightshade controlled had been turned into gardens, though Neven knew that every plant had been selected for its poisonous properties, and the plants thrived in part because of soil made fertile with the burial of a continuous stream of fresh corpses, those the blood witch did not deem "interesting" enough to turn into one of his sculptures.

"I'm making a sacrifice this morning," Nightshade said, "a very special one. To Colduraan. And to He Who Watches, one of his First Beings. I thought you might want to be present."

"What's so special about it? You kill people every day."

Nightshade gave him a censorious look. "Show respect for the magic. And the Elder Gods. Colduraan is the Lord of Chaos. I will ask his favor for the chaos we intend to create within Ravenwood."

"Seems like you've been doing a pretty good job on your own.'

"My lord is too kind," Nightshade inclined his head with false humility. "We bring monsters from beyond the Rift to serve our purposes. They are Colduraan's creatures. It would not be wise to take his bounty without showing our gratitude."

Nightshade led them to the high hedge that bounded his garden, and then through a gateway into the clearing beyond. This land had neither the careful plantings nor the sheep-trimmed lawns, remaining high with wild grasses.

"I thought you needed to do this sort of thing at midnight," Neven said.

"Midnight and noon are equivalent times of power," Nightshade replied. "Darkness is of importance only if one needs to hide one's work. I do not."

In the middle of the field, a stone altar held the bound, naked body of a panicked man. A gag and ropes secured him, but his struggle and muffled screams made his terror clear.

"What makes you think an Elder God is listening? Or might deign to respond?" Neven regarded the Guild gods as mere figureheads which lent a false sense of importance to the trades, and the Elder Gods as little more than legends embellished over the centuries by those who stood to gain from the fear and awe of the gullible.

Nightshade chuckled. "Oh, the Elder Gods exist. And they are hungry for devotion. Colduraan is a jealous god, and he rewards those who pay him his due. He Who Watches is also aware of the monsters we draw from beyond the Rift. A First Being is a powerful creature of ancient magic. He favors us with his attention."

"Then get on with it," Neven snapped, hiding his apprehension behind impatience. Employing a blood witch was much like making sausage: nice to have, but best if one did not look too closely at it.

"Stay here," Nightshade said, indicating a spot at a distance from the altar. "If the sacrifice is accepted, Colduraan may give us a gift. It would be wise to keep your distance."

With that, Nightshade walked briskly toward the altar, as the sun approached its zenith. Neven scowled at his back, though decided to indulge the witch and say nothing. Part of him remained curious, while a niggling sense of apprehension suggested he might be safer at an even greater distance. He steeled his nerve, unwilling to show his concern.

When the sun hung directly overhead, Nightshade began his chant. Four pillars with candles stood at the quarters around the altar. Nightshade moved widdershins between them, lighting each one with a word and asperging the space between them. As he walked he chanted, and his steps formed the rhythm to his motion. He picked up a censer and repeated the motions with incense that smelled to Neven of blood, rot, and the wet dirt of the grave.

Nightshade withdrew a knife from his belt and raised it in supplication to the sky. "Colduraan! Ancient among all, god of making and unmaking, of chaos and the void. Hear me and accept my sacrifice! He

Who Watches, ancient of days, first among the First Beings, turn your eyes upon us and grant us favor!"

He brought the knife down point first into the captive's chest, and then pulled it free and slit his throat. Blood spattered Nightshade's white robes and golden hair, painting him in crimson. His ecstatic expression suggested that he welcomed the warm red rivulets that tracked down his face and arms.

His chants grew faster, and he danced with the bloody knife in the space between the altar and the candles. With each circle, Nightshade's movements grew more frenzied, slashing about with the knife, raising his arms, and contorting his body. Neven watched with a mix of horror and revolted fascination.

On the next round, Nightshade brought the knife down, time and again, across his own flesh, cutting into the skin of his forearms until both were bleeding freely, staining his sleeves bright red. He seemed to care nothing for the pain, if he felt it at all in his transcendent state. He clasped his bloody hands together and shook his arms over the corpse, adding his blood to the crimson rivers flowing down the stone.

"Hear me, Lord of Chaos! He Who Consumes the Stars, hear my prayer! God of Unmaking, favor your servant with your presence."

Neven drew back a step, unnerved by the gyrations and hysterical cries. He had long ago ceased to be shocked by Nightshade's gory offerings, but seeing his blood witch in what could only be considered a fit of madness stirred fear on a primal level.

The air outside the circle shimmered, and as Neven gasped, a seam appeared, a black rip as if someone had grasped the sky and torn it asunder. Darkness spilled out, and the tall grasses all around it immediately withered and died, leaving a brown, burned circle. An unholy shriek sounded in the black of the other side, and red eyes glowed. Then with a leap, a creature with the squashed face and back-laid ears of a bat and the body of a black-haired sow sprang from the rip and stood poised to charge within the circle of destruction.

"Praise to Colduraan! Praise to He Who Watches! Thank you, Lord of Destruction, and First of the First Beings, for accepting this sacrifice!" Nightshade praised. And in the next instant, he threw himself at the monster, landing on its back, and brought his knife down over and over into the creature's hide.

The *vestir* shrieked and tried to shake Nightshade from astride him, but the blood witch held on with the strength of madness, stabbing again and again as the monster bucked and jerked to cast off its attacker.

Neven could not make out the words, but Nightshade chanted furiously throughout the attack, his eyes alight with frenzy, and his robes now sodden and dark with blood. One final blow brought the creature down, and Nightshade thrust his knife through its throat, allowing its blood to fountain over him like the blessing of the god he praised. In the next moment, he bent and swiftly drew the blade along the belly of the monster, spilling out its steaming guts onto the dead grass. He seized its entrails, cut them loose, and draped them around his neck and shoulders like a mantle.

"All praise and glory to Colduraan, He Who Drains the Seas and Crushes the Mountains. God of the Storm and the Maelstrom. Honor to He Who Watches, first among the Ancient Ones, for favoring us with his notice. We will prepare your way and make ready your feast."

Neven recoiled, no longer caring that he stared at the blood witch with wide, frightened eyes, mouth agape. He had suspected madness was either required to work blood magic or a consequence of its horrors, but he had no doubt now that Nightshade was utterly insane.

Insane, powerful, and favored by an Elder God of chaos and one of his original monsters.

The Rift closed, taking the dark tendrils of the taint with it. Just for an instant, before the rip in space snapped shut, Neven thought he saw inhuman orange eyes fixed on him, staring out of the primal darkness. Nightshade bowed forward, heaving for breath, eyes still bright with ecstasy. His body trembled as the cost of the magic and the physical exertion took its toll.

"Did you see?" he asked, straightened and turning toward Neven. His hair hung in dark, gory tangles and his robes clung to his body, soaked crimson. He looked like an avenging god or a berserk warrior, returned insane from battle. "He heard. He sent us a sign. My offering was accepted! We will be victorious—we have the favor of an Elder God and the attention of a First Being! Nothing can stand against us."

Neven's shock subsided. "I'll reserve judgment until our ends are accomplished," he snapped. "Clean yourself up, and see that the mess is taken care of." With that, he turned on his heel and walked back the way he had come, barely restraining himself from breaking into a run.

CHAPTER TWENTY-FIVE

"WE'RE BOTH AFTER the same men, and I know how to trap them."

Hant Jorgeson leaned back in his chair, doing his best to project cool certainty.

The rough man across from him, the emissary for the smugglers, regarded him with clear doubt. "If you know, why haven't you done it by now?"

Jorgeson shrugged. "Ravenwood is a big place. It took a while to find them. But we both have a score to settle with the Valmonde brothers and their outlaw friends. They're the ones who killed your fellows, and they're wanted for crimes back in the city. Help me, and I can make sure the Crown Prince never hears of your activities." The implied threat of what would occur without their help remained unspoken.

"Say on." The smuggler's eyes held an intelligent glint, and Jorgeson reminded himself not to underestimate the man.

"We believe someone has paid them to spy on you; likely a rival of your patron," Jorgeson lied. He suspected Merchant Prince Kadar benefitted from the smuggling, though he lacked hard evidence he could take to Aliyev. Then again, Kadar's dealings with the Crown Prince was none of his concern, and hardly what he needed to worry about to keep body and soul together. He owed Aliyev information, but that should not be confused with loyalty.

"My people have tracked them to this area. We can draw them out, make them vulnerable—and then we strike."

"And what is your intent?" the smuggler asked. "Kill or capture?"

"Capture—for the Valmondes and their gang. You're free to kill anyone else who helps them."

The smuggler rubbed a hand across his chin. "We don't want to attract attention. For obvious reasons."

"Yet you want vengeance for the men the Valmondes killed," Jorgeson said. "I'm offering you the best way to get it. Provide reinforcement, and we'll take credit for the kill. You fade back into the shadows knowing revenge was served. There'll be nothing to track back to your... enterprises... or your master."

"What's your plan?" The smuggler folded his arms across his chest, still unconvinced.

"The Valmondes fancy themselves monster hunters," Jorgeson replied. "There's a legend about an old mine near here that fools say is haunted. My... associates... will make sure it lives up to its reputation, causes problems for the villagers. That'll bring the Valmondes, thinking they're coming to the rescue. But instead, they'll only find us." He flashed a predatory smile.

"And what do we do? We're businessmen, not soldiers."

"Our success depends on making sure they can't get away. Your men help surround the area, and if the Valmondes and their fellow outlaws run your way, you stop them." His smile widened. "You're free to be as violent as you want about it, short of killing them. I need them questioned before they die."

"How do I know you won't turn on us?" the smuggler asked, and Jorgeson could see that the man was interested but wary.

"Your activities are not my concern," Jorgeson replied. "Once this is over, we will conveniently forget we ever met. I will take my prize back to the city, and you'll go on with your... business."

"All right," the smuggler said, nodding his head. "Let's talk about when and where."

———

THE OLD MINE loomed dark and silent, an empty socket sunk deep into the hillside. It sat a few miles from the nearest village, far enough that their activities were unlikely to be noted by townsfolk or farmers, but believably close to cause the havoc that would bring the Valmondes to their reckoning.

"You mean there's actually something down there?" Jorgeson asked Spider, watching the gangly witch emerge shaken from the mine's depths.

"More than one 'something,'" Spider replied. "I don't think they'll come easily to do our bidding. We'd be better off using magic to haunt the place ourselves."

"I want both," Jorgeson demanded. "They've slipped through our fingers too often for this to fail. You and Roach need to handle the evidence—slice up some cattle and sheep and leave the bodies. Snatch a child or two—kill the little bastards for all I care, but hide their corpses so the Valmondes can fancy themselves rescuers. Then push the damn ghosts out of the mine and turn them loose for a night or two before you stuff them back in."

"It doesn't work—"

"Then make it work!" Jorgeson roared. "I'll have a couple of the guards go down to the village pub ranting about haunts and monsters. That should get their attention."

"My lord," Spider objected, "we don't even know if the Valmondes have any contact with the village."

"They have an uncanny habit of showing up wherever a vengeful ghost or creature goes on a rampage," Jorgeson snapped. "So work a little blood magic while you're at it, conjure in a monster or two, for good measure. The Valmondes have witches of their own; maybe they can sense the power."

Roach looked at his master with barely concealed derision. "If they could 'sense' our magic, then why haven't we been able to sense theirs?"

Jorgeson fixed him with a wilting glare. "Because their witches are better than you."

"Or perhaps you're imagining a power that doesn't exist," Roach retorted. "They could be finding their hunts by luck."

Jorgeson shook his head. "No, their witches have a system of some sort. If they were just happening upon monsters, they wouldn't have made so many kills. And we've got eyes in enough pubs that we know they aren't making a habit of chatting up the locals looking for their next fight. But there've been five monster kills within a three day's ride of here in the last few weeks." He nodded. "That tells me they've found a base, and they're close. All we need to do is bait the trap."

"I don't like the ghost part," Spider whined. "Ghosts are unpredictable. Hard to control."

"Wouldn't it be wonderful if we had blood witches for that—oh wait, we do," Jorgeson snapped. "So make use of the balls you were born with and do your job."

He stalked away, leaving the two witches fuming behind him. The last word he had gotten from Aliyev—brought by rider from the city—excoriated him for incompetence and warned that the Crown Prince's patience grew thin. More worrisome was Aliyev's comment that the growing unrest in the villages—farmers and merchants taking up arms against the monsters, no doubt egged on by the Valmondes—would be seen as outright rebellion should King Rellan hear of it.

Jorgeson's years serving the late Lord Mayor Machison taught him to note what went unsaid. Between the "unrest" as the peasants took up arms and the impact Kadar's smugglers no doubt made on the rural Guild trades, Ravenwood was quite possibly in danger of defaulting on its agreement with Garenoth. Jorgeson grasped the consequences of that possibility perhaps more than did Aliyev.

Working around Blackholt had taught Jorgeson about the Balance and the Cull. If Ravenwood were to lose its League status, part of its disgrace would include being called upon to pay a higher death toll with the Cull. And that would surely be the spark in the tinder that pushed Ravenwood into outright revolt.

"Bloody Valmondes," Jorgeson muttered, retreating to the

peddler's wagon he had commandeered as his headquarters and lodging. He set a thick circle of salt and aconite mixture around his horses and his wagon, stirring in iron filings for good measure. After what he had seen the night Ravenwood City burned, he knew not to put his full trust in amulets or protective talismans. Salt and iron worked.

If he had his preference, he would be far away in much more comfortable lodgings. Sheer common sense would have him a league distant, not within sight of both the mine and the open space where Spider and Roach meant to work their blood magic.

Jorgeson took a swig from his flask and sighed, sitting back with a sword and dagger in hand. He had tried delegating, sending out guards and bounty hunters, to no avail. They either returned empty-handed or didn't return at all. Aliyev may have given him Spider and Roach to use, but from what he had seen of the blood witches' abilities, the gesture probably stemmed from a desire to keep them from mucking up their magic close at hand, rather than out of any belief they might provide help.

And if the witches are that deficient, it hardly suggests that he assigned me competent guards. This was Aliyev's excuse for getting rid of all of us—me included. A way to eliminate an embarrassment, while saving face for himself.

Jorgeson slept fitfully that night, twitching awake at every sound. He knew that out there in the darkness, the two blood witches and a few of the guards set the scene, killing livestock and a few unfortunates from the nearest village.

Well after midnight, the mages returned. Blood soaked their clothing and that of the two guards who accompanied them. They brought with them two young men, both in their teens. They, too, were bloodied, but still alive judging from their groans and weak struggle.

"Is it done?" Jorgeson asked when they came to present their captives.

"We killed a dozen sheep and four cows, left them cut up enough to make the farmers talk plenty about angry ghosts," Spider said, with a grin.

"We'll take care of the rest now since we've got the warm bodies we needed," Roach added, shaking one of the bound men who hung limply in the soldiers' grasp.

"See to it," Jorgeson snapped. "The night's wasting."

Jorgeson angled himself so he could watch Spider and Roach prepare their working. *If I'm lucky, this will draw out the Valmondes and be done with it.*

Guards stood in the bed of another wagon, also ringed with salt. They held their crossbows ready, though if the ghosts Spider and Roach summoned from the mine turned vengeful, quarrels would be of little help. The two blood witches hauled the unfortunate young captives into the field not far from the mouth of the mine, and set their warding, unwilling to expose themselves either to the angry ghosts or to whatever might come through from the other side of the Rift they intended to open. Spider and Roach might be underwhelming in their abilities, but they had a gift for self-preservation.

When the preparations were complete, Spider and Roach each grabbed one of the bound prisoners and hauled the terrified young men to their knees. Blood magic grew stronger from fear and pain; that much, Jorgeson had learned from his association with Blackholt. The witches' blades burned bright as fire as they chanted and traced sigils in the air before the knives faded once again into darkness.

Their voices rose and fell, and all the while the captives struggled unsuccessfully to break free. From the amount of blood on their clothing, Jorgeson could guess that the young men had put up a fight. Given the nature of the ritual, it was likely their capture had been more punishing than necessary to subdue them.

With a sharp cry, Spider and Roach brought their knives down in tandem, first making a deep slash across the prisoners' throats and then sinking their blades into the unlucky men's chests. Blood sprayed from the wounds, soaking the witches' clothing, and they clearly welcomed it, as if it were a cleansing rain.

The bodies slumped to the grass. Spider and Roach took up their chant once more, carving sigils into the air, and the night around them thickened and trembled. Jorgeson could not force down the fear that rose watching the sky itself twist and buckle.

A shriek echoed from the depths of the old mine, and despite himself, Jorgeson jumped in surprise. Instinct bid him run, and it took all of his will to remain where he was, keeping his grip firm on the reins to calm the horses. Even though the wagon team had been blindered and hobbled, they tossed their heads worriedly and whinnied in fear.

The air in front of Spider and Roach ripped apart, revealing the place beyond it to be even darker. Out of the depths, four *higani* scuttled at full speed, their white shells glistening in the night, joints clicking as they moved, *chittering* among themselves.

The guards cried out in fear, but only one deserted his post. The *higani* set on him immediately, moving faster than their round bodies and long, jointed legs seemed capable of going, quickly outpacing the terrified soldier.

One of the creatures slashed the back of the man's legs with its sharp, pointed foreleg, hamstringing him. The guard fell, screaming in vain for help. The rest of the *higani* swarmed over his thrashing body, sharp claws stabbing like daggers, plunging in again and again until the screams choked into nothing and the dying man lay twitching in a pool of blood.

Jorgeson held onto the reins and to his seat white-knuckled. No one else could hear the pounding of his pulse or see the sweat that beaded on his forehead, but he could not quell his fear when the world itself ripped asunder before his eyes. No more monsters poured out of the Rift, but even by the moonlight, Jorgeson saw that a foul black substance oozed from the split in the air, flowing like oil. Everything it touched died, withering the grass and saplings in a circle all around the Rift, contained only by a second salt circle around the area where the tear in the fabric of reality opened.

Roach took up chanting, arms raised as he faced the Rift. His voice did not crack, and he never faltered as the words of the Old Language poured out of his mouth. As quickly as it appeared, the dark tide withdrew, and the Rift snapped shut as if it had never been.

Spider faced the mine, and he shouted words in the ancient tongue, calling the restless spirits forth.

The temperature dropped in seconds, going from comfortably cool to cold enough that Jorgeson saw his breath. A gut-level sense of dread preceded the ghosts, an instinctive warning for the living to hide away from the horrors still to come.

Guards cursed and cried in fear, calling on the gods or shouting obscenities to buck up their courage, but they did not leave their posts. After what befell their comrade, it was obvious none of them wished to try their luck with either the *higani* or the ghosts.

Gray fog rolled from the mouth of the old mine. It curled and eddied, moving like no mist he had ever seen in nature. Now and again, Jorgeson glimpsed distorted faces and twisted bodies in the cold fog. He shuddered when they turned toward him, blank sockets still fixing on him as if they could make him out even within the protective circle. They rushed from their tomb with a frigid blast of wind that smelled like coal and rot.

Spider's full attention turned to the revenants, and he wove a complex mesh of sigils in the air, each one burning with fire. Whatever language he used to control the ghosts sounded harsh and guttural to Jorgeson, utterly unfamiliar. The ghosts surged as if they meant to overtake the guards in their protective circles, and the soldiers shuddered.

Spider stood quickly, legs splayed and arms upraised as if to bodily block the rush of spirits. They swirled around him, unable to break through the warding of salt and iron, held back by magic and the elements. Some of them encircled each of the guards, though they left Roach and the *higani* alone.

A cold wind swept past Jorgeson, stirring his cloak and riffling the horses' manes. Once again the spooked geldings whinnied, stomping their hooves and jerking against the reins, but Jorgeson and their hobbles kept them inside the protections of the salt circle.

Ghosts clamored all around the circle, pressing their misshapen faces against the warding as if it were glass. Their eyes held him in a baleful gaze, promising painful death if they could drag him from his sanctuary. The bony hands of withered corpses scrabbled against the warding, and Jorgeson heard their moans and cries, wailing like the damned. Many of the ghosts showed the injuries that had cost them their lives, broken bones and fractured skulls, crushed bodies and severed limbs. Their appearance shifted as he watched them, sometimes like fresh corpses, and then fading to skeletons and then to faded images made of mist.

Spider shouted, and the specters pulled back abruptly, sweeping down the small grade from Jorgeson's wagon toward the blood witch, then parting around his warding like water around a rock. The ghosts that tormented the guards also felt the pull of Spider's spell and joined the others in a ghastly, terrifying cavalcade toward the sleeping town in the distance.

The *higani* finished stripping flesh from the bones of the downed guard and the young sacrifices. Blood streaked their bone-white shells, and they moved ponderously, heavy with their feast, but they made their way down toward the fields, *clicking* and *chittering* as they went.

Spider and Roach continued their chant, though Jorgeson heard exhaustion in their voices. Roach finished first, shoulders slumping as he smudged open the salt circle and dispelled the warding. Spider's litany went on for several more minutes until his voice cracked with strain and he sounded utterly drained. He spat out the final words of the ritual, and as his wardings fell, so too did those around the guards and Jorgeson.

The ghosts were gone, the monsters fled in search of fresh meat, but the night still held its unnatural chill. Or at least that's what Jorgeson preferred to think as he felt the tremor through his body and saw his hands shaking.

Perhaps these two are not so useless as I thought.

The guards moved cautiously from their safe havens, crossbows still raised though they could have done no good against either *higani* or angry ghosts. They looked pale in the moonlight, eyes wide with barely contained terror, and from the smell of it, at least one man had pissed himself.

"What's to keep them from coming back this way?" One of the soldiers asked as Spider gathered up the materials he had brought to work the ritual.

"Nothing," answered Roach. That's why we're going to fall back, and we'll ward the camp. Let them do their worst tonight with us well out of reach. The Valmondes won't appear out of thin air; they'll need time to find out what's happened and travel here. So we wait. And when they come, we'll be ready."

Heady with the power of having ripped open the sky and restrained both monsters and the restless dead, Roach's voice held a new confidence that chilled Jorgeson.

"What you saw is nothing compared to what's coming for those farmers," Spider added, and his usual whiny pitch tonight took on a deeper, more certain tenor. Both witches seemed to thrum with power, as if the forces they had called, bound, and unleashed left them vibrating with its overflow. For the first time, Jorgeson felt afraid, and he thrust his fear down ruthlessly, refusing to give in to it.

I held my head up to Blackholt, and I'll be damned if I'll cower to these pox-faced half-grown boys, Jorgeson thought. He knew that now he had seen the full measure of the blood witches' power, he would not underestimate how dangerous they could be—to their enemies, or to him.

They pulled back about a mile from the mine. Jorgeson railed at the two witches that at this distance, they would be too far to gain their prize should the hunters show up to deal with both the ghosts and the monsters.

"If they show up, it won't be a quick thing," Spider assured him. "Let them wear themselves out battling the *higani* and fighting the ghosts. We don't want to be in the middle of that. Once they're worn and bloodied, you can sweep in and seize your prize, while we send the ghosts back into the depths of the mine and dispatch any monsters that remain."

"How will we know, since we're out of sight of the mine?" Jorgeson demanded.

"By scrying," Roach replied as if the answer were obvious. "One of us will watch the waters at all times. Don't worry; you'll have your hostages."

As the sun set the next evening, Jorgeson's temper frayed. "You said the Valmondes would find out," he fumed at Spider and Roach. "You were certain they would come." He threw up his hands. "We're wasting time."

"Patience," Spider replied, in a tone that only stoked Jorgeson's foul mood. "We don't know how the Valmondes are discovering where the monsters have come through, but their kills are too timely, too precise to be sheer accident. I suspect they're doing some scrying of their own, but exactly how I can't know."

"If they scry, they'll see us. They won't come," Jorgeson argued.

Roach shook his head. "We are warded, my lord. I've placed deflection sigils around us, and we both wear talismans that dampen others' ability to sense our magic. They will come."

Late that night, the two blood witches roused the camp to take their places. Jorgeson stormed from his wagon, armed for a fight, and saw nothing but the empty field in front of the darkened mine.

"Where are they?" he growled.

Roach gestured toward a shallow bowl into which he and Spider peered intently. Jorgeson moved to join them and felt a frisson of power down his back as he stepped into their space. He looked down, expecting a salt line, and saw nothing, but apparently, he had crossed an arcane protection.

"Look," Spider said, pointing to the bowl.

Jorgeson stared at the water, and images appeared on its tranquil surface. He saw cloaked figures working their way up the hill from the village, only minutes away.

"What of the monsters?"

"They've killed the monsters," Roach replied. "Quite a battle. We saw much of it. This is not the first time they've faced *higani*. Clearly, the hunters knew how to fight them."

"I didn't bring you here to praise them!" Jorgeson said, glowering. "Are their witches with them?"

Spider shook his head. "Not that we can tell. They might also have deflection spells, but at this distance, I believe we would still be able to sense them."

Jorgeson's smile was predatory. "Then this should be easy."

Not long after Jorgeson and his party hid themselves for the ambush, three men trudged up the hill. Even in the moonlight, Jorgeson could see the blood that streaked the men's faces and the torn fluttering of their cloaks, evidence that the fight against the *higani* had not been without cost.

I want to get my hands on their witches, Jorgeson thought, *but if we take the hunters, we can force the witches to come to us. This will work. This has to work. It's not too late.*

"There's the mine," one of the hunters said, gesturing toward the dark opening in the hillside. His hood fell back, revealing curly blond hair that fell to his collar. *Corran Valmonde,* Jorgeson thought.

"We'll watch your back." The speaker had the broad shoulders and muscular arms of a blacksmith, and Jorgeson guessed it was Ross, the farrier's son.

"Don't take too long. I don't like being out in the open." Jorgeson could not identify the third speaker, but it mattered little. He would force confirmation of their identities from them soon, and much more besides.

Corran Valmonde dug into his bag and withdrew four sturdy stakes, which he pushed into the ground at the quarters. He strung a stiff white rope between them, making a warded salt circle, large enough for him and his companions to stand inside, and began the chant to send the ghosts back into the mine and seal them away.

Jorgeson chafed at the delay. Roach and Spider had argued that it made sense to let Valmonde return the spirits to their prison, as it would further tire him, weakening his ability to resist capture afterward. As Jorgeson had no desire to find himself trapped between the angry ghosts and the hunters, he reluctantly agreed, though now he fought the instinct to call down his guards and seize the men while they remained easily within his grasp.

Corran continued his chant, and one by one, the stakes he had driven into the tall grasses began to glow: red, white, blue, and golden. The wind rose, and the temperature dropped, and fog rolled in from all sides, filled with the spirits of dead miners. They swirled and shrieked around the circle Valmonde cast, but to no avail. His words bound them, and as Jorgeson watched, fascinated by what he saw, the ghosts appeared to have no will to break away from the spell the undertaker cast.

As Spider and Roach had told him beforehand, this time, the ghosts paid no mind to them and their guards. The revenants swirled in a maelstrom around the three men within the circle, growing nearly solid, wailing and keening in grief and anger.

The chant reached its climax, and the circle flared.

"Those of you who are willing, I free you and consign you to the After," Corran's voice rose above the wind and shrieks. "Doharmu awaits."

Once more, the air above the clearing wavered, and a very different opening appeared. Jorgeson gasped despite himself and instinctively shrank back. This was no Rift, imposed upon nature by the will of sorcerers. It was as if the night opened of its own accord, a door unlocked from inside, and what lay beyond stretched dark and unknowable.

Jorgeson had no words to describe the primitive fear he felt, the almost physical compulsion to drop to his knees in worship and abase himself before the God of Death awaiting beyond the portal.

Tendrils of fog peeled away from the vortex surrounding the warded circle, streaming toward the black doorway that led to the After. As they passed the threshold, the ghosts fell silent, fading into the all-consuming darkness.

The rest of the ghosts raged at the hunters inside the warding, a storm of gray faces and glimpses of mangled limbs. Corran Valmonde lifted his hands once more and raised his voice in chant. The maelstrom of spirits tamed, slowing its swirling until row upon row of sullen ghosts stood surrounding the circle and glared balefully at the living men within.

"Go," Corran ordered. "If you will not go to your rest, to Doharmu, then return to where you died. Let it be your tomb. Trouble the living no more."

He might not be the full witch his brother was, but Corran's power compelled the dead to do as he bid. The spirits' faces and forms faded once more into mist as they swept back into the darkness of the abandoned mine. Jorgeson could not make out the next words Corran spoke, but he imagined them to be some sort of binding to compel the ghosts to remain within the mine.

With the ghosts gone and the monsters destroyed, Corran lowered his hands and slumped, apparently weary from the magic. One of his companions steadied him, and Corran dispelled the wardings with a word and a gesture, then gathered the marked stakes and coiled the rope, replacing them in his bag.

"Now!" Jorgeson and his guards rose from their hiding places and surrounded the three hunters, crossbows leveled at their chests. Shock gave way to anger, and grim resignation as Corran and his companions threw down their weapons and raised their hands in surrender. The smugglers moved in to bind their wrists, making it clear by their rough treatment that killing their companions would be avenged.

"Who are you?" Even on his knees, Corran Valmonde did not know his place.

"Hant Jorgeson. The man who's going to claim the bounty on your godsforsaken corpse."

Corran spat, aiming for Jorgeson's shoes. "Machison's lackey. I'm surprised you're still alive."

Jorgeson grabbed a handful of Corran's hair and yanked his head back. "I swore I would bring the outlaws to justice," he grated. "Your bounty is good, dead or alive. But before I kill you—before you beg to die—you're going to do a few things for me."

"Go to the Abyss," Ross yelled, earning himself a punch to the mouth. He looked up, bloodied but unrepentant.

"The other hunters were defiant too—at first," Jorgeson mused, "before we broke them. Do you remember? The ones we gibbeted in the square for treason."

"We remember." Corran's voice sounded like gravel. "And we'll avenge them."

Jorgeson smiled. "Not today." He drew his knife, and lightly traced its tip along Corran's jaw, down over the artery that pulsed in his neck, hovering at the hollow of his throat. "Before I cut you, before I make you beg for the chance to tell me everything you know to stop the pain, I'm going to let the men whose companions you killed work off a little frustration."

"Smugglers," Ross spat. He looked to Corran. "Told you we should have killed them all."

"All right boys," Jorgeson said, walking away. "Have your fun. Just leave them breathing. Live bait works better."

As Jorgeson walked past the blood witches, he barely spared them a glance. "Make sure the outlaws remain alive and don't break their jaws. I have questions that need answers. I want the rest of them, and I'm certain Valmonde has some kind of bond with his brother that will draw them here."

"As you wish, my lord," Spider replied, eyes alight. Both of the blood witches watched eagerly as the smugglers closed on the bound captives.

"The rest of you, keep your places. The other outlaws will come meaning to attack, so stay sharp," he warned his guards.

Jorgeson retired to a place out of range of the blood spatter. He leaned against a tree, watching as the witches drew close enough to monitor the beating, perhaps even to draw energy from the pain. Later, he would have the witches revive the prisoners so that he could interrogate them. He would learn their safe houses and their co-conspirators, the names of people and villages that had sheltered them and aided their raids, everything he needed to regain a measure of his damaged standing in the eyes of the Crown Prince.

The smugglers set on the captives with fists and kicks, practiced enough in striking to injure without killing. He suspected they had done this many times before, perhaps roughing up merchants late to pay for their goods. The outlaws took the thrashing stoically, refusing to cry out except when grunts of pain were forced from them by a punch to the gut or an involuntary reflex.

The smugglers were as brutal as they were efficient. Jorgeson crossed his arms and watched them work, as they split lips and broke noses, blackened eyes and wrapped their hands around the men's necks hard enough to leave fingerprints in the flesh. Even with their wrists and ankles bound, the hunters tried to fight back, lurching from side to side, head-butting those who got close, drawing up their knees and kicking. Yet in the end, they lay bleeding and battered, as the smugglers stood over them, dripping with sweat, heaving for breath, bloodied fists still clenched by their sides.

Amateurs, all of them, Jorgeson thought. While he had never relished torturing prisoners himself as Machison and Blackholt clearly did, he had mastered the techniques. Especially with the blood witches to help with the questioning, Jorgeson had no doubt the men would break. They all did, unless death took them. Though the hunters they had killed, the men whose corpses they displayed in the giblets, had given him precious little for all his work.

It will be different this time, he vowed.

Jorgeson moved away from the tree, eyeing the darkness that surrounded them. The smugglers had stepped away from the prisoners, and Jorgeson called the blood witches to him. "The hunters live?"

Spider nodded. "Yes. The damage is painful, but not too serious. Though they won't be trying to fight us tonight, I'd wager."

"Don't be so sure," Jorgeson replied. "They're a stubborn lot." He glanced around them. "Can you sense whether the others are coming?"

"Nothing, my lord," Roach replied. "Give it time. Even if there is a bond as you believe between the brothers, it will take time for the rest of their party to follow their tracks."

"Be ready," Jorgeson warned. "And stay close to me. I expect to win this. But I also expect to remain alive. One of you is to assure my safety at all times, no matter what."

"I'll guard you," Spider said, while Roach looked away. Jorgeson did not fancy that either of the blood witches liked his company or were happy about being given to him for his desperate quest, but Spider managed to hide his contempt better than Roach did.

"Make damn sure you do," Jorgeson snapped. "Capturing the fugitives is no good to me if I'm not able to present them to the Crown Prince." *And reclaim, if not exactly my honor, at least my freedom.*

Once more, the smugglers and guards melted into the shadows, awaiting new prey. Jorgeson had left his wagon hitched to the horses, ready to go should anything go awry. He learned long ago to plan for contingencies, and to design an escape in case of defeat as well as a path for a triumphant return. Jorgeson fingered the pendant that hung at this throat, an anti-magic charm for which he had paid dearly.

The wretch who made it for him swore on the life of his hostage child that the amulet was good enough to deflect the power of even an accomplished witch. Jorgeson had tried it by asking Spider to strike at him, while he held the hostage like a shield. The amulet worked, though expedience forced him to kill both the amulet maker and the child, regardless. He wore it always and favored it not only for protection but for how it seemed to make both Spider and Roach even more uncomfortable in his presence.

"Someone's coming," Spider muttered.

"The hunters' witches?" Jorgeson felt the thrill of the fight rise in his blood.

The roar of falling rock cut off Spider's reply as the mouth of the old mine collapsed. A streak of fire sizzled across the clearing, aiming right for Jorgeson, who leaped out of the way. Muted buzzing sounded in the night like strange bees, and four of the smugglers collapsed, with bloody gouges in the center of their foreheads.

"Shoot them!" Jorgeson shouted to his guards, who looked around at the darkness, still unable to make out their adversaries.

The twang of bows came as the buzzing resumed. An arrow flew toward Roach, then deflected against his warding. One of the guards fell with an arrow in his chest, while another clutched at a bleeding shoulder where an arrow had lodged. The buzzing—Jorgeson knew it now to be the whir of slings—sounded again, but none of the stones found their mark this time. To the left of where they stood, away from the mine entrance, fire leaped up from the dry grass, blazing bright and hot.

Too late, Jorgeson recognized the distraction. When he looked back to the clearing, two men stood with the prisoners, and he knew at once that the taller of the two was Rigan Valmonde.

"Kill him!" Jorgeson screamed to his witches and marksmen.

Rigan brought his hands down, and a ring of fire blazed around the two witches and the captives. The other man raised his hands, and a green warding crackled in a cylinder of energy all around them.

"You should not have come here," Rigan shouted. "Go back to the city, and take your guards with you."

Only two of the smugglers remained standing, and more than half a dozen of his guards. One of those clutched suddenly at his chest, stumbled, and then fell to the ground, gasping twice before he went still. Another doubled over, retching violently, bringing up the contents of his stomach over and over until only bile remained. *More witches, or can the two inside the ring keep up their walls and still attack my men?* Jorgeson wondered.

Shouts and jeers sounded from the darkness, dozens of voices strong. They yelled obscenities and cat-called, and for good measure, sent stones zinging through the air from slings and arrows flying toward their marks.

The rout Jorgeson had envisioned had turned into a debacle, and much as he was loathe to leave with his prize so close at hand, he knew a lost cause when he saw it.

"Get me out of here," Jorgeson growled to Spider and Roach. "Whatever it takes to get us to the wagon and clear of this godsforsaken place!"

They ran for the wagon. Up ahead, Jorgeson saw the dim silhouettes of people standing between them and the road. "Do something!" he hissed.

Roach uttered a word of power and swept out one hand, knocking everyone out of their way. Curses and cries of surprise sounded as they pounded past, but Roach had used sufficient force to keep those he downed from coming after them.

The wagon was on a farm lane that led away from the clearing and came out on another road. Jorgeson untethered the horses and climbed into the driver's seat, putting the wagon in motion even before the two blood witches were fully onboard.

"Keep them off our tail!" he yelled as Spider and Roach struggled to find a hold. The wagon lunged and jolted on the rutted road, but the horses kept the pace, and for a time, Jorgeson's concentration was so focused on not landing in a ditch or laming a horse that he had no idea what the witches did to dissuade pursuit.

They had put several miles between them and the outlaws by the time they reached the road and Jorgeson finally slowed the carriage. "What happened?" he snarled at the two witches, who looked worse for the wear after the harrowing ride.

"The hunters had help," Spider replied.

"I figured that already," Jorgeson bit back. "Villagers?"

"Most likely," Roach said. "My guess, from the slings and bows. Crude, but effective, especially in the dark."

"Why didn't you sense Rigan Valmonde coming?"

"We did, once he got fairly close," Spider replied, not bothering to hide the tension in his voice. "I suspect he and the other witch also used a deflection spell. They're common enough."

"And the others? The ones who just fell over dead or puking their suppers? What of them?" Jorgeson relished the chance to take out his foul mood on a deserving target, and his disappointment in both blood witches made them fair game.

"That's hedge witch stuff," Roach answered, derision clear in his voice.

"Hedge witch or no, they got the better of both of you," Jorgeson snapped. "Why didn't you attack?"

"We did, my lord, but there were too many of them to take on all at once," Spider protested.

"I saw nothing."

"Not all magic is flash and chant," Roach responded. "As soon as we realized others were coming, we sent a force against them to keep them back, but you said you wanted to take the fugitives alive, and we didn't know who was who. All we could do was throw obstacles in their way unless we risked killing them." He clearly blamed Jorgeson for the rout.

"Those bloody villagers took up arms against us," Jorgeson seethed. "I may not be able to find the Valmondes, but I know where their village is." He turned to the witches. "I want them to pay. Bring down the worst of the creatures on them. Wipe the village from the ground. All of them, kill all of them!"

"My lord—" Spider protested

"Just do it," Jorgeson hissed between gritted teeth. "And then figure out how we will find the Valmondes now that they've been put on alert. Because we will find them and when we do, we'll make them a sacrifice Colduraan will be proud of."

CHAPTER TWENTY-SIX

CORRAN STARTLED AWAKE with a panicked cry. Rigan grabbed his shoulders in a firm grip, anchoring him. "Easy. You're safe. Everything's all right."

Corran's wild eyes scanned the room and finally came back to Rigan's face. "The field. It was an ambush, they set a trap—"

Rigan nodded, still keeping his hands on Corran's shoulders. "You're out. You're safe. It's over." He could feel Corran shaking, and his pupils, blown wide with fear, made Rigan's gut wrench. He did not release his hold until Corran's breathing slowed and his pulse stopped throbbing so hard the vein jumped in his neck. That Corran did not try to move away told him something of his brother's state of mind.

"What happened?" Corran's voice sounded wrecked; a livid bruise and the marks where fingers had dug into his flesh still clearly showed on his skin.

"We were in the village. Polly and Elinor were working with the women, while Calfon and I trained the men. Aiden offered to see to their sick, and the ones who were hurt by the monsters. I—I had this feeling something was wrong," Rigan confessed. "And just when I was going to go ask Aiden about it, he came rushing in and said he'd had one of his visions." Rigan closed his eyes and swallowed hard. "He said… he saw you dying, near the mine." Rigan did not care that Corran heard the way his voice trembled. Corran laid a hand on his arm.

"We were."

Rigan took a deep breath. "Elinor and Polly gathered the women and their hedge witches. The men insisted on coming with us—said it was the least they could do since we'd driven off the monsters and dealt with the ghosts. They grabbed any weapons they had and… we all went to war."

"I don't remember much," Corran admitted. "We got to the field, and we worked the grave magic to send them on, or back into the mine. That went right. And then, everything fell apart." He shook his head. "Jorgeson's men set on us, too many of them to fight. And then, I don't remember anything until I woke up here."

Rigan closed his eyes and bowed his head. "It's probably better that way, although we put on quite a show," he added with a bitter smile. Corran listened silently while Rigan recounted the battle with the smugglers and Jorgeson's guards.

"So Jorgeson got away, and his blood witches?"

Rigan nodded. "Yeah. By the time we realized they were gone, it was too late and, well, we couldn't spare the time if we were going to save you and the others." He looked away and clenched his fist, willing himself to calm down. "It was bad," he said finally. "They'd beaten you three so badly; I was afraid we couldn't fix it."

"He told them not to kill us," Corran murmured. "Jorgeson. I heard that part. Said he wanted to question us. Bragged about how he killed Bant, Pav, and Jott."

Rigan swore under his breath. "When we find him, we'll make him pay," he promised.

Corran sank back onto the bed. Rigan got him a glass of water and steadied him as he drank. "How long?" Corran rasped.

"Three days. There were times when I was afraid you weren't going to wake up," Rigan said. He knew the strain of the past days showed in his red-rimmed eyes and the stubble he hadn't bothered to shave, and in the wrinkled clothes he'd slept in at his brother's bedside.

"The others?"

"They're awake. They didn't remember much more than what you said. Gods, Corran—that was too close."

"The villagers—"

"We've warned them," Rigan cut him off. "They're ready to fight to defend themselves, whether it's the Lord Mayor's guards or Jorgeson's strongmen."

"What about the smugglers?" Corran's voice was fading rapidly.

Rigan gave a bitter chuckle. "The villagers had enough of the smugglers. Seems they'd killed some young men who happened upon them, and the shopkeepers are angry about being undercut. So the townsfolk cut off the smugglers' heads. They sent one in a bag with a note to the Crown Prince to let him know what's going on, and the others they mounted on stakes along the riverbanks, as a warning to the rest."

"Neither of those things is going to end well."

"Probably not. But they told me that it felt damn good at the time."

Corran groaned as an attempt to sit up failed. "What now?"

"We've been keeping watch to make sure Jorgeson stays gone, and that no new guards show up," Rigan said. He stretched, muscles aching from his long vigil. "We all figured we should move on again as soon as the rest of you are well enough, since Jorgeson has to know we have a base within a few day's ride of the mine."

"Shit. I liked it here. And we'd only barely unpacked."

"Can't be helped." Rigan sighed. "We also got a message from Brock—the Sarolinian hunter?"

"The one who's part Wanderer?"

Rigan nodded. "With a wife who's a witch? Yeah. They said something really big is going to happen, and it has to do with the Rifts and the Balance. They want us to come to them, and they'll tell us more."

Corran shifted, trying to find a comfortable position. Although Rigan knew that Aiden had done everything he could for the three hunters after the beating, it had taken all of the healer's efforts just to keep them alive and reverse the worst of their injuries. Bruises, cracked ribs, and sore muscles would be painful for a while. "Do you think it's another trick?"

"No. Aiden and I were able to make contact with them through another dream walk."

Corran's eyes widened. "That's risky."

Rigan grimaced. "Couldn't be helped, given the circumstances. Aiden connected with Mina. Not enough to get the whole story, but enough to convince him that the request is real, and not a trap."

"So what's the plan? We can't move out of here and also meet up with Brock and Mina."

"Polly had a good idea on that," Rigan said with a tired grin. "She suggested that we leave whatever we can do without here, and move between several small temples that were desecrated when the Crown Princes seized the monasteries. We figure that if we aren't seen in the area for a few weeks, Jorgeson will move on, and we can come back."

"And in the meantime, we're taking refuge in the temples of the Elder Gods?"

"Do you have a better idea?"

"What about Brock and Mina?"

"As soon as you and Trent are up for it, we'll ride back for the border, along with Aiden and Ross. Calfon will help Polly and Elinor move our stuff to the temple. Polly already scouted it, and says there are chambers in the basement we can use."

"Sounds like you were busy while I was... out."

Rigan ran a hand through his hair, realizing he probably looked as ragged as he felt. "Don't joke about that," he said. "There wasn't anything funny about it."

Corran frowned as he studied his brother. "You look like shit. Is there something else—besides keeping a vigil for three days?"

Rigan looked away. "Ever since I came back from the Rift, I've had dreams."

"I know. You wake me up most nights, thrashing and screaming."

"Sorry. I don't know if any of us are going to sleep well ever again," Rigan said with a sigh. "But this... it's different. I'll be dreaming—good or bad—and then everything changes, and I'm alone in the dark, except I'm not really alone. There's something in the darkness, and it's watching. It's aware, and dangerous, and powerful, so powerful."

"I keep hearing that Colduraan reigns in the Rift. Do you think it's him?"

Rigan shook his head. "No. I mean, it doesn't feel like when we saw Eshtamon in the cemetery. I don't have a good way to describe it. But I think it's biding its time. And when that time is up, something really, really bad is going to happen."

Corran squeezed his forearm. "It could just be a bad dream. You're entitled to a few. Until we know for certain, don't make it into something bigger than it is."

Rigan nodded, although he didn't really believe what Corran said. *He doesn't know. He didn't feel it. It's real—and it's waiting.*

———

AFTER ANOTHER DAY to recuperate, Corran insisted he was well enough to travel, despite Rigan's protests. Aiden couldn't find a reason to overrule him, so while the others packed up enough gear to last them in hiding for a few weeks, Corran, Trent, Ross, Rigan, and Aiden set off for the Sarolinian border.

They kept to back roads, wary of patrols, watching for either bounty hunters or more of Jorgeson's men. A day and a half into their journey, they traveled along a dusty dirt trail that wound through farm fields and pastures. Rigan rode point, and he reined in his horse abruptly. The others stopped close behind.

"What's wrong?" Corran asked.

"Can't you smell it?"

Aiden met his gaze. "Blood. Not particularly fresh."

Rigan nodded. "And that buzzing—I don't think it's the wind."

They continued, weapons in hand. The stillness Rigan had found calming not long before now seemed ominous. When they rounded a bend in the road, their fears were realized. Dead cattle lay where they had been struck down by a force powerful enough to claw through their hides, rip open their rib cages, and tear them nearly limb from limb. Clouds of flies buzzed around them, darkening the sky.

"Sweet Oj and Ren," Aiden swore under his breath. "What do you think did this?"

Corran shook his head. "Ghouls wouldn't kill so many, or leave flesh on the bones. *Vestir* and *higani* would have dragged them away and eaten more. I have no idea."

"Whatever it was probably won't stop with one field of cattle," Ross said grimly. "I know you don't want to be delayed meeting Brock, but we'd better take care of this."

A few miles down the dirt road led them into a smattering of buildings that was more outpost than town. Rigan dismounted and went into the marketplace, a collection of farmers selling produce, fresh meat, and baked goods, and peddlers hawking their wares.

"What do you know about the field up the road, where the cattle died?" he asked, not in the mood for subtleties.

For a moment, Rigan thought no one would answer. Finally, a man behind one of the vegetable stands stood up. "Happened two nights ago. No one knows what we did to anger him, but we thought that, after the sheep, he would stop."

The answer made no sense, and Rigan felt certain he had missed something. "Anger who? Did this happen before, to your flock? What's going on?"

A woman in her middle years came around from behind the butcher's table. She held a bloody cleaver in her hand, and at first, Rigan thought she meant to threaten him, but she made no move to cause him harm. "You're a hunter, aren't you? One of them outlaws that goes around killing monsters and setting ghosts to rest."

After drawing attention to himself, he could hardly deny it. "Yes. That's why I'm asking. We can help."

"There's nothing to be done," a thin woman spoke up from where she sat, spinning carded wool into yarn. "We angered him, and now he's going to punish us until he thinks we've learned our lesson."

"Who's going to punish you? Is your Merchant Prince doing this? A landholder?" Rigan asked, aghast.

All of the merchants in the market were staring at him now, and they chuckled nervously. "No, lad. Not anyone living," another farmer replied, a burly man behind a table stacked high with cabbages. "The Woodsman is angry at us. He's been our protector, our guardian spirit, for as long as anyone remembers. And now, we've done something to make him turn on us. If you can figure out how we can set things right, we'd be in your debt."

The answer surprised Rigan, and he blinked for a moment as he gathered his wits. "Your village has a guardian spirit, and it's gotten angry and killed your herds?" he repeated, not believing what he heard.

The cabbage farmer nodded. "Aye. The stories say that he came through these parts and fell sick, and the people who lived here back then took him in and cared for him. He stayed on, after he was well, in a cabin out in the forest. He showed his gratitude by leaving firewood for the villagers in the middle of the night, without taking pay for it. When he died, his spirit remained here, watching over the town. He's saved us from wolves and storms, returned lost children, protected our crops from blight. He even drove away the monsters a fortnight ago. But then—"

"We didn't do right by him," the woman with the spinning wheel interrupted. "Weren't thankful enough for his help. People used to leave him offerings—a meal, some cakes, tobacco, whiskey. At the shrine where his cabin was. Folks don't do like they used to, don't show their thanks. And now look what's happened."

"We'd like to have a look," Rigan said. Finding a hunt on their way to meet with Brock and Mina was not in their plans, and he had hoped Corran would have longer to recuperate. With luck, the spirit could be easily appeased, and they would be on their way without incident.

A few of the merchants whispered among themselves. Finally, the cabbage farmer nodded. "Go ahead. We haven't been able to put it right, maybe you can. We ain't got money to pay you, but we can give you all the food you can carry."

"Let's see if we can fix the problem, and worry about that later," Rigan replied. He got directions to the Woodsman's cabin and returned to where the others were waiting. They listened incredulously as he recounted what he had learned.

"Is that even possible?" Ross asked. "I mean, I've heard about places that claimed to have a guardian spirit. Shit, my granny swore that her great-grandmam stayed around the house helping cakes rise and keeping the milk from spoiling. So having a ghost around to help out isn't the strange part. I've never heard about one turning on its people."

"Didn't he tell you that the Woodsman turned away monsters right before things went wrong?" Trent questioned.

Rigan nodded. "I don't know how long 'right before' was, whether that was days or candlemarks, but it sounded as if this all went wrong in the last fortnight."

Aiden met his gaze. "I think we need to go look at that shrine, and then have another look at the cows."

The directions led them to the stone foundation of what had once been a small house. By the look of it, the dwelling had been gone for a long time, with trees growing up among the stones. Outside the footprint of the foundation lay the remains of offerings brought to the Woodsman from the villagers. Food, trinkets, a jug of whiskey, and other items lay carefully positioned as if given to the gods. Some had been there for a long time, while others looked much more recent.

"Maybe he wanted better bribes," Corran said, looking at the moldering gifts.

Rigan elbowed him. "Show some respect," he murmured, mindful that the Woodsman's spirit might not be in the most charitable of moods.

"Can you sense anything?" Ross asked, looking from Rigan to Corran, counting on their grave magic.

Rigan closed his eyes and concentrated. A moment later, he opened them and shook his head. "There's no one here now."

They poked carefully around the ruins but found nothing to reveal what might have made the ghost change from guardian to persecutor. "Let's go have another look at that pasture," Aiden said finally. "There's got to be a reason for the change."

They rode back the way they came, and the rotting stench met them before the killing field came into view. After they tied their horses to trees near the fence, they cut through the swarms of flies, picking their way among the gutted and dismembered carcasses.

"It doesn't make any sense," Trent muttered, staring down at one of the savaged cows. "Why stay behind to protect the village for so long, and then suddenly turn on them?"

While Corran and Ross examined the remains, Trent stood guard. Aiden and Rigan ranged farther afield, spreading out across the pasture in hopes of finding an answer. "I think I've got something," Aiden called out, and the others hurried to him.

"What does that look like?" He pointed to a large circle of dead grass toward one end of the clearing. A strange black mold spread across the area but stopped at the edge of the dead zone. Even at a distance of several feet, Rigan fought the urge to recoil from the sense of wrongness that the circle gave off.

"A Rift opened here," Ross replied, his voice grim.

"And the taint is getting stronger," Corran added, with a nod toward the foul black mold.

"You think that the Woodsman's ghost somehow got corrupted by the taint?" Rigan asked.

Aiden nodded. "It's possible. In fact, I'd say it's our best explanation." He began to pace the perimeter of the circle.

"Imagine that the guardian spirit senses that something bad is about to happen. He's been fighting off threats for decades, maybe longer. So he goes to see what's wrong, and a Rift is open, with monsters spilling out and taint fouling the ground. He drives off the monsters, but somehow his energy gets tangled up either with whatever kills the plants around a Rift or by the black slop that oozes out when a Rift opens. Maybe since he's a ghost, he didn't worry about going close to it because he's dead and he figured nothing can hurt him."

"Except this is twisted magic, and he's energy, and bad things happened," Rigan finished his thought.

"Exactly." Aiden stood with his hands on his hips, surveying the ruined field. "We know the Woodsman has killed twice—the sheep, and now the cows. What's to stop him from turning on the villagers next?"

Much as Rigan hated to lose the time on their journey to meet up with Brock and his team of hunters, he knew they could not leave the villagers at the mercy of the twisted guardian spirit.

Corran hesitated. "Do you think it's a trap?"

Rigan stretched out his magic, sensing the touch of the Rift. "No."

Aiden shook his head. "Me, neither."

"Maybe this Woodsman is angry that something with magic is stomping around his territory," Corran suggested.

Rigan shook his head. "No. The power's darker than just anger. It won't go away on its own."

"All right then," Corran concurred. "Let's do it," he said, jittery the longer they stood near the tainted field. "We have what we need in our saddlebags. No need to wait until dark. Send the Woodsman to his rest, and at least the farmers are safe. Maybe Brock and the others will have word for us on how to seal Rifts. If so, we can come back this way."

They tethered their horses at a safe distance. By now, the sun hung low in the sky, and the shadows stretched long. Rigan flinched as the wind rustled in the branches overhead. He tensed at every forest sound, fearful that the guardian spirit knew they were coming. But neither he nor Corran sensed the presence of the spirit, which made him nervous for entirely different reasons. *Is he going to jump us here, or has he gone after the villagers? Are we too late?*

"Do you think he's buried here? Do we need to worry about a grave or just his cabin?" Corran mused.

Aiden and Ross poked around in the thick leaves as the brothers set a circle of the salt-aconite-amanita mixture around the broken stones and rotted wood. "I don't see anything that looks like a grave," Ross said. "Of course, it's been long enough the ground might not show it anymore. If he was up here alone, he might not have had anyone to bury him. Or if someone did, there isn't a marker."

They had laid so many ghosts to rest over the years, but the ones that bothered Rigan most were those who died alone. The Woodsman hadn't done harm to the village in his lifetime, and it wasn't his choice to turn against them. Rigan could only hope that making the passage into the After would remove the taint from his spirit and that Doharmu would give him the rest denied in life.

Rigan spoke the words of the summoning spell, as Corran and the others stood ready with iron and salt. They had piled leaves and dry branches inside the footprint of the cabin's foundation, ready to kindle into flames as soon as the ghost appeared.

Rigan anchored his magic, glad that here near the cabin, the taint had not yet taken hold. He raised his voice in the chant and felt the vengeful spirit fight against the compulsion. Rigan frowned, tightening his concentration, and felt Corran's hand on his arm, lending him his energy through their shared grave magic. Corran might not know how to confess spirits, but he was ready with the chant to send the Woodsman into the After once he appeared. Given the way the ghost fought Rigan's call, the banishing might take both undertakers.

No ghost had ever fought him so hard, and Rigan wondered if the Rift and the taint gave the corrupted spirit unnatural strength. Rigan felt a headache bloom behind his eyes, and as he concentrated his power to force the spirit to manifest, a warm trickle of blood ran from his nose.

"Rigan—" Corran protested.

Rigan did not slow his chant, even though the battle of wills took his full concentration. Corran's presence helped; this wasn't the first time Rigan had borrowed magical energy from his brother. But he feared that if it drained both of them to get the Woodsman to appear, Aiden, Trent, and Ross would be left to face him without the grave magic needed to send him on.

The temperature plummeted, and a thin film of frost formed on the plants near the foundation stones. Rigan felt the hair on the back of his neck prickle right before ghostly hands shoved him hard, sending him staggering. A moment later, Corran stumbled as well. Where the force had touched him felt like frostbite.

You want me? Come and get me, the ghost taunted.

"What's going on?" Ross held his iron sword at the ready, but the Woodsman remained invisible.

"The taint's given the ghost more energy than he should have. This isn't good," Rigan called back, regaining his feet and starting the chant again. Corran's voice joined his, as they both watched the woods around them, wary for another attack.

This is my home. You are not welcome! the ghost roared.

The wind picked up, and overhead, branches creaked and the limbs swayed. Rigan threw an arm up to shield his face from debris, and he saw the others do the same as the wind caught twigs and branches in its fury and turned the debris into shrapnel.

"Do something!" Trent shouted.

The temperature continued to drop. Rigan felt gooseflesh rise, and he shivered. The wind keened, whipping the trees from side to side.

"Watch out!" Aiden yelled as a large tree tipped with the force of the wind and started to fall. Rigan grabbed Corran's arm and yanked him out of the way as the others scattered. The heavy trunk crashed where they had stood seconds before.

Get out of my forest!

If he had any qualms about banishing the Woodsman's spirit before, they were gone now. The revenant was far too dangerous to be allowed to remain, and it would only be a matter of time before he turned on the villagers he had once protected.

"Two can play this game," Rigan muttered and thrust his magic deep into the ground. He had relied mostly on his grave magic before; now, he pulled on the power he had learned from Aiden and the witches Below. Conjuring fire would kill them all here in the forest, with the wind to turn a flame into a wildfire. Water would do no good since they had no choice about burning the ruins. Instead, Rigan sent his power down into the tangle of roots beneath his feet, tracing them, running along them to the trees they supported, skirting around the taint. He sent his magic into the forest itself, countering the ghostly wind, and making a prison of the clearing.

He could not hold this level of power long; he only hoped he could maintain it long enough.

The wind stopped suddenly, and Rigan realized how strong it had been when he stumbled forward, having braced himself against its fury.

When he opened his eyes, he saw the image of a stooped man with a gray beard and homespun clothing glaring at him, his mouth twisted in a sneer, eyes alight with madness.

"Take care of the ghost," Aiden murmured. "I'll handle the fire."

Corran had already begun to chant the banishing ritual once more, their voices growing louder as Rigan joined him. Rigan felt the outlay of power in every muscle and joint. Keeping his knees from buckling required concentration. His head throbbed. He focused on the chant and the magic that thrummed through his blood, pulsing in time with his heart.

His grave magic touched the ghost, and Rigan felt the stain of the taint on its spirit. Rigan called fire to him, sending it coursing through the Woodsman's ghost and past him into the kindling laid within the foundation's footprint. He kept his eyes closed, feeling the breath of flames along his skin, singeing the hairs on his arms. The smell of burning leaves and charred hair filled his nostrils, and in his inner sight he saw the Woodsman's outline limned in flame.

The ghost cried as the flames burned around him, and Aiden lent his power to the cause, as Corran continued to chant the banishing ritual.

Rigan sensed the doorway to the After open beyond the smoke. Then the fire let go of the Woodsman's spirit, and the ghost shone in Rigan's inner sight, free from the pollution of the Rift. The old man gave a weary smile, and raised his hand in farewell—and perhaps, in gratitude. Then he vanished, and the portal to the After disappeared.

Rigan and Corran dropped to their knees on the forest loam, spent.

"What in the name of the gods happened?" Ross still had his iron sword upraised, though the Woodsman had given him no opportunity to strike. Trent remained on guard, wary of new dangers. Aiden looked wan and weary, though the magic had not cost him as much as it had the brothers.

"The taint that turned him from a guardian to a threat gave him unnatural power," Rigan replied, his voice raw from screaming the chant above the wind. "We managed to burn it away and remove the poison, and send him on to Doharmu."

Corran plunked down on his ass, too tired to care whether it stained the seat of his pants. "I hope we don't have to do that again," he said, breathless. Aiden remained standing, eyeing the fire that burned among the foundation stones warily.

"We shouldn't leave until it's burned down," Aiden said. "The village won't thank us for saving them from a ghost if a forest fire robs them of their homes."

Ross frowned. "Would fire work against the tainted land?"

Rigan shook his head wearily, then regretted the movement as his temples throbbed. "Doubtful. That wasn't regular fire. I sent my magic into it—and I barely had the strength for it with Aiden and Corran lending me their help. The taint where the Rifts open is strong magic, very old, very powerful. There isn't enough of me to burn it away." The shadow of a memory teased at the back of his mind, something important and forgotten.

"You know this doesn't bode well," Trent said. "How long until the taint juices up the spirits and the monsters so much that we can't fight them? Or the Rifts rip apart the veil between realms to the point where the gateway doesn't close, and we're overrun? If that happens, I doubt the witches who called the damn things will be able to control them. It could wipe out all of Ravenwood—maybe all of Darkhurst."

Rigan remembered the presence in the realm beyond, the one that haunted his dreams. If it stirred to cross the Rift, he did not know whether there was enough magic in the world to force a First Creature back across the veil.

"Can you walk?" Ross asked, glancing toward the sky to gauge the time. "We still have a ride ahead of us to reach the border by nightfall."

Rigan and Corran got to their feet with their friends' help and waved off further assistance as they made their way out of the forest, back to where their horses waited. Rigan leaned heavily against his mount as he dug some hard sausage and water from his saddlebag to replenish him, and he passed both to the others, who accepted it eagerly.

"How many of those do you think are out there?" Trent asked as they swung up to their saddles. "Ghosts, affected by the Rifts?"

Corran shrugged. "No way to tell, except when we run into them."

"From the number of Rifts I could see opening when we were on the other side?" Rigan replied, "More than we want to think about, probably. It would depend. In this case, the ghost claimed an area to protect, not just a home or grave. If we're lucky, that would cut down on the number. I hope if we run into them again, it isn't tonight."

They ate a cold supper as they rode, unwilling to lose more time with the Sarolinian hunters waiting for them. Night fell, and the few travelers that had shared the road with them gradually dwindled to none. Rigan eyed the warm lights of a roadside inn enviously, imagining the luxury of a hot meal, a glass of whiskey, and an actual bed to sleep in.

"Maybe on the way back," Corran said, elbowing his brother as if he had read his mind. "Can't say I'd mind a night at an inn, if they don't know us for wanted men."

"I never considered us to be rich back in Ravenwood," Rigan said. "But I was wrong. Gods, I miss home sometimes!"

Corran smiled sadly. "I not only miss Kell, I miss his cooking—how bad is that?"

Rigan read the gentle jibe the way it was intended and managed a tired smile of his own. "Maybe not the mushrooms... or the shit stew." Though in truth, he would gladly endure the most vile of Kell's culinary mistakes just to have their brother back with them once more, and he knew Corran felt the same.

"Not much farther now," Aiden said, riding up behind them. "And if you've got the same headache I've got, I'll mix us all an elixir once I can get into my saddlebags. Gods, magic takes its toll!"

Presumably, Ross and Trent had escaped the blinding headache that throbbed with each heavy step of their horses. Trent rode point for that reason since the others were too spent for further magic if they encountered trouble, and could barely sit their horses, let alone fight. Ross brought up the rear, allowing the three riders in the middle to rest.

"I can see the break in the trees that should be near the border," Trent called back to them. "Let's hope your friends haven't given up on you."

The road sloped down as they approached the meeting point. Out here, far from cities, the border was marked by iron stakes and patrolled infrequently. In places closer to trading towns, a low stone or timber fence might provide a warning. Despite the squabbles that Rigan had heard raged between the city-states of the Bakaran League, no one wanted to pay for fortified boundaries or enough soldiers to guard them.

If anyone challenged their crossing, Rigan feared it might be Ravenwood soldiers, or perhaps even guards loyal to Jorgeson who might have learned of their plans or anticipated their movements. He sighed in relief when they saw no garrison waiting to block their progress across the border.

Until a dozen heavily armed men rose from the shadows once they crossed into Sarolinia. "Stop right there," the leader said. "Go no farther—if you value your lives."

CHAPTER TWENTY-SEVEN

CORRAN CURSED UNDER his breath. He reined in his horse and lifted his hands to indicate surrender. Much as he hated to do so, neither he nor any of the others could fight in their current condition. With luck, they could claim ignorance of the border and merely be turned back.

Before the standoff could turn ugly, Brock stepped out from behind the armed men.

"Forgive my methods, but there are real soldiers up the road, and none of us wish to encounter them," the Sarolinian hunter said with an apologetic smile. "They only just arrived, requiring that we move our camp in haste."

Corran felt relief drain away the buzz of tension as they followed Brock and the other hunters down a barely passable trail. At one point, they dismounted and led their horses along the pathway, until they saw the welcoming light of a campfire.

Mina rose and came to them, stopping first to clap a hand to her husband's arm, welcoming him home safely, and then stepping up to greet their guests. Immediately, her expression grew troubled.

"You've had a difficult journey," she said, meeting Corran's gaze with a look that said she knew she was understating the reality. Her gaze flitted to Rigan and held steady, and Corran wondered what the two witches saw in each other.

"You look like one of the Wanderers," Mina said to Rigan. "Both your face and your power mark you." Then she looked at Aiden, appraising him, a cool glance which the healer returned in kind. To Trent and Ross, she barely nodded to acknowledge their presence.

"Come," she said, beckoning them to the fire, where logs provided seating and a cauldron boiled on the embers. "First, we eat. Then, you tell us of your journey. After that, we must make plans. There is much to discuss."

Aiden fetched the powders to make headache potions from his bags, and one of the Sarolinian hunters brought him a bucket of water. While the two city-states had their own origin languages, enough trade led to a common language that was adequate for most communication. Corran had to listen closely to catch what was said, given the thick Sarolinian accent, and he saw their hosts doing the same, perplexed at times by the regional differences. But by the time Aiden finished his ministrations and everyone consumed a hearty stew, the Darkhurst hunters had managed to tell their tale.

Mina turned her attention to Rigan. "Darkness touched your soul." Her gaze strayed to Aiden. "Did you work blood magic to free yourself of the Rift? Tell me of your escape."

Corran did not miss the way some of the foreign hunters shifted so that their hands were closer to their weapons. Trent and Ross responded in kind, going tense in anticipation of an attack.

"Everyone stand down," Brock commanded, gaining him a glare from his wife and a questioning glance from the others. "I sense darkness, yes, but not corruption. We have all done dark things in these troubled days." He shared a look with Mina that spoke volumes. "Let them speak."

Mina leaned forward, wide-eyed. "You went inside the Realm. Tell us what you saw." Her voice held wonder and fear.

"I will, but it won't help you sleep at night, that's for certain." Rigan ran a hand through his hair and told a shortened version of the story, focusing mostly on the magic he attempted to bring them home and ending with Mir's death.

"And on the other side, I was trying everything I could find in the old books to open a Rift from this side so they could get out," Aiden added. "Including blood magic—but I swear, chickens and rabbits only."

"That's why I asked you for help," Corran interjected. "Because we had run out of options."

"If the monsters hadn't attacked and killed Mir right then, I'm not sure we would have gotten home," Rigan admitted, and Corran laid a hand on his arm in solidarity. "Although Corran bled himself pale short of that." Rigan glared at his brother, and Corran looked away.

"Colduraan's realm," Mina said, entranced by the story. "Full of monsters. Did you sense anything else, anything we can use against those who open the Rifts?"

"There's something on the other side that's worse than the monsters," Rigan said, avoiding her gaze. "I felt it watching us from the time we were pulled inside. But once we tried blood magic—even on a small scale—it haunted my dreams. It's ancient and hungry."

"A new kind of monster?" Brock suggested.

Rigan shook his head. "I don't think 'monster' is quite the word for it, though it might fall short of 'god'—but not by much."

Mina looked troubled. "Tell me."

Rigan did his best to explain the presence he had sensed, though words seemed inadequate. "Even though I'm back, I still see it in my dreams," he confessed, unwilling to look up.

"I didn't go through the Rift, but I did attempt forbidden magic to get our friends back," Aiden said. "And I've also felt the touch of something dark and powerful. It hasn't done anything, except draw closer sometimes. It just... watches."

Mina said something to Brock in the language of the Wanderers. He answered her, and several of their hunters joined the short but heated discussion. Mina turned back to their guests apologetically.

"I'm sorry," she said, her voice heavy with the Sarolinian accent.

"Not all of our hunters speak the common tongue well enough for such unusual conversations. They expressed dismay. The presence you sensed may be known to us through the legends. We call him 'He Who Watches' and he is one of Colduraan's First Beings, an Ancient One created before Order was wrested from chaos and the world that we know was formed."

"So he's not a god, but he is a creature made by the god of chaos," Corran recapped grimly.

Mina nodded. "Yes."

"Can he come through to our world?" Rigan asked, feeling queasy at the thought of that presence taking shape in Darkhurst.

"If the Rift is wide enough, and the boundaries weaken," Brock replied. They turned to look at him, surprised the answer did not come from Mina.

Brock sat back and clasped his hands around one knee. It looked as if he debated with himself for a moment about what to say, and Mina watched him, scarcely breathing, as she awaited his decision.

"You were acquainted with the Wanderers in Ravenwood, were you not?" he said finally.

The hunters nodded. "We saw them in the streets, but they kept to themselves," Rigan replied. "Once, I went to them to beg training, thinking they would help since our mother was of their blood. But they turned me away."

"For what it's worth, our brother died with the Wanderers when the Lord Mayor purged the city," Corran said, his voice as rough as ground glass.

Brock looked surprised, but seconds later his expression grew unreadable. "Our condolences on your loss." He licked his lips as if broaching a difficult subject. "Most consider the Wanderers little better than vagrants and thieves, meandering troublemakers. That is how they're treated throughout Darkhurst, now and for centuries past."

"The old Wanderer woman told me that they protect the Balance in their own way and that their sigils are more than curses," Rigan said.

Brock raised an eyebrow. "Then, despite your impression, she shared quite a bit with an outsider." He drew a long breath and looked off into the distance.

"The Wanderers—my people—don't simply 'protect' the Balance. In a very real way, they *are* the Balance, embodied. We were caught between two warring Elder Gods—Colduraan and Eshtamon. Colduraan cursed us because we would not side with chaos. For that reason, we wander, reviled wherever we go, homeless and stateless, hunted and vulnerable."

"But Eshtamon stepped in," Mina took up the tale. "He could not undo Colduraan's curse, but he made the Wanderers his own, and promised that they would not be eradicated. And in gratitude, they give him their service, maintaining the Balance against the worst of what Colduraan would send against us."

"We swore our souls to Eshtamon, to be his champions, the night Kell died," Corran replied, leveling a challenging gaze at Mina and Brock. "So we may not be full Wanderers. But we are Wanderer blood, and we serve the same Elder God. How do we seal the Rifts, remove the taint, and stop He Who Watches from coming across to our world?"

"I have some ideas," Brock said with a glance to Mina. "But discussing them is going to require more whiskey." He raised a hand, and one of his men brought a bottle from their supplies. Brock took a pull and passed it to Mina, who did the same without raising an eyebrow and handed it off to Corran.

Corran followed his hosts' example and tried not to gasp as the raw, potent liquor burned down his throat. He shoved the bottle at Rigan, who gulped down a swallow and needed to be thumped on the back to regain his breath. Aiden chuckled, and wisely took slow sips. Ross and Trent declined, appointing themselves to be on watch.

"Is there anything we can do about the taint?" Rigan asked. "It's getting worse. It's already turned a protective ghost vengeful. If it continues to foul the land, it's going to eventually foul the magic, too."

"It's already begun to do that," Aiden said. "Remember—I'm a healer. Sensing 'sickness' is part of my gift. Whatever is seeping from the Rifts won't just affect the land and the magic—sooner or later, it'll kill the crops, poison the water, and get into the animals. It's a blight—from another Realm."

Brock nodded. "You are correct—or as close as words can get to something magical and not of our world." He looked to Rigan. "Did you sense the taint when you were through the Rift?"

"We stayed in a cave and kept to the rocks as much as we could, and I avoided anchoring my magic in places that felt unclean. But... it was almost everywhere on the other side of the Rift."

"I examined Rigan and Trent when they returned," Aiden hurried to add. "And I saw none of the taint in either of them."

"Mir took sick," Rigan recalled. "Our friend who got pulled across with us. He didn't make it back." Rigan swallowed hard. "Mir got injured, and the wounds went bad. He had been... struggling... with how things had changed for us, and he didn't deal with it well. We thought he gave up hope." He glanced to Trent. "Maybe the Rift made things worse."

"You were fortunate," Mina said. She studied Rigan. "Perhaps it was Eshtamon's blessing that saved you—and your magic may have kept your friend safe as well. But you were only there for a short time. It would be unwise to count on such protection if the taint gets a hold in our realm."

"What is it?" Aiden asked.

Mina shrugged. "No one is sure. Maybe just another form of chaos. I believe it is tied to Colduraan and He Who Watches. Close the Rifts, cut off its source, and in time, the taint will fade."

"How can you be sure?" Corran pressed.

"This has happened before." Mina's lips twitched in a slight smile. "This is not the first time power-hungry men have tried to seize magic they were ill-prepared to understand. The Wanderer's stories remember those times, the heroes who saved them, and what came after."

"Does the taint make it harder to close Rifts? It's hard enough now. I hate to think it could get worse," Aiden said.

"It is difficult, but not for the reasons you think," Brock said. "The Balance is skewed. Blood magic calls on chaos energy. If you've attempted it, you know how much it drains the witch. That is meant as a limit. But when ambitious men and women won't be refused, then witches go looking for proxies. They called on the monsters to kill and spread fear, which increases the chaos energy, giving the witches more power."

"That validates what we had already figured out," Aiden said.

"There's more," Mina replied. "Natural monsters can't be easily summoned or controlled. They're smart, and they're not just beasts. So the blood witches had to summon creatures of chaos—from Colduraan's realm. They had to open the Rifts to do it, and sooner or later, with enough of them opening frequently, the taint was sure to seep through."

"The energy of the Balance keeps the Rifts from opening on their own. It's supposed to require great effort to rip a tear between realms." Brock took up the story again. "Part of Eshtamon's gift to the Wanderers was a measure of his power to help maintain the Balance and fight against Colduraan's incursions."

"But all the extra blood magic and opening the Rifts has sent that cockeyed," Aiden said.

Brock nodded. "Yes. And it gets worse."

Rigan groaned. "Really?"

"We intercepted a diplomatic courier carrying a message between the Sarolinian Crown Prince and one of his Merchant Princes. They both employ blood witches," Brock said, distaste coloring his voice. "The letter advised the Merchant Prince that because of the need to maintain the Balance, the Cull would be greater than usual, and suggested that to reduce the Cull, the Merchant Prince had better meet the terms of their League agreements."

Corran and Rigan exchanged a confused look. "That doesn't make any sense," Corran protested. "We were part of a Guild back in the city. We heard other Guild members talk. The Guilds that created goods for export were under pressure to live up to the trade agreements because if we lost our status, the things brought in from elsewhere would cost more and our shipments of everything—including food we couldn't grow ourselves—wouldn't be as nice."

"That's not the only consequence," Brock replied. "The blood witches can control where the Rifts open and where the monsters go. The death and fear they spread is the Cull. City-states with the lowest rankings in the League pay more of the Cull because their goods and labor are worth less in gold."

"So they pay with blood," Rigan replied, jaw set.

"Do the Guilds know this?" Corran demanded.

Brock shrugged. "Doubtful. For obvious reasons, the masters of the blood witches wouldn't want their subjects to know they were the ones sending the monsters to kill them."

"We knew the Lord Mayor of Ravenwood and his blood witch were summoning monsters and sending them against their enemies—or the Guild members that supported their rivals," Corran said. "When we overthrew them, we thought the problem was taken care of."

"And then we came out here and found more of the conjured monsters," Aiden added. "And realized someone else had to be calling them."

Brock nodded. "Many people, I'm afraid. Far more than the Balance can sustain, and the Cull can only replenish the energy to a degree. At some point, the Cull would have to kill too many people for the city-state to function. It's a seductive spiral that leads nowhere good."

"So what now? We're undertakers. We never meant to be revolutionaries," Corran said. "What are we supposed to do? Kill the Merchant Princes and their witches? The Crown Prince? The king?" He took another gulp of the potent liquor. "This isn't simply treason—it's madness."

Mina nodded somberly. "Yes, it is both. But we have a more immediate threat."

"This just keeps getting better and better," Corran muttered.

"In the same diplomatic pouch, there was a letter from the Sarolinian Crown Prince's blood witch to the witch who serves Merchant Prince Kadar in Darkhurst."

Rigan frowned. "Isn't that somewhat improper? Sarolinia may be a neighbor, but they're Darkhurst's long-time trading rival. The official relationship isn't exactly friendly." He swallowed as if remembering where they were.

Brock smiled reassuringly. "You're safe here, and we value you as allies. But the gist of the message between the two witches troubled me. Nightshade—the witch who serves our Crown Prince Neven—was reminding Wraithwind, the witch in Kadar's service—about a crucial rendezvous they had with each other. They had agreed to meet on the Solstice—next week."

"Why?" Corran asked, though he felt certain he did not want to know.

Brock met his gaze. "To summon the servant of the god."

It took Rigan a moment to find his voice. "You don't think—"

Mina nodded. "Yes. I do."

"But that's madness," Aiden gasped. "Why would anyone dream of doing such a thing?"

"They mean to call for Colduraan?" Corran asked.

Brock shook his head. "No. They intend to bring He Who Watches through a Rift into this realm."

CHAPTER TWENTY-EIGHT

"The reports have not been good." Guild Master Stanton watched Kadar warily as the Merchant Prince looked over the ledgers provided to him.

"What's the problem?" Kadar snapped, still frustrated over the loss of five guards without bringing the hunters to heel. "The weather has been fine, seas calm. There's no plague, no drought. But these numbers—"

"The city still hasn't got its feet back under it since the fires—and the death of the Lord Mayor, my lord," Stanton replied. "And without a steady hand at the helm—no slight meant to Crown Prince Aliyev, he's doing his best, I'm sure—but panic has set in. We've even heard of some Guild Members seeking passage on ships to other city-states."

"So stop them!"

Stanton clasped his hands in front of him. "It's not so easy, my lord. The Davona Accords allow Guild Members to move among the sister city-states in certain situations. War and unrest, in particular."

"Then suspend the Accords!" Kadar snapped, throwing his hands up. "Must I tell you everything?"

"The Crown Prince would have to be the one to do that," Stanton reminded him. "It's far beyond the control of the Guilds."

Kadar slammed the ledger closed and glared at Stanton. "I don't give a damn about the Guilds that get their trade from Gorog or Tamas. But the coopers and carpenters should have no excuse for not meeting their obligations. The harvest in the vineyards has been exceptional this year."

"When the city burned, we lost many shops and homes," Stanton answered. "Many of our members lost their workshops to the flames, along with their tools. Several of the blacksmiths' forges were damaged or destroyed—which affects the supply of nails and barrel hoops for the coopers."

"I expect the Guilds to deal with the minutia," Kadar snapped.

"My lord, we cannot make something out of nothing!" Stanton looked drawn and tired, like a man pushed past endurance. "We support you—"

"Damnable way you have of showing it!"

"We cannot bend reality to our will."

They stared at each other in silence for a moment as both men harnessed their tempers. "What will it take to set things right?" Kadar finally asked. The strain in his voice made his anger clear, but he needed Stanton, and taking his ire out on the other man would accomplish nothing.

"More time than we have," Stanton admitted. "Aliyev has all the men who were put out of work by the fires busy with the rebuilding, and it's happening as fast as something like that can, I suppose, but it's not enough. Not when tradesmen have deadlines to meet."

"Can Aliyev ask for extensions?" Kadar knew he was casting about for possibilities. "It's not unheard of. Storms, bad seas, plagues of locusts—there are many reasons outside of our control why deliveries might be late."

"Those are acts of the gods," Stanton replied. "But the fire that took out a third of Ravenwood was an act of men—first the Lord Mayor's guards, and then the hunters when they went to kill the Lord Mayor and his witch. I'm afraid that granting us leniency under the circumstances might be seen by some in the nobility as turning a blind eye toward acts of treason."

Kadar rose from his desk and paced. "Treason? That's putting too much stock in it. Those hunters were nothing but ruffians. Machison and Blackholt went too far. They got caught up in the game and forgot what really mattered. And Jorgeson—a buffoon. Look at him—months in exile, and he still can't bring those outlaws to heel to save his neck." Kadar shook his head. "No, not treason—incompetence. Malice. Surely the League—"

"My lord, that's what I've come to tell you," Stanton pressed. "Aliyev has already petitioned the League on our behalf—and been denied."

Kadar paled and put out a hand to steady himself against the desk. "Surely not!"

Stanton nodded. "I fear so, my lord. The Guild Masters have been in meetings day and night, trying to save Ravenwood. It looks likely that we will default on our obligation to Garenoth—and if we do, it will be within their rights to void the treaty and choose another favored partner."

Kadar brought his fist down on the desk. "And who would that be? I'll tell you—Sarolinia! This… it must be a plot. They've always been jealous of our standing in the League, our ranking, our favored status with Garenoth. They're an ambitious lot, trying to scrabble up from the bottom of the barrel."

"Perhaps," Stanton allowed. "On top of everything that's happened in Ravenwood, the Guild Masters are concerned because smugglers have been undercutting the price of the goods brought in for sale from Garenoth. If people buy the smuggled goods, then none of that profit returns to Garenoth, and our deficit grows larger."

For a moment, Kadar could not find his voice. *I never intended the smugglers to do more than line my pockets with some extra gold, make up for all the tariffs and fees to be paid to that tiresome exchequer. I didn't think it would matter. Didn't think anyone would notice. Surely those little boats couldn't have brought in enough goods to truly do damage?*

"Has Aliyev gotten to the heart of the smuggling ring yet?' Kadar asked, hoping he did not look as fearful as he felt.

"He's looking into it," Stanton replied. "Though everything points to Sarolinia being behind it. Aliyev told us the last we met with him that Sarolinian Crown Prince Neven was underwriting the smugglers—providing them with ships and capital."

Kadar's stomach lurched. "The Sarolinians?" he managed in a strangled voice. "Behind the smugglers?"

Stanton nodded. "I'm afraid so, my lord. It appears that Neven decided to act on his dislike of Ravenwood and destroy our standing, in order to elevate Sarolinia. Aliyev fears he may also be behind the additional monster attacks near the border."

Stanton was one of the relatively few who knew the truth of the monsters and their masters. "My vineyards are not far from the border," Kadar managed, his mouth suddenly dry.

"Then I would suggest extra patrols, my lord," Stanton said. "From what word we've received from the rural areas, it's grim out there."

Stanton took his leave, and as soon as he was out of sight, Kadar collapsed into the chair behind his desk. *How did this go so far awry? The smuggling was supposed to be a bit of extra coin—nothing anyone would notice, a way to cheat the tax man and come away with a score at the end of the month. Could I have been played for a fool by Sarolinia?*

In his heart, he knew the truth. The furtive meetings, the too convenient connections—he had thought them fortuitous before; now, he realized they had all been cleverly arranged, and him none the wiser.

"I've been a pawn," he said quietly. "A fool. And now—what can I salvage? The harvest in the fields is the best in five years. Surely that's worth something. I'll go to Aliyev, tell him of the harvest, offer it as a way to make amends to Garenoth. They're partial to our grapes. Perhaps there's still a way to fix this."

He sent a runner to fetch Wraithwind. The blood witch arrived a candlemark later, much longer than it should have taken to walk from his workshop. The witch carried himself like he was prepared for bad news, being summoned to appear in his master's chamber instead of Kadar coming to him in his workshop.

"You called for me?" Wraithwind asked, and he pulled himself up to his full height, which might have been intimidating if his bulk had been proportionate. He had pushed his long gray hair behind his ears, and his spectacles balanced precariously on his long nose.

"What do you know of the rural lands?" Kadar demanded. "Is Sarolinia calling monsters to harm my vineyards?"

Wraithwind raised an eyebrow. "I wouldn't know. That's not really my concern. You had me sending monsters against rival Guilds to the detriment of your fellow Merchant Princes. I have done as you ordered."

"A change of plans," Kadar announced. "Cut back on the monsters, in the city and the countryside, for now. Unless you can summon them across the border in Sarolinia."

"There's a limit to how much I can 'cut back' without affecting the Balance," Wraithwind warned him. "And the amount I can reduce is hardly likely to make a difference, whatever your intent."

"Do it," Kadar growled. "Or I shall withdraw privileges from your partner." He leaned back. "Micella has been very comfortable. It's up to you whether that continues."

Wraithwind blanched. "That's not necessary, my lord," he replied. "I'll do as you ask." He wetted his lips nervously before going on.

"As for conjuring monsters in Sarolinia—I had been intending to come see you this very afternoon," Wraithwind said. "I have it on good authority there's a relic at an old temple in the farmland. Very power-ful, very dangerous. Can't send just anyone after it. Would be quite an asset if we can collect it. So I thought to go myself."

"You loathe the countryside."

"Yes," Wraithwind replied. "But I'm willing to make an exception when the need is great."

"And what will I do in your absence?" Kadar demanded.

"One of my lesser witches will serve you. It shouldn't be a problem since you've asked that I reduce the conjuring," he pointed out. "I'll be back before you know it."

A prickle down his spine warned Kadar that nothing about the blood witch was as it seemed. Still, the request appeared innocuous enough, and if they intended to reduce the monsters summoned and sent against enemies—for the time being—he could think of no reason to forbid the trip.

Part of him feared testing his authority against the blood witch, fairly certain that "forbidding" the journey would not be heeded, forcing their struggle into the open.

"Very well," he said tiredly. "Go. But I expect this relic of yours will create a substantial advantage for me?"

Wraithwind's smile was difficult to decipher. "Oh yes," he assured. "It will change everything."

"Micella remains here," Kadar specified and saw fire glint in the witch's eyes. "Where she'll be safer."

Wraithwind stiffened, although his expression remained unreadable. Kadar knew the witch disliked leaving his partner as a hostage. Which made her all the more valuable. "As you wish, my lord."

By the time Joth Hanson arrived, Kadar's mood, already stormy, had turned black.

"Did you know?" He turned on Hanson as soon as the door closed behind him. Hanson took a step back, eyes wide.

"Know what, my lord?"

"Know what the smuggling was doing to the trade with Garenoth?"

Hanson raised his hands as if to surrender. "We knew that the smuggled goods would evade the tariffs and therefore sell at a higher profit," he said carefully. "That was the benefit of employing the smugglers."

"I've heard from Stanton," Kadar snapped. "The trade agreement with Garenoth is in danger. Just how much smuggling did you have going on?"

"Several boats a week, sometimes twice a week," Hanson replied. "Whatever we could slip past the harbor guards. The cargo varied, and the inland merchants were happy to buy the goods at a discount."

"The smuggling was never meant to destroy the trade agreement, merely skim a little off the top," Kadar raged. "What we make from the smuggling is a pittance compared to what I earn from the normal trade. It was meant to be an addition—not a replacement!"

"Guild Master Stanton no doubt has his own agenda for passing along the information," Hanson said. "Perhaps it suits his ends to alarm you. Certainly that would be true when it comes to any smuggled goods that affect the products of his Guild."

"I don't doubt that Stanton has an agenda," he snarled. "The Guild Masters *always* have a hidden plan. But I didn't think to ask before now what yours was."

"My lord?" Hanson stammered, backing up a step as Kadar advanced.

"You're the one who proposed the smuggling, the one who found the contacts, the one who brokered the deals," Kadar said, moving one step at a time and forcing Hanson back across the room.

"You made a comment about how you wished you could buy goods without having to pay the fees and tariffs," Hanson said, words tumbling over each other as he rushed to speak. "I took that to heart, found a way to make it happen—"

"I should have asked how you found the smugglers so quickly," Kadar said, fixing Hanson with a glare. "Should have wondered how a man like you has 'contacts' among that sort."

He had Hanson up against the wall, and the man's eyes were wide with fear. "I can explain—"

"Who's been paying you?" Kadar asked, bringing his knife up with the tip beneath Hanson's chin. "Was it Tamas? Gorog's son doesn't have the stones for something like this. Though I would have doubted Tamas had the brains." He jabbed the knife into the tender skin, raising a bead of blood.

"Was it Aliyev? Did he mean it for a test that I've failed?" Kadar watched Hanson flinch with every question, but something about his expression sent a chill creeping through the Merchant Prince as the pieces fell into place.

"Was it Sarolinia?" he breathed, barely a whisper. Hanson looked away, and Kadar felt his anger surge. "Answer me! Was it Sarolinia?"

Hanson met his gaze, and Kadar saw loathing in the man's eyes. "Yes," Hanson said, making no attempt to cover the contempt in his voice, knowing it was far too late to make amends. "The Crown Prince's people approached me not long after I took this position. They

had found out about my debts. I... owed people. Dangerous people."
He licked his lips nervously. "Gambling and... bad decisions. They
offered to pay off my debts, in exchange for me making suggestions
to you."

"Like the smuggling," Kadar said in a tight voice, his knife hand
shaking with fury.

"Yes. That, and other things."

"And did you carry tales of our conversations back to your
masters? Was that also part of your deal?" Kadar stood toe-to-toe with
Hanson, crushing him up against the wall, digging the tip of the knife
into his throat.

"Yes," Hanson replied. "I told them everything. They paid far
better than you did."

"Then consider this the final payment," Kadar growled. He pulled
back just far enough to plunge the knife into Hanson's chest, holding
him against the wall on the blade as the man jerked and gasped. He
withdrew his knife, and let the body slump to the floor.

Blood pooled at Kadar's feet, and his clothing stuck to his skin,
warm and sticky. "Take that message back to your real masters," Kadar
said, wiping the blade on Hanson's pants before he sheathed his knife.

He turned away and felt a tremor run through his body. Not
because of the murder; he had done as much before, maybe worse over
his life. No, what terrified him was that all he had built, all he had
worked for now crumbled under the weight of deception and betrayal.

*Surely it's not too late. I can salvage this. Hunt down the smugglers
and give them up to Aliyev—he may never need to know my part in this.
Prove my worth. The grapes are ready to harvest. It's been a good year. We
should have enough to press and still sell grapes to make up some of the
difference. Even with the fires, we have plenty of wine to send to Garenoth
—fine vintages—to fulfill our part of the agreement. And Stanton—I'll
work with him, with the Guilds. There's got to be a way to turn this around.*

Kadar poured himself a drink with trembling hands, knocking the
whiskey back in one shot to calm his nerves and slow his pounding
heart. He dropped into the chair, averting his eyes from Hanson's

corpse, running possible scenarios through his mind, discarding each one with fatal flaws. He felt a little strange taking it all in, and his mind began to wander.

Wraithwind went to seek a relic. Perhaps there's new magic, something that can cancel out what we've done, or enchant the Crown Prince—or better yet, the Garenoth powers so that they don't break the agreement. We'll make them give us more time, rescue us all, and Aliyev will be grateful to us and realize our worth.

Kadar stood and shook his head, trying to rid himself of the fog as he paced. His path took him past the window, and he paused, frowning as he realized that the sun had set.

It had been early afternoon when Hanson had arrived. Kadar's pulse quickened, wondering if he had truly been lost in his thoughts for candlemarks when someone pounded at his door.

"M'lord! Merchant Prince Kadar!"

Kadar recognized the voice of his captain of the guard, but he had never heard the man sound beside himself with fear, not in all the years the captain had served him. He opened the door and found half a dozen guardsmen standing pale and frightened in the hallway.

"What do you mean by this?" Kadar demanded.

"My lord," the captain said, too disquieted by whatever had occurred to fear his master's wrath, "we have all just come to ourselves, to find the entire afternoon gone. I swear we did not sleep, nor were we drinking. And it's all of us, m'lord. We've been bewitched!"

"Wraithwind," Kadar muttered. He turned to the terrified captain. "Go see what remains in the witch's workshop. Bring me news immediately." He looked to another soldier. "Go check on Wraithwind's partner. Now!"

The two men ran to do his bidding. As he waited for news, he turned to the other soldiers who stood at attention with expressions as if they faced a gallows.

"I want to know what's changed in the time we've lost," he snapped. "I suspect you'll find a horse and wagon are gone, at the very least. Get Hanson's body out of here, and then bring back that information."

They scrambled to obey, grateful to get out of his presence alive. Kadar went to the window and looked down over the courtyard, watching the soldiers running to carry out his orders. Before long, the captain and the second guard returned.

"M'lord," the captain said, out of breath. "Everything that could easily be carried is gone from the workshop."

"Micella—the witch's partner—is gone as well, and her guard was left with no memory of anything amiss," the second soldier reported, bracing himself for Kadar's wrath.

Reports came in from throughout the compound. As Kadar feared, one of the wagons and a brace of horses were indeed missing, along with provisions. The bridge leading from the manor's lands to the main road had collapsed, making pursuit too cumbersome to be useful.

Kadar retreated to his parlor and poured himself another stiff drink. "I'm ruined," he said to the empty room. His blood witch was gone, fled for gods knew what purpose. His chief advisor lay dead in another room, killed for a staggering betrayal. The glorious plans he had laid were in shambles, and all that remained was to watch the disintegration of his fortune and position.

"Still, there's the harvest," he murmured. "And the wine ready to ship. That may win me something, a small amount of Aliyev's favor for holding up my part of the bargain."

It wouldn't be enough to save him. Aliyev would replace him if he didn't send assassins to kill him, a more likely outcome. Kadar sat heavily into his chair, feeling cold sweat run down his back.

I've lost it all.

Panic gradually subsided into anger, which eventually yielded to resignation. Kadar had emptied the decanter of whiskey but felt none the better for it. Curiosity had raised a question he felt compelled to answer.

What was Wraithwind really after?

He should have asked more questions about the damned relic the blood witch claimed to need, should have demanded to know where it was supposedly hidden. Although Wraithwind could have easily lied. Perhaps the witch simply saw an opportunity to flee before Kadar's fortunes collapsed and managed to get himself and his partner out of harm's way rather than wait for Aliyev to send assassins.

Still, Kadar couldn't shake the feeling that he was missing something, that there was more to Wraithwind's sudden, desperate departure than mere escape. The witch usually groveled, terrified for the sake of his partner and afraid for his own life. But today, Wraithwind's deference had seemed forced, maybe even insincere.

As if he knew something Kadar did not, as if he had a gambit in reserve to save his own neck. He tried to remember what he had discussed of late with Wraithwind, if one could call their exchanges a "discussion."

We talked about monsters, and where to send them. The Balance— and he was short with me about what could and could not be done. The Cull, and how to avoid it falling too heavily on people I need for the harvest, tradespeople who provided services upon which I rely.

His eyes widened, remembering a part of the conversation he had dismissed as utter nonsense.

He went on about a bigger monster, one of Colduraan's get. A "First Being" he called it. Strange name, something about eyes, or seeing. He Who Watches, that's it.

Kadar staggered to the window, sober enough to realize how drunk he was. "Dear gods," he muttered aloud. "Did he really believe that rubbish? Is it even possible that he's gone to summon one of the Ancient Ones from beyond the Rift?"

CHAPTER TWENTY-NINE

"How did you find me?" Jorgeson eyed the blood witch with wary disdain.

"I'm a witch. That's part of what I do," Shadowsworn replied with a smirk. "And I come with a letter from Crown Prince Aliyev, ordering your support and protection." He had a stiff, straight stance and the precise manner of a money changer, or perhaps a lawyer. Hardly what Jorgeson expected from a blood witch of significant power. Shadowsworn would have looked at home among the Guild Masters, with the crisp press of his robes and the careful trim of his dark hair, just beginning to gray at the temples. Canny dark eyes looked out over a sharp nose and an angular face with a pointed chin. Those eyes spoke of cunning and patience, and danger.

Jorgeson blinked the sleep out of his eyes, still out of sorts from being awoken at an abominably early time of the morning by a witch whose arrival he had not expected. Bad enough that he hadn't shaved in several days, or that his hair fell long enough around his face that he could put it in a queue, or that his clothes showed the wear and dirt of months on the road.

Now in addition to the juvenile indignities inflicted upon him by Spider and Roach, he had his former patron's high-handed sorcerer to deal with, on an errand unlikely to have anything to do with his own, urgent mission.

"What do you need from me?" Jorgeson growled, taking the letter with a snap of his wrist. He knew that angering a witch of Shadowsworn's power courted danger. Gods, even Spider and Roach, could kill him if they didn't fear Aliyev's wrath. *Maybe that's why Aliyev sent his witch to me. Perhaps I've run out of time.*

But as he broke the seal on the letter, he knew that if his patron had come to the end of his patience, hiring a common assassin would be easier and less expensive than sending out his blood witch in a carriage suitable for one of the nobility. *Which is not going to help us be stealthy at all, not that I can say that out loud.*

Aliyev's brief note got right to the point. Jorgeson read it twice, then looked up, scowling. "So I'm supposed to offer you aid and protection. Have my men assist in any way necessary. None of this tells me why you're out here in the middle of nowhere."

"The Solstice is coming, a time for strong magic," Shadowsworn replied. "I will need the assistance of your blood witches, and I have sent for Wraithwind, the witch who assists Merchant Prince Kadar. Together with a master witch who will join us on the solstice for the ritual, we will put an end to Ravenwood's troubles, and usher in a golden age for all of Darkhurst."

Jorgeson remembered all too well the grand promises Thron Blackholt had made to Machison, promises which had either failed utterly or were twisted to his own ends. He repressed a shudder and knew better than to give voice to his misgivings.

"I hope you like sleeping outside," he said. "Because we don't have the sort of quarters you're used to."

"I've made arrangements," Shadowsworn said smoothly, everything in his manner and tone letting Jorgeson know he was of value only for the lowest assistance. "There's a manor house along the cliffs a few day's journey from here. In its heyday, Thornwood was one of the most elegant homes in Darkhurst. We'll be staying there. It is located auspiciously." He paused. "Thornwood belonged to a Merchant Prince who did quite well for himself—for a time."

"He's permitting us the use of his manor?" Jorgeson asked. After so many months sleeping in his wagon or at inns with mattresses alive with lice and bedbugs, the promise of a soft mattress and the luxury of a hot bath almost made him willing to agree to support whatever schemes Shadowsworn suggested.

The blood witch fixed him with a pitying gaze. "He fell into disgrace, lost his fortune, and hanged himself," he replied. "Not an uncommon end among the Merchant Princes... or those who serve them." The witch's gaze seemed to see down to Jorgeson's bones, reminding him of his lost status.

Jorgeson reined in his temper with effort. "So the new master of the manor—"

"No one has lived in the house for decades," Shadowsworn replied. "It's said to be haunted, by the unfortunate Merchant Prince, and others who died under unpleasant circumstances. Which makes it a well of supernatural energy from which we can draw, increasing its attractiveness."

The only thing less enticing than spending time with five blood witches was the idea of squatting in a filthy, haunted ruin. It crossed Jorgeson's mind that this might be one more torment Aliyev had arranged for him, but he doubted he was important enough to the Crown Prince to warrant that much notice.

"As you wish," Jorgeson said. "Will Kadar's man be joining us on the way, or meeting us at the manor?"

"Wraithwind will meet us at Thornwood. Ready your people to move on. We have much to prepare." With that, Shadowsworn swept past Jorgeson as if he were the lord and not the lackey, followed by the foppish attendants who seemed to serve no purpose except to provide theatrical flourish.

"Damn them all," Jorgeson grumbled under his breath. He hated witches, starting with Blackholt. While he held the late Lord Mayor Machison in a mix of pity and grudging regard, he felt nothing but revulsion at the memory of Machison's witch. Thron Blackholt had exceeded the bounds of Jorgeson's highly elastic morality, and he considered Blackholt as hardly better than the monsters his magic had

449

summoned.

"Damn their fancy names, too," he added. The overly dramatic pseudonyms affected by the blood witches made it hard not to roll his eyes. "They all sound like the villain in one of those awful plays on the village green," he muttered to himself as he saw to his horse's needs. "Do they lie awake at night and try to come up with the most ominous thing they can come up with, just to impress each other?"

Grudgingly accepting that his venting would change nothing, Jorgeson went to tell the others that they would be moving on right after lunch. Since the last, ill-fated battle with the hunters, he had hired on a dozen ruffians of questionable honor as muscle. They might be of help when he had the chance to corner the Valmondes and their friends again. Though running Shadowsworn and the witches upriver to a crumbling mansion meant less time to pursue his quarry—and win back his freedom.

Then again, if Aliyev gave his blessing to Shadowsworn's little jaunt, he's going to know damn well that it'll keep me from hunting the Valmondes, unless they conveniently happen to be heading the same direction.

He found the ruffian guards in the stable, betting at dice. They received word of the new plans with a shrug, unlikely to voice any reaction so long as they were paid in coin and whiskey. Spider and Roach sat near the cook fire, hanging onto Shadowsworn's every word. *What possible use can those two be to a witch with real power, except as sacrifices?* he wondered.

More than once, unfortunate witches had met their bloody end at the point of Blackholt's knives in the dungeons deep below Machison's palace. Jorgeson decided that after he caught the hunters, he would happily turn over the annoying witches to Shadowsworn or whoever wanted them, just to get them out of his sight.

When this is over, once I've run the hunters to ground and given them to Aliyev and cleared the death sentence from my name, I want to go somewhere far away from witches and monsters. I never want to see any of them ever again.

JORGESON HAD LOST track of the days out here, far from the city, but he reckoned they had about a fortnight until the solstice. He felt weary of the road, tired of his banishment, and as the days passed and they trudged farther from the last known location of the hunters, his doubts grew that he would succeed in satisfying Aliyev's orders.

He shouted to the hired men to keep up the pace and urged his mount ahead through the cold rain. Aliyev's note had not officially transferred command to Shadowsworn, but it became clear that Spider and Roach saw the witch as their true master, leaving Jorgeson to order the fighters about and see to the necessities of their journey.

Shadowsworn let his horse slow until he rode alongside Jorgeson as the sun set. "There's a village coming up. I have need of things from there."

"You've been stopping every few miles to collect leaves and twigs and toads," Jorgeson replied, letting his sore muscles and headache get the better of him. "What else do you need?"

Shadowsworn regarded him with amusement. "Bodies," he replied. "Captives—to begin with. Their blood must be fresh for the working. This ritual is particularly powerful. Such magic comes at great cost. And since it would not do to use your blood and that of your men, we'll have to come by it somewhere else."

"They won't just let us walk in there and take their people," Jorgeson warned.

"That's exactly what they'll do, once the others and I have cast our spells," Shadowsworn answered. "When they wake, they'll realize the loss, but by then, we'll be far away with nothing to tie us to the abductions."

"Except for the screaming captives in the wagon."

Shadowsworn gave a grim smile. "They'll be breathing. They will not be screaming. Not yet. I'll see to that."

Jorgeson fought instinct to keep from reacting as a chill slithered down his spine. "If your magic doesn't work, we'll have to fight our way out."

"It will work. Hardly the first time I've done something like this." The witch gave Jorgeson a look as if he were a simple child.

"You're concerned because you believe I am leading you astray from your quest, are you not?" Shadowsworn asked, surprising Jorgeson.

"We serve the same master," Jorgeson replied carefully. "But I saw nothing in the note offering an extension of the Crown Prince's expectations. The hunters have nearly been within my grasp more than once. I've learned their ways and their abilities. And I'm anxious to put that knowledge to use to bring them to account."

The blood witch's lips curled as if privy to Jorgeson's shaded truths. "You consider our trip to Thornwood a distraction, but I assure you that it will put to rights all that is awry. And when the time is right, it will draw your hunters to us, deliver them and their witches right into your hands, your reward for serving me."

Jorgeson held himself very still, keeping his expression neutral. Was this a trick? A probe to see where his loyalties lay, a way to further embarrass him in front of Aliyev, or somehow allege further failure? When he dared glance at Shadowsworn, he could not see anything to give away a lie.

"If that is true, then I will double my energies on your behalf," Jorgeson replied, wondering if the promise was merely a sop offered to assure his cooperation, one that would turn out to be empty words.

"Those who serve faithfully will be rewarded for their efforts," Shadowsworn said, with a glint in his eyes that made Jorgeson uneasy. "I keep my promises."

At nightfall, they stopped outside the town, as Jorgeson and his men prepared to do the witch's bidding.

"I need a boy and a girl—both virgins—a babe that has not reached its first birthday, a strong man and a woman in her childbearing years," Shadowsworn instructed.

"All from one village? No matter how quiet we are, someone will notice," Jorgeson protested.

"We have magic to account for that," the witch replied. "You'll have no difficulty."

Jorgeson led the guards to the outskirts of the village. Each of them carried rope in addition to their weapons. Six of them would head into the town to find the victims, then bring them back one at a time to the meeting point, from which the rest of the guards would carry them to the wagon waiting on the road.

"It's too quiet," one of the men murmured behind him. "Not natural. Something's wrong."

"The hocus said he was gonna hex them," another whispered. "Maybe he did."

For his own sake, Jorgeson hoped Shadowsworn's magic lived up to his promises. He imagined he felt a tingle of power slide over his skin as he entered the village, and wondered how the spell knew to quiet the villagers without putting him and his guards to sleep as well.

The unnatural quiet raised the hackles on the back of Jorgeson's neck. No dogs barked, no cats prowled the alleys, and no drunks stumbled across the green on their way to sleep off their liquor. Darkened windows in every house seemed all the more suspicious since the hour was not so late as to keep the townsfolk from indoor chores, or relaxing by their fires with a drink and a smoke. No one stirred, and no noise came from any of the buildings.

With hand signals and whispered commands, Jorgeson sent his men searching for the right prisoners. He knew of no way to find captives that suited Shadowsworn's needs without making a search of every home. He'd assigned each of his six men one of the captives to find, with the understanding that they would share information if they happened upon what one of the others needed.

The first home yielded nothing except a dowdy couple in their middle years, fast asleep in their chairs in front of the fire. The second house had only two old men and an equally old woman inside, but in the third cottage, he found a baby of the right age, quiet in his cradle. He lifted the child as carefully as he could, tensed to expect a shriek if the babe should awake to find himself in a stranger's grip. Despite his lack of experience handling children of any age, the child remained asleep, merely stretching before settling back down.

He returned to the meeting point and handed off his prize. "We've got the woman and man," one of his guards updated him. "But the virgins—how in blazes are we supposed to know who's one and who isn't?"

"Age," Jorgeson replied absently, watching the slumbering village for any sign that the spell might be waning. "It's not a guarantee, but no doubt Shadowsworn will be able to tell if we bring him someone sullied," he added with distaste.

Just as he debated going back after his two errant guards, they returned with their prizes. One held the sleeping form of a boy who looked to be about fifteen years old, while the other had a girl of perhaps twelve summers flung over his shoulder like a bag of flour.

"I reckon these will do," the guard holding the girl said. "The boy's got a proxy face, so I doubt he's a favorite with the ladies. And the girl didn't strike me as the kind to open her legs early."

"If he wants someone else, no doubt m'lord mage will let us know," Jorgeson replied. As much as he wanted to believe Shadowsworn's assurances that the hunters would deliver themselves into his hands, he knew far too much of Blackholt's lies and prevarications to trust anything the blood witch said. He noted that the hired men stuck closer to him than before, obviously frightened of the witch. That none of them had bolted, Jorgeson suspected was due to another kind of spell. He wondered if he, too, would find himself bound by magic if he were so foolish as to try to run away. Part of him feared Aliyev's wrath if he tried such a thing, but more of him feared Shadowsworn's.

"These will suffice," the blood witch said when all of the captives had been brought to the wagon. Spider and Roach hung a step behind him like acolytes, drinking in his every word, drunk on borrowed power.

"Then let's get out of here," Jorgeson said, unwilling to push their luck. "It's dark, but that doesn't mean there won't be travelers—and I've got no desire to meet either soldiers or brigands on the road."

———

THE NEXT DAY, Shadowsworn called for a stop after midday. "There's something I need—over there," he said, pointing.

Jorgeson stared, narrowing his eyes and raising a hand to shield his vision from the sun. "It's an empty field." He saw only a mound and a single tree, surrounded by the tall grasses of a meadow.

"There was a burying ground beneath that tree, long ago," Shadowsworn replied. "I need one of the bodies."

"It's broad daylight," Jorgeson protested. "Surely someone will see us—and while Aliyev may know of your plans, I doubt Kadar does, and even if he did, no one has told the guards."

Shadowsworn gave him the self-assured smile Jorgeson had come to loathe. Spider and Roach stood right behind him, mirroring their new mentor's stance and expression, making Jorgeson regret that he had not killed both of them when he had the chance. "We will make certain you're not disturbed."

Jorgeson and two men hiked to the top of the rise, and he tramped down the grass all around the tree. "There's nothing here," he called down to Shadowsworn. "No markers, no depression in the ground. Are you sure this is the right place?"

The blood witch nodded. "Absolutely certain. It calls to me. Go to the tree," he ordered. Jorgeson looked at him dubiously but complied.

"Move around it to your left—there!" Shadowsworn directed, and Jorgeson did as he was bid, though he felt like a fool. "Take six steps in your normal stride forward. Dig there."

Jorgeson walked six paces and looked down at the ground beneath him that appeared no different from the rest of the field. The two guards looked at him, and he shrugged. "You heard the witch. Dig here."

He stood back, clinging to the small bit of dignity that he retained by having the others do the labor for him. For a candlemark, the guards dug into the hard soil, and every time Jorgeson questioned the location, Shadowsworn reassured them of its correctness.

Finally, after two candlemarks of digging, one of the shovels struck old, rotted lumber. "Got something," the guard said. They hastened their work, sending dirt flying out of the hole, until they both stood up and stretched, wiping away sweat from their foreheads with grimy hands.

"Think this is what he's after?" he asked, with a nod toward the bottom of the hole. Jorgeson moved to stand on the edge of the open grave and looked down.

A weathered skull stared back at him, discolored from years beneath the ground. If clothing or a shroud had once covered the body, it had long ago disintegrated, leaving only bones. Even the wood of what might have been a plain casket was almost completely rotted.

"Must be," Jorgeson replied. "Bring him up—mind you don't lose any pieces—and let's get out of this godsforsaken place."

Shadowsworn's magic might dissuade travelers from crossing their path, but Jorgeson felt uneasy with the cool wind that stirred the old oak tree overhead, and the murder of crows that gathered on its boughs, watching them with accusing, soulless eyes. He had never considered himself a religious man, certainly not unusually sensitive to anything supernatural, but the longer he remained outside the city, the more he had seen of magic and ghosts. Like an acquired taste, he found that his senses adapted, honing an instinctive warning that he had learned not to disregard.

"Make it quick," he ordered. "I don't think the people buried here like having us disturb them."

The temperature suddenly plummeted, making a cool day cold as winter. The crows rose in a panicked flutter, flapping and cawing as they formed a shifting black cloud that engulfed the tree and then winged hurriedly away. Though the day had been clear, the area around the old graveyard fell under a shadow, and mist began to rise from the ground. Where before, Jorgeson would have sworn the land had been flat, now, he saw a dozen or more depressions the right size to be old graves.

"We need to get out of here," he said, wheeling to look for Shadowsworn. "The ghosts are rising." Jorgeson expected the witches to do something to protect them, to raise their athames and settle the revenants or chant to hold back the spirits until they could escape.

Instead, Shadowsworn and the other two witches merely waited at the edge of the copse, arms folded, eyes alight in anticipation.

"Screw this," Jorgeson muttered under his breath, motioning to the guards to pick up the old corpse and get moving. The air grew thick with mist, heavy like the approach of a storm.

"Run!" he shouted to the guards, angry to lose dignity in front of the witches, but unwilling to come to harm to preserve his pride. He could see the spirits now, rising from their graves, taking form in the mist. The specters reached for them with clawed hands and grasping arms, mouths open and teeth bared. Sepulchral wailing sounded from all around them, and the guards cried out in terror.

Jorgeson could see the edge of the disturbance, and to no surprise, the three witches stood beyond the boundaries of the mist. They watched eagerly, and he cursed silently as he realized that the ghostly attack had not been entirely unexpected.

The fog clung to them, miring them like heavy mud, making the small distance to safety an ordeal to cross. Jorgeson looked behind to see the guards struggling to make headway. The ghosts closed in on them, and he wondered if a sacrifice was part of the bargain to remove the shriveled corpse.

"Get out!" Jorgeson yelled, grabbing the guard who carried the remains and dragging him toward the edge of the mist. He shoved hard, and the man stumbled across the boundary, his steps picking up speed once he was clear as if suddenly freed of an encumbrance.

A scream of pure terror sent a shiver through Jorgeson. He turned back to the second guard, in time to see spectral hands tearing at his clothes, dragging him back toward the tree, out of Jorgeson's reach. The ghosts' bony fingers clawed at the guard's skin, opening bloody gashes, slicing deep.

With strength fueled by sheer survival instinct, Jorgeson hurled himself over the boundary. He dove across the last few feet of fog and landed hard in the dry grass beyond. He absorbed the fall on his shoulder and rolled with the momentum, coming up into a defensive crouch, already drawing a blade from his belt, though it would do little good against malicious spirits.

His eyes widened as he took in the sight of the guard in the midst of a swirl of fog and crimson spray as the revenants ripped the skin from his body in long bloody strips and pulled at his arms and legs as if they meant to quarter him.

"Do something!" Jorgeson shouted at the witches, who had drawn closer, standing at the very edge of the mist, entranced.

"Oh, we will." Shadowsworn raised a hand and began to chant. Spider and Roach said nothing, but they also raised their hands, palms out as if amplifying the power called by the senior mage. Abruptly, the ghosts turned their attention from the hapless guard to stare balefully at the three figures outside the fog. Jorgeson and the other guard stumbled backward, putting distance between them and whatever was about to happen.

Shadowsworn's chanted louder and faster, his eyes bright with fervor, expression ecstatic. Spider and Roach stood transfixed, wide-eyed and expectant. The ghosts no longer regarded the witches with anger; instead, their forms twisted and elongated, faces stretching and distorting.

Jorgeson felt the prickle of energy gathering around the clearing, and it suddenly released with an audible *pop*. The mist vanished, and as Jorgeson and the guard watched in horror, Shadowsworn, Spider, and Roach flung their arms wide and opened their mouths, pulling the wisps of ghostly energy toward them and then, in one fluttering, chill wind, swallowed down the spirits' essence until nothing remained.

Before Jorgeson could find his voice, Shadowsworn strode to the body of the dead guard and lifted it into his arms, then dropped his head to the dying man's neck and fed on his cooling blood.

"What in the name of the gods have you done?" Jorgeson managed when he could speak again. Spider and Roach shook themselves, awaking from their trance, faces still slack with ecstasy.

Shadowsworn looked up from where he knelt next to the guard's corpse. Fresh blood ringed his mouth, and his eyes shone with barely contained power. "We require energy for the summoning," he replied. He stood, shaking out his robes, and wiped his lips and chin on a kerchief.

"You said nothing of this kind of desecration—"

Shadowsworn fixed him with a look. "This kind of desecration," the witch echoed mockingly, "is nothing new for you. Machison and his blood witch bade you do something much the same to work a powerful spell for him."

"And look how well that turned out," Jorgeson snapped, too unnerved to watch his tongue.

"My spells and wardings do not fail," Shadowsworn replied. "And I assure you, we do not want to lack in materials or power when we work the summoning at Thornwood. This is necessary to leash the beast and turn it against our enemies."

"Go easy on the guards," Jorgeson retorted. "I'm running out of them. You wouldn't want to do any of the heavy lifting yourselves." Mustering the tatters of his dignity, Jorgeson turned on his heel and strode back to the horses, with the guard close on his heels.

They stopped once more at a cemetery, but this time no ghosts rose to attack them. Perhaps the spirits sensed their approach and fled in fear, or maybe the graves were old enough that the souls had passed on. The remaining guards clustered around Jorgeson, putting as much distance as they dared between themselves and the three witches. For once, Jorgeson did not send them away, taking a measure of comfort from their presence.

Several times a day, Shadowsworn called a halt to their journey and sent Spider and Roach into the surrounding area around the road to gather plants, leaves, and roots. Jorgeson knew little about magic, but he had seen enough in his time with Machison and Blackholt to recognize that what the witches' harvest was poisonous. The two junior witches took on the task with glee, especially when Shadowsworn directed them to trap several kinds of insects and grubs in bottles he provided.

"At this rate, it's going to take quite some time to reach Thornwood," Jorgeson chided. "Didn't you have a deadline for this magic of yours?" He made scant effort to hide the bite in his voice. If he had not already detested Shadowsworn before, he hated the witch more for having seen his fear.

"Patience," Shadowsworn counseled, in that infuriating tone Jorgeson loathed. "Magic like this has requirements that cannot be shortchanged."

"What next?" Jorgeson asked though he feared the answer.

"There's a town of some size not far from here," Shadowsworn replied. "Large enough to have what I require. The two witches will come with me to acquire the body of a freshly-hanged malefactor, while you and your guards abduct a condemned man on the eve of his execution."

Jorgeson stared at him, aghast. "You want what?"

"You heard me."

Jorgeson struggled to leash his anger. "You think you're just going to walk in there and cut down a body from a gallows and no one will notice or care?"

"They might care, but they will not notice," Shadowsworn replied confidently. "We will work at night, and our magic will distract them."

"And how, exactly, is that supposed to work for getting a man out of their jail?" Jorgeson demanded. "Since the guards and I don't have magic to cover for us? Or are you going to put them all to sleep, like last time?"

An unpleasant smile twitched at the corners of Shadowsworn's lips. "This village is too large for such a spell. I trust you to figure it out," he replied. "Do what you have to. Kill their constables, if that's what it takes. Just get what I need, or there will be consequences."

Fear curdled in Jorgeson's stomach, but he bit back his reply and stalked off to rouse the guards. He glanced at the sun, trying to estimate the hour by its position in the sky, a task made more difficult by the heavy clouds. Late afternoon, he guessed. While Shadowsworn might welcome a bloodbath, Jorgeson had no desire to test his small contingent of guards against the town's constabulary. And despite the witch's bluster, he doubted Shadowsworn would expend the energy necessary to cut down the body of the hanged man in broad daylight. Which meant that, once again, the witch was goading him, baiting to get a rise.

Do Aliyev and Kadar have any idea what they're toying with? he wondered. Shadowsworn struck him as a man who looked for the chance to ruffle feathers, eager to cause a ruckus for the sake of being at the center of the attention. Under other circumstances, it would merely be an annoying trait, but coupled with magic, that sort of attention-seeking could be devastating.

Worse, Jorgeson saw no way around giving in to Shadowsworn's demands.

Cursing under his breath, Jorgeson found the guards who weren't on watch, eating their rations beneath a tree.

"Holcomb, Sonders, I've got a job for you," he snapped. The two men hurriedly swallowed the last bites of their food and jumped up. "Holcomb—there's a town up the road. I need reconnaissance. Try not to attract attention. I need to know where the jail is, how many cells, and how many guards. Figure out the best approach to get in and out with minimal exposure. Go now, and come back as quickly as you can."

Holcomb nodded and set off at once.

"Sonders."

"Sir?"

"You're the best lock pick in the group. Once Holcomb gets back, and it's dark, you're coming into the town with me. We've got a man to break out of jail."

Several candlemarks later, Jorgeson, Sonders, and Holcomb made their way toward the village of Hoffnee. The village was situated near a swiftly running stream with a large grist mill and a winepress surrounded by grain fields and vineyards. More of Kadar's lands, Jorgeson supposed.

Holcomb's recon had proven exceptionally thorough. The jail was at the edge of town, the only stroke of good luck about the situation. He had counted five constables, both at the jail and making their rounds of the town. What a village the size of Hoffnee needed with that many constables, Jorgeson could not imagine, unless the villagers were all remarkably dishonest. More likely, the town's mayor liked to keep his fellow citizens solidly under his thumb.

If so, the mayor was in for a very bad evening.

Holcomb had even managed to find out about the hanged man and the poor wretch they were about to kidnap. Thieves, both of them, with the misfortune to steal from a well-to-do trader in town after one of them had carried on a lengthy, unsanctioned affair with the man's daughter. The light-fingered lover had been the first to die, hanged the day before. His brother and accomplice sat in the jail for an extra two days, giving him plenty of time to realize the consequences of their actions.

Jorgeson felt certain whatever Shadowsworn had in store for the convicted man held an outcome far worse than the noose. He wondered if the fact that the hanged man and the convict were brothers would matter to Shadowsworn, whether that connection might provide some extra magical energy boost because of the shared blood. Maybe the witch had known about the men in advance, making Jorgeson and the guards find out for themselves as part of his twisted sense of humor. Gods, he hated witches, and once they reached Thornwood, he would have two more to contend with, including one whom Shadowsworn considered extremely powerful.

Not for the first time, Jorgeson felt certain consigning him to mind the witches was part of Aliyev's idea of punishment.

"Go," he told Holcomb once full dark fell and the village quieted. Holcomb ran a few streets to the east where he had seen a granary and made quick work of setting a fire. A few shouts and the sight of flames jumping into the sky brought the constables running, leaving their prisoner locked in his cell.

The man looked up as Jorgeson and Sonders entered. "Who are you?" he asked warily.

Sonders didn't answer; instead, he glanced around for a key and when he saw none, knelt next to the lock on the cell door and pulled out his lock pick. Jorgeson took up watch in the doorway, in case any of the constables came back.

"You're complaining about getting out?" Jorgeson asked over his shoulder. "There's a gallows waiting for you."

"Did he send you?" the prisoner asked, retreating against the far wall of his cell.

"He, who?" Sonders replied as the pick clicked the lock free.

"Gods have mercy, he did, didn't he?" the condemned man groaned. "Please, I'm already going to die. You don't have to do this."

Sonders and Jorgeson exchanged a confused glance. "You think the man you robbed sent us?" Jorgeson asked.

The prisoner nodded, plastering himself farther into the corner. "Said he'd cut off my balls and shove them down my throat and see me hanged by my prick instead of my neck." His voice trembled and he had gone a ghastly shade of pale.

"Lucky you, we don't work for him. Our orders are to get you out and bring you with us."

The relief on the man's face would have been funny if Jorgeson did not know the reason behind his mysterious rescue. "Did Jamie get away then? Slip the noose and send you for me?"

"Ah, no." Sonders stood and pulled the door open. "Come on. Let's go."

The confused prisoner hung back, eyes wide. "Jamie's dead?" he asked, his voice hollow. "Then who—"

"We don't have time for this," Jorgeson snapped. "Grab him and let's go."

Sonders lunged for the prisoner, who fought back, struggling to get free. "No—I'm not going anywhere until I know who sent you. Where do you think—"

The prisoner went silent and limp when Sonders brought the grip of his knife down hard on the side of the man's head. He hefted the unconscious prisoner over his shoulder. "The hocus wanted him alive," he said with an apologetic look at Jorgeson. "Didn't say anything about awake."

Holcomb joined them in the dark street behind the jail, and they ran for where their horses were hidden on the outskirts of town. Jorgeson glanced over his shoulder. The fire had spread, consuming the large granary building and jumping to the roofs of several nearby structures. If there were the slightest wind, the entire town might be cinders by morning.

"Did you have to burn down the biggest damn building in the village?" he huffed as they ran.

Holcomb grinned. "I figured it would keep the constables busy longer, and by the time they finally get back to the jail, we'll be long gone."

"If the wind shifts, the jail will go up with everything else," Sonders said, carrying the convict's weight as if it were nothing. "Doubt they'd have gone back for him. So in a way, we've saved his life."

Jorgeson snorted. "By handing him over to the witch? Hardly."

"Better him than us, I say," Holcomb replied.

No one pursued them, as the town focused its attention on the fire. Holcomb draped the prisoner over the saddle of one of their waiting horses, securing him with rope and binding his wrists and ankles for good measure. When they met up with the others, Shadowsworn gave a grudging nod of approval.

"Very good," the witch said. "We have all the materials that we need. It's time to prepare the location for the ritual."

"Ritual?" The prisoner thrashed against his bindings, trying to see. They had tied him, but not gagged him. Jorgeson decided that had been a mistake.

"Nothing for your concern," Jorgeson snapped.

"Is that Jamie's body? Oh gods, why do you have Jamie's body?" the prisoner cried out, spotting the corpse near Shadowsworn's feet.

"Gag him," Jorgeson ordered, and Holcomb scrambled to comply. The prisoner continued to shout garbled threats and pleas against the gag until Spider walked over and touched the man's head with his fingertips. Immediately, the convict fell still and silent.

"He's still alive," Spider replied as he walked away. "Didn't hurt him, just shut him up. Couldn't take that yammering all night."

A silent caravan of horses and wagons took the steep, winding road to the top of the cliffs that overlooked the river. Jorgeson had glimpsed their destination from afar, and he liked it less with every step.

Thornwood sat poised on a bluff above the river, dense forest behind. Holcomb and Sonders spoke of the forest in hushed tones, but

Jorgeson heard enough to get the gist of their whisperings. The woods ran along the divide between Kadar's lands and those of his rival, Gorog. Much of Gorog's trade came from lumber, but according to the tales told, the deepest, oldest sections of the forest were off-limits and remained uncut. Those who ventured in did not return.

Jorgeson knew enough about the outdoors to recognize the dangers of the forest: wild animals, sinkholes, sudden drop-offs, swift and treacherous streams, and disorientating vastness. But the stories the two guards told each other spoke of shapeshifters in the forms of monstrous wolves and bears, or darker, bloodthirsty *guin* which looked like living men and women but fed on blood and flesh like ghouls.

Rubbish, all of it, Jorgeson thought. But as they climbed the path, their horses became skittish and easily spooked. The night air felt charged as if a storm brewed. When they reached the top, Jorgeson cast a wary glance along the lightless edge of the deep woods, and could not shake the feeling that they were being watched.

Two strangers awaited, and by their robes and mannerisms, Jorgeson deduced they were the other witches. One was a tall, slender man in white robes with long, blond hair. His voice carried on the air as Shadowsworn went to greet him, enough to let Jorgeson know the blond mage had a heavy Sarolinian accent.

The second witch, an older man who looked extremely nervous, made Jorgeson take a second glance. He only remembered meeting Merchant Prince Kadar's blood witch once, several years ago, but the man had changed little since then. Jorgeson had heard that the witch—Wraithwind, if he remembered the name correctly—remained in service to Kadar because a loved one had been taken as a hostage.

"We have much to make ready," Shadowsworn said, raising his voice to address the entire group, including the two dozen guards who nervously watched the open meeting place. "My colleagues and their assistants will ready our workplace. Jorgeson—see to the security of the grounds."

With that, Shadowsworn and the other witches strode toward the dark manor house with their lackeys scurrying to catch up. Jorgeson felt the questioning gaze of the soldiers who turned toward him.

GAIL Z. MARTIN

"I want a hundred-foot perimeter on all sides of the house," Jorgeson ordered. "Including the cliff face—send someone down with ropes; I don't want to find out there's an army waiting to scale them," he snapped, cutting off any protests. "Once that's secured, you'll draw for watches and rest, and we'll see about food. Get to it!"

He folded his arms across his chest, supervising as the guards ran to their places to do as they were bid. But Jorgeson could not help the way his gaze returned again and again to the darkness of the forest or the way every instinct urged him to flee.

"Nothing good can come of this," he muttered.

466

CHAPTER THIRTY

"You're tellin' me that the monsters that been eatin' our children and killing our neighbors are being sent by the Princes?" The woman stood with her hands on her hips, feet wide apart as if she expected a physical challenge. Faded rags bound up her hair, leaving only a few curly gray wisps escaping. A life of work in the sun etched the deep lines on her face, but her bright blue eyes glinted with anger, and the set of her jaw spelled trouble for whoever had caused affliction for her village.

"Yes, that's exactly it," Corran replied, leaning against the bar in a rundown pub in the village of Brookside, which sat amid Merchant Prince Kadar's treasured vineyards, not far from the Sarolinian border. They had fought off a dozen *higani* that had been savaging the farmland and had cost Brookside most of its sheep and some of its children.

"Why?"

"The Merchant Princes want to get the better of each other," Corran replied. "So they have blood witches who use dark powers to do favors for them. But something has to pay back that power, and it's not the Princes or their witches doing the paying. It's you. All of you, and your neighbors and your kin. That's why we're out here, fighting the monsters—and you can fight them, too."

"How do we know you ain't tellin' tales?" one of the men shouted from the back of the crowd. Most of the adults in the small village had jammed into the pub's common room, the largest gathering space available.

"We saw it ourselves, back in the city," Rigan took up the story. "The Lord Mayor of Ravenwood used his blood witch to call down those monsters on his own people, in his own city, because the price of all that magic is blood. The higher-ups don't want to pay with their blood, so if things don't go like they want, they send the monsters after more and more of us to pay for the magic they steal. Those things out there, they aren't natural. The blood witches rip open the sky and bring them here, spit them out in your fields to eat your cattle and sheep. And when they've killed all your herds, they come looking for you and your children. All to pay for stolen magic."

"That ain't right," the woman in the headscarf said, and the crowd nodded and murmured in agreement.

"No it ain't," a young woman tending bar declared with a stamp of her foot. "We pay taxes. We work hard to keep body and soul together. Ain't no man got the right to take our lives, use up our blood for their magic to get them more when they already got plenty."

"Well none of that will change—unless you help stop it," Corran answered. "And every time they tear open the sky to bring more monsters through, it makes the dead spots in your fields, kills the grass in a big circle in your pastures, and when it touches your cows or your goats—or your children—it makes them sick, or makes them disappear."

"What can we do?" one of the women in the back asked. She might have been five years older than Polly, Corran thought, with a baby on one hip, a brat pulling at her skirts and a swollen belly that told of one on the way. "We rise up to stop the monsters; the guards'll kill us, take our men away, maybe throw us all in jail."

"And where will you be if the monsters come again?" Trent argued. "They'll take your men—and your women and children, your cows and your sheep—and then what?"

"What can we do?" A broad-shouldered man stepped up beside the woman in the bandana. His hands were broadened and calloused by work, and his hazel eyes held a shrewd glint.

"We fight," Ross replied. "We can teach you how to fight the monsters and win, and how to keep clear of the guards, so you don't get caught."

"Can you?" the man asked.

"We've done it—and we can show you how," Corran confirmed.

"I'm in," the man said. He turned to the three men behind him. "And you're in, too—'cause I'm not doing this alone."

"We're all in," the old woman in the bandana said, and Corran felt the tension in the room shift as if having the matriarch make her decision settled the matter for everyone else. "Teach us what we need to know."

"I'm not waiting for the monsters to come to us," a young man declared from the back of the room where he stood with a handful of his friends. "We should go looking for them before they do any more damage."

"People around here weren't much fond of Prince Kadar to begin with," another man shouted. "He's got no friends now, if he's the one what profits from sending those things after us."

A murmur ran through the crowd at that, growing restless and angry. Corran saw the young man and his friends whisper among themselves, then slip out the back. He glanced at Rigan and Calfon, but they had no way to follow without wading through the shoulder-to-shoulder bodies. Corran wondered what the men intended to do, and hoped it would not provoke a fight.

The hunters split the townsfolk into groups according to their interests and abilities. Rigan worked with the hedge witches. Corran and the others explained the weaknesses of the different kinds of monsters they had fought and told those who gathered how to use their farm tools and butchering knowledge to protect themselves from the creatures.

As they packed up to leave, the smell of smoke caught their attention and they saw a glow in the west long after the sun had set.

"That's the direction of Kadar's vineyards," one of the men said, eyes wide with alarm. "Oh gods, someone's burned the vineyards!"

They ran outside, where the smoke hung thick in the night air and the smell of burned wood mingled with the acidic tang of overcooked grapes. They ran up a flight of stairs and crowded around a window for a better view. In the distance, rows of grapevines burned, with flames leaping high into the sky the length of the fields.

"Those stupid bastards," Corran growled. "They'll bring Kadar's guards—and monsters—for certain."

"And the Cull," Rigan said quietly. "Because Kadar's never going to make next year's quota for shipment with that much of the vineyard burned." He shook his head. "Those vines take years to mature. Ravenwood—and Kadar—are going to be a long time coming back from this."

"You need to get out of here," Murt, the pub owner, decreed, looking to Corran and the other hunters. "You getting caught isn't going to do anyone any good. Leave while you still can. We'll hand over the ones who burned the vineyard to the guards—damn fool ruffians. But you hunters—get going. And, thanks."

Corran felt a twinge of guilt at running, but he knew Murt was right. He glanced back over his shoulder as they rode out of town in the opposite direction of the flames, hoping that the villagers would be able to protect themselves.

They rode for a candlemark back to their camp. Kadar and Jorgeson had stepped up patrols, increasing the danger of being caught with every foray. Corran agreed with Calfon that trying to return to their base at the monastery each night made the odds of discovery much higher, so they expanded their range to a two-day ride and resigned themselves to making a cold camp in the woods mid-journey.

To the hunters' surprise, they found Brock and Mina waiting for them, along with two older men who had the look of Wanderers. Corran and Rigan exchanged glances, wondering what had moved the Sarolinians to cross the border and venture into foreign territory to find them.

"We've got a big problem," Brock said after a hurried greeting. "Our Crown Prince's blood witch, Nightshade, has arrived in Ravenwood—and from the magic we've scryed, it looks like our guess was right that he means to summon a First Creature on the solstice." He shook his head. "Believe me when I say I would give anything to be wrong about that."

———

"WE BARELY MANAGED to kill Blackholt. How are we going to go up against five blood witches?" Rigan asked, running a hand back through his hair. He and the other hunters had listened in shocked silence as Mina and Brock laid out their news.

"You won't be alone," Mina promised. "I will stand with you, and we have put out word to Brock's people."

"I thought he left the Wanderers and they didn't forgive that kind of thing," Corran said. "At least, they sure didn't forgive our grandmother."

"Different people, different circumstances," Brock replied, though his cheeks colored with embarrassment. "My people can be hard-headed, but not suicidal. Stopping a First Creature from coming through a Rift is big enough to put aside petty differences." His mouth twisted in a bitter smile. "After we save the world, they can go back to shunning me again." Mina laid a hand on his arm, and he leaned into the touch. No matter how long ago the break had occurred, it obviously still bothered Brock.

"Will they help?" Corran asked, his voice still sharp. "Because when we tried to talk to them, begged for help, they were too wrapped up in their secrets to bother."

Mina and Brock exchanged a look that seemed to convey an entire unspoken conversation. "I won't defend their ways except to say that over the centuries keeping their own counsel has helped them survive," Brock said. "Obviously, I had my differences, or I wouldn't have left. But my issues were personal. My people take their duty to Eshtamon seriously. They would have sensed his hand on you both, and whether they told you, they would have looked into the matter."

"Looked into it how?" Rigan asked.

"They drew sigils throughout the city, am I right?" Brock said.

Rigan and the others nodded. "And everyone thought they were curse signs, I imagine," he added with a sigh.

He pursed his lips and frowned as if having an internal debate about how much to say. "Some *are* curses," he said finally. "Others are wardings for protection, or to deflect awareness or evil. And some are what we call 'third eyes'—spells that monitor and record what happens in front of them, which a practitioner can read, thus 'seeing' many places at once."

"Then why in the name of the Old Ones didn't they save our brother? Or their men who were taken—Kell died with at least a dozen Wanderer men."

Mina leaned forward, looking at Corran intently. "I understand your grief—and your anger. We don't agree with how most of the Wanderers do things; that's why Brock left, why those who have joined us have also risked being shunned to do as they believed to be right. And perhaps if the Wanderers in the city had fought back with might or magic, they could have saved their men and your brother. Or perhaps they would all also be dead. We'll never know. But now, here, we will fight. Can you let go of the past long enough to fight beside us?"

A muscle twitched in Corran's jaw, and his eyes narrowed. For a moment, Rigan feared his brother's answer. Then Corran closed his eyes, nodding. "Yes."

Rigan let out a breath he had not realized he was holding, and Mina relaxed, managing a hopeful smile.

"You were going to tell us how the Wanderers you're gathering can help," Trent said, redirecting the conversation. "Can you use your sigils and scrying to see what the blood witches are doing? Can your magic help us stop them?"

Mina nodded. "In a way, the Wanderers embody the Balance, the equilibrium of power between creation and chaos. Without the meddling of blood witches, Rifts would still form on their own, but it would happen once in a great while. A small number of monsters would slip through, be hunted down, or die off. The Wanderers roamed to seal and bless those Rifts, to counter any taint that slipped through, and if necessary, to destroy monsters if no one else did."

"So what happened?" Ross asked, "because whatever they were doing stopped working."

"Too much blood magic, too few of my people," Brock replied. "The Rifts opened so often, and in so many places, they couldn't be everywhere. So they used some of the sigils to store their power, like a bandage over a wound to hold it shut. Not perfect, but better than allowing it to gape open."

"Then how does all this blood magic and the taint from the rifts affect your power?" Rigan asked.

"Yet another reason we have had to choose our battles very carefully," Brock replied. "The pollution from beyond the Rift puts a strain on our magic. Over time, it weakens us, saps our strength. We fight if we must, but we are most powerful as healers—of energy, of fractured and damaged magic, of that which is out of alignment."

"So this battle against the blood witches, it's part of the Wanderers' mission from Eshtamon," Rigan supplied.

Brock nodded. "Yes. Believe me when I say it's the sort of task you hope you never actually have to complete."

"Perhaps individually none of us is as strong as the most powerful of the blood witches," Mina added. "But pooling our magic, we are much more. And perhaps we will have Eshtamon's favor as well, since the struggle with Colduraan and his First Beings is old and bitter." She smiled, and for the first time since they began the conversation, Rigan felt a spark of hope. "We will stop this."

"Do we even know where the witches are?" Calfon asked.

"They'll go to Thornwood," Brock said. "It's well-placed for harnessing powerful magic. Thornwood was constructed to be an anchor for power. There are caves in the cliff beneath it that have been used for ceremonies for centuries—perhaps even to the time when creatures like He Who Watches were worshipped as gods."

"That doesn't sound good," Corran said.

"Take heart," Mina interjected. "We can also draw on the site to anchor, as well as on the deep forest at the edge of the estate. It, too, is a place of old power. And we have allies there. I have called to them, and they will help."

"I'd heard that those who went into the old forest didn't come out," Ross observed.

Mina gave a predator's smile. "The forest is protected, and we call on its protectors for aid. They have common cause with us in this matter and no love for either blood magic or Colduraan. Remember— the enemy of my enemy is my friend."

One of Brock's hunters slipped up beside him to whisper a message. Brock nodded and said something in reply, then turned back toward Corran and the others. "It appears some of those reinforcements have arrived—and emissaries for others as well."

"Emissaries?" Trent echoed.

"I believe he meant me." A stranger stepped out of the darkness. Calfon and the other hunters jumped to their feet and reached for their weapons.

Mina and Brock put themselves between the hunters and the newcomer without a second of hesitation. "Stand down," Brock ordered. "He's an ally."

"I don't know what he is, but 'ally' wouldn't have been the first word to come to mind," Calfon murmured.

Even the warm glow of the fire could not add color to the man's corpse-pale skin. He stood well over six feet tall, with a narrow build and long, slender fingers. An angular face with dark eyes and hollow cheeks that did not look entirely human—or completely alive.

Rigan sensed magic, old and alien. "What are you?" he asked, taking a cautious step forward.

"Call me Leland. It's as good a name as any," the stranger said in a voice that sounded... amused. "As for the 'what,' I believe your word is '*guin.*'"

"You're a sanguinary," Rigan murmured. "I've read the lore in the old texts, but I wasn't sure they were telling the truth."

"Want to fill the rest of us in?" Corran prompted, irritation clear in his tone.

"Leland comes from the Old Wood beyond Thornwood," Mina said, remaining between the hunters and the *guin*. "His people take refuge there, and serve the forest energy."

"His race subsists on blood," Rigan explained. "Hence the name."

"A vampire, like that damn strix we fought?" Ross asked sharply.

"We are nothing like the strix," Leland said archly, as if the comment gave great offense. "We serve the forest, as guardians. If it puts your mind to rest, we only hunt what comes into the oldest part of the woodland, where humans are forbidden."

"They're trustworthy," Mina assured the hunters, who looked skeptical. None of them drew their weapons, but they did not move their hands far from the grip of their swords.

"Like the man-wolf we met," Rigan said. "If the lore is right, the *guin* are strong and scary fast, top predators. If they're willing to come out of the Old Wood for this fight, we could use their help."

"Our mystics have foreseen the abomination the blood witches seek to summon," Leland said, his voice thick with contempt. "It cannot be permitted. Thornwood lies at the edge of the Old Wood. It is within our role as guardians to be of assistance in the fight."

"And the others, will they come?" Mina asked.

"Others?" Corran's eyes darted from Rigan standing dangerously close to a blood-drinking forest predator to the Wanderer and his witch-wife, and back to Leland, whose expression betrayed nothing.

"The man-wolves of which this one spoke," Leland replied tonelessly. "They call themselves *thropes*. A large pack shares the forest with my people—and the obligation of guardianship. It is a good partnership," he said, and his smile exposed sharp teeth. "We hunt together. We take the blood; they take the meat and bone. Nothing wasted."

"Do we have a truce?" Rigan asked, daring a glance to Brock and Mina. "If you fight beside us, can we count on your people and the pack not to harm ours?"

Leland smiled. "You are careful. Precise. As it should be. And yet, we already have an agreement with your people."

"We're not Wanderers," Corran replied, knowing that in magic and in dealings with supernatural creatures, precise language mattered.

"Your blood smells of them."

"My brother and I have Wanderer blood, but our friends do not, and we aren't accepted as part of their clan," Rigan replied. "Do we have an accord of safe passage with your Guardians?"

Leland chuckled. "Yes, witchling, your hunters will be protected, as we will protect those who Wander."

"Tomorrow, we will ride for Thornwood," Brock said. "Others will join us along the way, and by the time we arrive, we'll lay our battle plans. Tonight, eat and sleep. Prepare for what lies ahead."

Brock, Mina, and the other Wanderers withdrew to their wagons, while Corran, Rigan, and the rest of the hunters did the same.

"Do you trust them?" Calfon asked once the Wanderers were no longer in sight. Even so, he kept his voice quiet.

"Mostly," Corran replied. Rigan nodded in assent. "Do I think there's information they aren't telling us? Yes. Do we have a choice? No. So it'll have to be enough." He looked to Rigan and the other witches. "Did you pick up anything with your magic?"

"I sensed some evasion," Rigan replied. "Not untruth. The way someone might skirt a sensitive family topic. Mina's a powerful witch, and while Brock may have left the Wanderers, he's still got their magic. Except..."

"What?" Ross asked.

"I've never been around a Wanderer for long—other than Corran and Kell, who aren't full blood," Rigan said. "Usually, when I sense magic in someone, it runs like a bright river. The color varies, but it's like a bolt of lightning trapped inside a body. With the Wanderers, it's... different. The magic isn't separate in a streak; more like it's soaked into every fiber. There's no distinction between 'it' and 'them.'"

"But if they've been carrying out the will of an Elder God for generations, then maybe he changed them to suit his purpose," Corran said.

"What about Aiden and Elinor?" Trent asked. "Can they help?"

Rigan considered for a moment, then nodded. "I think so, even if they could each single out just one of the witches to weaken. It's going to take all of the blood witches to contain the power they're raising and break through the Rift. If we can stop them before they contact the creature, maybe we can keep them from bringing it through."

"Fight it in its realm, on its home territory, or fight it in our world, where it will destroy everything in its path," Corran said.

"The legends said that if the Balance wasn't kept, something horrible would happen, a catastrophe. Do you think this kind of thing was what they had in mind?" Rigan asked.

"Even First Beings might die when they run out of food," Ross observed.

"And we're going to stop that—three witches, a handful of hunters and a few dozen Wanderers?" Calfon challenged.

"It'll have to be enough," Corran said. "We're all there is."

Corran and the other hunters finished setting up their sparse camp. Rigan wandered back to where Corran sat by the small fire. "You all right?" he asked, jostling Corran's shoulder companionably.

Corran shrugged. "Are you?"

Rigan grimaced. "Not particularly. Didn't have this in mind when we started out."

Corran stared off into the distance, sure Rigan knew him well enough to see the fear and worry Corran hid behind a stony expression. "Neither did I. Wouldn't have mattered, I guess. Not sure we could have done anything differently." He shook his head. "I'm sorry. When Mama and Papa died, I was supposed to take care of you and Kell. And look how that turned out."

"You did your best. Better than best."

Corran gave a derisive snort. "Not good enough."

Rigan closed his hand around Corran's forearm. "No. You listen to me. You, me, Kell—we did the best we could. That's all anyone can do. But we're together; we're alive, we've got friends on our side. I don't know how this is going to go." He gave a sharp, desperate laugh. "We're going up against a god and his creature, and I'm saying that I don't know how this is going to end. I must be crazy."

"Maybe." Corran managed a wistful smile.

"The point is—we'll see this through. And there's no one I'd rather have watching my back." He squeezed Corran's arm for emphasis, moving so his brother could not avoid meeting his gaze. Corran could see everything Rigan usually hid: fear, uncertainty, resignation, and beneath it all, fierce pride and love.

"Hey, we've got an Elder God of vengeance on our side," Corran said. "It's not over yet."

"Damn right."

Rigan withdrew his hand and looked away, but sat so that their shoulders brushed. They watched the fire until it burned to embers and Corran rose to take his turn at watch. "Get some sleep," Corran said. "We've got to save the world tomorrow. Or not. Either way, it's going to be a busy day."

CHAPTER THIRTY-ONE

HOWEVER GREAT ITS former luxury, Thornwood had fallen far from its days of glory. Cold, dusty, and damp, the rambling, abandoned hulk of a manor seemed a fitting stage from which five mad blood witches might summon the minion of a chaos god.

Five of the ruffians Jorgeson had hired as guards had deserted on the road to the manor, prudently worried that they might not live long enough to spend any coin they earned. Jorgeson wished with all his heart he could go with them.

He suspected the remaining men stayed out of fear of the witches. Or perhaps, like himself, they believed no escape to be possible. Jorgeson threw himself into erecting what defenses they could muster around the overgrown lawns of the old mansion. He could do little with such a small force to guard the manor, but Jorgeson had the sense that the witches had a plan that required minimal reliance on mere mortal efforts.

"Damned witches," Jorgeson muttered under his breath. Spider and Roach were, of course, in awe of the elder magic-users, who accepted the adoration as their due. Shadowsworn, Nightshade, and Wraithwind, all of them were pretentious bastards with overblown names that likely hid a very mundane background. They reminded him of the foppish hangers-on in the Lord Mayor's court, the men and women overly taken with their own importance and cleverness who lived to make an impression and thrived on gossip.

"At least I'm not likely to have to put up with them for long," he remarked to himself, a bleak assessment of how he saw their endeavor unfolding.

The witches went to ready a suitable room for their magic, dismissing Jorgeson to manage the grounds. Spider and the guards hauled the living captives into the shadows of the manor, while Roach slung the corpse of the hanged thief over his shoulder, protesting loudly about the smell. Holcomb and Sonders dragged the rest of the materials the witches had gathered along the way, then made a hasty retreat.

Jorgeson wondered if, like him, they suspected that Nightshade and the others might decide the captives they had were not enough. He would die here. Once that certainty settled over him, Jorgeson felt a part of him relax, if not exactly into peace then into the knowledge that most of the things he had worried about no longer mattered. It had become clear to him some time ago that regardless of his success hunting the Valmondes and the rest of the outlaws, he would never get a full pardon from Aliyev. He had not liked Machison, and he had loathed Blackholt, so without the chance to redeem himself, his quest to avenge their deaths offered no vindication.

The cold knot of grim satisfaction in his gut lay in knowing that Shadowsworn had defied Aliyev to attempt this grand dark magic. Nightshade and Wraithwind had likewise deserted their masters to tempt a monster beyond reckoning to cross the Rift. He did not understand the madness that drove them or the delusion that a First Being could be leashed by mortals, regardless of their magic. But such a creature would lay waste to Kadar's lands, then those belonging to Gorog and Tamas, assuring that Ravenwood defaulted not only on its agreement with Garenoth, but on all of its League contracts. Everything Aliyev had worked so hard to rebuild would be gone, and maybe the city itself as well. Perhaps the accursed Valmondes, too. If Jorgeson could not free himself, then he would assure that Ravenwood—and maybe all of Darkhurst—went down with him. Too bad he wouldn't live to see it.

"I want one barrier ring around the manor," Nightshade told Jorgeson. "Physical obstacles, not magic. Then make a second ring fifty feet out from the first."

"I don't have many men left," Jorgeson said, finding courage in the fact that if he was going to die anyway, he refused to cower. "That's a lot of territory and a short period of time."

"If you insist," Nightshade replied. "I'll send one of your witches out with some additional help. Mind you don't let the helpers get too close to your guards, or there'll be problems."

Jorgeson didn't like the ominous sound to that. Nightshade presented a contrast that made Jorgeson's head hurt. Tall, elegant, and beautiful with blond hair and pristine white robes, the blood witch's appearance contradicted his ruthless demand for human sacrifices. He was startlingly handsome, the type of man who would certainly attract attention in the Crown Prince's court, or even the court of a king. But his eyes held the fire of madness, and the tight line of his thin lips hinted at his cruelty. Nightshade strode back to the manor before anything more could be said, robes billowing around him, managing to make a dramatic exit from even a mundane conversation.

"We need to make sure nothing disturbs the witches," Jorgeson shouted to his small work crew. With the help of the wagon teams, they hauled sledges piled with stones, large branches, and uprooted trees from the edge of the property.

"Don't like the look of those woods," one of the guards said, standing a respectful distance from the dark verge of the forest. "Anyone who goes in there gets eaten."

Jorgeson eyed the tree line and shoved down his intuition that told him to run. "Go into any woods with bears, wolves, and wild cats, and you'll get eaten. Get back to work."

The man moved off, looking relieved to move away from the edge of the woods. Jorgeson glanced back at the deep shadows beneath the trees and wondered whether magic of some sort caused their fear, or was there really something big and bad watching them from the darkness?

They had laid obstacles around nearly a third of the distance before Jorgeson heard startled cries from his guards that quickly turned to gasps and curses. He looked up and saw Spider loping toward him followed by a dozen walking corpses.

The smell of rotting flesh carried on the wind, making Jorgeson's gorge rise. The guards scrambled back, putting distance between themselves and the blood witch's contingent.

"I brought you more workers, as promised." Spider's smile told Jorgeson the young witch enjoyed every moment of discomfort his entourage caused.

Jorgeson loosed a string of expletives before getting to the subject. "Are you mad? What am I supposed to do with corpses?"

Spider clucked his tongue. "That's not very nice," he said, and added a mocking "m'lord." "They'll work until they drop—or rather until parts of them drop off." He wrinkled his nose. "So long as I command them, they pose no threat to the rest of you, and they won't tire or want to break for supper."

Jorgeson looked at the reanimated dead who stood unnaturally still behind Spider. Their skin had a gray-blue cast where settled blood hadn't mottled it, but they were freshly dead enough that decomposition had not advanced too far to make them useless. Sightless eyes stared back at him, unblinking.

"Get them on the outer perimeter," Jorgeson ordered, managing not to shudder. "It's larger, so it will need more hands and take more time. Salvage anything we can use, but stay out of the forest."

"As you wish, m'lord," Spider said with an exaggerated bow. He spoke words of power, and the walking corpses turned in unison to stare at him, then shuffled forward at his command. Jorgeson watched until he saw Spider set them to dragging stones and hauling branches, or making barricades from old boards.

He was relieved to have the undead workers as far away from him as possible. From the looks on his soldiers' faces, he knew they felt the same.

They finished the fortifications by late afternoon. Roach joined Spider shortly before the reanimated workers finished the outside ring. It did not seem to bother the walking corpses that they were on the far side of the barrier. The two blood witches left them standing there, slack-faced and still, and began to move along the tangle of refuse that made up the barricade, chanting as they went.

"Looks like those dead folk are too dumb to realize they're on the wrong side of the fence," one of the guards chuckled.

"Are they?" Jorgeson wondered aloud. "Because we're trapped in here, and I'm not sure who's safer."

"What you think the witches are gonna do?" another guard asked, bravado not entirely hiding the fear in his voice.

"Don't know for sure," Jorgeson replied. "Something big."

"But we're going home when it's over, ain't we?" a third man asked.

Jorgeson had noted the lack of a quantity of foodstuffs in the wagons heading to Thornwood. Whatever the witches planned, it did not include feeding a large number of people or provisioning anyone for very long.

"I think we'll be away from here quickly," he replied, and if the man misread his meaning, perhaps it offered comfort.

Jorgeson looked out over the manor's meager defenses. The obstacles would never hold against any real assault. Properly armored soldiers on horseback could ride down most of the barricades without breaking stride, and any decent war wagon would break through with little difficulty. If he had fifty trained archers with longbows, he might be able to use the cover provided by the barricade to harry an approaching force, but the ruffians he had dragooned would be no use for much aside from hurling rocks. Even then, he doubted their aim.

"I don't know what kind of resistance they expect, but anything headed this way is going to be coming from the road we used," Jorgeson said. "We'll hold the line there."

"M'lord—look!" One of the men pointed beyond the second row of barricades. He had gone pale, and his eyes widened with terror.

The other guards gasped and cried out at the sight of a dozen ghouls scrabbling up the overgrown lawn. Jorgeson drew his sword, expecting for the creatures to easily scale the obstacles, but Spider stood on the other side of the makeshift fence and extended his hand, chanting under his breath. The ghouls turned around, facing down the slope, and stood pliant and quiet.

"Over there!" another guard called, and Jorgeson turned to see what new terror descended on them. Half a dozen *higani*, their white shells glistening in the sunlight, skittered through the tall grass. Behind them came a cavalcade of horrors, the red-eyed huge black sows of the *vestir*, the undulating arm-sized maggot-like *lida*, razor-teethed *hancha* and monstrous, massive snake-creatures some called *azrikk*. By rights, they should have turned on each other, fighting in a spray of blood and ichor, picking dead and tainted flesh from bones. Instead, they ignored the other monsters, oblivious to everything except for the call of the two skinny blood witches who mastered them as Spider and Roach prepared for their moment of triumph.

Are they protectors, or an offering to a bigger, more terrifying monster? Jorgeson wondered. *Or perhaps fodder to stall any opponents foolish enough to try to stop the madmen in the manor?*

A cold wind rose from nowhere, bending the tall, dead grass and whipping through the bare branches of the trees in the godsforsaken forest behind them. The bitter chill cut through him, forcing a shiver that was not entirely from the temperature. From deep within the shadows of the Old Woods, he swore he heard moans and cries, unlike anything to come from a human throat.

The wind held a charge like the air in the midst of a lightning storm. The hair on Jorgeson's arms rose and prickled against his skin. He turned to look back at the old manor and glimpsed ripples of blue energy coursing along its walls, drawn to the single glowing window in the tallest point in its tower where Nightshade, Shadowsworn, and Wraithwind worked their infernal magic.

The sun hung low in the sky, and as he watched the glow fade, Jorgeson wondered whether he would live to see the dawn. *Probably not,* he thought, surprised to find he regarded the idea with detachment. Death in battle held purpose, even if only to ruin his faithless prince. It would be a good death, fitting for a lifelong soldier, far better than dangling at the end of a noose or dying on his knees bent over the executioner's block. He bared his teeth in a rictus grin and lifted his sword high with a battle roar.

"Let's give anyone who comes up that hill the fight of our lives," he shouted above the wind. "Make this a battle they'll tell stories about for years to come."

CHAPTER THIRTY-TWO

"SHIT, THAT'S A lot of monsters." Corran peered into Mina's scrying bowl and felt his stomach tighten. Thornwood's paltry physical defenses were bolstered by dozens of creatures who by all rights should have been tearing each other to shreds. Instead, they paced restlessly.

"Two witches," Mina said, staring intently at the image. "Not terribly strong magic—someone else no doubt fashioned the spells for them to control the monsters. They aren't powerful enough to have laid the original geas on the beasts, but their magic is sufficient to maintain it."

"Kill the witches, and the magic fails," Brock said.

Corran's head snapped up. "And then what? That will turn them all loose against us."

"If the witches live, they'll still send the beasts against us, but they'll control them, make sure they do more damage than they would on their own."

"Can you strike the witches from a distance?" Corran asked, looking from Mina to Rigan.

Mina shook her head. "No—at least, not from far enough away to avoid being in the thick of the fight. They've set protections—and once again, the wards are stronger than they have the power themselves to raise. They're drawing from the more powerful witches."

Corran muttered curses under his breath. "How close do we have to get?"

"Closer than you're going to like," Mina replied.

"Can we use the link the lesser witches have to the stronger ones?" Rigan mused. "After all, channels flow in both directions. And if the other witches are trying to summon and leash a First Being, they aren't going to be able to afford distraction or a drain on their power."

A crafty smile touched Mina's lips. "I like that. We can use it. A two-pronged attack. We're going to need every advantage we can find."

Nervous energy buzzed through the camp. Calfon, Trent, and Ross had gone to gather as many of the villagers they had trained as would come with them. Corran pushed down a surge of guilt at putting inexperienced volunteers into the front lines. Yet if they failed, if He Who Watches came through the Rift, then it wouldn't be a question of whether the men and their villages would die, only an issue of when. Perhaps together, they had a slim chance. Without reinforcements, Corran knew that he and the hunters and Wanderers could only hope to mount a doomed, valiantly suicidal attack that he doubted even the favor of an Elder God could salvage.

Only a few candlemarks remained before the blood witches would summon the creature, and the defenders were still desperately gathering their forces. Leland had returned to the Old Woods to make the case to the nests and packs that sheltered there. If they chose to intervene, it would not be for love of the human lives that would be spared; rather, their help would spring from pure self-preservation, since loosing a First Being on the world would imperil even the *guin* and the *thropes*.

We discovered that the monsters had masters. And now we ally with other monsters against those masters. How in the name of the gods did we get mixed up in this? Corran wondered.

He glanced at Rigan. His brother's features were tight with concentration, as he and Mina worked out the last details of the assault. He and Rigan had talked late into the night, both aware of the very real risk that the next day would see one or both of them dead. Corran had told Rigan how proud he was of his brother's magic, and he hoped it helped to dispel any remainder of Rigan's ambivalence about his power. He knew Rigan had at one time feared Corran's reaction to his growing magic, and Corran had wanted to make sure that his brother knew the truth, that Corran accepted it, without fear or judgment. Saying things plainly didn't come easily to Corran, but the thought of dying with them unsaid was unbearable.

Rigan noticed Corran watching him, and spared a faint smile and a nod. "Are you sensing anything? From... Him?" Corran asked, knowing Rigan took his meaning.

"The nightmares are getting worse," Rigan confessed. "He seems closer, like in the Rift. And I think he's... anticipating what's going to happen." He frowned. "What I do pick up, it's so alien it hurts to try to make sense of it."

"I'm sorry to ask, but keep trying," Corran said. "There's a chance something you hear through the link will make a difference."

Rigan nodded. "I will. It's just that when I'm listening for him, he starts to realize I exist, and that presence I felt turns its eye on me." He tried to repress a shiver. "It's not something you want looking at you."

———

WITHIN A CANDLEMARK, the hodgepodge army moved out. Corran and his hunters led the hastily assembled ranks of volunteer villagers who had rallied to their call. Some wielded long knives and sharp scythes, but many had only farm tools, sharpened wooden pikes, or iron bars taken from the blacksmith's stock. Calfon, Trent, and Ross had long-bows as well as their swords and knives, while Corran had a variety of blades and a crossbow from the stash of weapons they brought with them. Leland had promised reinforcements from the forest, but right now their help felt more theoretical than real.

"You're not coming with us?" Corran asked Brock, surprised and disappointed.

Brock shook his head. "Storr will lead my hunters, and they will ride with you," he said. "I trust Storr with my life. He's a good man, and a good friend," he said with a nod toward a blond man Corran had often seen among Brock's group. "I'm going with the Wanderers."

Corran raised an eyebrow. Brock gave a self-conscious chuckle. "Yeah. I won't say it's comfortable, for me or them. But… we are blood, and it's the blood that carries the old magic. We've got at least thirty Wanderers already, and more are straggling in. Some of the matriarchs remembered old stories when something like this happened long ago. They think there's a way we can work some tribal magic to counter what the blood witches are doing." He gave a wan smile. "I don't really understand. I don't have to. I just know it's where I have to be."

"We'll clear the way for you to get into Thornwood," Corran promised. "We'll handle the monsters so you can get to the blood witches and kick their asses."

Brock clapped a hand on his shoulder. Corran returned the gesture. "Then may Eshtamon's favor be upon you. I'll see you on the other side," Brock said, leaving unsaid whether that reunion would take place in this realm or the next.

Brock walked back toward the camp, while Corran swung up into his saddle, and Storr did the same. Those with horses packed as much of the salt-amanita-aconite mixture as they could carry, along with their precious, dwindling supply of green vitriol. Their restless fighters assembled behind them, some on horseback but most on foot. Corran glanced toward Calfon, Trent, and Ross, who nodded in readiness.

"We've got monsters to fight," Corran shouted. "Let's get started."

They smelled the monsters long before they reached the manor grounds. The reek of rotting flesh and old blood spooked the horses so badly that they had to set their mounts loose earlier than they planned, going the rest of the way on foot. Corran heard murmurs and whispers behind him as the villagers realized the source of the stench. Calfon and the other hunters moved among the skittish volunteers offering encouragement, reminding them of what was at stake, doing their best to keep the newcomers in ranks and to strengthen their resolve.

Privately, Corran was amazed that the whole lot of them didn't flee in pants-pissing terror.

Cold purpose settled in Corran's chest. It didn't completely push out the fear; Corran still felt the thrum of adrenaline in every vein and the readiness for the fight in the pounding of his heart. Along with the fear, Corran could not shake the sense of being watched. It unsettled him enough for him to feel certain it was more than nervous tension. Ghosts, perhaps, drawn by his grave magic. Or maybe the *guin* and *thropes*, scrying to determine when to join the fight. A darker possibility presented itself. Perhaps, because he had attempted blood magic, He Who Watches turned his attention from beyond the Rift onto any who dared try to stop his ascendency. He resolutely turned his thoughts to the battle, vowing to ignore the rest.

Rigan rode out with Mina, the Wanderers, and the handful of hedge witches from the village who had answered their call to arms. Aiden and Elinor rode with Corran. Both of the witches stayed up late the night before making poppets and readying the materials Elinor would need for sympathetic magic. She had badly weakened Blackholt with poisons to thin the blood and damage the heart, working her magic at a distance through the rag dolls, and planned to do the same to Jorgeson's two witches.

Aiden mixed potions to coat their blades, making their weapons more effective against monsters. He would look for ways to turn his healer's magic against the dark witches and their creations. If any of them survived the battle, having a healer nearby would be a bonus. Corran couldn't let himself think that far ahead. Too much killing lay between now and then.

"Stay back," Corran cautioned Aiden and Elinor as they let their horses go.

"We need to have a specific target in mind to work Elinor's magic," Aiden said, "and I can't do much either if I can't see what's going on."

"This will work." Elinor's voice came from above, and Corran looked up to find her high in the branches of a tree. "I can see the approach to the manor from here. They can't go far to the right without falling off the cliff, and there's not much room to the left before the

Old Woods." She wriggled into a more secure position. "Hand up my materials."

Aiden passed up a small wooden lap desk that gave Elinor a flat surface on which to work, and a knapsack that clinked with bottles and jars filled with the elixirs and extracts she needed to work her sympathetic magic.

Elinor took out small bundles of dried plants, several crude cloth poppets, shallow bowls, and a stout candle. She sat with her back to the trunk and her legs supported on a sturdy branch. She had a good view of the main battlefield, while the smaller limbs hid her from prying eyes unless someone knew exactly where to look.

"I'm going for heart and lungs again since that worked well before," Elinor said, selecting two of the poppets to represent Jorgeson's two blood witches. "I'll thin the blood, so any injuries will bleed more. Slow the heart, freeze the lungs, and cause some internal bleeding. It won't be immediate, so give me about half a candlemark before you expect to see effects," she warned.

"I'll strike right away," Aiden added. "Boils, itching, and hives, to distract from what Elinor's doing, and then I can target the major organs as well." He sounded confident, although Corran knew the healer hated what he considered to be "misusing" his gifts.

"We're going to need every advantage you can give us," Corran replied.

"I never tried using magic while I was up a tree," Aiden muttered. "But whatever it takes..." He jumped for a low-hanging branch in a tree several feet away from Elinor and hauled himself up, then climbed until he found a secure perch with a view. "It'll do," he called down.

"Let's hope none of the monsters climb," Corran muttered.

"I heard you," Aiden said. "Don't go saying things like that." He paused. "We'll do our best to cover you. Good luck."

Corran gave a curt nod and turned to the frightened men who waited for orders. "Move out!"

The monsters rallied to meet them as the fighters ran toward where the creatures massed all along the ramshackle barricades. Calfon led a contingent of farmers against three huge, red-eyed *vestir*. He kept his bow slung over his shoulder and fought with his sword until he could clear space around him and get close enough to manage a shot at the blood witches inside the first perimeter. Ross split away from another group, drawing off a cluster of white-shelled *higani*. Some of the villagers carried torches, lighting the battlefield and fending off the creatures with flames.

Corran and his men headed for the ghouls and *hancha*. They were the most numerous of the monsters that had gathered, and while they were less challenging to kill individually than the *vestir* or the *higani*, Corran could not risk the damage the ghouls and *hancha* could do if they swarmed.

"Strike for the head and the heart," Corran yelled as he slashed one of the creatures, barely slowing its advance. "They're not really dead until you've cut off the head."

Corran swung again, sending the ghoul's head flying as two more of the monsters closed in. Sharp claws tore at his clothing, leaving gashes in his arm and shoulder. He wheeled, stabbing one of the ghouls through the chest and sending the second sprawling with a kick to the groin that would have put a mortal man down for good. The first ghoul ripped free from his blade, wounded but not stopped, while the second rose to its feet with a growl and came running back for more.

"Shit," Corran muttered, striking again with his sword and cleaving one of the ghouls shoulder to hip while his knife dug into the skinny neck of the second ghoul and tore loose, leaving the head flopping on its nearly-severed spine.

Behind them, men screamed as they stumbled into a roiling tangle of *lida*, bloated slug-like creatures as wide as a man's arm and several feet long. The monsters' skin secreted acid, and their suction mouths could drain a man dry in minutes. Torches converged, and the *lida* shrieked as the fire burned them, sending up an oily, stinking smoke.

Corran resisted the urge to look back toward where he had left Aiden and Elinor. The ghouls fought with more cunning than usual, and even the beast-like *vestir* seemed to act less on impulse, as if directed from afar. He looked toward the hulking shadow that was Thornwood, high on the cliff, blotting out the stars. Threads of lightning fire darted up and down its dark stone walls, crackling along its length and breadth, and above it all, in the tall tower, a window glowed with a sickly green light.

"Cover me!" Calfon shouted to his men, close enough now to draw his bow in the midst of the fray. He loosed an arrow and let out a whoop of victory as it found its mark in one of the blood witches on the other side of the barricade.

Seconds later, his triumph turned to a cry of pain as the monsters converged, sent in vengeance against the witches' attacker. One of the soldiers went down as the creatures swarmed them, as fighters hacked and swung desperately against the hard-shelled *higani* and their sharp, segmented legs.

Corran tried to fight his way closer to help, but the ghouls and *higani* redoubled their attack, changing tactics to overwhelm with speed and sheer numbers. Two of the men to Corran's right fell screaming as *hancha* drove their sharp talons into soft bellies or unprotected chests, tearing free with bloody hunks of flesh or organs ripped from bodies. The battlefield stank of blood and piss, rotting flesh and the foul black sludge that flowed when monsters bled. Torchlight cast the killing grounds in flame and shadow, and smoke hung heavy in the cold night air.

Corran struggled to see the two blood witches that controlled the monsters. He could make out a tall, gangly young man and another shorter, dark-haired man. Neither looked older than Rigan. Both affected the trappings of witches, standing on a battlefield in billowing cloaks and ostentatious outfits that looked as if they had been pieced together from scavenged finery.

Still, their power sufficed to call and control the monsters, making the two witches deadly enemies. Corran's fighters attempted to strike them with arrows and stones hurled from slings, but the projectiles bounced away from the wardings erected after Calfon's lucky shot.

He wrenched his attention away as Ross gave a victorious shout when he and his group of fighters hacked through the wave of *higani*. Swords cut through the hard shells in their most vulnerable places, severing jointed, insectoid legs, and heavy iron rods crushed immobilized bodies.

Corran and Calfon fought back-to-back, as a torrent of ghouls surged, unnaturally strong and completely tireless. Corran lost track of time, blocking and slashing, barely looking up as one ghoul fell before the next took its place. His head pounded, and he felt an aching pressure behind his eyes. The sense of being watched was stronger now, and he had the feeling whatever creature regarded him was taking his measure.

The bodies of the ghouls lay where they fell, and their monstrous companions scrabbled over the corpses to get to the fresh meat. They had only begun the fight, but Corran's arms were soaked red to the elbow, and gore spattered his tunic and trews.

He dared a glance toward the young blood witches and grinned as he saw evidence of Aiden's and Elinor's magic. The blond man's face oozed with fresh boils, and blood trickled from the corner of his mouth. The dark-haired witch's arms bore bright red hives, and he looked unsteady on his feet.

"Too many ghouls," Calfon grunted. Sweat and blood soaked his shirt and plastered his hair to his head.

"Fall back then, and let's burn them down," Corran said. He reached into his pack and pulled out several small oil pots, while Calfon covered him. He lit the wicks from a torch that burned nearby.

"Clear!" he shouted, hurling the pots in quick succession, making sure they hit where the container would shatter to spread and ignite the oil.

Flames engulfed the ghouls, and their shrieks echoed as they burned. One of the blood witches turned, hands raised to regain control of the monsters. Pustules ravaged the blond witch's face, and blood ran from his ears and nose. Corran felt the crackle of magic in the air, a potent tension as the blood witch tried to keep his hold over the ghouls. The creatures staggered forward, monstrous animated torches, as flames charred skin and burned limbs down to bone.

The tainted magic strained and twisted, as the failing blood witch struggled to keep control. Recoil sent Corran reeling a step back, and it felt as if an invisible tether snapped as the hold of the blond blood witch faltered. The burning ghouls collapsed, too damaged to continue without the witch's compulsion. Corran had only seconds to rejoice, as other monsters, freed from their master's reins, reverted to their nature and set about themselves with murderous fury, attacking both hunters and each other with equal, bloody abandon.

One of Jorgeson's pet witches still stood, his dark hair wild around his poxy face, blood marking trails from the corners of both eyes. Crimson tinted his lips, and he appeared to barely be able to keep his feet, but he struggled to retain his hold on the monsters, fists raised and clenched in the air as he urged his creatures on for vengeance.

Witch lightning from Thornwood's walls and flames from pyres of the ghoul's bodies lit the battlefield, as the fight turned into carnage. Corran lost sight of Calfon, Ross, and Trent in the mayhem, and spotted far fewer of the farmers than had begun the fight. Blood, viscera, and ichor slicked the ground beneath his boots as he moved on instinct: thrust, slash, parry, swing. The world narrowed to the immediate threat, and time slowed second by bloody second. Gobbets of flesh and congealing blood covered Corran. *Lida* squirmed and writhed in the dry grass, and Corran kicked one of the maggot-like creatures into a pile of burning ghouls. It swelled and exploded, rewarding him with a rain of gore.

Toward the forest, two of the snake-like *azrikk* were winning their fight against a handful of grimly determined fighters. The creatures were each as thick as a man's body, with an inner and outer wide-hinged maw ringed with viscously sharp fangs. Their scaled hide made them hard to kill since little destroyed them aside from sawing off their heads. The bodies of men crushed by the snake-monsters or ripped apart by their teeth made it clear that the hunters could not hold out much longer.

The dark-haired witch staggered. Pain and fury drew his face into a grimace, baring blood-slicked teeth. Crimson tears oozed from eyes. He raised his face to the sky, let out a howl, and called the monsters to converge.

"Shit," Calfon muttered as he and Corran once again stood back-to-back, facing an onslaught. Few of the farmers and villagers remained, but Corran spotted Trent and Ross amid the scrum of monsters. Calfon and Corran wielded torches in one hand and their swords in the other, slashing and jabbing to hold their ground.

"Cover me!" Corran shouted above the shrieks and screams of the creatures. He reached for more oil pots, knowing his supply was dwindling quickly. He lit the pots and hurled them into the thick of the creatures' stampede, past fearing that the fire would spread and engulf them all. Trent and Ross lobbed their pots, and the twilight sky lit with flames as the fire spread and caught in matted fur or tangled hair.

Corran heard the hum of a sling and saw a red wound blossom on the forehead of the dark-haired blood witch as the sling's stone hit its target. Thinned by Elinor's magic, blood poured from the wound, and the witch swayed, then tumbled forward to the ground. Ross threw an oil pot, and the blood witch's body ignited.

Monsters still outnumbered the hunters, and while some of the creatures had turned on each other or stopped to feast on the flesh of the fallen beasts, Corran doubted enough hunters remained to battle the creatures. He felt a wave of grief and acceptance at the knowledge.

Bloodcurdling shrieks rang from the verge of the Old Wood. Loud howls answered. Corran blinked, and when he looked again, shadowy shapes poured from the darkness beneath the trees. He ducked a murderous swipe of claws from one of the *hancha*, and drove his sword through its wide-open mouth and out the back of its skull, giving a savage, two-handed twist that snapped the head from its rotting spine. When he looked up again, a flare of firelight revealed lithe, graceful creatures with the pale, elongated features of the *guin* running with immortal speed straight for the battle. Farther down the treeline, a pack of unnaturally large wolves bounded toward the snake monsters. The *azrikk* broke off their attack on the hunters, as if aware that a more dangerous threat had joined the fight.

In moments, the *thropes* were on the huge snakes, five or six shapeshifters tackling each *azrikk*, bearing the writhing, coiling creatures to the ground beneath their weight, teeth, and claws, sending up a spray of blood.

The *guin* went after the *vestir* and the *lida*, as if the remaining ghouls and *hancha* were beneath their notice. Freed from the control of the blood witches, the *vestir* tried to run, but the *guin* stalked them in pairs, herding them like cattle, steering them away from the human fighters until they finally gave an inhuman leap and landed astride the backs of the *vestir*, their sharp fangs piercing through the beasts' coarse, matted hair and tough skin.

The remaining hunters let out a whoop of exultation at the surprising turn of the battle. Corran feared the farmers might see the *thropes* and the *guin* as new monsters to be fought, but so few of the fighters remained against such an overwhelming enemy that they welcomed whatever help appeared.

Corran ran toward a ghoul, sword raised to strike, when the creature wavered, then collapsed without being touched. Corran stumbled to a stop, staring wide-eyed as all around him, the ghouls and *hancha* froze in their tracks, then began to shake violently as blood or ichor spilled from their mouths, eyes, and ears. They dropped, twitching and trembling, before falling still. Corran imagined that he must be grinning like a madman as he realized that somehow, Aiden and Elinor's magic had found a way to bring down the most human-like of their opponents.

Corran spotted Ross, Calfon, and Trent near the barricade, along with a handful of village hunters. On the other side of the makeshift wall, he saw movement, and he lifted his sword as a rallying point for the surviving fighters.

"Over the fence!" he shouted, finding a reserve of energy in the giddy surprise of still being alive. "We've got to clear the road for Rigan!"

He scrambled over the tree trunks and stumps. A glance behind told Corran that the *guin* and the *thropes* were making quick work of the last of the monsters, which looked to be focused more on trying to escape than in engaging the fearsome predators.

Corran jumped down from the barricade, landing on the wet remains of a ghoul. He straightened, weapons ready in his grip. In the dim light, he caught sight of Ross, Calfon, and Trent once more. They moved and carried themselves as if they had been wounded and were exhausted, but the fact that they were still alive and fighting mattered most. Several more volunteers rallied behind them, getting their bearings as they looked for enemies.

Together they ran toward Thornwood's entrance, intent on sweeping away resistance so Rigan and the Wanderers could get close enough to take on the three senior blood witches inside. The closer Corran got to the manor, the more his head throbbed. The sense of being observed grew stifling, an oppressive alien touch that he could only guess originated from one of the First Creatures, peering through the Rift.

Half a dozen ragged soldiers ran out of the smoke to block the approach to Thornwood. They threw themselves into the fray with wild eyes and frantic movements, dangerously unpredictable.

Corran beat back an attack as one of the soldiers flailed madly with his broadsword, jabbing and slashing in sheer panic. The strikes came with the strength of lunacy, clanging against Corran's blade and shuddering through his bones as he dodged and wove to keep the swings from doing real damage. Even so, the tip opened a gash on Corran's arm, and the blade grazed his shoulder as the frenzied attacker showed no sign of backing down.

Corran feinted left, and thrust into his opponent's unguarded flank when the man left himself open. The blade sank deep, opening an artery. A second swing of Corran's sword sent the man's head toppling into the dust. Corran wiped his bloodied hands on his pants and spotted his friends amidst the fighting. Ross and Trent fought as a team, bloodied but still on their feet. Calfon battled one of the ruffian soldiers a few feet away, and Corran ran to flank his attacker.

Together, Corran and Calfon hemmed in the soldier, who fought with abandon, as if he knew he was already damned. Up close, Corran wondered how Calfon remained on his feet. Pale with blood loss and shock, limping from a wound in his leg, Corran feared his friend's injuries would challenge even Aiden's skill, and might well claim him before they could reach the healer.

Corran swung low; Calfon swung high. The soldier missed

blocking Corran's swing, but his blade skidded down Calfon's, turning away the strike and jabbing the point into Calfon's left shoulder. Corran's strike slit the man's belly wide open, spilling out his steaming guts as the soldier screamed and collapsed.

"Corran, watch out!" Calfon threw himself forward, knocking Corran nearly off his feet, as a new attacker emerged from the stinking smoke. The newcomer's sword caught Calfon between the ribs, and the wound blossomed red with blood as the strike took Calfon through the heart. Corran cried out as he saw Calfon fall dead, and lunged toward his friend's killer, sword raised.

"Valmonde!"

The burly, broad-shouldered man in a stained and threadbare uniform closed on him, murderous intent in his eyes. His attack showed both training and experience, backed up with a muscular build that put power enough behind the strokes to cleave a man in two. Corran found himself unexpectedly on the defensive, blocking and parrying with all his skill as the man rained down one blow after another.

Madness sparked in the man's eyes, and his thrust nearly caught Corran in the throat, cutting a gash into his shoulder as Corran dodged at the last instant. Corran scored cuts on the man's forearm and thigh and took new slices on both arms as he fought for his life.

That allowed little time for Corran to recall where he had seen his attacker before. Smoke stung his eyes and made it hard to breathe. His heart thundered in his chest, and he felt the flood of adrenaline that kept him on his feet and moving despite exhaustion and injury.

"You've destroyed everything!" the man shouted, and cursed Corran by all the gods, old and new. "I'm a walking dead man thanks to you and your brother and your godsdamned hunters!"

Steel clashed, punctuating each phrase as Corran and the man circled and struck at each other. Both bled from new, deep cuts. The stranger attacked with the ferocity of a man who had nothing to lose, and Corran realized with a frisson of fear that his opponent would welcome death if only he could kill them both.

Jorgeson. The name finally came to Corran as his mind pieced the clues together. Lord Mayor Machison's attack dog, the man in charge of the hated city guard.

"Vermin," Jorgeson spat, swinging with manic strength.

Corran blocked the strike, but Jorgeson's blade rang against his own, reverberating through Corran's arm with enough force he thought the bone might snap.

"Ruffians. Troublemakers. You've brought Ravenwood to its knees!" Jorgeson growled, launching another flurry of blows that forced Corran back a step.

Everything felt wrong. The mental assault of the First Creature had grown to constant, throbbing pain that dulled Corran's thinking and threatened to slow his reactions. Whatever had begun within Thornwood's walls added new, crackling energy to the confusion of the battlefield, making Corran feel as if someone had set a match to his nerves. And something about Jorgeson sent a warning to Corran's gut, even as Jorgeson pulled an amulet from his pocket and snapped the talisman in two.

Gray specters rose from the blood-soaked ground, swirling around Jorgeson like a maelstrom, shrieking so loudly Corran could barely think. *Wraiths*, Corran thought, breathing heaving as he tried to control the psychic pain crowding in from all sides. Wraiths were the rabid dogs of the spirit world, shells of their former selves driven mad by anger and vengefulness until only a thirst for blood remained, driving out any memory of the people they had once been.

The wraiths swept forward, clawed hands solid enough to rip flesh from bones, intent on taking their revenge on any living creature. Jorgeson's triumphant laughter rose above the sounds of battle and the keening of the wraiths, welcoming his own bloody death if he could take his enemies with him into the After.

Instinct took over, and Corran reached for the only weapon left to him, his grave magic. He had rarely sought to summon spirits, but now he called to any and all within the range of his power, offering them swift passage to the Golden Shores in exchange for their protection.

Ghosts flocked to the battlefield, from the cellars beneath Thornwood and the rocky seas beyond the cliff, from the forgotten bones beneath the ground of old sacrifices and the buried remains at the edge of the Old Wood. They heard Corran's summons, and they came, swarming the wraiths, carrying them away on a wind as cold as the grave. The shrieks of the wraiths vied with the howls of the restless dead, and even the undead *guin* drew closer, as if entranced by the pull of the grave magic.

Corran shouted the words of the Old Language above the chaos, fighting with every breath against the overwhelming pressure of the hungry darkness from beyond the Rift that lapped at the edges of his consciousness. He saw the passageway to the After open, and the ghosts swept the wraiths along with them toward the darkness and Doharmu, who awaited them. Too late, the wraiths realized the intent and tried to fight their way back to wreak their fury on the living, but the ghosts, desperate for surcease, clung all the harder until the howling storm of tortured souls vanished, and the portal to the After vanished.

"No!" Jorgeson's scream forced Corran back to the battle, as he flung himself forward, intent on murder. Corran parried, barely averting a fatal blow, pressed to block a series of hard, fast strokes that forced him backward. He saw his chance, and lunged, thrusting with his sword and sinking the blade deep into Jorgeson's chest. Jorgeson's body went rigid, wide-eyed with shock and pain, shaking with death tremors. A final instant of clarity burned in Jorgeson's eyes, long enough for his expression to twist in contempt as he spat in Corran's face.

"Go to the Abyss," Jorgeson grated. In the next instant, his body slumped, sliding free of the bloody sword that had held him on his feet.

The two opponents who weren't dead fell to their knees in surrender.

"Clear the road!" Corran shouted, staggering forward as Rigan, Mina, and the Wanderers ran for Thornwood's entrance, finally able to cross through the battle zone without squandering their magic against lesser foes. Storr's ragtag band of Wanderer-fighters and surviving volunteers closed ranks to hold the approach, assuring that their witches would not have to worry about new enemies at their backs.

"Sweet Oj and Ren, what is *that*?" Ross's voice trembled as he pointed toward Thornwood's turret.

Threads of blue-white energy rippled up the tower, arcing into the sky. Where they converged, the air shimmered and roiled. As Corran and the others watched in horrified fascination, a jagged, bright line formed like a streak of fire in the heavens, and the fabric of the sky itself appeared to bulge and shift as if something massive lurched against it. The fire lanced through Corran's thoughts, and he swore it burned through every vein in his body, pressure and pain that nearly stripped him of consciousness.

"We're out of time," Corran breathed. "The First Being. He's here."

CHAPTER THIRTY-THREE

RIDING AWAY FROM Corran and his friends on the cusp of battle might
have been the hardest thing Rigan ever had to do. Even when they had
gone against Machison and Blackholt, splitting their efforts, they had
each only expected to face one man, a few guards, and some dangerous
magic. Frightening as that had been, it seemed like nothing compared
to Corran going up against an army of monsters, while Rigan went
with strangers to face down powerful blood witches and stop an
eldritch being from a nightmare realm.

"Vorn, Demetras, make sure the sigils are chalked as we move
forward," Mina ordered, and two of the Wanderer-witches moved to
either side of their group and set to marking spell signs on tree trunks
and boulders along the route. "Store energy to replenish us when we
return, and ward off evil from the path we've cleared."

"Tennera, Holton, and your climbers—gather the gear. We'll create
a deflection while you head down the cliff. Watch for ghouls. You
know the plan. Gods go with you." Six more men and women left the
main group, coils of rope slung over their shoulders, and headed
toward where the ground met the sky, high above the river.

Rigan knew that Mina spoke the Wanderer's language like a native
though she was not of their blood, but she addressed their cadre of

fighter-witches in the common tongue, for his sake and that of the other newcomers.

"You wanted to learn from the Wanderers," Brock said, riding up beside him. "Well, now's your chance."

"I don't know the language. I can't chant the words," Rigan fretted.

"The words are merely a focus point; the magic is in the intent," Mina said, dropping back to join them. "Hone in on the energy the group raises, and reinforce it with your power. If we heal the Rift, we seal the First Creature inside. Killing the blood witches behind this assures that they won't try it again." Taking out powerful blood witches would also slow the arrival of new monsters, and reduce the number of times small Rifts opened, spreading the taint.

"Are there others in your group like me?" Rigan asked.

Mina frowned. "Meaning?"

Rigan felt his cheeks color. "Um... with extra magic? I've never really gotten an answer on whether mine is strange by Wanderer standards—because it certainly is compared to my grave magic."

Mina's expression softened. "Now isn't the time for long explanations, but I can tell you this: your magic is still... unusual... in its strength."

Rigan turned his focus back on Thornwood. The cliff side dropped off nearby, and he could hear the rush of the river far beneath them. Tennera's group would rappel down the cliff to the caves below and come up through the tunnels that led into the manor. Rigan had no doubt that both teams faced an enemy awaiting their attack, but he was happy to be remaining above ground.

The sound of fighting carried on the wind across the hills. Not the clang of steel, but the shrieks and howls of monsters and the shouts and screams of the men who fought them. Corran was out there somewhere. Rigan swallowed hard, willing his thoughts away from worry.

The blood witches had left a maze of traps for them all along the approach, along with more monsters roaming the area than Rigan had seen in one place. Fighting cost time and precious energy, and left them all tired and wounded before they got to the real battle.

"Shit," Rigan muttered. "What in the name of the Abyss is that?"

Blue-white veins of energy laced up and down the manor's walls. Even from a distance, he could feel the wrongness of the blood magic. It felt fouled and twisted, making him want to recoil.

"We're running out of time," Mina said, casting an anxious glance toward the manor and the dark sky above it. "We've got to get inside."

Rigan stretched out his senses, "listening" for familiar magic and looking for threats. He felt the strains of Aiden's and Elinor's power, and the fading energy of blood magic coming from the battlefield outside the manor, where the monsters gathered the thickest. He felt grave magic stir, and it released a knot in his gut, assuring him that Corran must still be alive.

The stench of blood magic overlay everything. The closer they got to the manor, the stronger the echoes of the power he had felt beyond the Rift grew, and he shuddered to remember how it had felt to have the attention of He Who Watches upon him.

He sensed that presence growing stronger with each day that they traveled closer to Thornwood. Once its dark tendrils touched his mind or its monstrous eyes beheld him, he was bound to it by a mental contamination as potent as the taint that leaked through the Rifts. Maybe the First Creature's notice slowly stripped away the sanity of those it touched, driving them mad, he thought. Aiden and Corran had argued otherwise, but Rigan knew this fight was as much his personal battle against madness as it was a last-ditch effort to save the world.

"I can feel him. He's coming," Rigan murmured. Mina looked at him with concern and nodded as if she recognized how he knew. "We've got to get to the tower. Might be too late already."

"Not too late. Not yet," Mina replied.

The remains of barricades hunkered on each side of the entrance to the manor. In some places, the uprooted trees and jumble of boards and broken wagons still smoldered. Other sections stank from the black blood that soaked them, evidence of the battle that had torn them apart.

Smoke hung heavy over the battlefield, choking them with the stench of burning bodies, barely covering the smell of rot and decay. Underlying all of it, Rigan caught the bitter, acrid odor of the ichor that ran through the veins of the monsters, a scent that haunted his night-mares and brought the memories of his time in the Rift far too close.

Rigan and the witches rode hard for the manor, urged on by the survivors of the battle. He glimpsed Corran, Trent, and Ross among the blood-smeared survivors, and the sight gave him courage for the real fight that lay ahead. This close to the manor, blood magic shimmered in the air around them as the blue-white threads of power crackled up and down Thornwood's walls as if grounding lighting.

He felt the call that hummed through those threads, an unholy summons to a creature from the fever dreams of madmen. The blood witches must be insane to heed that voice. And then Rigan knew: the blood witches had also felt the presence that haunted him, but they had opened themselves to it, given themselves up to its service. And now, as acolytes to the darkness from beyond, they were prepared to usher in the end of the world.

"Hurry," Rigan grated, feeling the pressure building in his mind. Now that he knew what it was, the presence loomed closer than even when he had been inside the Rift. It *recognized* him, and that made his stomach roil. Knew him, wanted him, and had set its taint like barbed hooks into the fabric of his mind, coveting his sanity and his magic.

Just as Rigan felt despair nearly choke him, he sensed another, familiar presence. *Corran.* His brother worked grave magic nearby, and the strands of power that came from years of sharing the magic in their blood loosened the hold of the darkness that had threatened to claim him. Rigan drew in a deep breath and spoke a centering litany, reinforcing the walls in his mind, the safeguards around his magic. The darkness receded.

He Who Waits could afford to be patient and allow Rigan to come to it.

"This is too easy," Brock muttered. They had left the horses beyond the front gates, crossing the last bit of ground on foot, sidling up the steps, waiting for an ambush. Rigan wondered if the witches had gotten to the caves without a fight, if they had been able to make it underneath the manor, where old stories said a passageway led to the river. Maybe they were already in position, awaiting the signal.

Maybe they were already dead.

"The blood witches are waiting for us. For me," Rigan said quietly. Mina snapped to look at him, and he saw the truth in her eyes. "They can't bring He Who Watches across with just the three of them, and the two witches in the yard didn't have the power. I crossed a line when I worked blood magic in the Rift. It found me, knew me. Needed me."

"You're not alone," Mina urged. "We have your back. The Wanderers share your blood. When the time comes, open yourself to them. Eshtamon had a reason for his choice."

Fear left Rigan dry-mouthed and forced the breath from his lungs. He remembered how his magic had joined with Corran's and Aiden's in the final moments of the battle against Blackholt.

"Together," he managed, although he had no clear idea of exactly what that meant. All he knew was that word mattered, and he hung onto it like a raft in a flood.

"Together," Brock and Mina echoed.

The too-quiet manor beckoned for them to enter, while the tainted power rose around them with every step. Rigan could feel the vines of magic that shimmered against the outer walls like fire in his veins. They had seen a light in the window of the tower, but Rigan knew it was a decoy. The blood magic pulled him like gravity toward what he guessed might have once been a ballroom. That's where the other Wanderers would circle and meet them, waiting until signaled for back-up.

Rigan and Mina led the way, with the rest of the Wanderer-witches close behind them. Even within the manor, two of the witches trailed behind, marking sigils as they went. The Wanderer chant started like a low hum and grew in intensity, magic weaving between them like a soft, golden light. It prickled his skin and raised the hairs on his arms and the back of his neck. As the glow brightened, he saw it pulse, a counterpoint to the blue glow enveloping Thornwood.

Rigan did not know the words to the chant, but he let himself fall into a trance, listening to the cadence, to the beat of his heart, feeling the strengthening pulse of the shared energy. He sensed the magic rising around him and through him, and gave himself over to it, allowing it to pull from his power.

He called to that magic and sent it in a blast that flung open the doors to the ballroom. The stench of a charnel house billowed out, heavy with the copper tang of blood and the bitter edge of shit and piss. Bodies lay scattered across the parquet floor, dropped where they had been sacrificed. Gall and wormwood burned in a censer, around an altar heaped with skulls and hearts.

Nightshade's blond hair and sullied robes hung heavy against his spare frame, sodden with the gore that had sprayed his face and spattered the walls. A wild smile creased his features, and the mad spark in his eyes bordered on ecstatic. Wraithwind looked like a scholar caught in an abattoir, with a cloud of tangled gray hair above spectacles dripping with blood and wide, unfocused eyes that looked drugged. The two witches continued to chant and dance in an orgiastic frenzy, paying no attention to the newcomers, wholly intent on the culmination of their summoning. Shadowsworn alone appeared to be in full command of his faculties, not yet lost to the excess of the ritual, and his head snapped up as the door slammed open.

A glowing tide of power surged as Rigan and the Wanderers burst into the room. A cry from Mina called to their reinforcements, who swept into the ballroom from the other side, sending their wave of magic flooding toward the three bloodied witches. The power hit an invisible obstacle and parted around the altar and its supplicants like water around rock.

"We've been waiting. He said you'd come." Shadowsworn's eyes were bright with power, filled with the energy stolen from the wretches whose bodies and blood fed his magic.

Rigan heard Mina raise her voice, and the witches from the caves appeared at the opposite door, forming a line to seal the room. They sent the full blast of their power forward, only to see it deflected short of its target. Some of the magic spent itself against the shimmering defensive wards that protected the ritual, while the rest shook the walls and sent a snow of dust down on them as cracks appeared in the ceiling.

Three blood witches should not be able to repel so many Wanderers, unless they had gained a taste of the power promised to them by the beast they summoned. From the satisfied glint in Shadowsworn's eyes, Rigan guessed that He Who Watches had given his loyal acolytes a portion of his magic to finish the summoning.

The oppressive weight of the First Creature's presence filled the room, and Rigan winced as the pain in his head intensified, like daggers stabbing through his eyes. It felt as if the huge totality of He Who Watches had slipped its dark tendrils inside his skull to prise it apart until the First Being could fit inside. Rigan gasped and staggered, then drew on his magic and stubborn will to straighten and shove back against the entity clawing at his mind.

He Who Watches didn't want him as a sacrifice, or an offering. He wanted the power that eluded him in the Rift, and the soul that battled for control. If the First Being won, it would crack open Rigan's bones and drain his magic like marrow. And there would be no champions left to fight against the darkness.

"You're too late. You can't stop the rising," Shadowsworn said. "But we want the gravedigger. Our master has need of his power."

"No." Rigan's voice, low and determined, carried even over the chanting and cries of the wild-eyed blood witches.

Behind him, he felt the Wanderer-witches' power gather once more, and at the same time, Rigan felt the appearance of the Rift like a physical blow. An irregular stain appeared in the ceiling and in the middle of it, a pinprick of blood red light gradually tore down through the blackness like a gash cut by a knife. The energy running along the walls of the manor suddenly heaved and shifted, arcing, and Rigan saw the Rift with both his eyes and his magic. He felt the reaction of the witches linked to his power, a mix of fear, dismay, and resolve. The chanting grew louder, faster, and the power rose.

The line in the ceiling glowed blue, then a sickly, foxfire green, finally blazing red like a raw wound. The Rift looked like a ragged cut in the night itself, and the air around it bulged as if something were pushing against a barrier from the other side.

The Wanderers' chanting rose above the wind, and energy crackled all around them, in shimmering, diaphanous waves, coalescing over-head in a sparking cloud. The sigils all around them glowed with inner fire.

Eshtamon, if you're paying attention, we could really use your help. The Elder God's attention had been sporadic at best thus far, but Rigan figured a silent plea couldn't hurt.

Rigan had never felt magic in quite the same way, surrounded by dozens of other witches, physically linked as they called to their power, melding will and mind through the repetition of the chant and the trance state it produced. He felt larger than his body, too big to be contained within his own skin, and he could detect the consciousness of those around him and sensed their essences brushing against his own.

In his mind, he saw a swirl of golden, pulsing power rising above the Wanderers; it had a center bulge that slowly gathered more of the glow to itself in spiraling arms that twisted faster and faster like a maelstrom. Beyond it, the Rift had grown nearly too bright to look at, blood-red and seeping energy. The air around the gash appeared distorted, and the red line of the Rift broadened, and tendrils of some-thing dark and foul wriggled free, pushing against the opening.

Rigan felt the power of the Wanderer witches throughout his whole being. He drew on the energy of the ring of grave sigils he had marked on his body, as he had done the night they battled Blackholt, and felt the rising power of the marks the Wanderers chalked as they reflected and strengthened the magic. He thought again about the battle raging at the lower wall and realized that the monsters had not been summoned merely as protectors. They were sacrifices, like the men who fought them, called to slaughter to feed the power of the blood witches in the tower that sought to free an abomination. A source of power—and as that realization dawned on him, Rigan determined to use that power, even if it damned his soul to do it.

He stretched out his grave magic, calling to the souls of the men who had died in the battle, and praying that Corran was not among them. The souls flocked to him, lending him their energy and Rigan felt the warmth of it thrumming through him grow to a heat that seemed to set his body on fire from the inside.

Rigan felt the blood magic tearing at the essence of the dead and dying monsters, ripping the last glimmer of existence free of their savaged corpses, and sensed that the monsters fought that desecration fiercely, using up their waning power and straining that of their would-be masters.

The golden, glowing energy shifted, and the Wanderer sigils glowed blindingly bright, focusing reflected magic on Rigan. The spiral arms of the coalescing magic twined clockwise around him, as the black, putrid tendrils from the thing beyond the Rift also snared him, twisting in the opposite direction.

Though his feet remained planted on the ground, Rigan felt his essence pull loose of his body, rising until he hung between the heavens and the ground beneath. The two powers warred against his skin, and he struggled to harness more of his grave magic, sending out a silent summons to all the restless spirits who would heed his call.

The Rift grew wider, and the tendrils that pushed through thickened. Everywhere the dark tentacles touched Rigan they burned his skin with a fire that burrowed agonizingly deep, trying to draw out his magic and life, perhaps his very soul. The First Being stank like the taint, smelling of wet rot, old corpses, and putrefaction.

Their touch opened his mind's eye, and Rigan glimpsed He Who Watches. He had no words or frame of understanding for the terrifying creature, and the horror of it felt too big for his skull to contain. He screamed in pure, primal fear as a single, blood-red eye beheld him and the notice of a First Being fell upon him. Then the notice passed, the eye turned away, and Rigan felt overwhelming relief.

The glowing strands lent him energy, twining a golden cage around his heart and the pulse he thought of as his essence. The two powers warred across his body even as the witches clashed around him, and Rigan knew they were all running out of time.

Rigan drew the spirits of the dead closer, bidding them to step into the golden power, promising their release to the After. They came to him, first by ones and twos, then in larger clusters, those long denied their rest and those finally ready to give up their unfinished business. From each he received a flicker of power as they left the world of the living behind and he opened their passage to the After. Those pulses of energy strengthened him, shoring up his war against the poisonous tendrils of darkness.

Rigan's body and soul had become the battleground, torn between ground and sky. He felt the Wanderers channeling all their energy into him, as the cavalcade of spirits increased, strengthening him flicker by flicker. He pulled the dying and the newly dead of the battlefield to him, the villagers and farmers who fought alongside the hunters, the Wanderers who had taken up arms, and those of their allies, the *guin* and the *thropes* that had fallen in battle. They came to him willingly, offering up the last of themselves if it could turn the tide of the battle.

With each soul that passed through the gateway he had made of his being, the dark tendrils shrank and withered, as the golden strands lengthened and grew thicker. Rigan felt the cosmic powers warring around and through him. He knew that no human was meant to contain or sustain such power for long. He would burn to ashes, a husk sucked dry, and it would be worth the sacrifice if only he could seal the Rift and keep Corran, Elinor, and the others safe.

Rigan opened himself to take in all the remnant soul energy, feeling the magic swell around him and the dark tendrils draw back as the Wanderers channeled all the energy they could muster to him and through him. Caught up in the tide of magic, the golden power ran up his body like an athame, assaulting the bloody gash of the Rift.

Distantly, he realized that the foundations of the manor shook with the power channeling through it, as the walls trembled and chunks of the ceiling began to fall around them. Glass shattered, and curtains caught fire. All of it felt too far away to concern him.

Magic burned against his skin and bone like lightning, blazing from his eyes and mouth, consuming him as its conduit. The light warred against the tendrils and the Rift, a clash of titanic powers. In the background, Rigan sensed the old power of Colduraan and Eshtamon as they watched their champions war for dominance.

Screams echoed in the crumbling manor as He Who Watches drew on the magic of the three blood witches, draining their power and then their lives, releasing them only when the screaming stopped, and nothing remained except brittle husks.

The influx of ghosts waned, and Rigan knew he dared not let his magic falter, not now. He had one last chance, one remaining card to play. Fear and sorrow rose in his chest. If he could add his own soul to the power assaulting the Rift, it might be enough to turn the tide of the battle, no more of a sacrifice than the men who had lost their lives to the claws and teeth of the monsters they battled on the ground below him.

I'm sorry, Corran, Elinor. Be safe.

Rigan's head fell back. He threw his arms wide, arching his chest as the golden power tore through him. The chants of the Wanderers echoed in his mind as raw energy and pure magic burned away the last of the dark tendrils from his body. The bolt struck the center of the Rift, and fire blazed at the contact, cauterizing the gash like a raw wound with a hot poker.

An inhuman shriek of anger and frustrated hunger escaped from beyond the Rift, the cry of He Who Watches as he realized victory would be denied, a sound like thousands of creatures screaming in agony. The Rift burned closed, and the screaming cut off abruptly.

The ceiling ripped away overhead, unable to contain the surge of power, sending a hail of rock and plaster that gashed and pummeled him, but Rigan did not feel the pain. Brutal magic stripped through him, securing the seal on the Rift, past his ability to control. He gave himself over to it completely, holding nothing back.

What consciousness remained slammed back into his damaged body. Rigan no longer felt the beating of his heart or the rise of his breath. Fire withdrew, leaving him so very cold. The golden glow lowered him to the ground, and it was the last thing he knew before everything went dark.

CHAPTER THIRTY-FOUR

RIGAN WOKE SLOWLY, aware of voices nearby. He could not make out the words, but the tone disturbed him. A man's voice, ragged with grief and exhaustion. Women's voices, some with authority, and another thick with worry.

He drifted. Sometimes the voices sounded closer; at other times they receded until he could barely hear them. The tone changed. They argued, pleaded, consoled, and sobbed. Rigan wondered why they did not move away and just let him sleep in peace.

Rigan floated in warmth and darkness, broken only by the fire of sigils that circled his resting place. The sigils burned with a golden glow that soothed where it bathed his skin and calmed when it touched his mind. Nothing else existed, and he could not remember anything before the darkness and the sigils, nor could he imagine why remembering might be important.

Gradually, the warmth and glow receded, and Rigan felt sad at their loss. He felt smaller, contained. The vessel into which his essence poured seemed weak and limited. Feeling returned, followed by pain. He longed to go back into to the darkness, though the voices begged him to stay.

For the first time in a long while, Rigan felt solid, not a thing of light and energy, but a heavy, sluggish body. A heartbeat pounded in his ears, and he was aware of the inhale and exhale as shallow breaths rose and fell. Everything ached, more in some places than in others. The heat of the blankets could not match the enveloping warmth he had left behind in the darkness.

"Rigan?"

It took him a few seconds to recognize the strained, rough voice as Corran's. He had only heard his brother sound like that a few times. The night they buried their mother. The night they lost Kell.

Rigan opened his eyes with effort, and saw Corran leaning over him, with an expression of hope and fear. His eyes were red-rimmed and his face thinner than before, but the wide, relieved smile made Rigan's heart stir in response.

"Rigan." Corran's hands closed on his shoulders, gripping him as if to hold onto his essence, to keep him from slipping away. He swallowed hard, and his breath caught. "Thank the gods. You were... gone... for a while."

Rigan wanted to reply, but all that came from his dry throat was a groan. Corran's face lit up at the sound, and he let go of Rigan's shoulder long enough to drag a hand across his eyes. "Aiden! Elinor! He's awake!"

He heard running footsteps, and then two anxious faces appeared beside Corran. Corran stepped back but kept a hand on his shoulder like he feared Rigan might vanish if he let go.

"Just now," Corran said, responding to something Aiden said that Rigan did not catch.

Elinor pressed a kiss to Rigan's dry lips, making no attempt to hide her tears. She brushed a hand through his hair. "I'm glad you're back," she managed as her voice cracked.

Aiden's face filled his line of sight. "Got a million questions for you, but they can wait. It's good to see you. Don't go anywhere," he added with a wan smile, clapping Rigan on the shoulder. Rigan closed his eyes and drifted back to sleep, anchored by Corran's firm grip on his forearm, and Elinor's hand in his.

———

"YOU GAVE US all quite a scare," Aiden remarked. Rigan was unsure how much time had passed since he first opened his eyes. He had slept and woken, each time to find Corran and Elinor holding him, whispering their concern, stroking his hair like a sick child. Other times, Aiden prodded him into awareness tending to his needs.

"What happened?" Rigan's hoarse voice sounded brittle with disuse.

"We won," Corran replied. He sounded dead tired. Rigan looked over and saw Elinor asleep in a nearby chair. Corran sat nearby, and the dark circles under his eyes suggested a long vigil. "The Rift sealed. He Who Watches didn't get through. The monsters are dead—and when we got inside Thornwood's defenses, Aiden and Elinor killed the two minor blood witches who were controlling the monsters, and it was a free-for-all for a while, but the Wanderers sent us good fighters, and then the *guin* and the *thropes* saved our asses."

"And didn't eat us in the bargain," Aiden chimed in as he moved around the room, coming in and out of Rigan's line of sight.

Corran's laugh suggested that might have been a near thing. "Yeah. They kept their promise and went back to the Old Woods. As long as everyone leaves them alone, there won't be any trouble." He reached for a cup of tea and took a sip to ease his throat. "That's when the sky got freaky. And then the golden light came, and the manor blew apart." His voice caught. "We didn't know whether any of you made it through, with so much magic loose. We didn't know how much of it was you until after, when Mina and Brock told us."

He looked away, gathering his composure before he went on. "Then we got inside Thornwood, and we found the other three blood witches—the ones who really had power—but they were nothing but dried up shells. Guess they didn't figure on being part of the sacrifice to bring He Who Watches through the Rift."

"So it's over," Aiden added. "At least the plot to let a First Being through is finished."

"Other blood witches," Rigan croaked. "More monsters. Bounty hunters."

Corran shook his head. "Jorgeson is dead. Killed him myself, and we captured what was left of his guards. I don't think any of his crew will be coming after us."

"As for the blood witches and monsters, we'll deal with them when they cross our path," Aiden added, mixing up an elixir and holding a cup to Rigan's mouth for him to drink. "That's a battle for another day."

"Calfon's dead," Rigan said when he had swallowed the medicine. Corran looked startled and then nodded.

"You used your grave magic, there at the end. I felt it and tried to give you what I could to help. Yes, Calfon died in the battle. Ross, Trent, and Polly got pretty banged up, but they'll live," Corran replied.

"Elinor—"

Aiden chuckled. "She and I did our part in the battle from a distance, and then moved in to help the survivors as soon as the fighting was done. She was terribly worried about you, and with good cause," he added, arching an eyebrow. "Once we got you back from the Wanderers, she and Corran stayed with you the whole time, until you woke up."

"How long?" Rigan croaked.

Corran and Aiden exchanged a glance. "A week," Corran replied. "You wouldn't wake up. We were afraid you might not. The Wanderers told us not to give up, that you were a fighter." A wan smile touched his lips. "They were right."

"You owe your life to Mina and the Wanderers, not me," Aiden said, sitting on the end of Corran's bed. "And to Eshtamon, since Mina said you weren't breathing and you didn't have a heartbeat when the Rift vanished. So much for the need to make a 'total sacrifice,'" Aiden said with a grimace. "The Wanderers got your heart started again and helped you draw air, and that strengthened you enough for me to take over." He ran a hand over his eyes. "Even so, it was rough going."

"I remember a little of it," Rigan said, his voice faint. "The glow from the Wanderers' power. Calling the grave magic. Calfon's spirit.

The Rift sealing." He gave a weak shake of his head. "Not much after that."

Corran squeezed his forearm. "Mina and Brock told us all about it. We'll fill you in when you feel better, but for now, you can rest up knowing that you saved the world."

Rigan snorted. "I feel more like I got hit with a boulder."

Aiden laid a hand on his shoulder again. "With rest and food, you should feel much better soon, and I'm certain when Elinor wakes up and finds out you're back among the living, she'll see to it that you've got incentive to make a full recovery," he added with a grin, and Rigan blushed.

They fell quiet for a while, Corran's hand still on Rigan's arm as if he were afraid to let go, Elinor asleep nearby in the chair, Aiden moving quietly around the room. The part of his mind that channeled magic felt stripped raw and burned, and he winced away from examining it too closely. He felt a faint presence from the Wanderers, a thread of power lending him strength and helping to sustain him. Otherwise, he sensed only exhaustion, something fairly easy to fix.

"What now?" Rigan asked, beginning to fade.

"We're in what's left of Thornwood, protected by Wanderers and the witches and farmers who survived the battle," Corran said. "When you're well enough, Polly says she has a new monastery picked out for us. Without Jorgeson, someone else will have to take up the hunt for us —if we're still a priority with all the other things going on. And with three powerful blood witches dead, there won't be new monsters—at least for a while." He managed a tired smile. "Gives us time to regroup."

"When the monsters come back, we'll be ready," Rigan added in a whisper as his eyes drifted shut.

"Yeah," Corran said, staying close as Rigan drifted off to sleep. "We know the game now. We'll be ready."

EPILOGUE

MERCHANT PRINCE KADAR paced, stopping every few minutes to peer out the window as if he could see the smoke rising from his ruined vineyards.

"You're certain? A total loss?"

Pior Tolen—Joth Hanson's reluctant replacement—nodded, carefully keeping his face expressionless. Pity at his reversal of fortune would have infuriated Kadar; compassion might have undone his fragile reserve. "Yes, my lord. That vineyard and the next closest. Our men contained the fire at that point, but..." He spread his hands in a gesture of helplessness, the message clear. The damage had already been done.

Kadar turned from the window and ran his hands back through his hair. "We can't meet our future quota without that harvest." He hated the desperation in his voice. He'd been up all night, getting reports from sooty-faced riders who had been able to make out the fires from the watchtowers and come to bear the grim news. It would be a week at best before any of his people who had been at the vineyards could return with a full report; and that only if they rode at full speed and switched out mounts.

The details could only make it worse, magnifying the catastrophe.

Vineyards took years to come to maturity, and the lands that burned were among his oldest, bearing grapes that became his best wines. He had other lands, as yet untouched, but recovering from this setback would not be easy or quick.

"What do you hear?" he asked, afraid to ask and even more fearful of remaining ignorant.

"Nothing good," Tolen replied, and Kadar marveled at the man's ability to keep his voice neutral. "Several smugglers were captured by Aliyev's men near the harbor; they not only gave up the name of your contact but also the Sarolinian man who sent them our way. He's one of Crown Prince Neven's loyal retainers."

Kadar bit back a cry of utter despair. He could see it all clearly now, how he had been played. Neven's men had exploited his ambition, his need to show up Gorog and Tamas, his desire to spite Aliyev. The extra profits the smuggling venture had netted now looked paltry compared to the damage inflicted—on his own fortunes, Ravenwood's economy, and the trade agreements.

I've been a fool, an utter idiot, Kadar groaned silently. The platitudes about pride presaging a comeuppance proved true once again, on a devastating scale. "What of Wraithwind? Have you been able to track him?"

"No. But my people have learned that Shadowsworn left Ravenwood City abruptly not long before Wraithwind vanished, and our spies in Sarolinia report that Crown Prince Neven's blood witch also suddenly left on a long journey."

Kadar turned to look out the window to hide his reaction. "They're up to something."

"The lesser witches picked up on a large flare of energy some distance to the north," Tolen replied. "No idea what to make of it."

"Nothing good," Kadar murmured. "What of Aliyev?"

Tolen's hesitation confirmed Kadar's fears. "Ravenwood is in rebellion, my lord, even as the farmlands rise in revolt. The Guilds refuse the Crown Prince's orders, hunters roam the streets killing monsters and fighting the guards with impunity, and we are well and truly fucked when it comes to meeting our trade agreements."

"It's all coming apart," Kadar murmured. "It wasn't supposed to happen like this."

"We received a messenger from Aliyev this morning." Tolen handed over the parchment, sealed with wax embossed with the Crown Prince's signet imprint.

Kadar broke the seal, read the paper twice, and let his hand fall, barely biting back a cry. "Aliyev wants the ledgers early," he croaked. "He must be desperate for money, or for proof he can supply enough goods to the king to salvage the situation with Garenoth." Kadar dropped the parchment and ran a hand over his eyes. "Gods. The king. Rellan will have our heads."

"One other bit of news," Tolen continued, and Kadar wondered whether the man enjoyed being the bearer of bad tidings or realized his fortunes fell with those of his masters. "Aliyev declared Hant Jorgeson rogue and put a bounty on his head. It appears he hasn't been successful capturing those bloody undertakers and their outlaw friends, and they've been marauding across the countryside, raising insurrection and telling the villagers the truth about the Balance and the Cull."

"They're behind this," Kadar said, as fear, loss, and humiliation fueled the viciousness in his voice. "The Valmondes. It's all been a plot to destroy Ravenwood. First Machison and Gorog. Now Aliyev and me. Tamas and Gorog the younger are hardly worth the bother." The possibility that someone else might have been responsible for his reversal of fortune fueled him with vindictive purpose.

"My lord—"

"They can't be working on their own," Kadar continued, paying Tolen no attention as his mind raced. "No. They must be working for someone, paid by someone. But who?"

"My lord, we've investigated them. They are the last of many generations of undertakers in their family, Guild members. They couldn't—"

"Of course they could!" Kadar shouted, eyes alight with purpose akin to madness. "This is too complicated to be the plotting of some disgruntled tradesmen. Someone wanted to wipe the slate clean, and that's what they've done." He clasped his hands behind his back and paced quickly back and forth as he worked out the details.

"This is big. Devious. Who could be behind it?" He wheeled on Tolen. "I want to know who among the nobility might fancy themselves a rival to King Rellan. And who in Sarolinia might be supporting Neven, if he's got a hand in this."

He nodded as the pieces fell into place. "That's our saving grace," he said with a feral smile. "Identify the traitor and the outside threat. Prove myself helpful. I'll bring proof of the plot and the names of the traitors to Aliyev and the king, and they'll be so grateful, they'll forgive the smuggling. They'll have to, because I'll be the one who saves them, who reveals the plot."

Tolen stared at him, speechless.

"Don't just stand there!" Kadar roared. "I want your best spies on this matter; I want names and evidence. By Oj and Ren, protect our warehouses and those barrels! I want the rest of your men out in the farmland, protecting the remaining vineyards and putting down the rebellion. And I want your assassins to hunt and kill those bloody Valmondes. I will not let some outlaw undertakers destroy me!"

Tolen nodded, though he had gone pale and his eyes widened with something akin to fear. "As you wish, my lord." He bowed, then hurried from the room.

Alone, Kadar continued to pace in front of the window. *This has to work. I've come too far to lose now. We'll turn this around. We have to be able to fix this—and come out on top. I'll show Aliyev and the king how valuable I can be with the rebuilding. They'll be grateful for my help—especially when I deliver the heads of those traitorous undertakers. It's not over. I won't admit defeat, not unless or until all of Ravenwood goes down in flames with me.*

Kadar heard the thud of a crossbow firing an instant before the quarrel pierced his chest. Blood fountained over his hands as he grasped at the bolt and its sharp tip. He fell to his knees, unable to breathe, as his heart slowed. Without a doubt, the assassin's shot had been calculated to let him live just long enough to understand what had happened, to know that Aliyev had contracted his murder.

With the last of his strength, Kadar swept the lamp from a nearby stand and watched as it dashed against the curtains. Flames jumped from the draperies to the woodwork and tapestries. Kadar fell forward, as his heart stuttered and his vision dimmed.

Now we all burn together.

AFTERWORD

It takes a village to produce a book. Many thanks to my wonderful husband and partner, Larry N. Martin, for all the editing, formatting, uploading, and proofreading that goes on behind the scenes. Thanks also to Jean Rabe, our editor, for an excellent, professional read as always, and to my agent, Ethan Ellenberg for his staunch support.

Thank you to our Shadow Alliance street team, who are a constant source of friendship, solidarity, and encouragement. Many thanks to our beta readers, Chris L., Nancy N., Trevor C., Andrea L., Sharon M., and Julie M. for helping make the book its best. Thanks also to Mindy Mymudes for being a fantastic coordinator!

People do judge a book by its cover, so thanks to artist Sam Gretton for the front cover and to designer Melissa Gilbert for the print wrap.

Deep appreciation to the convention organizers and volunteers, bloggers, reviewers, and bookstore staff who help spread the word. Eternal gratitude to the crew of authors who make the conventions, events and road trips fun. We couldn't do this without you.

Most importantly, thanks to our readers for believing in us, looking for new releases, telling their friends, and letting us know when you've enjoyed a book. Because you read, we write.

Thank you for supporting independent authors!

This book was written and published by an independent author. Independent authors work outside the large, traditional publishing industry, which means we can be more responsive to our fans and readers, bringing you more of the kinds of stories you want to read.

When you support independent authors, you're helping them make a living, providing an income for their families, and helping to guarantee that they can continue writing the books you enjoy reading.

By helping spread the word about the books and authors you enjoy, either in reviews on book sites and Goodreads or by personal recommendation, you help others discover these books for themselves, and you help make it possible for the writers you enjoy to keep on writing. This is especially important for independent authors, because we don't have a big name publisher promoting our books or the benefit of being shelved in bookstores.

If you've enjoyed this book, or other books by independent authors, the biggest way to show your thanks is by reviewing online and spreading the word. And please, never download "free" books off of pirate sites. Doing so harms the author by robbing him or her of the sale, and makes it harder for authors to stay in business, writing the books you love.

ABOUT THE AUTHOR

Gail Z. Martin is the author of *Vengeance*, the sequel to *Scourge* in her Darkhurst epic fantasy series, and *Assassin's Honor* in the new Assassins of Landria series. *Tangled Web* is the newest novel in the series that includes both *Deadly Curiosities* and *Vendetta* and two collections, *Trifles and Folly* and *Trifles and Folly 2*, the latest in her urban fantasy series set in Charleston, SC. *Shadow and Flame* is the fourth book in the Ascendant Kingdoms Saga and *The Shadowed Path* and *The Dark Road* are in the Jonmarc Vahanian Adventures series. Co-authored with Larry N. Martin are *Iron and Blood*, the first novel in the Jake Desmet Adventures series and the *Storm and Fury* collection; and the *Spells, Salt, & Steel: New Templars series (Mark Wojcik, monster hunter)*. Under her urban fantasy M/M paranormal romance pen name of Morgan Brice, *Witchbane* and *Badlands* are the newest releases.

She is also the author of *Ice Forged, Reign of Ash,* and *War of Shadows* in The Ascendant Kingdoms Saga, The Chronicles of The Necromancer series (*The Summoner, The Blood King, Dark Haven, Dark Lady's Chosen*) and The Fallen Kings Cycle (*The Sworn, The Dread*).

Gail's work has appeared in over 35 US/UK anthologies. Newest anthologies include: *The Big Bad 2, Athena's Daughters, Heroes, Space, Contact Light, With Great Power, The Weird Wild West, The Side of Good/The Side of Evil, Alien Artifacts, Cinched: Imagination Unbound, Realms of Imagination, Clockwork Universe: Steampunk vs. Aliens, Gaslight and Grimm, Baker Street Irregulars, Journeys, Hath no Fury,* and *Afterpunk: Steampunk Tales of the Afterlife.*

Find out more at www.GailZMartin.com, at DisquietingVisions.com, on Twitter @GailZMartin, on Facebook as the WinterKingdoms, and on Goodreads https://www.goodreads.com/GailZMartin.

OTHER BOOKS BY GAIL Z. MARTIN

Other books by Gail Z. Martin

Darkhurst

Scourge

Vengeance

Ascendant Kingdoms

Ice Forged

Reign of Ash

War of Shadows

Shadow and Flame

Chronicles of the Necromancer / Fallen Kings Cycle

The Summoner

The Blood King

Dark Haven

Dark Lady's Chosen

The Sworn

The Dread

The Shadowed Path

The Dark Road

Deadly Curiosities

Deadly Curiosities

Vendetta

Tangled Web

Trifles and Folly

Trifles and Folly 2

Other books by Gail Z. Martin and Larry N. Martin

Jake Desmet Adventures

Iron & Blood

Storm & Fury

Spells, Salt, & Steel: New Templars

Spells, Salt, & Steel

Open Season

Deep Trouble

83843544R00331

Made in the USA
San Bernardino, CA
31 July 2018